"Now that you've had a chance to spend some time in Devil's Door and meet its citizens, what do you think?"

"I really like it. The people are friendly," Avery said.

"And curious about our new houseguest," Brand added with a laugh.

"I can see that not much happens around here without the whole town knowing about it."

"That can be a good thing, if the news is positive, or a really annoying thing if it's not something you wanted to share with your neighbors."

Avery glanced over. "Were you ever the object of ugly gossip?"

He shrugged. "Not ugly, I suppose. But the three Merrick brothers, as you may have noticed, weren't born with halos and wings." He turned. "How about you? Is there a little devil behind that innocent face?"

She laughed. "You think I'm going to tell you all my secrets?"

"I should have known. A woman of mystery."

"I think everyone should have a few secrets."

He wiggled his brows like a villain. "I'll tell mine if you tell yours."

She gave another laugh. "Nice try, cowboy."

RAVES FOR R. C. RYAN'S NOVELS

BORN TO BE A COWBOY

"Readers who prefer their Westerns with a dash of suspense will find this latest from Ryan an ideal choice. The action and danger ramp up from the beginning and never let down."
—*Library Journal*

"Smooth like good whiskey."
—*Keeper Bookshelf*

THE COWBOY NEXT DOOR

"Satisfying...This sweetly domestic story should win Ryan many new fans."
—*Publishers Weekly*

"*The Cowboy Next Door* is a work of art."
—Fresh Fiction

COWBOY ON MY MIND

"A strong, protective hero and an independent heroine fight for their future in this modern rough-and-tumble Western."
—*Library Journal*

"This talented writer...invites you to join a little journey that has you biting at the bit for more."
—Fresh Fiction

REED

"4 stars! Ryan's latest book in her Malloys of Montana series contains a heartwarming plot filled with down-to-earth cowboys and warm, memorable characters. Reed and Ally are engaging and endearing, and their sweet, fiery chemistry heats up the pages, which will leave readers' hearts melting...A delightful read."
—RT Book Reviews

LUKE

"Ryan creates vivid characters against the lovingly rendered backdrop of sweeping Montana ranchlands. The passion between Ryan's protagonists, which they keep discreet, is tender and heartwarming. The plot is drawn in broad strokes, but Ryan expertly brings it to a satisfying conclusion."
—Publishers Weekly

MATT

"Ryan has created a gripping love story fraught with danger and lust, pain and sweet, sweet triumph."
—Library Journal, starred review

my kind of
COWBOY

R. C. RYAN

FOREVER
New York Boston

Copyright © 2020 Ruth Ryan Langan

Cover photography by Rob Lang. Cover design by Elizabeth Turner Stokes. Cover copyright © 2019 by Hachette Book Group, Inc.

Forever
Hachette Book Group
1290 Avenue of the Americas, New York, NY 10104
read-forever.com
twitter.com/readforeverpub

First Edition: April 2020

Forever is an imprint of Grand Central Publishing. The Forever name and logo are trademarks of Hachette Book Group, Inc.

The publisher is not responsible for websites (or their content) that are not owned by the publisher.

The Hachette Speakers Bureau provides a wide range of authors for speaking events. To find out more, go to www.hachettespeakersbureau.com or call (866) 376-6591.

ISBNs: 978-1-5387-1684-7 (mass market), 978-1-5387-1683-0 (ebook)

Printed in the United States of America

OPM

10 9 8 7 6 5 4 3 2 1

For Skyler, Jackson, Avery, and Rowan—a new generation and the next chapter.

And for Tom, who wrote the prologue to my best love story ever.

my kind of
COWBOY

PROLOGUE

The Old Butcher Ranch—Wyoming
Twenty years previous

You'll make a fine life for yourself here, Bo." Egan Merrick clapped a hand on his son's shoulder while looking around at the old-fashioned furnishings left behind by the previous owner. "Leigh and the boys seem happy here."

Bo Merrick glanced across the room at his beautiful wife laughing with his mother, Meg, and his sister, Liz. It warmed his heart to see their close bond. Family mattered to Bo. He and Liz had grown up in their grandfather's home. It was where his father had brought his bride and where Bo had brought his. Even after the birth of their three sons, they'd continued living on the family ranch. And now, finally, they were enjoying their first taste of their own place.

"We're loving it, Pops. When old Wayne Butcher decided to pull up stakes and move in with his daughter in Montana, I figured it was fate. With our range lands adjoining, we're close enough to share ranch chores."

Egan pointed to where Bo's three sons, Brand, Casey, and Jonah, were playing with a set of ancient wooden trucks left behind by the previous owner. "I can see it's already starting to feel like home to all of you."

"Yes, sir." Bo nodded.

Bo and Leigh had hosted a family supper, followed by endless rounds of stories about the early days when Hammond Merrick, patriarch of the family, had become something of a legend in these parts. These were stories none of them ever tired of hearing. The three little boys considered their great-grandfather a superhero. Despite his cantankerous ways, it was plain to see the love between all of them. They were easy in one another's company.

The older man stifled a yawn, and Meg stepped closer. "Ready to go, Hammond?" Meg was the only family member who called him by his given name. To everyone else he was Ham. No sweet, cuddly nicknames for him.

Ham nodded. "Ranch chores start early." He hugged his grandson's wife. "A grand supper, as always, Leigh. I thank you."

The three little boys gathered around their great-grandfather to share his famous bear hugs before he trailed behind Egan, Meg, and Liz as they made their way to their truck for the drive back to the family ranch.

As they drove away, Bo drew his wife close. "Life doesn't get much better, babe."

"I was just thinking the same thing." Leigh brushed a quick kiss over his mouth before calling to her boys, "Time for bed. Let's head upstairs and I'll hear your prayers."

Six-year-old Brand was asleep, tucked up beside his two younger brothers. Their room was in the attic of the ancient ranch house they now called home.

Something had disturbed Brand's sleep, and he now lay listening to the creaking of rotted timbers above his head. His father had said that this house may be more than a hundred years old, but it was sturdy enough to give them shelter until he could finish the new house he was building on the other side of the rickety barn. His pa said they were lucky to be able to buy this ranch, located right next door to his family ranch. By merging the two, the Merrick family would own one of the biggest spreads in Wyoming.

Just thinking about his ma and pa asleep in the big bedroom downstairs had Brand smiling as he began to slip back into sleep.

The creaking of the timbers grew louder, and Brand sat up, wondering at the other sound. The wind? If so, it was howling loud enough to blow the house down.

Through the closed curtains, he saw a strange orange glow, and he rubbed his eyes before slipping out of bed and crossing to the window.

Fire!

Flames were licking along the outer wall, and bits of burning wood and shingles were flying through the air, landing like gunshots above his head. He could hear the crackling sound that told him the roof was already on fire.

"Casey. Jonah." Brand was shaking his brothers roughly, pulling aside the covers and forcing them both to a sitting position. Though they weren't yet awake, he started dragging them toward the door. When little Jonah whined and dropped to the floor, Brand picked him up. Staggering beneath the load, he half carried, half dragged his two little brothers down the stairs until they reached the closed front door.

Leaving them there, he raced to his parents' room, shouting for them to wake up.

"Ma! Pa!" He started tugging on his father's arm until Bo sat up in a daze.

After a punishing dawn-to-dark workday, it was no wonder Bo had to struggle to focus. There were never enough hours in the day. Sleep was a luxury he often did without. "What's wrong? Are you crazy, son?"

"Fire, Pa. It's up on the roof."

Bo was out of bed and stumbling toward the door, all the while shouting to his wife, "Leigh, wake up. There's a fire."

She sat up, struggling to get her bearings. Suddenly she bolted out of bed. "The boys."

"They're okay, Ma." Relieved that his parents were awake and ready to take charge, Brand raced out of their bedroom and hurried to where he'd left his little brothers.

Jonah had fallen asleep.

Casey was sitting beside his little brother, looking completely bewildered by the smoke swirling about the room.

"Come on." Brand threw open the big front door and was buffeted by a rush of wind.

He grabbed Jonah by one hand and Casey by the other, dragging them outside. Despite their protests, he continued dragging them clear across the yard before shoving them into their pa's truck for safekeeping.

Unsure whether or not to leave his little brothers alone, he stood shivering outside the vehicle, watching for his parents.

To a boy of six, the next few minutes seemed like an hour. Finally, after shouting to Casey to stay inside the truck with Jonah, he ran toward the house, shouting, "Pa! Ma! Where are you?"

At first as he stepped inside, all he could hear was the

roar of the fire, sounding like a train bearing down on him. Cowering in the doorway, he cupped his hands to his mouth and continued shouting.

A flash of lights had him turning as a truck came barreling across a flat stretch of meadow and came to a screeching halt alongside his father's truck.

The doors opened and Brand's grandparents came rushing toward him, followed by his great-grandfather and his aunt Liz.

Gram Meg wrapped her arms around Brand, gathering him close. "Your brothers?"

"In Pa's truck."

She gave a cry to Liz and the two turned away, racing toward the terrified little boys who could be seen peering through the windows of the truck.

Hammond caught Brand by the shoulders. "Your folks?"

"Inside. I woke them. Then I brought Casey and Jonah out here."

Egan started inside, followed by Hammond. The flames were now everywhere, and thick smoke billowed, leaving the entire house in darkness.

Hammond turned around, pointing a finger-of-God order at Brand. "Go to the truck, boy."

"But Ma and Pa—"

Stern old Hammond hollered, "You heard me, boy. Get out of here. Now."

The old man disappeared inside the inferno, and though the need to find his parents was all consuming, it never occurred to Brand to disobey his elders.

He hurried toward his grandmother and aunt, who were each holding one of his brothers, murmuring words meant to soothe.

Barefoot and shivering, Brand focused all his attention on the front door.

A short time later he saw three figures emerge.

Though Gram Meg tried to hold him back, he wrenched free and raced toward the house to find his father, grandfather, and great-grandfather lying on the ground, coughing and retching.

"Pa." Brand knelt beside his father. "Where's Ma?"

Bo's head came up. "She's not out here with you?"

"No, Pa."

"She told me she was heading up to fetch you boys."

"I said they were okay. I had Casey and Jonah with me."

"My God. She must not have heard you and went upstairs…" Before Bo could race back into the house, there was a great rush of flames and the roof collapsed inward, sending streams of flaming timbers and glowing embers raining down on everyone.

Hammond gave his great-grandson a shove. "Run, boy. Get in the truck."

Looking over his shoulder, Brand saw his grandfather and great-grandfather dragging Bo toward the shelter of the truck. Twice Bo broke free and darted back toward the fire, and twice he was caught and held until the three men were forced to leap back and watch as the walls caved inward and the house dissolved into a pile of fiery rubble.

"Leigh!" Bo's hoarse voice echoed and re-echoed in the night sky as he dropped to his knees and buried his face in his hands, while the others stood by helplessly.

The sound of his father's sobs had young Brand frozen in place. It was, he knew, a sound that would remain in his memory forever.

*　　*　　*

The endless days that followed were spent at the ranch, where the family did their best to ease Bo and his sons through the pain of loss.

Though everyone, including the volunteer fire department inspector, said the fire had been fueled by sparks from the wood-burning fireplace, the Merrick family wasn't fully convinced. When Bo met Leigh Johnson, the great love of his life, she'd been engaged to Des Dempsey, whose father owned the bank in Devil's Door. When she broke her engagement to Des to marry Bo, the entire Dempsey family turned their backs on the Merrick family, refusing them any of the financing necessary to a rancher's existence. Since their bank was now closed to the Merricks, Bo had been forced to go far beyond the town to borrow the money he'd needed to buy the old Butcher ranch.

Bo, Egan, and Hammond were seated at the kitchen table, talking in low tones.

Bo's voice was raw with fury. "I haven't a doubt who did this. This was Des Dempsey's final revenge."

"Now you don't know—" Hammond's words broke off.

Bo turned to see what caused the interruption and caught sight of young Brand standing hesitantly in the doorway. He shoved away from the table and crossed to the boy. "You should be in bed, son."

"I can't sleep, Pa. I want to stay down here with you."

Bo knelt and gathered his son close. "I understand, but you need your rest." He picked up Brand and turned toward the stairs. "Come on. I'll sit with you until you fall asleep."

When he was tucked in his bed, Brand looked up at his father. "Why did Mr. Dempsey cause the fire?"

"I don't know. I have my suspicions but..."

Brand's voice trembled. "Is Ma never coming back to us?"

"No, son." Bo's voice was tight with grief.

"Will we ever go home again?"

Bo sighed. "This will be our home now."

"But what about having our own place?"

"I'll need my mother and your aunt Liz to help with you and your brothers."

"I can help you. We'll all help."

"I know you will. You're a good boy, Brand. We'll merge the two pieces of land, and we'll stay on here. It'll be fine. You'll see." Bo pressed a kiss to his son's cheek. "We'll still be a family, only bigger. Sleep now. Good night, Brand."

"'Night, Pa."

After his father went downstairs, Brand lay awake, trying to sort out all that had happened. His big, strong father had always been the one to crack jokes and tease. Now he looked sad and broken.

Brand came to a decision. He would help with Casey and Jonah. He would learn all he could about being a rancher, while keeping an eye out for bad old Mr. Dempsey. And someday he would be big like his pa, and he would do whatever it took to ease his father's sorrow.

At last he fell asleep to the rumble of masculine voices below. Despite the ache in his heart, he felt a sense of safety here in the home where his father had grown to manhood.

CHAPTER ONE

Merrick Ranch—Wyoming. Spring, present day

Hold on, Brand." Ranch foreman Chet Doyle pulled his mount beside Brand's and said in a whisper, "Look over there."

A band of mustangs melted into the woods and became invisible as two horses and riders crested the hill.

"I see them." Lifting his hat to wipe at the sweat that beaded his forehead, Brand nudged his horse forward.

Ordinarily Brand's vision would have sharpened at the slight movement of fresh green foliage, and he would have paused to watch the herd disappear. Everyone on the Merrick ranch shared his love of the herds of wild horses that roamed these hills. They were the favorite subject of his aunt's photographs, featured in glossy wildlife magazines. The love of mustangs had been the motivating force behind Casey's decision to become a veterinarian, and they were featured prominently in Jonah's first best-selling novel. But it had been a particularly long day with the cattle in the high meadow, now lush with grass, and Brand was distracted by the pain pulsing down his leg. Even the beauty of the countryside, always such a thrill in springtime, failed to lift his spirits.

Usually the sight of the Grand Tetons towering in

the distance and the Merrick family ranch spread out below, spanning thousands of acres of spectacular hills and valleys, meadows and highlands, would be enough to have him grinning from ear to ear. Today, his handsome face was etched with pain.

Seeing it, Chet fell silent. The rugged foreman, best friend to Bo and Liz since childhood, had been with the Merrick family long enough to read their various moods. And he'd watched Brand fighting this lingering pain ever since that fall from his mount.

When the ranch buildings came into view, Brand's horse, sensing food, lengthened its strides, adding to Brand's torment.

"I know you want this to end, Domino. So do I. But slow it, boy." He pulled on the reins, and the horse fell back to a plodding walk.

Back at the barn, Brand and Chet unsaddled their mounts and toweled the overheated animals before filling troughs with food and water.

At the house, they paused in the mudroom to roll their sleeves and scrub away the dust of the trail before stepping into the kitchen, where they were greeted by the chorus of voices that had resounded through this house for a lifetime.

"Took you long enough, boy." Across the room, Hammond Merrick looked up from the tray of longnecks being passed by his granddaughter Liz. "We were getting ready to eat without you."

Liz shot a soothing smile at Chet and her nephew. "Don't you believe a word of it. We knew you were on your way."

"Thanks." Brand managed a smile before helping himself to a beer and tipping it up to take a long pull. "You know you can always get started without us. After a day in the hills, even leftovers would be a feast."

Beside him, Chet nodded his agreement before quenching his thirst.

Brand's grandmother, Meg, touched a hand to her grandson's arm. "Speaking of feasts, Billy made something special." Her smile was radiant. "Your favorite. Pot roast with all the trimmings."

Brand arched a brow. "You usually ask Billy to make that when you're about to hand me some bad news." He gave her a steady look. "What's wrong?"

"Wrong?" Meg glanced at her husband, who was frowning.

"Supper's ready." Billy Caldwell, cook for the Merrick family for twenty years, waited until the family had taken their places around the table before passing platters of roast beef, mashed potatoes, carrots and snap peas, and a salad of greens and tomatoes grown right in the little greenhouse alongside one of the barns. A basket of flaky rolls was placed in the center of the big table, along with cruets of balsamic vinegar and oil.

With a chorus of praise for Billy's hard work, the family spent the next few minutes holding the platters for one another until all their plates were filled.

They paused.

Hammond's deep baritone intoned the words of the familiar blessing. "Bless all of us gathered here, and those no longer with us."

Brand noted the narrowing of his father's eyes, the only sign of the pain he still suffered at the loss of his beloved Leigh. To this day, Bo was compulsive about checking the many fireplaces in their sprawling ranch house and seeing to it that every fire was banked before going to his bed.

Seeing how his father poured himself into his work in order to overcome his feelings of helplessness, Brand grew up doing the same. And when age began to slow down the oldest members of their family, Brand smoothly took up the slack. Whether a sudden spring snowstorm or a late-summer range fire, Brand was always in the thick of the action.

It was just such a storm that had Brand taking a nasty fall from his horse, crashing into a rock, splintering several bones in his right leg. Old Dr. Peterson, at the Devil's Door Clinic, had sent Brand to a specialist in Casper, who used titanium rods and pins to repair the damage, before recommending six weeks of physical therapy. That had added precious time Brand was forced to spend away from the ranch, and after just four weeks, he'd come home.

Over their meal, the men talked of the crops and the weather.

Casey, freshly showered after a long day, buttered a roll. "With a wet spring like the one we're having, I'm figuring we'll have a long, hot summer."

Twenty-three-year-old Jonah, the youngest, was grinning. "I hope you're right. The hotter the better."

Hammond's stern face relaxed into a smile. "I can't remember the last time the range grass was knee-high before June. This promises a good summer and a healthy herd."

"And a lot of smelly, sweaty laundry," Billy muttered, bringing a round of laughter from the others.

During a lull in the conversation, Brand turned to his grandmother. "I take it you're saving whatever bad news you have until dessert, hoping to soften the blow."

Instead of the usual laughter, she took a sip of her

tea before saying, "I can't help noticing how, since your accident, you've been favoring your leg."

Under cover of the table, he slid his hand along his right leg, from his thigh to his knee. He frowned. "It's fine."

"It isn't fine."

"Give it time, Gram Meg."

She shook her head. "Time's up, Brand. Dr. Peterson warned you about this when you cut short your therapy in Casper. There was no one in Devil's Door trained to follow up. Now you're limping and gritting your teeth when you think nobody is looking. There's no sense pretending that it will go away all by itself."

As if to hold off the approaching storm, Billy began circling the table, serving slices of carrot cake topped with mounds of vanilla ice cream.

Brand picked up his fork and dug into his dessert. "We're through with this discussion, Gram Meg. My leg will heal."

"Yes, it will. Because I've asked Dr. Peterson to send someone trained in physical therapy to come here to the ranch and work with you."

He lowered his fork. "A physical therapist? Here? And when do you suppose I'll have time for such nonsense? Before I muck stalls at dawn? While I'm repairing the wheel on that tractor after breakfast? After I ride herd on a bunch of ornery cattle until dark?"

"Yes." She folded her hands in her lap, a sure sign that she intended to dig in and not back down. "Before, during, or after. I don't care how you make it work. I know only that you will have to make time in your busy day for regular therapy sessions until your leg is one hundred percent healed."

"In case you haven't noticed, I'm no longer that little

eight-year-old you and Pops used to hold down while forcing nasty cough syrup down my throat."

"Really? You're acting just like him."

Brand lifted his chin, biting back the curses that couldn't be uttered in front of his grandmother. "I won't be pestered by some physical therapist asking me to walk on a treadmill or do a series of squats."

"He's already on his way. Dr. Peterson told me that Avery Grant will be here tomorrow. Billy and Liz gave me a hand cleaning out Hammond's old suite of rooms on the third floor. I'm sure our visitor will be comfortable up there for the next six weeks."

"Six weeks?" Brand's voice frosted over. "You're wasting his time and mine. Not to mention a whole lot of money for nothing."

"No matter. It's done."

He tossed aside his napkin and shoved away from the table. His eyes narrowed on his grandmother. "I can't believe you'd do this behind my back."

"You left me no choice, Brand. Once you started avoiding the issue, I realized I'd have to take a stand."

Without a backward glance, he stalked out of the room, his limp so pronounced the entire family could see him fighting to hide his pain.

After hearing his footsteps on the stairs and the slam of his door on the upper level, Bo turned to his mother. "We can all see that his leg's giving him plenty of trouble. But the decision should have been his."

The older woman gave a nod of her head. "I know. I hate hurting him like this. But my years of nursing training told me he'll never heal properly without help."

Old Hammond pointed with his fork. "I agree with Bo. You crossed a line, Margaret Mary."

Bo laid a hand on his mother's arm, hoping to soften his grandfather's words. "I realize you're the medical expert in the family, and I know you consulted with Dr. Peterson before doing this. If it's any comfort, I agree that Brand needs help. But I also feel it should have been Brand's choice."

Egan rushed to his wife's defense. "Meg's just doing what she knows is right."

At the sudden silence in the room, Meg gave a long, deep sigh. "Being right doesn't make it any easier."

From the head of the table, Hammond declared firmly, "The deed's done, thanks to your meddling, Margaret Mary. Now, either our Brand will learn to work with this therapist or decide to fight him tooth and nail. And I wouldn't blame him one bit if he refused to be bullied into this. In my day, pain was a part of life, especially life on a ranch."

It was on the tip of her tongue to remind her father-in-law that times had changed, but Meg held back, having learned after almost fifty years in the family that her response would fall on deaf ears.

To defuse the situation, Casey turned to his great-grandfather with a grin. "My money's on a knock-down dirty fight between the two. And nobody comes away from a fight with Brand without being bloodied."

Jonah nodded. "I'm with you, bro. I pity this poor stranger who thinks he'll be able to give orders to our grumpy big brother."

The two fist-bumped, while beside them Liz gave a shudder. "As if life around here isn't crazy enough in spring. I can't imagine how having a stranger getting in the way can be anything except trouble. But I have to admit, with Brand in such a rotten mood, it should prove to be an interesting few weeks."

"Easy enough for you to avoid whenever it gets ugly." Meg turned to her daughter. "You can drive off into the hills and snap all those lovely photographs. But I'll be stuck here, mediating between your headstrong nephew and this poor young man sent here to help him."

"You could always go along with me and hide out in the hills. I guarantee one thing. You'll enjoy some spectacular scenery." Liz turned to Chet. "Are the trails dry enough for me to drive on?"

He shrugged. The men in this family weren't the only headstrong ones. This woman, so much like her grandfather, wouldn't care if her truck got stuck for weeks in the wilderness. Whenever she was ready to escape, she did so without asking any of them for their help. "You'll have to keep an eye out for runoff. Some of the trails are too soft to maneuver."

Jonah arched a brow. "You could always go along with her, Chet. Like a bodyguard."

Though the foreman's expression never changed, a slight flush darkened his neck.

"As if he doesn't have enough to do wrangling those herds." Hammond pointed a fork at his granddaughter. "Why, I was exploring those hills when I was only—"

"Half my age. I know, Ham." Liz blew the old man a kiss. "And we're so glad you did. I can't imagine living anywhere else in the world than right here." She turned to her mother. "I think I'll head out in a couple of days. Want to come along?"

Meg merely shrugged. "I guess I'll wait and see how Brand and this therapist get along before deciding whether to stick around or run and hide."

Casey was grinning. "I'm picturing this guy Avery with no neck, bulging biceps, and wearing thick glasses."

Jonah added, "And carrying a megaphone as he belches out orders for Brand, chained to a treadmill."

That had the others chuckling at the image planted in their minds. As they began pushing away from the table, they called their thanks to Billy before going their separate ways.

All but Meg, who poured a second cup of coffee and sat, brow furrowed, deep in thought.

She hoped she hadn't started an all-out war with the hiring of this therapist. Over the years, she'd seen how quickly an ugly incident could get out of control, burning everything in its path, like a range fire.

CHAPTER TWO

Avery Grant plugged in the directions given by Dr. Peterson and studied the GPS map before heading toward the Merrick ranch.

According to the good doctor, Brand Merrick fit the stereotype of every cowboy in this part of the country. Hardworking. Dedicated to family. Also tough. Stubborn to a fault. And absolutely determined to continue working as he always has, despite whatever pain he was forced to endure. A pain he felt compelled to overcome without a therapist, thank you very much.

"You've come highly recommended," Dr. Peterson had said. "But I doubt you've ever had to deal with a fourth-generation Wyoming rancher, who knows nothing but backbreaking, never-ending work that would stagger a giant. When it comes to describing Brand Merrick, I'd call him a man among men. Everyone who knows him respects him. Men and women alike. But he is nothing if not rock-solid in his opinions."

"Is that a polite way of saying he's stubborn, Dr. Peterson? If so, I've managed to work with some pretty tough customers. I've met men like him who feel their manhood is being insulted every time they have to go through a series of simple workouts, especially when handed to them by a woman."

"Avery, forget whatever you've learned and just try to figure out a way to get Brand Merrick to work with you without every session turning into a battle of wills. It isn't that you're female. His grandmother conveyed his views, apparently shared by his father, his grandfather, and especially his great-grandfather, that accepting help from a physical therapist is a drain on his time." The doctor's voice was warm with laughter. "We don't call Hammond Merrick 'the Hammer' around here for nothing. He's the toughest, most determined old codger you'll ever meet. And he has nothing but disdain for anything he considers a waste of time."

"I've heard it all before. But thanks for the warning, Doctor. I'll do my best to make a believer of Brand Merrick. And his great-grandfather, if necessary."

"I wish you well." Dr. Peterson had been smiling as he offered a handshake. "Good luck. You're going to need it."

Avery sighed and lowered the window, allowing the fresh spring breeze to blow through the rental car. She'd begun to think her luck had run out. Then she'd received the call to take on this assignment in the middle of nowhere. Even though she was feeling completely out of her element, she was determined to put the next six weeks to good use.

She'd left home expecting a certain amount of discomfort. After all, the Michigan college town of Rose Arbor, where she grew up and followed her father into medicine, had offered a wealth of intellectual pursuits. Libraries, museums, theaters. The town bustled with shops and restaurants, and though the university buildings were ivy-covered and quaint, the city that grew up around them was modern and high-tech.

If she were to describe what she'd seen so far in Devil's Door, she'd call it the exact opposite. Low-tech. A single church, a high school right next door to an elementary school, and both of them single-story buildings with small flower and vegetable gardens. What a concept, she thought with an approving smile. A movie theater, a diner, a small drugstore, a family store that carried new and "slightly used" clothing and household items, a combination hardware and grain and feed store, a small bakery, and a sweet shop. And of course a very busy, very lively bar. The only newer buildings in town seemed to be the bank and a medical clinic. She hadn't noticed a single fast-food chain restaurant or big-box store.

Being here, so far from all that was familiar, she felt like the proverbial fish out of water.

That pretty much described not only this situation but also her life lately. Her father hadn't held back his disapproval. He'd called her a fool for leaving home to take a job clear across the country, in a little town nobody had ever heard of, in a state with more cows than people. He'd told her in no uncertain terms that she was accepting a job that was beneath his only child's considerable talent.

Needless to say, their last meeting had been less than loving. Though he'd tried to be civil, his hug lacked warmth, and he'd told her that whenever she regained her senses, he would welcome her back.

His rejection hurt. He'd wanted, in fact had expected, his daughter to be his clone. Instead, here she was, clear across the country in Wyoming, hoping to bring the gift of health to yet another patient.

What had Dr. Peterson called this rancher? She was grinning. Stubborn as a Missouri mule.

Well, so was she. She'd dealt with plenty of tough cookies. She took pride in her ability to win over even the most hardened patient. She had no doubt her professionalism, her dedication, and her firm-but-gentle manner would win over even this mule-headed rancher.

There was another reason she'd been eager to take on this assignment, though she wasn't quite ready to admit it, even to herself. Wyoming was as far away from Michigan as she could get. And right now, for her peace of mind, she needed that distance.

Following the GPS instructions, Avery turned off the main road and onto a strip of asphalt. Hers was the only vehicle on the road.

She slowed her car to stare in wonder at the amazing countryside. Miles and miles of the greenest grass she'd ever seen, waist-high and dotted with colorful wildflowers. The hills black with cattle. And set as the backdrop to it all, the snowcapped Grand Teton Mountains, looking so majestic they took her breath away.

She'd never expected the Merrick ranch to be so close to the mountains. As she rounded a bend, she had her first glimpse of the house. A graceful mix of stone and wood, soaring to three stories and offering oversized windows to better enjoy nature's view. A wide wooden porch with big, man-sized rockers and gliders encircled the building, offering an invitation to come and sit awhile.

Avery couldn't help shaking her head in wonder.

For some strange reason, when she'd accepted this job, she'd pictured a Midwestern farm. But this was so much bigger, so much more impressive. Like the land, she thought. Like the people who had cleared it and tamed it. All larger than life.

As she pulled around to the back of the house, she saw several trucks parked one behind the other by the back porch. She turned off the car at the end of the convoy and pocketed the keys before making her way up the porch steps.

Just then, a tanned, handsome cowboy in faded jeans and plaid shirt came barreling out the door and nearly collided with her before stopping short and catching her by the elbows.

"Hey. Sorry about that. I wasn't expecting to find a pretty woman directly in my path."

Avery chuckled and pulled back before offering a handshake. "Hi. You must be Brand Merrick. I'm Avery Grant."

"You're Avery?" His smile was quick and easy, adding to his charm. "I'm Casey Merrick. Brand's my brother. It's really great to meet you. Come on inside and meet the family."

She arched a brow. "Weren't you racing off somewhere?"

"Hmm? Oh yeah." His smile widened. "But now that I know who you are, I'd rather stick around and watch the fire…" He paused and added, "I mean, until you've had a chance to meet Brand."

He seemed almost gleeful as he held the door and followed her inside.

It was a big mudroom, with hooks along the wall for hats and parkas, and a shelf below for assorted boots. Across the room was a big sink where a man stood with his back to her, his sleeves rolled to the elbows. The backside of his jeans and shirt were filthy.

Without turning, he began to shuck his shirt.

Before he could undress, Casey stopped him. "Uh, Brand, you might want to wait until you're upstairs to strip. You wouldn't want to shock our visitor."

"What the..." The man turned, and Avery had a quick impression of a man badly in need of a shave. With his shirt open, the muscles of his hair-roughened chest and torso were clearly visible.

"Sorry. Didn't see you there." He stepped closer, and when he smiled and stuck out his hand, that first impression was instantly wiped away. The sweat, the dirt, couldn't hide the fact that, if possible, he was even more handsome than his brother. "Brand Merrick."

"It's nice to meet you, Brand. I'm Avery Grant."

"Avery..." His smile faded. He swung a glance at his brother. "Is this one of your elaborate jokes, bro?"

"I wish I'd thought of it. But, hey, this is even better than a joke. It's the real deal."

Brand's gaze narrowed on the woman. "You're Avery? The...physical therapist my grandmother hired?"

"That's me." She looked from Casey to Brand. "Is there a problem?"

Instead of an answer, Brand turned his back on her and stepped through the doorway.

Casey put a hand beneath Avery's elbow and steered her into the big kitchen, where an army of people were milling about on the far side of the room, talking and laughing and tipping up a variety of drinks, from beer to lemonade.

Brand's curt voice cut through the noise. "Gram Meg, your therapist is here." He emphasized 'your' before saying, "Avery Grant. My family. I'll let Casey handle the introductions."

In the silence that followed, he strode from the room, and his footsteps could be heard on the stairs as the cluster of people simply stared after him before turning, wide-eyed, toward Avery.

A petite woman with soft white hair and an eye-crinkling smile stepped forward. "Well, so you're Avery. I'm Meg Merrick, Brand's grandmother."

"Meg. It's so nice to meet you."

The woman turned to handle the introductions. "This is my husband, Egan, and his father, Hammond. Everyone, including his great-grandsons, call him Ham. He'll expect you to do the same."

"Egan. Ham." Avery gave him a wide smile and was surprised by the dark, angry scowl the older man didn't bother to hide before his gray-haired son, Egan, stepped forward to offer a handshake.

Meg went on with the introductions. "My daughter, Liz."

A blond-haired woman who appeared to be in her mid-forties nodded. She wore faded jeans and a plaid shirt. Her short hair was tousled, her pretty face completely free of makeup.

"And this is my son, Bo, father to Brand, Casey, and Jonah. I see you've met Casey, and this is Jonah, Bo's youngest. And this," she said, turning to include another cowboy, "is Chet Doyle, our ranch foreman."

The foreman was lean and muscled with curly brown hair framing a tanned, handsome face.

Meg turned. "Avery, this is Billy Caldwell, our cook and all-around housekeeper. Billy's been with us for almost twenty years, and we can't imagine how we'd get along without him." She led Avery toward a rail-thin man wearing a spotless white apron over his plaid shirt and jeans. Shaggy hair in a bowl cut framed a lean face with sparkling blue eyes.

He wiped his hand on his apron before extending it. "Welcome to the Merrick ranch, Avery. Or do you prefer Dr. Grant?"

"Just Avery. I studied medicine, but I'm not a doctor. Nice to meet you, Billy. Something smells amazing."

"Slow-cooked beef stew and biscuits."

"My mouth has been watering since I walked in."

As she turned away, Casey said teasingly, "Don't worry about all the names, Avery. We'll wait a day or two before testing you to see how many you remember."

That broke the ice as they began laughing, even as they studied Avery with looks that ranged from amusement to curiosity, and in Hammond's case, downright hostility.

Meg took in a breath. "I must admit, you've caught us by surprise, Avery."

"You weren't expecting me today?"

"Oh, yes." Meg put a hand on Avery's arm to soften her words. "It's just that the woman who set up this appointment called you Avery, and I made the wrong assumption that you were a man."

"A bookish man," Casey added with a grin, "with round, owlish glasses and big soft hands. At least that's how I saw you."

Avery could feel her cheeks growing warmer by the minute. "I see. Is this going to be a problem?"

Meg was quick to give a shake of her head. "No. Not at all. The woman I spoke with assured me you were highly qualified. It's just that…" She paused before saying in a rush, "Leaving friends and family behind to travel across country, especially since we're so far from civilization out here, I'd hoped to ease your loneliness by inviting you to spend your after hours hanging out with my grandsons."

"Oh." Avery managed a small smile as the realization dawned. "Doing guy things, I suppose."

Meg nodded. "Just so you could relax and form a bond."

Jonah, watching with the others, broke his silence. "Don't worry, Avery. Gram Meg and Aunt Liz have survived all these years without doing guy things like getting drunk at Nonie's Wild Horses Saloon or engaging in any bar fights." He arched a brow while looking from his grandmother to his aunt. "At least that I know of."

That brought another round of laughter.

"Oh, I don't know." Casey turned to his brother. "Remember that time Aunt Liz got between you and Marcus Canaday when the two of you were rolling around in the dirt exchanging punches? You had a bloody nose and swore he'd broken it. Then all of a sudden there was our sweet aunt to the rescue, and by the time she'd separated the two of you, she had a torn shirt, was caked with mud, and had a black eye for weeks."

Jonah nodded. "It was a beautiful shiner." He turned to Liz. "And you were my hero."

She joined the others in raucous laughter.

Jonah punched his brother's arm. "And everyone in town was convinced that she'd had a fight with a boyfriend."

At that, Liz shrank back before shooting him a dark look.

Bo put his arm around his sister and squeezed her shoulder. "That's how rumors get started, little sis."

By now, everyone was laughing, including Avery, and without warning, the tension seemed to evaporate from everyone except Liz, who stared at a spot on the floor.

Seeing her embarrassment, Chet crossed to her and offered her a glass of lemonade.

From across the room, Billy called, "Dinner's ready."

As the others gathered around the table and claimed their places, Meg suggested that Avery take one of the two vacant seats next to Casey.

Moments after she was seated, Brand strode in, freshly shaved and showered. Droplets of water glistened in his dark hair. His face without the stubble looked even more lean and handsome than before.

Without a word, he settled himself beside Avery.

When his leg bumped hers, she looked over with a smile, only to be met with a scowl.

As the family began passing bowls of steaming stew and rolls fresh from the oven, along with a garden salad and an array of dressings, the conversation centered on ranch chores.

At the head of the table, Hammond turned to Casey. "What did you think of that new antibiotic? Did it work?"

His great-grandson nodded. "So far. I intend to keep watching and recording the results."

"Good." Hammond turned to the ranch foreman. "And those calves? Any more of 'em showing signs of sickness?"

Chet shook his head. "No new ones since Casey started the treatment."

The old man nodded his approval.

In an aside, Jonah explained to Avery, "Casey recently completed his veterinary studies. Now we don't have to rely on old Doc Streeter, who was the only vet in this county for years."

"I'm sure it's handy for the family to have their own." Avery smiled. "And Chet? Is he family, too?"

"He grew up with Dad and Aunt Liz. He and Dad have been best friends since they were old enough to walk. When Chet came back from three tours of Afghanistan, he was just in time to replace Paddy Clancy, who was as old as Ham."

"And how old is that?"

"He'll be ninety this year, and still going strong."

"Ninety." Avery gave a shake of her head. "He looks amazing."

"Wait till you see him work. He's up every morning before dawn along with the rest of us and out mucking stalls before breakfast, if we don't beat him to it."

Avery shot the young man a look of surprise. "Are you saying you all get up before dawn?"

Overhearing, Casey laughed. "We have no choice. If one Merrick gets up, everybody else does, too." Seeing the look on Avery's face, his smile widened. "You'll see tomorrow morning. We Merricks are a noisy bunch."

"Thanks for the warning."

She was still smiling when she turned in time to see the frown on Brand's face. Throughout the meal he'd remained silent, allowing the rest of the family to carry on the conversation while he brooded.

Turning her head, she decided to completely ignore him and do her best to interact with the others.

Her first rule had always been to never let the patient see a trace of unease.

Across the table, Jonah called to Casey. "You going to Nonie's tonight?"

Casey brightened. "Wouldn't miss it."

"It wouldn't be because of that pretty little redhead who waltzed in last night with Marcus, would it?"

Casey merely smiled. "She may have let him buy her a longneck, but she was eyeing me at the bar."

"And at the pool table, and on the dance floor, where you made a fool of yourself with Gina and Tina."

"Nonie's twin nieces who bartend," he muttered to Avery before saying to his brother, "It got the redhead's attention, didn't it? Maybe, if she's there again tonight, I'll dance with her instead of them."

"Maybe if she's there tonight you ought to ask her name before you ask her to dance."

Casey ignored the laughter of the family. "The important thing is that she knows my name."

"And knows how lame a dancer you are."

Avery joined in the laughter, grateful to have something to serve as a distraction from her unwilling patient beside her, who was making absolutely no effort to hide his intention to ignore everybody.

She found herself grateful for his two brothers, who were proving to be delightful company and provided the perfect distraction.

CHAPTER THREE

As dinner was ending, Meg turned to Billy. "Since it's such a pretty evening, why don't we take our dessert on the back porch?"

At the cook's nod of approval, Jonah looked over. "What's for dessert tonight, Billy?"

"Fudge brownies and ice cream."

Jonah nudged Casey before saying, "Let's postpone our drive to town until after dessert."

The two shared a grin, and Egan chuckled. "Smart move, boys."

Surprised and pleased to have the chance to relax outside, Avery joined the others as they settled on gliders and rockers.

Brand walked out to find all the other chairs and rockers taken. He was forced to take a seat beside Avery on the glider.

The cook rolled a serving cart onto the porch and began passing around bowls of brownies liberally mounded with vanilla ice cream and topped with hot fudge.

Everyone fell silent except for many oohs and aahs as they savored the dessert.

Afterward, sipping strong, hot coffee, Meg turned to Avery.

"Tell us a little about yourself, Avery. Your family. Your home."

Feeling pleasantly content, Avery set her cup on a side table. "There's just my father and me. My mother died when I was twelve." She was aware that Brand beside her had become suddenly alert.

"No sisters or brothers?" Meg asked.

Avery shook her head. "I'm an only."

"Only." Bo chuckled. "Liz used to want to be an only whenever she thought I was trying to boss her around."

"Which was every day." Liz polished off her dessert.

Bo merely grinned. "Things changed whenever you wanted me to do your chores so you could sneak off to meet Boyd Crandall."

Liz looked annoyed. "Boyd promised to teach me how to whistle through my fingers."

"I'll bet that's not all he taught you, Aunt Liz." Casey's remark brought a round of laughter.

"I was only thirteen," Liz protested.

"That would make Boyd fourteen. A dangerous age with all that testosterone raging."

Liz arched a brow at her nephew. "For you, maybe, but Boyd was only interested in teaching me to whistle the way my big brother did, since he'd refused to teach me."

"You got that right." Bo grinned at his sons. "I loved being able to do something Liz couldn't do."

"And now I can, thanks to Boyd."

"Show us, Aunt Liz."

At Casey's urging, Liz put her two fingers to her mouth and gave a whistle so loud and shrill it carried to the hills.

Bo turned to Avery and winked. "Now she's done it.

In no time we'll have half the coyote population around here coming out of their dens to see what's up."

His father was shaking his head at their back-and-forth. "As I recall, Lizzie, you were always looking to Bo to make things right whenever you were in trouble, or wanted a favor." He turned to his wife. "Isn't that about right, Meggie?"

Meg, seated in a rocker beside his, tucked her hand in his. "You're right. Liz never came to us. Always to Bo. Sometimes I was almost jealous of the way she trusted her brother over us."

Avery sat watching this family and their interactions. Hammond looked stern and regal as the conversation flowed around him. With his slightly shaggy hair as white as snow, and thick white eyebrows that framed dark, piercing eyes, he appeared, to Avery, like a king of ancient times surrounded by his noble family, except that they all wore jeans instead of flowing robes.

As she looked around, she could see the similarity among all these Merrick men. Well over six feet, with lean, muscled bodies honed from years of hard physical labor. The same piercing eyes that pinned her, making it impossible to look away. All of them with thick hair in need of a trim. But where Hammond's hair was white, his son Egan had steel gray hair, and his grandson Bo's dark hair was threaded with just a few strands of gray at the temples, giving him a distinguished look.

Brand seemed the most like his great-grandfather. Stern. Unyielding. And when he looked at her, he seemed to be taking her measure, which only made her more determined to stand her ground.

Liz looked like her mother. Petite, a slim, almost boyish figure in faded jeans and a plaid shirt. Her honey hair was short and tousled, most likely because of her habit of running her fingers through it. There was a shyness about her that was endearing. And when she smiled, which seemed rare, her eyes crinkled the same way as her mother's.

Meg set aside her empty cup. "Where's home, Avery?"

"Michigan."

"Are your sunsets as pretty as that?" She pointed to the sun beginning to dip below the top ridges of the Tetons.

Avery sighed. "We have some beautiful sunsets. But I have to admit we have no mountains to compete with yours. This is simply breathtaking."

"That it is." Hammond stretched out his long legs. "And our Liz has the photographs to prove it."

"You're a photographer?" Avery turned to Liz with a smile. "I'd love to see some of your work."

The color rose on the young woman's cheeks as she stared down at her hands.

Meg quickly added, "Since you're going to be here for six weeks, I'm sure Liz will find time to show you."

Jonah nudged Casey. "Time to head to town." He turned to Brand. "Coming with us, bro?"

Brand, his face in shadow, shook his head. "Not tonight."

"Your loss." Jonah looked at Chet. "You coming?"

The foreman grinned. "I'll pass."

"Gramps? Pa?"

As they shook their heads, Jonah said to Casey, "No takers, I guess. Unless you'd like to come with us, Ham."

The old man shook his head. "There was a time I wouldn't have missed watching all the action. But not tonight, boy."

Casey saluted the cook. "Great dessert. Thanks, Billy."

After calling out their good nights, Jonah and Casey strolled to a truck and took off along the gravel driveway.

Hammond eased himself out of his rocker and started toward the door. He tipped his wide-brimmed hat in a courtly gesture as he passed Avery, though there was no accompanying smile. "Good night, young lady. I hope you'll be comfortable here on our ranch."

She smiled at him. "I'm sure I will. Thank you for your hospitality."

Egan took Meg's hand. "I'm beat. You coming upstairs, Meggie?"

Meg nodded before calling her good night to the others. To Avery she added, "If there's anything at all you need, don't be afraid to ask."

Liz got to her feet and started behind her parents, as though unwilling to be left behind.

As soon as Liz took her leave, Chet called good night and strolled toward the bunkhouse.

Bo set aside his empty mug on the wheeled cart. "I'm sure you two will want to talk about some sort of schedule, so I'll say good night now."

Billy followed, rolling the cart with their empty dishes through the doorway.

As soon as the door closed behind him, Brand broke his silence. "My day starts at dawn and ends at dark. It doesn't leave room for any kind of schedule."

Avery had already planned her remarks, hoping to deflect his negative attitude. "I can't even imagine how much work it takes to keep a ranch of this size running smoothly. If you don't mind, maybe I'll just take a couple of days to observe, and then we'll figure out something that will work for you."

"What would work…" He bit back his words, visibly reining in his temper.

He stood and paused to look down at her. "I'm sorry my grandmother brought you all this way, but I'm not about to ask my family to pick up my chores while I waste my time doing some…stretching exercises with a coach."

Avery sat very still, counting to ten.

Forcing a smile, she stood to face him, refusing to give him the advantage of towering over her. Even standing, she realized the top of her head barely reached his chin. She was aware of not only his size, but also the feeling of strength and power emanating from him. She thought about what Dr. Peterson had called him. A man among men. The sudden realization of those words hit her with the force of a physical blow.

"I have no intention of interfering with your busy schedule. But you'll soon see that there's a lot more to physical therapy than a few stretching exercises. What I can teach you about simple movements could prove useful for a lifetime."

Before he could protest, she turned toward the door, aware that she was taking the coward's way out by running. But she wanted to make an exit before he could leave her standing alone in the dark. "Good night, Brand. I'll see you in the morning."

Brand was scowling as the door closed behind Avery.

He turned away, muttering several rich, ripe curses as he limped to the barn. He saddled Domino and led him from the barn before pulling himself into the saddle and turning him toward the hills.

A fast run in the cool night air was just what he needed to clear his head.

While he and his mount raced through the tall range grass, he thought about this latest disruption in his life. If that fall hadn't been painful enough, now he was being asked to revisit the pain. As if some skinny city girl could magically undo all the damage that had been done.

Old Doc Peterson had sold his grandmother some nonsense that therapy was the be-all and end-all of modern medicine. And now that sweet old lady was gung ho to have her miracle.

He paused at the top of Fox Hill and stared down at the family ranch below. The house was in darkness except for a light in the window of the upper floor. He could imagine Avery up there, looking around at the simple surroundings and wondering what in the world she'd been thinking, leaving her easy city routine for six weeks on a ranch in the middle of nowhere.

Slowly, as his anger dissipated, he found himself smiling.

She'd offered to observe his work before figuring out a schedule. Observe? At predawn while mucking stalls? Riding up to the herds at the hottest time of day under an unrelenting sun? Arriving back at the ranch, hot and sweaty and filthy, hoping for a long shower and a nap, and learning that she was expected to join his family for dinner?

He was laughing as he turned Domino toward home. Avery Grant had just given him the opportunity to send her packing without uttering a single word against her.

He would be the perfect gentleman as he invited her into his world. He would smile and nod and be a gracious host as he introduced her to a hostile environment of ever-changing weather, unpredictable emergencies, and a wilderness that refused to be tamed.

Oh, he couldn't wait to see how she reacted after a day or two of real life on a working ranch.

An hour later, as he lay in his bed listening to the faint sound of footsteps one floor above, he fell asleep with a smile.

There was nothing he liked better than a challenge. Especially when he could already taste sweet victory.

CHAPTER FOUR

Narrow bands of rose and amber sliced through the predawn darkness.

As usual, Casey was cracking jokes as he and Jonah trudged into the barn.

"…and Tina was trying to explain that they'd run out of Jack Daniel's, and this cowboy kept insisting his name was Mac, not Jack."

Jonah gave a shake of his head. "Was he drunk, or just couldn't hear?"

"How could anybody hear over the jukebox? It was cranked up so high, I couldn't hear old Carstairs, who was sitting next to me at the bar."

The two brothers were laughing until they spotted Brand in one of the stalls.

Jonah grabbed a pitchfork from a hook along the wall. "A little early, even for you. What's up, bro?"

"Nothing's up." Brand tossed a load of dung and straw into a wagon. "Just wanted to get a head start on morning chores."

Jonah shared a knowing look with Casey. "Eager to see what the city girl has in store for you, huh?"

The two grinned.

Seeing it, Brand's frown deepened. "I don't have time for foolishness."

"Gram Meg seems to think it'll be good for you."

He huffed a breath as he leaned into his work. "Then maybe Gram Meg can come up with an old injury her therapist can work on. As for me, I want no part of it."

Seeing his temper, Casey and Jonah moved into adjoining stalls and decided to give him a wide berth as he worked off his anger.

Avery awoke with a start and inhaled the wonderful fragrance of coffee from below.

Slipping out of bed, she hurried into the shower. A short time later, dressed in yoga pants and a crisp white cotton tunic, she ran a brush through her hair and made her way down the stairs toward the kitchen.

Seeing nobody around, she helped herself to a steaming mug of coffee and sat at the table, waiting for the rest of the family.

Billy stepped into the kitchen carrying supplies. Spotting her, he gave her a wide smile before setting them aside.

"Morning, Avery. I'm glad you helped yourself to coffee. Would you like me to cut up some fruit before I start breakfast?"

"Oh, no thanks, Billy." She held up her cup. "As long as I have caffeine, I'm fine. When will the rest of the family be up?"

He began lifting pots and skillets from a drawer. "Most of 'em are already out and about handling chores."

Avery nearly bobbled her coffee. "I thought I was the first one downstairs."

He chuckled. "You'd have a hard time doing that. I

spotted Brand heading to the barn almost an hour ago. Casey and Jonah not long after."

Avery inwardly groaned. She'd wanted to observe Brand's day, to see when she could slide in a session or two.

She shoved away from the table. "I guess I'll head to the barn."

Billy turned. "Better make a stop in the mudroom and find some cover for that nice white shirt. The same with those shoes."

She looked down at her feet. "I didn't bring any boots."

"There are plenty in the mudroom. Just find a pair that fit. And pull an old denim jacket over those things, or you'll be changing again in an hour."

She drained her coffee and set the mug in the dishwasher. "Thanks, Billy."

A short time later, wearing a pair of oversize boots and a parka zipped up to her neck, she made her way to the barn. Even before she drew near she was gagging on the smell that permeated the morning air.

How, she wondered, could ranchers ever get used to this?

Taking what she knew would be her last good breath for a while, she stepped inside the cavernous barn and paused in the doorway to allow her eyes to adjust to the gloom.

"…think somebody would come all the way from Michigan to work here?" Jonah's voice drifted from one of the stalls.

"Good question." Casey shrugged. "Maybe there aren't enough patients in need of therapy in her hometown."

"Who knows? Maybe she just wants to see how far she can push some hardheaded cowboy." Jonah chuckled at his own joke.

Brand's head came up sharply. "Well, she's not pushing this cowboy." With a vicious oath, he tossed another load of dung and straw before spotting Avery standing in the doorway, looking like a deer in headlights.

"Sorry. Didn't know you were there."

"Obviously." She lifted her chin like a prizefighter. "To answer all your questions, I'm part of a team of therapists who are certified to offer our services anywhere in the country in need of us. I'm here because your grandmother found out about us and offered me a very generous salary to fly to Wyoming to try to bring relief to what she described as her 'much loved grandson's lingering pain, which he is attempting to hide from himself, as well as from all of us.'"

After a moment of strained silence, Brand found his voice.

"That sounds like something Gram Meg would say. I guess I've been too hard on her." He motioned with a shoulder. "If you'd like to get a taste of what we do around here, you can join us in mucking stalls. Or have you been trained to just stand and observe?"

It was on the tip of her tongue to accept his challenge. Then, seeing the sweat on Brand's face as he set aside his pitchfork and lifted the wagon loaded with wet, heavy straw, she bit back her response.

He shoved the wagon out the back door, moving with an ease that was astonishing. Minutes later he returned the empty wagon and resumed his chores along with his brothers.

Avery stepped closer, directing her words to Casey and Jonah while watching Brand. "Do you do this every morning, even in winter?"

Casey, always ready to joke, shrugged. "It beats having

to diaper all our animals. And even then, somebody would have to change those diapers. And it wouldn't be their mamas."

That had Avery laughing. "Good point. Sorry. I must sound like such an amateur."

Jonah assumed a drawl. "Around these parts we call 'em city slickers, ma'am."

She laughed again. "Point taken. I just wish I was slicker."

"Well, ma'am, I'm thinking I'd call you a looker. You're easier to look at than the cows up in the hills we're usually stuck with."

"Gee, thanks for that left-handed compliment."

At that, they all laughed.

Avery glanced over to see Brand's frown morph into a grin. Maybe not a big deal, but it was a start.

She decided to try again. "I'm not ready to shovel manure, but if there's something I can do, just name it."

Casey nodded toward the empty stalls. "We have to spread fresh straw and fill the troughs before bringing the stock back in. Think you're up to spreading straw in those?"

She nodded. "I'll give it a try."

Against the far wall were bales of straw that looked as though they weighed more than a full-grown man. Before she could figure out how she was going to handle one of these, Brand crossed the space between them and jammed an implement into a bale before lifting it with ease.

She shot him a look of surprise. "Thanks."

He looked her up and down. "I don't think you're up to carrying this much weight."

In the first clean stall he set it down, freed the bale, and handed her a pair of work gloves before walking away.

She stood a moment, watching as he returned to his work. Without a word, she pulled on the gloves and began spreading fresh straw. As soon as she'd used up all the straw, Brand was there to carry a fresh bale over. By the time she'd reached the last stall, the three brothers had finished cleaning and had returned their pitchforks to hooks along the wall. After filling the troughs with feed and water, they looked around with satisfaction.

Jonah patted Avery's arm as he started past her. "You do good work. For a city girl."

That had her laughing again. "Thanks, Jonah. I think this city slicker could get the hang of things."

"Don't let the praise go to your head. You've just taken baby steps," Casey said with a grin.

"You're right about that." As she pulled off her work gloves, Brand was beside her.

"I'll take those." He tucked them in his back pocket and put a hand beneath her elbow in a courtly gesture as they walked from the barn. He cleared his throat and squinted against the rising sun. "I hope you can forget what I said earlier."

"When you didn't know I was listening?"

He nodded.

"I hope this means you'd like to start over."

He gave a shake of his head. "I don't want..."

She put a hand on his arm, just the briefest touch, and was surprised by the feel of all those muscles, which caused a flare of heat along her fingertips.

Just as quickly he gave her a sharp look, and she quickly withdrew her hand before tucking it into the pocket of her parka. "Look, I know having therapy wasn't your idea. But since I'm here and being paid very good money, I hope you'll at least give me a chance to prove that I can ease your pain." At his frown she added, "It will certainly ease your grandmother's guilt at having brought a woman here, thinking I was a man."

He couldn't control the grin. "Maybe I enjoy guilting her."

Avery could hear the warmth in his tone and see it in his eyes as well. "You love her too much to guilt her."

"You're right. Not for long, anyway. But at least for a little while, I intend to milk it for all it's worth. It's really kind of satisfying, since she did all this without even consulting with me." He paused before adding, "If you're serious about wanting to see what a typical workday is, I'll be heading into the hills later, if you'd care to join me."

Avery knew he could read her stunned surprise. Before she could say a word, he added, "Have you ever ridden a horse? Or would you rather ride in a truck with some of the wranglers?"

"I know how to ride a horse." The minute the words were out of her mouth, she wanted to take them back. But she'd fallen into his challenge without thinking.

"We don't use fancy English saddles out here."

"I can sit a Western saddle." Oh, she was burying herself and couldn't seem to stop.

"Good." He gave her a sideways look before holding open the door.

By the time they stepped inside the house and paused to shed boots and parkas and wash up at the big sink, Avery was feeling like a rabbit caught in a trap.

And wasn't Brand Merrick the sly one? He'd coaxed her into it without any bait at all, except a challenging look she couldn't seem to resist.

She took comfort in the fact that at least he wasn't as angry as he'd appeared yesterday.

Suddenly she was feeling ravenous.

Maybe it was the work she'd done in the barn. Or maybe, she admitted, it was knowing she and Brand had taken that first step in working together toward a common goal.

Or was he just playing her? The only way to find out was to follow through and see where this took her.

CHAPTER FIVE

Avery was greeted by a chorus of voices as the family stood sipping frosty glasses of freshly squeezed orange juice or draining mugs of steaming coffee.

When Meg spotted Avery walking in, with Jonah and Casey in front of her and Brand beside her, she couldn't hide her look of surprise. "Good morning, Avery. Have you been out for a walk?"

"I walked as far as the barn."

"Where we put her to work," Jonah announced as he reached for a mug of coffee and practically inhaled it.

"To...work?"

Casey downed a glass of juice before adding, "Avery volunteered to muck stalls, but we thought we'd ease her into things by giving her the job of spreading fresh straw."

"In case you've forgotten"—Meg gave her grandsons the hairy eyeball—"Avery already has a job. And it doesn't involve barn chores."

"Her choice," Casey said with a laugh.

Avery nodded. "I wanted to get an idea of the type of work my patient does, before setting up a schedule."

Liz eyed her crisp white tunic. "You worked in those clothes?"

Avery grinned. "Thanks to Billy, I wore a parka and

somebody's old boots before heading to the barn. Otherwise I'd be upstairs right now changing into fresh clothes."

Billy turned to wink. "You're welcome, Avery."

They exchanged knowing smiles.

Avery helped herself to a mug of coffee before crossing to where the others had gathered.

Satisfied that the choice of chores had been hers, the conversation turned to weather, a big factor in every rancher's life.

Hammond turned to Brand. "Chet and I were out in the equipment barn. He said you were thinking of working on that tractor later."

Brand nodded. "That's the plan. In fact, Jonah and Casey are going to give me a hand with it before I head up into the hills." He looked smug. "With Avery. She volunteered to go along."

"Chet got a report of a storm heading into the hills. He's already on his way to join the wranglers."

Brand glanced out the window, noting the clouds that obscured the peaks of the Tetons.

He turned to Avery. "I don't mind introducing you to ranch life. But these spring storms can get pretty rough. Looks like our plans just changed."

The minute the words were out of his mouth, Jonah called, "Let's get moving."

He and Casey started for the door.

Before they were halfway there, Billy dashed after them, holding out a handled bag. "Here's your breakfast for the trail. Sausage and eggs on a bun."

Brand had already helped himself to a cinnamon roll, oozing warm frosting. As he turned away, he called to the family, "I can't promise we'll be back tonight. If the storm lasts, we could be up in the hills for a couple of days." He shot a grin at his grandmother. "Looks like the verdict will stay out on that miracle cure."

Meg pinned Brand with a look. "I never said physical therapy would be a miracle."

He didn't bother with a response.

Minutes later he and his brothers could be seen leading their horses from the barn before climbing into the saddle and heading across a field of lush grass.

In the kitchen, Avery exhaled slowly. That pending storm just saved her hide. At least for today. From now on she'd have to be more aware of just how vulnerable she was to accepting Brand's challenges. Next time, if there happened to be a next time, she'd swallow her pride and admit that she wasn't up to handling a quick course in Ranching for Dummies.

"A fine breakfast as always, Billy." Hammond pushed away from the table.

Egan followed his father's lead and set aside his empty cup. "You ready to head into Devil's Door, Ham?"

The older man nodded. "I want to talk to Spriggs about the parts for the backhoe."

Egan paused to press a kiss to his wife's cheek. "Need anything in town, Meggie?"

She nodded. "I made a list." She turned. "Billy?"

The cook reached for a notepad and tore off a page. "All set."

Egan dropped an arm around Meg's shoulders. "Why don't you come along with us? That way Ham and I can take care of our business while you handle whatever you and Billy need."

Meg's smile widened. "I'm fine with that. As long as you throw in lunch, cowboy."

Egan chuckled as he gathered her close to press a kiss to her temple. "It's a date."

As the three walked away, Avery stared after them before turning to Liz. "Your parents are so cute together."

"Yeah." Liz picked up a lidded to-go cup of coffee and hurried out of the room, nearly running in her haste to get away.

Alone with Billy, Avery topped off her coffee and stood by the window, watching as Hammond, Egan, and Meg climbed into a truck and drove away.

Beside her, Billy nodded toward the moving vehicle. "Egan and Miss Meg are a great couple. Theirs is a real love match."

Avery glanced over. "Childhood sweethearts?"

Billy gave a short laugh. "Hardly. I've heard their story a hundred times or more. Miss Meg was studying to be a nurse in Philadelphia when she joined some friends heading to a rodeo in Cheyenne."

"From Philadelphia to Wyoming? That's some trip."

"She says she did it on a whim, to ease the pressure of dealing with finals and to escape her overly strict parents." Billy grinned. "Like you, she was an only child, and she was always trying, and failing, to please them."

That struck a chord with Avery. "So, they met at the rodeo?"

Billy nodded. "She said she watched this handsome young cowboy leading a parade of horsemen into the arena, all carrying flags, and when he glanced her way, she could feel her face burning. Later, when he filled in for an injured friend and agreed to ride a bull, she thought her heart would stop when he was thrown."

"Was he hurt?"

Billy laughed. "Only his pride. But Egan claims the

minute he saw Margaret Mary Finnegan, he was struck by Cupid's arrow. He couldn't even see anyone else except her. It was a whirlwind weekend, and he managed to find out her plans so he could show up at every event, even dinner, on her last night in town. They said a tearful goodbye, and then a week later he showed up at her home to declare his love. Miss Meg's father wouldn't allow him to spend the night under his roof, so Egan took a room at what he called some 'fleabag hotel,' and Miss Meg followed him there. The next day she told her parents she was leaving for Wyoming with 'her cowboy' and never looked back."

"Oh my." Avery gave a gasp of astonishment. "How brave and reckless of her."

"Reckless, indeed. She didn't even bother to take her exams or to graduate nursing school. Her parents never forgave their only daughter, and they both died without ever seeing her again."

Avery put a hand to her mouth. "How horrible. And how sad that her parents carried that anger to their deaths, depriving themselves of the joy of getting to know their grandchildren."

"Yeah." Billy grew thoughtful. "It made Miss Meg more determined than ever to cherish her own family. I've watched her through the years become a fierce mama bear about all of them, and especially Brand, Jonah, and Casey."

"I didn't want to ask. Do you mind telling me where their mother is?"

Billy relayed the story of the house fire and the loss of Leigh, Bo's wife, and how that event shaped all their lives.

"Leigh and Miss Meg and young Liz bonded, as the only women in this family, and were best friends. When Leigh died in that fire, everyone lost someone precious."

"I'm so sorry." Avery thought about all she'd learned. "This family history is fascinating. I could listen to it for hours."

Billy snorted. "Oh, I guarantee you, once Ham gets started, it will turn out to be hours. He has more yarns about the early days here than the history books."

"I can't wait to hear them all." Avery hesitated before saying, "Is it my imagination, or is Liz cool toward me?"

Billy chose his words carefully. "Bo's wife Leigh wasn't the only person Liz loved and lost in her younger days. And it's made her...cautious. Except for family, she doesn't open up much. She's especially wary of strangers."

"I'm sorry she's been shaped by loss. Is there something I should know?"

Billy shook his head. "It isn't my story to tell. And it isn't something she ever talks about."

"I see." She finished her coffee and set the cup in the dishwasher. "Thanks for filling me in on some of the family history, Billy. Now it's time for me to get to work."

Billy arched a brow. "What work can you do without your patient?"

"Now that I've met Brand, I can fill in some of the blanks. Height, weight, physical makeup. Even though there are standard routines, I plan each session around the individual patient's ability."

As she climbed the stairs to her upper rooms, she mulled over all she'd learned.

Every family had a rich and fascinating history, and the Merrick family was no exception. Knowing how tragically Brand and his brothers had lost their mother at a young age, she could better understand that fierce sense of independence she had seen in Brand. It would be a stretch for him to accept help from a stranger, especially if it meant admitting a weakness.

Still, despite his protests, Brand seemed to have softened his stance, at least a little. Whether or not he was willing to give up a little time to at least see if therapy could help was another matter.

From what she'd seen of his limp, he was in a lot more pain than he admitted. The proper exercises could lessen that.

When she reached her suite of rooms, she crossed to the lovely antique rolltop desk and began going over her paperwork.

Pausing, she dropped the pen and walked to the big window overlooking the magnificent countryside. The peaks of the Tetons were cloaked in ominous clouds. Already the highest peaks were covered in a fresh layer of snow.

Snow in springtime. The thought had her smiling as a little thrill shot through her. She was far enough from home to feel like she'd landed in an alien landscape.

She thought about all Billy had told her. She couldn't wait to hear Hammond's tales of his early days here in the wilderness. So many family members living together on this vast land, and all with a story to tell.

The mere thought had her wishing, once again, that she had scads of relatives—aunts, uncles, cousins, grandparents—to fill in all the gaps in her own family history. All she knew from her father was that she came from a long line of scholars and doctors. She couldn't imagine any of them clearing a wilderness and sinking roots in such a challenging place.

Strange, she thought, how different the Merrick family history was from her own. Yet here she was, doing her best to fit in. And hoping her time here could make a difference.

CHAPTER SIX

As their horses steadily climbed, Casey passed around the egg and sausage biscuits Billy had prepared for them.

"So." Jonah pulled his mount alongside Brand's. "What do you think of your new therapist?"

He frowned. "Seems to me she's trying awfully hard to look like she belongs here."

Casey polished off a second biscuit. "I thought it was cute the way she offered to help with this morning's chores."

"Cute?" Brand shot his brother a cutting look. "I had half a mind to let her try to lift that bale of straw by herself."

"But you didn't." Casey exchanged a look with Jonah. "In fact, you were across the barn in a flash. From where I stood, you were acting like Sir Galahad."

Brand's frown deepened. "I didn't want to be mean. I can appreciate that she's trying to make this work. But nothing can change the fact that she's here because of Gram Meg, and I'm the one stuck with pretending to let her help me so she can put in her time and get out of my way."

"So you're not really going to cooperate?"

Brand gave a bitter smile and thought about the trap

he'd set for the city girl before the weather had saved her hide. For now.

"Like I said. I don't want to be mean. I'll do as much as I can. But if she pushes too hard, I can't guarantee I won't push back."

"Or"—Casey exchanged a look with Jonah—"you could just do as she asks and see if it helps relieve your pain."

Brand urged his horse into a trot. Over his shoulder he called, "Maybe she can do something about you. Have I told you lately that you're becoming a pain?"

With hoots of laughter, Jonah and Casey caught up with him and then passed him by as they raced toward the herd of cattle in the distance.

Avery circled around behind the barns and began walking across a meadow. Finding a trail of sorts made by tire tracks, she followed it upward until she reached higher ground.

Looking down at the ranch, she realized that this would make a perfect exercise track for Brand, once they'd worked out some of the bad habits he'd acquired. From her own therapy, she recalled the first rule. When a limb is injured, a body automatically compensates by putting more pressure on the other limb, often causing pain and inflammation to the healthy part of the body. Brand would need to relearn how to walk, using both legs equally. From experience with other patients, Avery knew his first response would be annoyance that something as simple as walking could be part of the sessions.

She watched as, far below, Billy stepped out of the greenhouse alongside the barn. In his hand was a basket of vegetables.

The thought of this man growing the food they ate had her smiling. Though it sounded like a simple thing, she knew that it would take planning and a lot of elbow grease to set up such a process. Planting, weeding, coddling the plants through the stingy winter sunlight, and then starting over again each year. It was proof of how seriously the ranch cook took his responsibilities. And it spoke to something primal in her heart. Maybe because she'd grown up in a thriving city, it was somehow almost romantic to think about coaxing life from the simplest seeds.

She started across the meadow, following the same path, until she reached the back porch, where Billy was busy scraping carrots and peeling tiny potatoes.

"Did you build that greenhouse on your own?"

He looked up. "I had the idea for it for years. But it was Bo and his sons who surprised me with it for my birthday four years ago." His smile widened. "Best gift ever."

"I'll bet. I hope you'll let me see the inside one day."

"Whenever you'd like, Avery. Feel free. There's nothing off-limits here." He placed all the peelings in a paper bag before setting it aside.

At Avery's arched brow, he explained. "Compost. I save everything from egg shells to potato peels to toss into my compost pile. Then I mix it all back into the soil to enrich it without having to use fertilizer. These are nature's fertilizer."

He turned and headed inside, calling, "I baked cheese biscuits if you'd like some."

"I'd love some." She followed him through the mudroom and into the big kitchen, perfumed with the wonderful fragrance of baking.

Billy put the kettle on the stove and placed a couple of biscuits on a plate. When the kettle whistled, he filled a teapot and carried two cups, along with a little tray of cream, sugar, and cinnamon sticks.

"Thank you." Intrigued, Avery stirred her tea with the cinnamon stick and breathed in the sweet smell before lifting the cup to her lips and tasting. "I'm afraid my plain old tea will never seem enough now that I've tried it your way."

That had the cook smiling. "I'm glad. I think everything we eat or drink should be soul-satisfying as well as nutritious."

"Soul-satisfying." She nodded as he passed her the plate of biscuits. "Are you joining me?"

"I am." He filled his cup and took the seat across from her. "What do you think of the Merrick ranch?"

"I'm in awe. It's so much bigger than I'd expected. And so comfortable. I was preparing myself for something...almost primitive, I guess. A rustic place where I'd be sharing a bathroom with an entire family and setting up my exercises in a corner of the living room." She blushed. "The rooms I've been given upstairs are bigger than my entire apartment."

"You don't live with your father?"

"No." She stared down into her cup, idly stirring the cinnamon stick. "With my mother gone, my father sold our house when I left for college and took a place closer to the hospital. After medical school, I found my own apartment."

"Your father never married again?"

She looked over with a laugh. "He's married to his career. There is not a more driven surgeon at the hospital than Alexander Avery Grant."

"Alexander Avery. So, if you'd been a boy, you'd have been a junior."

"Though my parents didn't give me the first name

Alexander, I'm still expected to be a junior." Her smile faded slightly.

Sensing that he'd hit a nerve, Billy changed the subject. "When will you and Brand begin therapy?"

"Whenever he can find the time. Since he's made his reluctance clear, I'm hoping to wait a day or two, just so he can ease into it." She broke open a biscuit and nibbled. "Oh, these are wonderful."

His smile was quick. "Thank you."

"How did you happen to become a cook on a ranch? Did you grow up around here?"

"I grew up in Oklahoma, on a ranch small enough to fit in one corner of this place." Billy stirred his tea, smiling at the memory. "My grandmother lived with us and oh, how she loved to cook. She would start early in the morning, and by suppertime the house would smell so good that even if you'd just finished a feast, you'd be hungry to try whatever she was cooking."

"She was your teacher?"

He nodded. "After Granny died, and then my folks, I couldn't maintain the ranch. I was seventeen and learned the hard way about taxes, insurance, supplies, buying good breeding stock. It was all too much to handle, even if my passion had been ranching. Which it wasn't," he added with a laugh. "Cooking was my passion. So I sold the place and moved to town, got a job in a diner, then moved on to a big, fancy restaurant."

"Did you like it?"

He shrugged. "It was a living. But the owner had a nasty temper, which he often took out on the staff, and one day he tossed an entire pot of beef stew against the wall because he'd had a fight with his partner. Then he ordered the kitchen crew to clean up the mess. I remember taking off my apron and walking into his office to tell him I'd had enough of his tantrums and was through. He reminded me that his uncle was a big shot in the state government, and said if I left, he'd see to it that I'd never get work in his state again."

"Did you?"

Billy grinned. "I didn't give him a chance to prove his threat. I drove to the bank, cashed my last check, and then started driving. Days later I found myself in Devil's Door, Wyoming. I walked into a little diner to ask if they needed a cook. The old guy there said he didn't need anybody, but he'd heard the Merrick family needed some help at their place, what with all of them living under one roof. I drove here, walked up to Hammond in the barn, who sent me inside to talk to his daughter-in-law Margaret Mary, who hired me on the spot. She told me she'd been cooking for all of them since the fire and homeschooling her three grandsons, and it was all proving to be too much for her."

"You told me that a fire took Bo's wife, but I'm missing a lot of details."

Billy sipped his tea. "I wasn't here when it happened, but I've heard the story. Bo and Leigh moved into the old Butcher ranch that adjoined the Merrick property. The Butcher family and the Merrick family had shared range-land for as long as they'd been in Wyoming. The Butcher house was over a hundred years old, and apparently sparks from the fireplace ignited the roof before burning down the entire place. Bo and the boys escaped and came back here to live."

"How terrible for all of them. How old were the boys?"

"Just little guys. As I understand it, Brand hauled his two younger brothers downstairs and woke his folks before dragging Casey and Jonah outside. The rest of the family living here saw the smoke and rushed over, but they were too late to save Leigh."

Avery touched a hand to her heart. "I know how devastated I was losing my mother to illness. I can't imagine losing her in such a tragic way as a house fire."

"Yeah. It left its mark on all of them."

Avery leaned forward. "Why did they stay on here? Didn't Bo want to return to his own place and rebuild?"

Billy shook his head. "The Merrick family absorbed the land and took down the rest of the buildings, hoping to put that sad history out of their minds."

"Do they ever talk about it?"

"No need to. I'm sure it's still in their hearts. But the Merrick men put all their energy into work. It's the great healer for them." Billy drained his cup. "Speaking of work, I'd better get to mine. Would you like anything else?"

"No, thank you, Billy. And thank you again for filling me in on a little of the family history." She set her empty cup in the dishwasher. "And for the record, I'm glad you drove to Devil's Door looking for work."

"So am I. I'll tell you this. Since starting here, I've never looked back."

As Avery walked out of the kitchen, she could hear him humming a little tune as he began his chores.

Everyone, it seemed, had a story. And through luck and a lot of hard work, they were able to write their happy ending.

CHAPTER SEVEN

Avery paused in her work upstairs.

This space had been a complete surprise. A small room beside the bathroom had turned out to be a sauna, complete with temperature controls and a long bench for reclining.

When Avery raved about it to Billy, he explained that the upper floor had once been Hammond's, until climbing so many stairs proved to be too taxing at the old man's age. He abandoned the upstairs for a room on the main floor. Since then, these rooms had been used for nothing more than storage until they were cleaned out for her use.

While he chopped vegetables, he added, "That suite of rooms is a little gem that has been completely overlooked for years."

"Billy, this 'little gem,' as you call it, would rent for a huge sum where I live. Someone in the family might want to think about moving up there when I leave."

That had Billy chuckling. "I can't imagine who'd be willing to trade their current rooms for it. When Liz was little, her parents spoiled her and gave her a space they called her princess rooms. She may have replaced the canopy bed and twinkle lights on the ceiling for a modern king-sized bed and a walk-in closet, but it's still a great space. The same goes for all the other family members.

A house of this size offers a lot of privacy, no matter how many people there are."

Avery nodded. "You're right about the privacy. The rooms Miss Meg gave me are just perfect."

"I'm glad they suit you, Avery."

This more than suited her. Besides the big bedroom and adjoining bathroom, there was a second room that she'd decided would be perfect for her sessions with Brand.

It had probably once served as the elderly Merrick's office or library. A stone fireplace dominated one wall, with bookshelves on either side, crammed with dusty, leather-bound tomes with titles like *Soil Conservation* and *Utilizing Mountain Snowpack and Runoff*. It would seem the Merrick family knew how to tap into the research of experts. What's more, it would appear they were dedicated caretakers of the land.

Avery was drawn to the wall of floor-to-ceiling windows that offered a spectacular view of the countryside. It must have given Hammond a sense of pride to survey all his hard work from this vantage point. Rolling hills and meadows folded into each other, and all of them dotted with vast herds of cattle. Men moved about on horseback or in trucks, seeing to the million and one chores needed to keep everything running smoothly. One flat stretch of land had been planted, its rows of crops in perfect symmetry. A giant machine could be seen moving between the rows. The head and torso of a lone man inside the cab had Avery smiling. What would it feel like to operate something so enormous? From this distance, the driver seemed as relaxed as a man driving a car on a country road.

In the distance were the Grand Tetons. The very sight of them had Avery catching her breath. Clouds drifted past, obscuring the highest peaks.

Did Brand and his brothers climb the mountain? Were they even aware of how awesome their countryside appeared to someone from the Midwest?

Avery took another look around the spare room with a sense of satisfaction. On her flight here, she'd fretted that she might be forced to work with her patient somewhere in the house that was occupied by other family members. Having this space on the third floor guaranteed that she and Brand could work together without the others stopping by and possibly making him feel defensive about doing simple exercises.

Exercises. From the little she'd seen, that was the last thing a hardworking rancher needed. The work here on this vast stretch of land appeared to be never-ending, from dawn to dark. And yet, exercise was exactly what was needed to undo some of the bad habits Brand had picked up since his fall.

She was determined to keep things as easy as possible. She eyed the elastic bands that he could use for stretching his leg muscles. A stool for stair-stepping. A chair. A low bench. Beyond that, they would walk outside, as far and as often as time and weather would permit.

Satisfied that she'd done all she could, she stepped from the room and started down the stairs. Hearing a text on her phone, she looked down to pull it from her pocket. In that same instant, she collided with Brand, who was just opening the door to his room. Her phone spun out of her hand and landed on the floor.

"Hey." Brand's big, calloused hands instinctively closed around her shoulders, holding her still.

For the space of a heartbeat, she felt as confused as if she'd run into a brick wall.

His voice held a rumble of laughter. "I guess since

you threw yourself into my arms like this, you're happy to see me."

"I...Sorry." Struggling to regain her composure, she pushed free of his grasp and took a step back, though her head was still spinning from the impact.

"You dropped this." He bent and returned her phone to her.

Seeing the smudges he'd left on her sleeves, he frowned. "Sorry. I got that pretty little shirt all dirty. I'm just back from the hills, and it's hot, sweaty work."

"There's no need to apologize. It was my fault. I wasn't looking."

"No harm done. If you're looking for the family, they're downstairs in the kitchen."

"Thank you." She managed a smile. "I guess I'll...join them." She paused. "Are you coming down?"

He gave her an answering smile. "If I came down smelling like this, they'd make me eat in the barn." He shoved open the door to his room. "I'll shower and change first."

As she walked away, he paused and watched until she was out of sight. Stepping into his room, he closed the door and stood a moment, grinning.

He knew he smelled like a barnyard. Quite a contrast to the woman who'd just sailed right into him, all fresh and sweet-smelling. There was no denying it had surprised the hell out of her, making her look vulnerable. But once she got her bearings, she'd turned back into Miss Prim-and-Proper, I'm-Totally-in-Charge.

That collision had surprised him, too. He was still vibrating from it. And it wasn't from the force of their encounter. She weighed no more than a feather, but he could feel every dip and curve of that slender form as it slammed into him. His body had reacted in a purely masculine way.

He ought to feel bad about leaving his dirty finger-prints on that starched top. But in truth...? If she didn't watch where she was going, hell, next time he might be tempted to leave his fingerprints all over her.

Wondering where that thought had come from, he stripped and stepped under the warm spray.

When Avery reached the bottom step, she paused and put a hand to the wall, waiting for her heart rate to settle.

Her breathing was ragged, as if she'd just run a marathon. She had to struggle for breath. She wasn't about to join the Merrick family until she got her nerves under control.

But why this over-the-top reaction to a simple collision?

Maybe, she realized, because it hadn't been simple. Oh, it had been an accident. And it should have been nothing more than a sorry, see-you-later apology. But that had all changed when she'd looked up into Brand's eyes. Though he'd been as surprised as she, instead of annoy-ance there had been amusement in his eyes. And then his lips had curved into that sexy grin.

Was that when she'd felt overwhelmed? Or had it been when he'd pointed out the imprints left on her shirt? Somehow, though he'd tried to make it a joke, there had been an implied intimacy that stirred her blood.

The very look of him, work-weary, muddy, unshaven, did strange things to her heart. There had been about him a look of solid dependability. Though she'd slammed into him, losing her balance, his quick thinking had kept her from falling. He had the look of a man who would never let a woman fall, no matter the circumstances.

As her breathing returned to normal, she put a hand to her throat. Bumping into Brand must have rattled her brain as well. That was the only explanation for these nerves.

Next time, she would be better prepared. In fact, she resolved, there would be no next time. Once was enough. This man was a patient in need of care. Nothing more.

Feeling more in control, she smoothed down her tunic, took a deep breath, tucked her phone into her pocket, and stepped into the kitchen, where the family had already gathered.

"Hey, Avery." Jonah looked up and motioned to the tray of drinks on the counter. "There's beer, wine, and ice water. Help yourself."

"Thank you." Avery chose a frosty glass of water and settled herself in an upholstered chair beside Hammond's.

The elder Merrick gave her a stern look. "What do you think of your rooms?"

"I love them. Billy told me they used to be yours."

He nodded. "I always liked being on the top floor." Thinking about it, his smile came slowly. "In truth, I enjoyed looking down on the land I'd tamed."

"You have every right to enjoy it. This land is breathtaking. It's bigger than I could have ever imagined. All these hills, and herds of cattle that seem to stretch for miles, and those mountains…" She stopped, embarrassed to be caught going on like this.

He arched a bushy white brow. "Falling under its spell, are you?"

Knowing she was blushing, she ducked her head, hoping someone else would take up the conversation.

Meg took the hint. Turning to her grandson, she said, "What was the big emergency today that had all of you rushing to the Old North Road?"

Bo glanced at his sons. "Chet found flooding from the

mountain runoff. He needed Brand to bring the backhoe and Casey and Jonah to haul away the broken culvert and replace it with a new one. If not for his quick thinking, the wranglers up in the hills wouldn't have been able to get their trucks down for days."

Hammond shook his head from side to side. "As always, Chet to the rescue."

Casey, always the tease, added, "And as always, Brand and Jonah and I were left to handle the dirty grunt work nobody else wanted."

Egan turned to Bo. "Your son sounds an awful lot like you when you were his age."

Bo was laughing. "And I tell him exactly what you always said to me, Pops. Doing all those dirty jobs will make you a better man."

"If that's true"—Casey grinned at Jonah just as Brand stepped into the room—"we were better than most men by the time we were teens."

"Or younger." Brand snagged a beer from the tray. "As I recall, Dad, I was doing your dirty work by the time I was ten or twelve."

"And look at you." Bo exchanged a smile with his father and grandfather. "You're none the worse for it."

"Except for that limp." Casey punched his brother in the shoulder, and Brand punched him back.

"But the good doctor here is going to take care of that," Casey added.

Avery was smiling as she shook her head. "I'm not a doctor. I'm a physical therapist."

"That makes you medical. And that's good enough for me, Dr. Grant." Casey emptied his beer.

"I'll remind you of that if you ask me to stitch up a nasty cut while I'm here."

"Ouch." While the others were laughing, Casey's gaze fixed on her shoulder. "Those smudges on your shirt look suspiciously like fingerprints." He glanced at Brand, then back. "Is my crude brother responsible for that?"

Avery felt her face flame. "I wasn't looking where I was going and ran into him on the stairway. Thank goodness Brand caught me or I think I'd have fallen the rest of the way down the stairs."

"Good reflexes, bro."

Before Brand could respond, Jonah said, "Leave it to Casey. There's nothing off-limits to him. The rest of us were being too polite to mention those smudges, but count on Casey to tease you. So be warned, Avery."

"Thanks for the heads-up." Avery found herself laughing. "I'll be ready the next time."

As the family made their way to the big table, Brand leaned close to mutter, "Sorry again. Casey is good at making a big deal out of everything."

"It's all right." Avery managed a smile. "No harm done."

As they took their places and began passing bowls of salad and garden vegetables and platters of roast beef and garlic potatoes, Avery could feel Brand beside her.

Each time their hands touched as they passed a platter or their thighs brushed, she was reminded of the strength she'd felt in him. Not a brick wall, she thought. A warm, flesh and blood man who had, for that brief instant, stirred something inside her that she very much didn't want to think about.

CHAPTER EIGHT

As the family began dispersing to their rooms or to the porch to watch the sunset, Avery turned to Brand. "I was hoping you might try a session of therapy. You up to it?"

He frowned. "After the day I put in, what's a little more pain?"

Hearing his sarcasm, Avery was quick to say, "If you'd rather relax with your family on the porch…"

"I do love watching the sunset after a day of hard work. But I'm curious about just how you figure to ease my pain by inflicting even more."

"Ouch." With a grimace, she pushed away from the table. "I guess I'd better up my game. Let's head upstairs."

As she climbed the steps, she was uncomfortably aware of Brand trailing behind. When she passed his door, she found herself blushing at the way she'd barreled into him. Talk about clumsy.

She stiffened her spine, determined to put that little scene out of her mind and concentrate on her plans for his therapy.

As they stepped into the room, Brand paused to look around. "I spent a lot of time up here when I was a kid."

"You did?"

He nodded. "Gram Meg wasn't just our substitute mother. She was also our teacher. My brothers and I were homeschooled. Whenever I wanted to get away from the classes, I'd come up here with Ham." Brand wandered across the room. "This rolltop desk was here. When Ham gave up the stairs, this was too heavy to move downstairs, so he had to settle for a smaller desk. He kept a jar of lollipops right here, and he and I would choose our favorite colors and stand at this bank of windows, just staring out at the hills and enjoying candy from his stash."

"That's sweet."

He was smiling at the memory. "Ham has always been special to me. Oh, he was a stickler for rules. He's the toughest guy I know. He has this old-fashioned code of ethics and isn't shy about lecturing us every chance he gets. But when he was willing to let go and relax, I think he really enjoyed the time he spent with his great-grandsons. Of course, he probably didn't expect to still be around at ninety. But he certainly made every day with us count."

"And here he is, as strong and healthy as ever."

Brand shook his head. "Not even by half. He was the strongest man I've ever known. He could lift a cow out of a mudhole without asking for help. I've watched him haul a fence post as tall as a tree, dig the hole, set the post, and all without using anything except his own two hands and a shovel. There aren't many wranglers who can claim that kind of strength. But now he has to be content with mucking stalls and driving into the hills with Chet."

Avery gave a dry laugh. "You make it sound like he's helpless now. Don't forget. I watched you and your brothers muck stalls. It's hard physical labor. How many ninety-year-olds can still do that?"

Brand threw back his head and laughed while holding up both hands in a gesture of surrender. "Hey. Don't shoot the messenger. I'm still in awe of Ham. I'm just saying I've had a chance to watch him through the years, and lately he's had to make some concessions for his age."

"All right." She joined in his laughter. "I guess, since I wasn't around in his younger days, I'll take your word for it that he's slowed down a bit. But I'm still impressed with all the things he can do at his age."

"He impresses the hell out of me, too. He's the man." Brand looked around, changing the subject. "What are those for?" He pointed at the wide elastic bands.

"For stretching your leg muscles."

He saw the way she stared at his legs, encased in snug, faded denims. "You think my muscles need stretching?" He couldn't hide his dismissive tone.

"It's not what it sounds like. Proper stretching of the muscles is the key to becoming pain-free." She picked up one of the bands and handed it to him. "Put your foot here and resist while pulling the band upward."

He easily did as she asked.

"Did you feel that pull in the calf muscles?"

He nodded.

"Now do it again, only slowly, half a dozen times before moving to the other foot."

When he'd finished, he shot her a teasing grin. "I'm still standing. It's a miracle."

His sarcasm had her laughing. "Okay. I claim no miracles here. But I do claim that if you do these exercises faithfully, and gradually expand them, you'll begin to notice your thigh muscles strengthen, especially in your damaged leg. And when that happens, you'll start trusting it to hold you, and you'll stop putting extra weight on your good leg."

He shot her a probing look. "Is that what I've been doing?"

"Yes. Not consciously, of course. It's an automatic response to injury. Even as the injury begins to heal, you try to avoid anticipated pain by treating the damaged limb with care and forcing the healthy limb to do more than usual."

He was silent as he set aside the band. Silent and thoughtful.

He looked around. "What else will we be doing?"

"Some stair steps with that stool. Again, forcing the damaged limb to do as much as the healthy one."

"Sounds too simple."

"I hear that sarcasm. So, if it's too easy, it must be useless?"

He shrugged. "I guess I was expecting to walk around with a weight in my boot. Or doing squats for hours on end. Anything that would add to my pain."

Now she laughed aloud. "I'd be happy to add that to your sessions if it makes you happy."

He joined in the laughter. "Forget I said any of that. I prefer what you have in mind rather than the torture I was expecting."

"Oh, don't get your hopes too high. I'm sure there will be days you'll be cursing my name at the end of a session."

"Not if you deliver what you promise." He ran a hand down his thigh before turning to give her a probing stare. "Do you really think a few simple exercises will completely eliminate this limp?"

"I do. In fact, I believe walking outdoors, especially on hilly terrain, will be another exercise to add to your sessions."

"Isn't that what I do every day?"

"It is. But I plan on having you walk with specific goals in mind. One of them will be to put equal pressure on both legs."

"Sounds too easy to make a difference."

"I guess we'll just have to see." She nodded toward the doorway. "I discovered your great-grandfather's sauna. It would be a great way to relax those muscles after a workout."

Brand nodded. "This old thing hasn't been used since he moved downstairs. Have you tested it? Does it still work?"

She shrugged. "I haven't checked it out. I guess I'd better ask before I try to use it."

He walked past her and held the door. Together they crossed to the sauna.

After fiddling with the dials, he stood back and watched as the heat began to rise and with it the steam.

With a smile, he turned. "Casey and Jonah are going to be so jealous when they realize this still works. I'd better warn you. The room may be crowded with hot, sweaty bodies after a day of bone-jarring work."

"I'm sure that's what it's here for. I bet even Hammond will be willing to climb the stairs for a little time in his old sauna."

Brand nodded. "I'm betting you're right about that." He turned the dials and waited as the steam began to dissipate.

He looked over. "Anything else you'd like me to do tonight?"

She shook her head. "I think after the day you and your brothers put in on that flooded road, you're ready to call it a night."

"You got that right." He followed her from the room.

At the head of the stairs, he paused. "Thanks for my first session, Avery. It wasn't at all what I'd anticipated."

"You're welcome."

"Good night."

As he started down the stairs, Avery stood watching until he paused at the landing and stepped into his room.

When his door closed, she crossed her arms over her chest and turned away with a sense of relief. She'd expected Brand to find fault with everything she'd suggested. Now that he seemed willing to cooperate, she needed to adjust her thinking.

If things continued to go this smoothly, the next six weeks would fly by.

CHAPTER NINE

Brand lay in bed, hands beneath his head. After the day he'd put in, he should have been sound asleep by now. Instead he found himself thinking about Avery Grant. When he'd first seen her, he'd thought her too pretty to be taken seriously. She looked like she ought to be on the cover of a magazine, modeling scrubs for a medical supply magazine. That slender body. The porcelain skin without a trace of makeup.

She was too city-pretty to ever fit in here on the ranch. When she'd offered to help in the barn, he hadn't believed her. But she'd tackled the chore like she'd been born to it, and impressed his brothers in the bargain.

He'd told himself he didn't share their admiration, but he couldn't deny that she was winning him over.

Could Gram Meg be right about the need for therapy?

He ran a hand down his thigh and felt the familiar dull ache. Was it less painful than a month ago? Worse? After all this time, he couldn't be certain. Pain, whether dull or sharp, had become his constant companion. But something Avery said tonight had caught him by surprise.

Had he been overusing his good leg to compensate for anticipated pain in the damaged leg?

It was true that the pain had been unrelenting since the accident. It made sense to avoid it by putting as much pressure as possible on his left leg. He ran a hand down his left thigh and felt a twinge. Was this new pain caused by him overusing it, or was it the result of those leg stretches earlier?

Annoyed, he rolled to his side and tried to think of something else.

But thoughts of Avery couldn't be ignored. The image of her hovered at the edges of his mind. The way she'd felt when she collided with him on the stairway, all soft and pliant. When he'd caught her by the shoulders, he'd had a quick impression of big, startled eyes and was forced to fight the crazy urge to drag her close and kiss her breathless.

Maybe it was the sweet smell of her. Like a field of wildflowers on a spring morning. Or all that long silken hair flowing down her back. Or that willowy body that she covered in long tunics.

Whatever the reason, he'd never before had this quick sexual reaction to a woman he barely knew.

He had scant weeks to get to know who Avery Grant really was. Weeks to work with her, if he chose. Or he could go with his first instinct and push back against this intrusion in his busy life. Since she was the intruder here, maybe he would follow through on his plan to take her out of her comfort zone and into his. Riding into the hills wasn't the same as following a string of rental horses on a manicured path at some dude ranch.

Let's see what you're made of, city girl.

That thought had his mouth curving into a smile as sleep claimed him.

* * *

Avery sat on the side of her bed and was about to set her phone on the night table when she remembered the text that had caused that awkward collision with Brand earlier. In her confusion, she'd forgotten to read it.

She touched the screen, and the words jumped out at her.

Wyoming's not nearly far enough.

After her initial jolt of fear, she looked for the identity of the sender. The message had come from an unfamiliar number. No name. No caller ID.

But she knew this was the same person who had sent her into a panic back home.

It was the reason she'd jumped at the chance to live and work so far away. She'd hoped that enough time and distance would put an end to this…this cruel game that wasn't really a game.

She shivered as she turned out the light and crawled beneath the covers.

Maybe this was a last desperate attempt to rattle her. Maybe, if she didn't respond, he would let this go.

Or maybe what she'd feared from the beginning was closer to the truth. Someone, hiding behind a veil of anonymity, was harassing her, stalking her, either to wear her down or to cause her harm by doing something more.

Something more.

That's what kept her awake at night. That's what had sent her to the authorities in the first place, until their investigation had come up empty. The keying of her car, leaving a deep scratch from front to rear. The message on her front door, written in her own lipstick. In both instances, the police detective assigned to the case had been careful in his remarks. This could be an ex-boyfriend. Someone she had crossed paths with in the past who just wanted to make her uncomfortable. He suggested a security camera and told her to be cautious.

Since installing the camera, there had been no further incidents. But several times, when she'd returned from work after dark, she'd had the distinct impression that she was being followed. Or had she become so paranoid she had begun magnifying every footfall, every sound in the night?

She'd hoped six weeks far from home would bring an end to all this. And now, with a simple text, she was right back where she'd started. Feeling alone and vulnerable. And scared to death.

She rolled to her side, hands balled into fists, her body rigid with tension.

Gradually, using the meditation she'd been practicing, she uncurled her fingers and stretched out her legs, willing herself to relax. In time she was able to slip away into a happy, safe space within her mind as sleep overtook her.

"Good morning, Liz." Avery stepped into the kitchen and managed a smile, though she was still feeling sleep deprived.

"'Morning." Liz barely looked up from the table before returning her attention to her breakfast.

Avery turned to the cook. "Good morning, Billy. I see I'm late again. Are the others out in the barn?"

"Not today, Avery." He indicated a tray of juice and coffee on the counter. "Help yourself. Bo, Brand, Casey, and Jonah had to head back up to the hills with Chet. All that rain overnight has them worrying about more flooding." He nodded out the window. "Hammond and Egan are taking over the barn chores."

Ignoring Avery, Liz pushed away from the table.

"Thanks for those amazing waffles, Billy." She picked up a mug. "And thanks for the coffee."

"You're welcome. Heading to your studio?"

She nodded and, without a word to Avery, breezed from the room, dressed in the now-familiar faded jeans and flannel shirt.

Avery watched her go before turning to Billy. "I hope I'm not the reason she left so abruptly."

"That's just her way. Liz is shy and pretty much a loner. She can be pretty short with people she doesn't know well." He pointed to the waffle iron. "Ready for a sweet treat?"

"I am. I saw what Liz had on her plate, and I realized I'm hungry."

"Good. I'll have these ready in a jiffy." He poured batter onto the waffle iron and closed the lid.

Minutes later he set a plate in front of her with golden waffles covered with fresh blueberries and dripping in syrup.

Avery took a taste before looking over at Billy, busy cleaning the stove. "Oh, Billy, these are heavenly."

He turned with a smile. "I'm glad you like them."

"Like them? I've never tasted anything so wonderful." She returned her full attention to the waffles, until she'd eaten every bite.

She rinsed her dishes and placed them in the dishwasher.

"What are you up to today?" Billy asked her.

"Since everybody's gone, I guess I can just take my time exploring. Mind if I walk through your greenhouse?"

"Not at all. Take all the time you want in there."

"Thanks, Billy. And then I'll just walk around. Being on a real working ranch is all so new and exciting to me."

"Then enjoy exploring. You can't get lost. This old house is so big, it would be impossible not to see it no matter how far you wander."

As she started away, he pointed to the counter. "Want to take along a coffee?"

She picked up the lidded mug. "Thank you, Billy. I'll return this later."

She left the house and, sipping coffee, strolled toward the barns in the distance. Nestled beside the bigger of the two barns was the greenhouse. Inside, the humid air was redolent with the earthy scent of growing things. Snap peas climbed a clever trellis. Bright red-orange tomatoes spilled in and over metal cages. There were tidy rows of carrots, onions, beets, all marked with stakes at the head of every row, as well as green lines of lettuce, spinach, and chard.

Avery walked the length of the rows and back, amazed at the variety of vegetables ready to pick, despite the fact that it was still early spring.

When she'd taken the time to see everything, she stepped out of the greenhouse and began walking past the barn. Some distance away was a second barn, and she wondered what it was used for.

Seeing a door open, she decided to peek inside.

There was so much equipment stored inside that it resembled a factory. Besides a row of trucks, there were tractors, trailers, a combine, a hay baler, a front-end loader, a backhoe, and the giant machine she'd seen from her window.

She walked among them, feeling dwarfed by their enormous size, until she came across another open door.

Stepping through the doorway, she stared around in surprise.

After the gloom of the barn, this room was brighter

than day, thanks to a bank of overhead lights flooding the room with a fluorescent glow.

Standing off to one side of the room was Liz, frowning as she caught sight of her intruder.

"Oh, Liz. I'm so sorry. I thought…" Avery swept a hand to indicate a row of shelves along the walls, with every inch of space covered with photos encased in clear plastic. There was a big work table and tall stool in the middle of the room, as well as cupboards and cabinets for supplies.

Avery stood near the doorway, drinking it all in as the truth dawned. "This is your studio."

Liz merely nodded.

"It's… wonderful." Avery stepped back. "But I didn't mean to intrude. I had no idea this was here. I thought it was just another room in the barn. I'll leave you to your work."

Embarrassed, she turned away. Before she could escape, she felt a hand on her back.

"Sorry." The soft voice trembled slightly. "I'm not used to having visitors to my studio. But now that you're here, you may as well come inside and satisfy your curiosity."

Avery shook her head. "I'll be in your way."

"No." Liz stared hard at the floor. "I'm not working today. I'm just trying to pick out what photos to send to my agent."

Avery's brows shot up. "You have an agent? That's impressive."

Liz offered a fleeting smile while she twisted and untwisted her hands. "Evelyn Carter has been my agent for fifteen years. She's assembling my work for a showing in California."

"Do you show your work often?"

Liz shrugged. "Evelyn usually arranges a showing or two a year. One here in the States and the other somewhere in Europe. She keeps telling me it's the perfect excuse to travel abroad. She's acquired quite a list of collectors willing to buy my work."

"How exciting. When will you go?"

"Oh, I don't go to the showings. I leave all that to Evelyn. I'm only interested in taking my photos. She handles the business end of things." As she spoke, Liz led the way back to her studio.

Avery paused inside to look around before walking slowly past a row of photos. "Oh, Liz, these are fabulous." She stopped for a closer look. "And this." She pointed to a black and white photo of a frozen waterfall. "Was this taken in the Tetons?"

Liz nodded and walked over to join her. "While I was there, the temperature dropped to fifteen below zero. I stepped out of my tent and saw all around me this magical ice kingdom. I grabbed my equipment and started shooting everything I could before the light changed."

She pointed to a second black and white farther along. "These icicles had formed on that rock ledge. The sunlight above was melting the snow, but before the runoff could reach the ground, the frigid air froze it in place."

Avery peered at the photo with a look of awe. "It's as delicate as crystal. I could swear that water is going to drip right off the page."

Liz beamed, showing an animated side Avery could hardly believe. "That's exactly what I was going for."

"How did you get started?"

Liz stood a little apart, hands behind her back, head bowed, obviously reluctant to talk about herself. "When I was just a kid, my parents bought me a small box camera for my birthday. Our ranch was so isolated, I had nobody to play with except my brother, Bo. But Bo had his best friend, Chet, and the two of them weren't happy that I followed them everywhere. With my trusty camera, I started following Ham around on his chores, snapping photos of anything that caught my fancy. The next Christmas, Gram Meg bought me a more intricate camera, with a couple of lenses to filter out reds and excessive sunlight. Within a few years, I'd saved enough money to buy myself a really expensive camera with all the bells and whistles. And after I won first prize in a state contest, I got serious about pursuing photography as a career instead of a hobby."

"Are all of your photos of wildlife and the mountains?"

"Pretty much. But I do love doing portraits, too. One of my favorite subjects is Ham. His white hair and sun-bronzed skin and those big, workworn hands. And his look of concentration when he's tending a sick calf or mending a fence. My nephew Casey has that same look."

Liz led the way to a second shelf. "This is Ham visiting our family cemetery up in the meadow."

Avery joined her to study the picture of Hammond Merrick, wide-brimmed hat in hand as he paused, head lowered, beside a row of weathered headstones.

"His wife?"

Liz nodded. "Amanda. He calls her his Mandy. There are a lot of Merricks buried in that meadow. My sister-in-law Leigh, along with a few of my ancestors. Every so often, summer or winter, I'll see Ham trudge up the hill and disappear over a ridge, and I know he's paying a call on his Mandy."

Avery continued staring at the photo. "That's so sweet." She cleared her throat before adding, "I can't remember the last time my father went with me to visit my mother's grave."

"Maybe it's too hard for your father to think about his wife in the grave. Some folks just can't do it."

"Or maybe they just don't care because they have more important things to do in their life."

Liz touched a hand to her arm, then just as quickly withdrew it. "I think I'd have a hard time visiting a big, impersonal cemetery. It's different here. This is our land. All the dead buried here are ours."

For a moment Avery couldn't find any words. She didn't know what surprised her more. The fact that this aloof woman had actually reached out to touch her for the second time or that Liz could feel such empathy for someone she'd never met.

Avery stared at the photo of Hammond, hat in hand, visiting his wife's gravesite, and knew the image would remain etched in her mind. "I can only imagine how comforting it must be to live in the same place as all those who went before you. And to know that they carved out this space from pure wilderness."

Liz said softly, "Once you leave the ranch, it's still wilderness around us. It's a shame you can't take the time away from your work to go with me into the mountains. Up there, it isn't uncommon to see mustangs, mountain goats, wolves, and even a big cat or two. And all of them living as free as their ancestors hundreds of years ago."

Avery sighed. "I can't even imagine seeing such beautiful wild creatures in the flesh. All I've ever seen of them are photographs." When she realized what she'd just said, she laughed. "The photos I've seen may have been yours."

Liz shrugged. "An awful lot of my prints have appeared in wildlife magazines."

"You must be so proud."

"I am." Liz didn't meet her eyes, instead turning toward the shelves of photographs. "I guess I'd better get busy picking out which ones to send to Evelyn."

Taking this as a signal that she had overstayed her visit, Avery turned toward the door. "Thanks for allowing me to see your work, Liz. It's really wonderful."

When there was no answering response, she added, "I'll see you at the house later."

As she made her way from the barn, Avery found herself thinking about Liz Merrick. Despite her initial annoyance at having Avery intrude on her privacy, she'd made a valiant attempt to make up for it.

Her voice, her entire demeanor, had changed when talking about her work. There was such vitality, such fire, when she spoke about the various photographs.

Maybe the truth was that Liz was only comfortable in her studio or out in the wild, photographing her beloved mountains. But she had permitted Avery to see, for those few moments, another side to her personality.

What a shame they couldn't form a bond. It would have been such a comfort to have a friend in this place. Especially one as complicated as Liz Merrick.

It was only a few weeks, Avery reminded herself. Not long enough to form any lasting bond, friendship or otherwise. Here in this isolated place, it would be weeks of work and enforced solitude.

Not a bad thing, she consoled herself, considering the tension she'd left behind.

CHAPTER TEN

Avery woke to the sound of masculine voices, raucous laughter, and doors opening and closing. She lay a moment, struggling to get her bearings. Not home. A ranch in Wyoming. She was smiling as she stretched her arms above her head and came fully awake.

Yesterday had been a day of exploring the barns and the many outbuildings, as well as the pastures nearby. She'd spent several lazy hours watching the antics of a foal learning to run alongside its mother. He was as frisky as a child, pausing to sniff at everything new and interesting. He would run full-out across the pasture, then suddenly leap into the air, as though trying to fly. And all the while the mare nibbled grass nearby and kept an eye on her curious child.

As the day wore on, Avery found herself falling into an easy rhythm of life away from the city. It occurred to her that, without the traffic sounds, the blaring of horns, the shrill sirens piercing the air, she could actually hear the chorus of birds and the hum of insects. She felt as though she'd landed on an alien planet.

Alien or not, she was eager for another day.

After a hasty shower, she dressed in a T-shirt and

the only pair of jeans she'd thought to pack. Tying her hair back, she slipped out of her room and hurried down the stairs.

From the voices in the kitchen, she knew Brand and his brothers hadn't yet left to see to the barn chores.

The voices ceased abruptly when she walked into the room, before Casey and Jonah called out a greeting.

Billy finished filling mugs with coffee before looking over at her. "Good morning, Avery."

"'Morning, Billy."

Brand looked surprised to see her. "You're up early."

"I thought it was time to get with the program. I can help with morning chores."

Brand's smile came quickly, realizing this was the perfect chance to test her. "Casey and Jonah have the barn chores covered. But if you'd like, you can ride with me to the herds."

She hesitated a moment. "Ride?"

His smile grew. "Since you boasted that you're comfortable riding a horse, we'll skip the truck and I'll saddle up one of our horses for you."

"But breakfast…"

"We can eat along the way. Billy always has food ready for the trail." He nodded toward the tray of steaming mugs. "Help yourself to coffee, and you can join me out back in a few minutes."

As he and his brothers ambled away, she stood sipping coffee and staring out the windows at the surrounding hills. Just how far away was the herd? How long would she be in the saddle?

She turned to Billy. "Do you think I need a jacket?"

He shrugged. "Hard to say. Mornings and nights are usually cooler in the hills than down here. But later in the day, when the sun is high, it could be steaming up there while it's turned cool down here." He nodded toward the mudroom. "There are half a dozen denim jackets hanging there. Help yourself to whatever fits you."

He glanced down at her canvas sneakers. "Since you're riding, you may want to try on a few Western boots as well. Something sturdy enough to handle the cow patties you'll no doubt step in a time or two."

The two shared a laugh while Avery set aside her half-finished coffee and made her way from the kitchen. In the mudroom she sat on a wooden bench trying on leather boots until she found a pair that fit. Slipping on a denim jacket, she made her way outside to watch as Brand approached, holding the reins of two saddled horses.

"You're starting to look like a born rancher." He gave her a long look that had her cheeks coloring. You'll need a hat. The sun's already out." He handed her a wide-brimmed hat he'd snagged from a hook in the mudroom earlier.

As Avery set it on her head, he turned. "This is Honey. She's a sweet mare who won't insist on having her own way."

"That's good, I think." She stroked Honey's muzzle. "Hi, Honey. I hope you live up to your sweet reputation."

Before she could pull herself into the saddle, Brand was beside her, his hands at her waist, lifting her with ease.

"Thank you." She managed a smile of thanks, though in truth she could still feel the imprint of his hands where he'd touched her. Silly, she knew, but he'd caught her by surprise. Something he seemed to do often.

Next time, she promised herself, she'd be more prepared for that sudden jolt of heat when he touched her. If he touched her.

He settled himself into the saddle of his gelding. "This is Domino. He and I have ridden these hills since I was a kid." With a touch of his knee, his horse turned and began the ascent across a flower-strewn meadow.

Honey followed behind at a leisurely pace.

As the trail became wider, Brand halted his mount until Honey caught up.

He shot an admiring look at the way Avery handled the reins. They were held loosely in her hands as she swayed gently in the big saddle. He'd half expected her to be clutching the saddle horn, the way many inexperienced riders did.

"You look like you were born here."

"Pure illusion." She gave a laugh. "I'm working very hard at not thinking about how sore I'll be tonight."

"Whenever you get tired, let me know and we'll walk."

"I don't think you want to walk all the way up this mountain to your herd."

He laughed. "You're right. But just say the word and we'll dismount for a while, so your muscles adjust."

"I'm not worried about any of my muscles except my backside. I'm sure I'm going to pay for this tonight."

He joined in her laughter. "There's not much I can do about that." He paused, surprised by her honesty. "Want to go back and exchange the horses for a truck?"

She shook her head. "Too late. I'm in this for the long haul. And if I'm too sore to get out of bed tomorrow, I'll remember that I have nobody to blame but myself."

She lifted a hand to indicate the scene around them. "Do you ever stop to just enjoy this spectacular countryside?"

"Probably not as much as I should. Some days I feel like all I do is put out fires. A broken culvert. A flooded road. A fence down. A herd in distress."

"You're lucky to have so many family members around to lend a hand."

"Yeah." He squinted into the sun. "We all do our share. And when one of us is down, there's always someone around to handle double duty."

"That's got to be a comfort."

"It is." Their horses moved through a stand of dense trees, coming out the other side of the woods into a flat stretch of green meadow, dotted with wildflowers.

"Oh." Avery drew back on the reins. "Just look at this."

"One of my favorite spots." Brand paused Domino beside her. "Why don't we stop here and enjoy what Billy packed for breakfast?"

He slid from the saddle before reaching up to ease her to the ground.

After tethering the two horses, he led her to a sunny spot in the grass and unrolled a zippered bag. Inside were half a dozen biscuits filled with thick slices of ham and eggs, along with slices of tomato and cheese.

Seeing it, Avery couldn't help laughing. "Does Billy expect us to eat all this?"

"He does. And we never disappoint him."

As she nibbled her food, Brand handed her a lidded cup of coffee.

"Oh, this is wonderful." She polished off the biscuit and sat back, feeling revived. "I think I could learn to love living like this."

Brand looked around with a smile of satisfaction. "I can't imagine living anywhere else. When my brothers and I were kids, we'd head up to the herd with Pop and Gramps and Ham, and they'd teach us exactly how they wanted us to do things. Ham would order us to cut a weak calf out of the herd or put an injured one behind our saddle. We were helping deliver calves before we were teens. And at branding time, all of us worked like dogs. It was hot, sweaty, filthy work. But then, in the middle of all those exhausting chores, he would surprise us with a big, hearty lunch right here in this meadow." Brand smiled at the memory. "We'd gather around him, sitting in a circle in the tall grass, and just eat and laugh and listen to his tales of the early days here." Brand shook his head. "I never got tired of hearing his stories." He grinned. "And still don't."

"You're so lucky to have so much family."

He looked over. "What about you? Grandparents?"

She shook her head.

"Aunts and uncles and cousins?"

Another shake of her head. "When my mother was alive, she made everything so much fun, it never occurred to me to want anyone else. Even when my father would miss an event, like my first dance recital or the spelling bee I won, she would be there beaming with pride, and it was enough, just having her there."

"That's nice." He arched a brow. "Why did your dad miss those things?"

"He's a teaching surgeon. As he said, saving someone's life is more important than watching a bunch of little girls in tutus looking lost onstage."

"Couldn't he do both? Save a life and cheer on his daughter?"

She shrugged and looked away. "He had to make a choice."

Seeing the pain in her eyes, Brand handed her a second biscuit.

She surprised herself by eating it, along with a handful of strawberries Billy had placed in a plastic bag. When she'd finished, she gave a sound of surprise. "Did I really eat all that?"

Brand chuckled. "You may not realize it, but riding burns up a lot of calories. Not to mention the effects of all this fresh air on a body. It's why we consider a cook like Billy a real treasure. He understands hungry ranchers."

He wrapped up the rest of the food and returned it to his saddlebag. "Ready to ride?"

She nodded.

Again he helped her into the saddle.

This time she told herself to be ready, but nothing could prepare her for the heat that spread through her limbs at the first touch of his hands to her waist.

She lifted the reins. "How much longer until we get to the herd?"

"Just up over this ridge." Brand nudged Domino into a trot, and Honey picked up her speed to follow the leader.

At the top of the hill, they could see, spread out before them, the land looking like a sea of cattle. Moving around the perimeter were wranglers on horseback, keeping an eye on the herd.

For a moment Avery was speechless at the amazing sight, like something out of a movie.

When she found her voice, she managed to say, "There must be a thousand or more cows down there."

"More," he said with a grin. "A whole lot more."

She heard the pride in his tone. "And you and your brothers were up here working with the wranglers when you were just kids."

"Didn't you ever go to the hospital with your father?"

She nodded. "As often as he'd allow it."

He gave a shrug. "Same thing. That's your family business. This one's ours."

His words had her laughing. "Somehow, walking around a sterile hospital isn't quite the same as making your way through a herd of cattle, and actually helping deliver a calf."

He joined her laughter. "Okay. I'll admit our family business is messy. And our uniforms are different. But the results are the same. Because of what we do here, people are fed and clothed. And we eat, we sleep, we pay the bills. Best of all, we're doing something we love."

Avery was grateful that Brand had insisted on getting her a hat. Without it, she'd have been burning under the afternoon sun. She'd removed her denim jacket, tying it behind the saddle as she'd seen Brand do with his.

She'd chatted with Chet and met the wranglers, some of them college students, pausing in their work to slather on sunscreen, while others, who had been around for years, had ruddy skin and heavy beards.

She'd watched as Brand moved comfortably among both the wranglers and the cattle. A man completely at ease in his own skin.

When Chet had ordered a wrangler to lasso a cow and isolate it from the herd, the bearded man had been almost courtly, tipping his hat to her before riding off to follow the foreman's orders.

She'd turned to Brand with a smile. "Such manners."

He was watching her reaction. "A cowboy's code, ma'am. Fiercely protective of women and children. Especially pretty women."

That had her laughing along with him. But she'd sensed that beneath the mellow charm, he'd meant something more. It sent a shiver along her spine.

"I'm amazed at the sense of teamwork."

"We're all working for the same thing up here. If a man doesn't care about the job at hand, he doesn't last long. Chet has no patience with slackers."

"I can see that." She could actually sense the camaraderie among the crew as they moved among the cattle, doing whatever was needed.

As they started away from the herd and back down the mountain, Avery couldn't believe how quickly the day had flown. Could it really be edging toward suppertime?

She couldn't remember a day slipping away so easily.

Brand slowed his mount and waited for Avery to catch up. As they moved along the familiar trail, he glanced over. "Feeling tired?"

She shook her head. "Not even a little. I'm so glad I had the chance to see this. Thank you, Brand."

"You're welcome." He experienced a twinge of guilt. He'd conned her into riding, thinking she'd be ready to throw in the towel hours ago. He'd expected to feel like a victor, lording it over a smart-ass city girl. Instead, she'd been intrigued, curious, and actively engaged in every step of the ranch operation. From the questions she'd asked and the attention she'd paid to their answers, the wranglers had gone out of their way to engage her in conversation.

Avery continually surprised him. She wasn't at all what she'd first appeared. Instead of a standoffish woman who was all business, she'd mingled with the wranglers as though she'd been born here.

When she let down her guard over breakfast, he'd discovered something very wounded and vulnerable about Avery Grant. Could that cool demeanor all be an act to hide a wounded heart?

He knew what it felt like to lose a mother. But he and

his brothers had been lucky to have this large and loving family around them to ease the pain of loss. How would a young woman cope when the only one around after such a loss was a father more in tune with his patients than his own daughter?

As they neared the barns, Brand came to a decision. For the few weeks she was here, instead of exerting all that energy fighting her, he would do his best to go along with the program.

Hell, what would it hurt to let her do her job and let her think she was actually improving his life? Once she was gone, he could get back to doing things the way he had before she came here.

He was smiling as he helped her down and began unsaddling the horses.

She startled him by reaching for the cinch. "I'll unsaddle Honey, and you can take care of Domino."

"Sure thing. How'd you learn to unsaddle a horse?"

"When I was ten, I went through a period of being really horse-crazy, and my mother indulged me by driving me to a stable outside of town. The rule was, if I wanted to ride, I first had to learn to saddle and unsaddle my mount." She laughed, remembering. "I think the saddle weighed as much as me, and I had to stand on an overturned bucket to hang it over the rail of the stall."

Brand was chuckling. "I'm trying to picture that."

"When my lesson was over, I also had to muck the stall and fill the trough with feed and water. All part of the lessons, but it was also a help to the stable owner, who had to put up with a bunch of silly little girls playing at being cowboys."

As he worked alongside her, his smile grew. Avery Grant was just full of surprises.

CHAPTER ELEVEN

Brand pushed away from the table along with the rest of his family. "That was a fine supper, Billy."

Instead of following the others to the great room, he paused beside Avery. "I think it's time we got in our first serious session."

Her brows lifted. "Now?"

He nodded. "After a day in the saddle, I'm paying the price."

She chuckled. "I know what you mean." He saw her wince as she took a step. "I think I could use a few stretches myself."

He allowed her to lead the way up the stairs to her suite of rooms. As he trailed behind, he couldn't help admiring her trim backside in those skinny pants. As long as he was trapped spending time with this woman, at least she was easy to look at and not at all the tough drill instructor he'd been envisioning.

Once in the room she'd designated for their therapy sessions, she handed him the bands. "We'll start with some simple stretches."

Instead of standing back to watch him, she picked up a second pair of bands and faced him, showing him exactly how she wanted him to move. "We'll begin with some calf stretches. Remember, it isn't the number of times we do an exercise. It's more important that everything be done slowly and deliberately, to allow for the resistance of the muscles involved."

He couldn't help grinning at the ease with which she did each exercise. "Not fair. It's pretty obvious you've done these a time or two."

"Yeah." She paused to watch as he mirrored her movements. "You're not bad yourself. Are you sure you haven't been practicing in secret?"

"Does slogging through fields of mud count?"

That had her laughing along with him.

After a dozen repetitions on each leg, she began showing him a second routine, bending slightly, pausing, then taking the bend lower, with another pause.

"The fact that you've always been physically active really works in your favor, Brand. Except for teaching certain muscles to work in tandem with other muscles, you've already got it all together. You won't feel the after-effects of these sessions nearly as much as someone who sits at a desk all day."

"Sitting all day?" He gave a mock shudder that had her smiling.

"The guy at the desk might say the same about spending his days with a herd of bawling cattle. One man's dream is another man's nightmare."

He paused to wink at her. "I'll take my nightmare over anyone else's, thank you."

She absorbed a tingle of warmth along her spine. Even though she knew his wink was a purely spontaneous gesture, it felt like a beam of light aimed directly at her heart.

She brushed aside the thought. She was here for one reason only.

After a second round of stretches, she suggested he walk slowly across the room and back. As soon as he started, it was apparent to Avery that he was still forcing his left leg to pick up the slack for his injured right leg.

"Stop a moment."

He stopped and turned to face her with a quizzical look.

"As you begin to walk, think about putting equal pressure on your injured leg."

He did as she said, while she kept her gaze fixed on his hips for any sign that he was correcting his gait.

A mistake, she realized. The minute she allowed herself to be distracted by that toned body, she forgot to focus on him as a patient in need of real therapy. All those muscles encased in a pair of faded jeans were messing with her mind.

She blinked, determined to remain professional.

He turned and walked back to her. "Better?"

She swallowed. "Yes. I can see you were really trying. Just don't overcorrect. Let's try it again."

As he turned and walked away, she was relieved that he couldn't see the heat that had risen to her cheeks. She felt like the worst sort of liar. While he was trusting her to help ease his pain, she was acting like a teen with her first crush. Not only was she being unprofessional, but she was also being sexist. Maybe she could be forgiven for her thoughts, as long as she resolved to never act on them. After all, it wasn't the thoughts that counted. It was the action taken.

There. She felt somewhat better about her unwanted distraction.

He turned and ambled back to her, looking satisfied and a bit smug. "Definitely better. Right?"

She nodded, afraid to trust her voice.

"All right. Now what?"

"I think that's it for our first session."

"Okay."

She looked over as two faces peered around the open doorway.

Casey was grinning. "I win."

Jonah slapped a ten-dollar bill in his brother's hand before saying to Avery, "I figured by now you'd have Brand doing some fancy pose."

Avery laughed. "You've got this confused with a yoga class. We're finished now, but we were working on controlling certain muscles."

"Certain muscles?" Casey turned to Jonah with a wicked grin. "I don't know. That's asking a lot of a guy. Poor Brand. I feel for you, bro."

The two brothers burst into laughter.

Avery bit back her own laugh to say, "I can see where your lecherous minds have gone."

"Sorry." Casey didn't look a bit sorry. "It's a guy thing." He nodded toward the sauna. "If you two are finished, Jonah and I thought we'd spend some time in there to ease our aching muscles."

Jonah nodded. "After a day in the saddle, I could use some moist heat. How about it? Want to join us?"

She brightened. "It sounds perfect. But I didn't bring a bathing suit."

Casey wiggled his brows like a movie villain. "We won't complain if you don't, ma'am."

That had her laughing. "I think I'd probably violate some sort of professional code of conduct if I wore my birthday suit."

"Believe me, Jonah and I won't rat you out to your professional review board."

"Nice try." She couldn't hide her smile. "But it's still a no."

Brand stepped past her to open a closet. Inside was an array of bathing suits and terry robes hanging on hooks. "They're not one size fits all, but something in here ought to work."

He reached for a simple woman's tank suit. "I think this belongs to my aunt Liz, but she won't mind if you borrow it, especially since it's been hanging here for years."

Casey fiddled with the dials for the sauna. "It should get nice and steamy in no time." He grabbed several pairs of bathing trunks and handed them around to Brand and Jonah before heading for the stairs. "We'll see you inside."

As they strolled out the door, Avery made her way to the other room to strip.

A short time later, as she sat in the cloud of steam, wearing the borrowed bathing suit, the door opened and Brand stepped inside, wearing bathing trunks and carrying a towel.

Avery knew she was staring, but she couldn't look away from that perfectly sculpted body, that hair-roughened chest. She thought about all the young interns at the university hospital, spending their off hours working out with a trainer in the gym. What they wouldn't give for a body like Brand's. But, of course, it came from a lifetime of ranch chores.

"Ah. Now this was worth all the work." He sat on a

bamboo bench facing her and stretched out his long legs before draping the towel around his shoulders.

She watched the muscles in his arms flex with each movement, and thought again, as she had up in the hills, that this was a man completely comfortable in his own skin. Because of the years of physical labor, his body was beautiful. And he had no idea, which made him all the more appealing.

The door opened, sending steam billowing, as Casey and Jonah stepped inside. Both were wearing bathing trunks and carrying towels.

Brand made room on the bench. "I thought maybe you'd decided not to come."

Casey punched his older brother's arm. "And let you two have all the fun?"

"Next time I'll keep my big mouth shut."

"Hey." Jonah took a seat beside Avery and nudged her elbow. "He's just kidding. We know he wanted us to join the two of you."

"Exactly," Casey added. "If two's company, four's a party."

Avery looked from one brother to the other. All three were toned and fit, with the same sexy smiles and eyes that crinkled at the corners whenever they laughed. And they always seemed to be laughing.

Jonah leaned back and closed his eyes. "I can't believe we haven't been taking advantage of this for the past year or two."

"More like three or four years," Brand added. "Since Ham relocated to those rooms on the main floor."

Casey nudged his older brother. "Maybe when Avery's six weeks are up, I'll ask Gram Meg about taking over these rooms. I like the idea of having my own sauna."

Brand shot him the evil eye. "Get in line, bro. Since I'm the oldest, it stands to reason that I should move in here."

"You've already got the biggest room in the house."

"Because Gram Meg loves him the most," Jonah said with a laugh.

"That's right." Brand gave Casey a brotherly punch to the arm. "And don't you forget it."

"How could I forget?" Casey shared a grin with Jonah. "That's because Gram Meg feels sorry that you didn't get our brains or good looks and is always trying to make it up to you."

The two brothers chuckled at his little joke before turning their attention to Avery.

Casey gave her a long look. "Aren't you a little bit embarrassed to be wearing that baggy bathing suit?"

"It never occurred to me to pack one of my own. And don't call it baggy unless you want to insult your aunt, Doctor Casey."

He winked. "The only ones who call me doctor are the animals. As for that baggy bathing suit, you need to do a little shopping. You've got six weeks before your job here is finished."

Casey and Jonah exchanged knowing looks before Casey added, "Speaking of your job, Avery. Maybe you should look at my shoulder." He leaned forward and twisted slightly, all the while flexing his muscles like a bodybuilder. "I bet you know a good massage technique that could ease the tight feeling here in my pecs."

"How about the emptiness between your ears?" Brand said with a laugh.

"The girls at Nonie's don't have a problem with my brains."

"Or lack thereof." Brand shared a grin with Avery. "As long as a guy has a few dollars in his jeans."

"Speaking of Nonie's…" Jonah turned to Avery beside him. "You really need to visit our glorious little town."

"I drove through it on the way here."

"Driving through is not the same as experiencing it." He looked over at Brand.

Brand nodded. "Especially now that it's become famous, thanks to a certain bestselling author."

At Avery's blank look, he chuckled. "I see you haven't heard. Devil's Door was the fictional town in last year's blockbuster thriller *Overload*."

"Oh. I'm so glad you told me that. I brought it with me to read while I'm here. Everyone back home is raving about the book by J. R. Merrick."

The moment the words were out of her mouth, she stopped and gaped at Jonah. "No. Are you … ?"

All three brothers wore matching wide smiles.

It was Brand who asked, "You really didn't know?"

She was shaking her head. "Not a clue. I just know all my friends were raving about the book and its hot new author."

"Hot." Casey turned to Jonah. "I like the sound of that." Jonah merely grinned.

Avery was still staring at him with a stunned expression. "Are you working on another novel?"

"Yeah."

Because he knew his brother was reluctant to talk about himself, Casey stepped in to say, "When he's out in the barns mucking stalls or riding up in the hills with the herd, we can all see the wheels turning in that brain of his. He may be here physically, but in his mind he's already working out the details of his next book."

Avery asked hesitantly, "Would you mind signing my copy of *Overload* before I leave here?"

"I'd be happy to."

"And maybe make reference to Devil's Door?"

He nodded, all the while grinning.

Casey clapped a hand on Brand's shoulder. "Speaking of Devil's Door, maybe when you're picking up Billy's supplies tomorrow, you could take Avery along. I'm betting she could find herself a hot little bikini at Stuff."

"Stuff?" She looked up.

"Stuff has been in town since Ham was a boy," Brand explained. "Sheila Mason is the fourth generation to own and operate our general store, and her great-grandfather called it Stuff for Ranchers. The name stuck. New and used clothes for the entire family, as well as every kind of Western boots and hats ever made. In the back room they carry new and slightly used household goods."

Avery arched a brow. "Sounds interesting."

"It is. When Gram Meg heads to town, she can spend hours in Stuff. According to Pops Egan, she needs a truck to haul home all her bargains."

"And," Casey added, "she usually forgets to buy whatever had her going to town in the first place."

"That's Gram Meg." The three brothers were nodding and laughing.

"And every time it happens," Jonah said to Avery, "Ham meets her at the door, her arms filled with shopping bags, asking for his pipe tobacco, or his favorite chewing gum, or whatever else he asked her to get him."

Laughing, Casey added, "And she gets that deer-in-the-headlights look, and Ham walks away muttering under his breath…" In a perfect imitation of Hammond, Casey began, "Frivolous woman. She can spend money on everything in that blankety-blank town except for the little things I asked her to get me. When will I ever learn? I should have just taken care of it myself instead of trusting my list to Margaret Mary Finnegan."

By this time all of them were laughing so hard they were rocking the bamboo benches.

When the timer went off and the steam began to dissipate, they draped their towels around their hips and started out of the sauna.

"Good night, Avery," Casey called.

"See you tomorrow, Avery," Jonah added.

Brand waited until his brothers had descended the stairs. "I hope you didn't mind them joining us."

"Mind? They were such fun. Like they said, four's a party. And if they hadn't come up here, I may have never learned about your brother being the famous author J. R. Merrick."

Brand's tone was filled with pride. "In case you didn't notice, he's not one to blow his own horn."

"I noticed. I think it's very sweet." Her smile bloomed. "And it's also sweet that you and Casey are so proud of him."

"We are." He was grinning. "I don't know about you, but my muscles are already thanking me for that sauna."

Avery nodded. "Mine too. I'm sure I'll sleep comfortably tonight."

"I'll see you in the morning." Brand turned away. "And the invitation stands, if you'd like to go with me to town tomorrow."

"Thanks. I'd like that."

When she was alone, she hung the towel on a hook and slipped into a cami and boxer shorts before tying up her damp hair and preparing for bed.

A short time later she lay in the big bed and thought about the past hour spent with Brand and his brothers. They were so easy to be with. And so humble. Despite their success, they did the work of every other wrangler on their crew. Her respect for the Merrick family went up another notch.

It occurred to her that she hadn't had such simple, mindless fun in years. Without watching TV or even once thinking about her phone.

And she had weeks ahead of her to enjoy it all again.

CHAPTER TWELVE

"Good morning." Avery stepped into the kitchen just as Meg and Liz were shoving away from the table.

"'Morning, Avery." Meg turned to call, "Thank you for that great breakfast, Billy." At the door, she paused. "We're heading to Liz's studio. She wants my opinion on a couple of photos for her showing. Would you care to join us?"

Avery smiled at them both. "I appreciate the invitation, but I promised Brand I'd go to town with him."

She couldn't help noticing that Liz seemed relieved. It occurred to Avery that she'd probably been allowed her one and only visit to the reclusive photographer's studio.

Meg nodded in understanding. "A trip to town always takes up the better part of the day. I guess we won't see you again until dinnertime."

When the two women were gone, Avery enjoyed her coffee while standing by the tall windows, enjoying the view of the Tetons in the distance.

Within minutes, Brand drove a truck alongside the back porch and stepped out before sauntering into the kitchen.

"'Morning, Avery."

At his long, steady look, she felt her cheeks grow warm. "Good morning."

He turned to the housekeeper. "Got your list, Billy?"

Billy handed him a slip of paper. Brand tucked it into his pocket before leading the way through the mudroom and outside.

He held the passenger door and Avery climbed up to the seat.

As he rounded the truck and settled himself beside her, he pulled sunglasses from his pocket before turning the key in the ignition.

They rolled along a mile or more of gravel road until they reached the highway.

Avery glanced around. "There's not a single vehicle in sight."

He arched a brow. "And that means...?"

She gave a shake of her head. "It means I must be in Wyoming."

"So, in that place you come from, you never see an empty highway?"

His question had her laughing. "Maybe at four in the morning. Though to be honest, I doubt there's an empty highway even then. And by six in the morning, it's rush hour."

"Rush hour." He gave a shake of his head. "Out here, that's hard to imagine."

"You've never driven in bumper-to-bumper traffic for hours?"

He chuckled. "Not even for minutes. The only time I've ever been stuck on the highway was when Buster Mandel's herd broke through a fence and decided to meander home on a nice, clear ribbon of asphalt. I acted like one of those herd dogs, honking whenever they slowed down just to keep them moving along. Buster sure was surprised to find his cows milling about his back door. And his wife had fire in her eyes when she realized they'd walked right through her freshly planted garden. By the time the herd was back in their pasture, Trudy Mandel was outside doing her best to save the few scraggly plants that had survived that stampede of hooves."

Avery joined in his laughter. "It sounds like something out of a sitcom."

"Except that out here it's the reality of everyday life. And whenever it happens, we just have to roll with it."

"It's much more interesting than our rush-hour traffic on an expressway. That's just mostly horns blowing, rude hand gestures, and the occasional nasty words exchanged."

He snorted. "At least the cows can't talk back."

He fiddled with the radio before glancing over. "What's the most surprising thing you've found here in Wyoming?"

She lifted a hand to the passing scenery. "All this. Everything seems so much bigger here. Maybe it's because there are so few buildings, and cars, and people."

"Plenty of cattle, though."

She laughed. "I'll say. But there's such a feeling of space here. Take your family's house. Four generations living under one roof, and you're not tripping over each other." She shook her head for emphasis. "The minute I started college, my father couldn't wait to sell our big house and move to an apartment."

"Maybe he felt lonely there. Or maybe the memories haunted him."

She looked over. "I think that's so. Also, he's so married to his career, he prefers no distractions. But it was hard letting go of my childhood home and all its memories."

He reached out and closed a hand over hers. "I'm sorry. That must have been a shock for you."

She was so surprised by his unexpected gesture of comfort that she felt frozen in place. She glanced at their hands, then over at his face, and saw something for just a moment. Not so much sympathy as empathy. Then he blinked, and the look was gone.

She folded her hands in her lap and turned to look out the window. "I don't want to sound like a victim. I'm not. After I adjusted to my new reality, I decided to get on with my life. And I did."

"I'd say medical school was a step in the right direction. A tough, determined step."

"It wasn't as hard as it sounds. With a father in the profession, I didn't have to prove anything to anyone except to myself."

Brand gave her a thoughtful look. "Sometimes we're our own toughest critics."

She looked over. "You sound like you've been there a time or two."

He shrugged. "You've met my father, grandfather, and great-grandfather. They've set the bar awfully high."

"You don't seem to have any trouble meeting it."

"It's not enough to meet it. I want to surpass it."

She studied him with new respect. "I get it."

"I figured you would."

As they passed a sign announcing they were nearing Devil's Door, she couldn't help asking, "How did your town get its name?"

He kept his eyes on the road. "Back in the 1800s, Fritz Sutter was headed toward the Grand Tetons, forging a trail for his fellow Missouri relatives who were due to arrive months later. When his wagon broke, he unhitched his mule team and found that his tools had spilled out somewhere along the trail. Since he couldn't repair the wagon, he was forced to settle down right where he was. Shortly after, a spring blizzard blew down from the Tetons and destroyed the rest of his belongings. By the time his relatives arrived months later, it was late summer. The fields were lush. There was an abundance of game to hunt. They insisted on settling here, even though old Fritz warned them it was hell in both winter and summer. Despite the fact that he called it Devil's Door, they refused to move on."

"Did he stay, too?" Her brows shot up. "Or did he move on?"

"Family was obviously more important to old Fritz than the threat of weather. They say he stayed on and had more than a hundred family members before he died."

"Oh, that's so sweet." She was smiling now, shaking her head in disbelief. "A town is named after a killer blizzard."

"So the history books tell us." He winked at her. "And to this day, Devil's Door is on every map of Wyoming. I'm betting the early mapmakers only added it because of the crazy history behind the name."

She studied his face, which could be as stern as his great-grandfather's when he was angry. But when he laughed, as he did now, he could melt hearts. Or at least hers.

At that thought, she turned away, hoping her cheeks weren't as red as they felt.

Gradually they passed small ranches, alerting them to the fact that they were nearing town.

"That's the Harper ranch." Brand pointed as they drove past a modest house and a number of fenced pastures. "Ben Harper owns the hardware store in town."

"Those fences look brand-new."

"It's no accident. Ben keeps them that way by replacing any broken boards or posts so everyone will follow his lead and buy new fencing at his store."

"Pretty smart."

Brand chuckled. "Ben Harper is a businessman through and through. And that's a good thing, since he's not much of a rancher."

He turned the truck off the highway and drove a few miles before heading into town.

As they drove along the main street, he pointed. "That big building used to be Tremont's Grain and Feed. Wilson Tremont sold it to Ben Harper, so he could concentrate on taking care of his wife, who's been sick for a couple of years now. Wilson is also the town mayor and has been for years, since nobody else wants the job."

"You're kidding." She was grinning. "You mean he runs unopposed?"

"Wilson doesn't run for office. He just continues along as he always has."

"What if somebody decides they want his job?"

Brand shrugged. "Then he'll either hand over the title, or if he decides to compete, I guess we'll have ourselves a horse race."

He pointed to a line of vehicles parked along a fence. "That's Harvey Sprigg's farm equipment sales. He sells used and new equipment."

"I'll bet he does a brisk business."

Brand nodded. "For small ranchers, it's good to have

a place where they can buy and sell their old equipment, since the new ones cost a fortune."

As they continued along, Brand pointed out the landmarks. "Our police chief's office and the jail alongside it. Over there is the courthouse and city office. Just down there is Julie's hair shop and beyond it is the new spa run by Julie's daughter and son-in-law."

"The bank looks new."

Brand frowned. "Yeah. Des Dempsey and his family own it."

"From the look on your face, Des Dempsey must not be one of your favorite people."

"Our family doesn't do business with him. We do our banking in Stockwell, about fifty miles from here."

"That's quite a ways to drive just to do your banking."

"We don't mind the distance." He pointed. "Here's our old Devil's Door elementary and high schools."

"I noticed the pretty gardens on my first drive through town."

He nodded. "The students and their parents plant vegetable and flower gardens every spring. The kids get a chance to harvest what they grow, and the lunchroom serves fresh veggies from their gardens until the first frost."

Avery was shaking her head. "That's inspired."

"Yeah. They're good lessons for ranch kids to learn." He pointed. "Up on the hill are the church and cemetery." He turned to her with a wicked grin. "We've got it all covered, from birth to death."

She chuckled. "I can see that."

He drove to the end of the street and backed his truck into one of the loading docks. "This is Ben Harper's Hardware and Grain and Feed. I'll give him my order, and he can fill the back of the truck with our supplies while we shop."

As they stepped out of the truck, Brand was forced to stop every few feet to call out a greeting or shake a hand.

Once inside, they watched as a rail-thin man in round glasses and a baseball cap pulled down over his forehead climbed down a ladder and started toward them. An apron with deep pockets filled to the brim with scissors, twine, a stapler, and an assortment of pens was tied around his narrow waist.

"'Morning, Brand." His voice was surprisingly deep and reminded Avery of a radio announcer.

"'Morning, Ben. I'd like you to meet Avery Grant."

The man's eyes widened and a huge grin split his lips as he tipped his hat to her, revealing a bald head. "The physical therapy guy Doc Peterson recommended to your grandmother?" He speared Avery with a look. "I guess old Doc needs his glasses replaced."

"Or my grandmother needs to ask a few more questions before closing a deal."

"Don't let Miss Meg hear you say that, Brand."

The two men shared a laugh, and Avery joined in.

Ben nudged Brand. "How'd the Hammer take the surprise?"

"Pretty much the way you'd expect. Ham hates surprises. And doesn't much approve of changing the way things were always done."

Ben Harper chuckled. "Now that's an understatement. I'm betting he won't let poor Miss Meg live this one down for quite a while."

"Don't worry about Gram Meg. If anyone can handle Ham, it's her." Brand handed the man a slip of paper.

"Here's the order, Ben. Avery and I have some shopping to do. We'll probably be back sometime after lunch."

"Your order will be ready, Brand." He replaced his baseball cap. "Nice meeting you, Avery."

"Nice meeting you, too, Ben."

She followed Brand from the cavernous building and out into the street.

"Come on." He offered his arm.

Surprised and pleased, she looped her arm through his and experienced a tingle of awareness along her spine.

As they started along the sidewalk, he said, "It's time you saw Devil's Door up close and personal."

CHAPTER THIRTEEN

'Morning Brand."

"Noble." Brand paused to shake hands with a tall, muscled man wearing a perfectly pressed police uniform and badge. His gray hair was cut military short. "Avery, this is our police chief, Noble Crain. Noble, this is Avery Grant."

"Avery? The physical therapist?" The chief broke into a wide grin. "You don't say."

Avery smiled. "Like the others, you were expecting a man."

"I was. And I have to say you're a very pleasant surprise."

"Thank you."

"Welcome to Devil's Door, Miss Grant. What do you think of our little town?"

"I like it. And I love the history of how it got its name."

"It makes for a good story." At a ping from his phone, he looked down, then said, "Excuse me. I need to respond to this. Nice meeting you, Avery. I hope I see you around."

As she and Brand continued along the sidewalk, they paused half a dozen more times as Brand shook hands and introduced her to friends and neighbors. A man named Aaron, who did roofing and siding. A white-haired woman named Aurora, who was a friend of Miss Meg. An elderly couple who asked about Hammond's health. A cowboy who went on and on about this endless rainy season the ranchers had to deal with. In each instance, Brand smiled and nodded and handled the introductions, which brought the now-expected response.

Avery's head was spinning from all the names and faces. "I'm sure I won't be able to remember any of those people if I meet them again."

Brand leaned close. "No need to worry. They'll remember you."

"Yeah. I'm the infamous man who turned out to be a woman."

They shared a laugh as they paused outside a shop with a pretty striped awning and a bright neon pink sign reading STUFF.

Brand held the door before following Avery inside.

A young woman with red hair and a parade of freckles across her nose looked up from behind a counter. "Hey, Brand. How're all your family?"

"They're all great, Sheila." He crossed the room. "Sheila Mason, this is Avery Grant."

"The physical therapist. Hi, Avery. It's nice to meet you. Though I must say—"

"—You thought I'd be a guy." Avery finished for her, and the two women burst into laughter.

"I've bet you heard that before."

"Half a dozen times already."

Sheila looked from Avery to Brand. "What are you two shopping for?"

Brand held up his hands. "I'm not staying. I thought

while I was in town I'd head on over to Julie's and get a haircut while Avery shops."

He turned away. "Text me when you finish getting what you want."

As soon as he was gone, Sheila grinned. "Just like a guy. The thought of spending more than a few minutes shopping makes them antsy."

Avery nodded. "I noticed how quickly he was backing away. He couldn't get out of here fast enough."

The two women shared another laugh before Sheila asked, "So, what are you looking for?"

"A bathing suit. It never occurred to me to bring one, but since there's a sauna at the Merrick place, I'm going to need one. And while I'm here, I think I'll look for a pair of jeans and some tees as well."

Sheila indicated the shelves across the room. "Everything on that side is new. The ones over there are slightly used. The fitting rooms are back there. Feel free to take as much time as you need. And I'm here if you have any questions."

"Thanks, Sheila."

For the next hour, Avery went through the shelves and racks, choosing an assortment of clothes before heading toward one of the fitting rooms.

Every so often, Sheila would stop by the fitting room to carry a few items to the counter until, much later, Avery emerged, wearing a pair of skinny jeans and a lime-green T-shirt. On her feet were comfortable Western boots, and in her hand a wide-brimmed hat.

"Oh, don't you look pretty," the shopkeeper called as she approached the counter.

Avery paused to study her reflection in a mirror across the room. "You don't think it's too much?"

"Too much? Avery, you look like you were born here. You made some great choices."

Avery burst into laughter. "And that proves that you're really good at your job, Sheila."

"Fourth generation," she announced proudly, pointing to a row of pictures behind the counter. One of a bearded man standing in the doorway of what must have been the original wooden mercantile. Another of a young woman surrounded by her children, all smiling for the camera.

"Oh, you must be so proud." Avery handed her a credit card.

Sheila nodded as she ran the card and handed Avery a receipt. "I am. My great-grandfather wasn't much of a rancher, so he turned his talent for selling into his shop, calling it Stuff for Ranchers. Everybody around these parts called it plain old Stuff. My grandmother on my mother's side was widowed when she was just past forty and raised ten children by running Stuff. She was proud of selling things that folks around here needed. Her oldest daughter, my mother, started working here when she was still in school. And I did the same. It's in our blood."

They both looked up as Brand strolled through the front door.

For a moment he fell silent as he studied Avery. Then his face creased into a wide smile. "Who are you and what have you done with that city woman who came in here an hour ago?"

She put a hand on her hip and did a slow turn. "I thought I might look silly, like I was trying to pretend to be one of you, but Sheila assures me I look fine."

"Better than." He gave her one last smoldering look before turning to the counter to pick up the half dozen handled bags.

Avery put a hand over Sheila's. "Thanks so much. I love your store. I know I'll be back before I leave for home."

"I'm glad. I look forward to seeing you again, Avery." To Brand, Sheila called, "Say hi to those good-looking brothers, Brand."

"I will." Brand held the door and the two walked outside into bright sunshine.

Avery was surprised to see the ranch truck parked at the curb.

Brand deposited the bags in the truck and closed the door. "Ben called and said my order was ready, so I figured, since you hadn't texted me yet, I had time to pick up the truck and drive it here while you finished your shopping."

"And your haircut?"

He removed his hat and she nodded. "Julie does good work."

"Actually, it was her son, Greg, who cut my hair." He replaced his hat and offered his arm. "Ready for some lunch?"

"I am. Shopping always gives me an appetite."

"From the number of bags, you must be famished. Now the big decision." He pointed to the pretty little building down the street, with red and green awnings and a green door. "That's Antonio's. Pizza, pasta, and the best meatball sandwiches in the west. Or"—he pointed in the opposite direction—"Nonie's Wild Horses Saloon and Café, our local watering hole. Burgers, chili, and whatever Nonie fixes for her daily special. Along with ice-cold longnecks."

Avery gave it only a moment's thought before saying, "On a day like this, a burger and beer menu sounds like a feast. Besides, I have to see the place Casey and Jonah talk about."

"A woman after my own heart." She nearly stumbled on the uneven sidewalk and he quickly caught her hand. "You need to watch out. This sidewalk is nearly as old as the town." He started off down the street, keeping her hand in his. "Okay. Nonie's it is."

It occurred to Avery that she hadn't had a man hold her hand in a very long time. And even though he was only looking out for her safety, she liked it.

Nonie's Wild Horses Saloon and Café was impossible to miss. The name flashed in bright neon yellow and orange on a sign hung from a peak on the roof. It was repeated on a wooden door that squealed in protest each time it was opened.

Inside, a long bar ran the length of the room on one side, while on the other side were booths offering a hint of privacy. In the center of the big room were tables and chairs, and in the rear, a row of pool tables and a square wooden dance floor beside a raised bandstand.

The chorus of muttered curses and bursts of laughter from the cowboys seated at the bar were a counterpoint to Dolly Parton's unmistakable voice coming from the jukebox, lamenting about always loving you.

The distinctive smell of onions on the grill permeated the air.

Before Avery's eyes could adjust to the dim lighting, a woman was across the room grabbing Brand in a bear hug.

"Brand Merrick." The voice was bluesy and husky and came from a surprisingly pretty woman with short, auburn hair, who looked like she'd be more at home running a daycare center. Her eyes, a startling blue, crinkled with laugh lines as she held Brand at arm's length and studied him with warmth. "Where've you been hiding, you devil you?"

"Just ranch chores, Nonie. You know I'd never hide from you."

"You'd better not try. And tell that good-looking father of yours the same thing. He'd better not stay away too long or I'll come looking for that cowboy."

Brand was grinning. "Nonie, I'd like you to meet Avery Grant."

Before greeting Avery, Nonie said in a mock whisper, "The guy Miss Meg hired who turned out to be this beautiful stranger?"

Then she stuck out her hand. "Nice to meet you, Avery."

"Nice to meet you, too, Nonie. I guess there are no secrets in Devil's Door."

"None. Welcome to my Wild Horses Saloon and Café."

"Thanks." Avery looked around. "I like your place."

Nonie slapped Brand's arm. "Okay. She just moved up a notch in my book. You want a table, or are you looking for privacy?"

"We'll take a booth."

"Smart move. You'd best hide her from the local cowboys, or they'll be swarming around this pretty thing like bees to honey." Nonie led the way across the room.

When they were seated, she said, "The burgers are freshly ground sirloin. And the special today is firehouse chili. It comes with a warning. More than one bowl, you'll need the volunteer fire department to put out the blaze."

Avery and Brand shared a laugh.

Brand was still grinning. "You've sold me. I'll have a bowl of chili and a longneck."

Avery didn't hesitate. "I'll have the same."

Nonie gave her a long, appraising look before turning to Brand. "This should be interesting."

As she walked away, Brand leaned close to whisper, "I hope you realize the entire place will be watching to see if you finish that chili without melting down."

She patted his hand. "I'll try to keep from making a fool of myself."

He closed his other hand over hers.

She absorbed the quick sizzle of heat and saw the way his eyes narrowed, as though he'd felt it, too, before quickly withdrawing his hand.

"Tell me about Nonie."

He smiled. "She's really respected in town. This was her husband's place, and she helped out with the cooking. They owned a little ranch outside of town. He died in an accident on the interstate, along with his brother and wife, who left twin babies orphaned. Even though Nonie was numb with grief, she took in the two little girls, Gina and Tina, and raised them like her own. She couldn't manage both the ranch and this place, so she sold the ranch and did double duty here as saloon owner and mom. They're back from college now and working for her while they figure out their future."

"Nonie sounds like a really loving person."

Brand nodded. "She's the best."

Avery gave him a sly smile. "Is it my imagination, or is she sweet on your father?"

He gave a deep laugh and without thinking reached again for her hand. "She never fails to ask about him."

"Is the interest mutual?"

He gave a shake of his head while his thumb ran over her wrist. "If he is, he keeps it hidden."

They both looked up, startled, when Nonie set two ice-cold longnecks in front of them before walking away. Both of them took their time sipping before leaning back and looking anywhere but at each other.

"I like Nonie's Wild Horses Saloon and Café." Avery groaned inwardly. Small talk had never been her strong suit.

"Yeah. I've been coming here since I was a kid."

Avery's brows lifted. "Are kids welcome in here?"

"It's a café as well as a saloon. And we only came in here when we were with Dad. As you've noticed, if my dad had wanted to come in here riding his horse, Nonie would've found a way to make him feel welcome."

They both smiled.

Ben Harper crossed the room and paused beside their table. "I see you paid a visit to Stuff, Avery."

Before she could ask how he knew that, he merely grinned. "You came in my store looking like you just got off a bus from the city. Now you look like a citizen of Devil's Door."

"Why thank you, Ben." She could feel the heat on her cheeks. "I'll take that as a compliment."

"That's how it was meant." He tipped his hat. "Avery. Brand."

As he sauntered away, she looked across the table at Brand. "I guess folks around here don't miss much."

"You're topic A right now. Most folks are wondering how my grandmother is holding up under the withering looks she's getting from the Hammer."

Avery shook her head. "He certainly hasn't tried to hide what he thinks of me."

Brand was quick to put a hand over hers. "It isn't personal, Avery. Ham is old school. He honestly believes pain is the price a rancher has to pay for the work he does. And he believes that paying someone to teach you how to walk without pain is some kind of foolish weakness."

"How does he ever allow himself to see a doctor?"

Brand winced. "He has to be in fear of dying before he gives in and relies on Doc Peterson."

"But he allows a veterinarian to tend his animals?"

At her question, Brand threw back his head and roared with laughter. "I guess he figures only ranchers should suffer. Besides, since the vet is his great-grandson, who wouldn't dream of charging him a fee, he figures he's getting a bargain."

Avery was grinning. "As I recall, you shared your great-grandfather's belief when I arrived." She gave him a probing look. "Have you changed your mind, or are you just hoping to go along with your grandmother's program until my time's up?"

He studied their joined hands. "For now, I'm the guy in the middle of a fierce tug-of-war. But I'm trying to keep an open mind."

She felt herself relax. "Fair enough."

When Nonie walked up with their order, he released Avery's hand and sat back as Nonie set down a tray containing two bowls of steaming chili along with assorted toppings and a basket of crackers.

She set a tall glass of water in front of Avery. "I think you'll be needing this." She was grinning as she walked away.

Brand watched as Avery took her first taste.

"Well?"

She swallowed, smiled, and nodded. "Hotter than I'm used to, but really good."

"Is your mouth on fire?"

"I'll tell you after a few more bites."

With a laugh they both dug into their meal. And though Avery emptied her bowl of chili, she also emptied her tall glass of water, along with the beer.

A short time later, Nonie ambled over to ask if they wanted anything else before setting the bill in front of Brand.

"I think we're good." He placed his money on the bill.

"Thanks, honey." Nonie turned to Avery. "And thanks to you, I'm ten dollars richer."

At Avery's arched brow, she added with a laugh, "The guys at the bar had a bet going that you'd never be able to finish that bowl of chili. I'm good at reading people, and I bet them ten you would. So thanks."

That brought a smile. "My pleasure."

"Way to go, tenderfoot," Brand whispered as he stood beside her.

She felt a little thrill at the press of his lips to her temple, as well as the unexpected nickname.

She was still shivering as she and Brand made their way to the door, feeling the curious stares of every cowboy at the bar until they stepped out into the sunlight.

CHAPTER FOURTEEN

As their truck moved along the main street, Brand slipped on his sunglasses before turning to Avery. "Now that you've had a chance to spend some time in Devil's Door and meet its citizens, what do you think?"

"I really like it. The people are friendly."

"And curious about the Hammer's houseguest," Brand added with a laugh.

"I can see that not much happens around here without the whole town knowing about it."

"That can be a good thing, if the news is positive, or a really annoying thing if it's not something you wanted to share with your neighbors."

Avery glanced over. "Were you ever the subject of ugly gossip?"

He shrugged. "Not ugly, I suppose. But the three Merrick brothers, as you may have noticed, weren't born with halos and wings."

She gave a mock gasp. "What? You're not angels?"

"More like little devils, according to local lore. We got into our share of fistfights, and trouble." He turned. "How about you? Is there a little demon hiding behind that innocent face?"

She laughed. "You think I'm going to tell you all my secrets?"

"I should have known. A woman of mystery."

"I think everyone should have a few secrets."

He wiggled his brows like a villain. "I'll tell you mine if you tell me yours."

She gave another laugh. "Nice try, cowboy."

He sighed. "It was worth a try."

As they left the town behind and turned onto the highway, Avery motioned toward the Tetons in the distance. "Have you and your brothers ever climbed them?"

He nodded. "Lots of times. Whenever we had time away from our chores. It's like having this giant playground in our backyard."

"Didn't your family consider it too dangerous?"

He shrugged. "They taught us to use caution. But they also taught us that there's danger everywhere. Buster Mandel's son Charley was thrown from a horse when he was thirteen and died after hitting his head on a boulder. He was just at home, doing his regular routine. The same with Julie Franklyn's youngest son, Hank. He lost an arm after swimming in Devil's Creek. He picked up some kind of parasite that found its way into an open wound, and by the time Dr. Peterson examined him and had him transported to a hospital in Casper, they were forced to amputate in order to keep it from spreading through his body. We can't stop living just because there's danger around us."

Avery kept her gaze fixed on the mountains, but she had gone so quiet that Brand looked over with concern. "Something I said?"

"Hmm?" She turned to him and he could see the little frown line between her brows.

He touched a finger to the spot. "Looks like I triggered something in that mind of yours, tenderfoot."

"Just..." She crossed her arms over her chest. "Nothing important."

"Want to talk about it?"

She shook her head.

"Okay." After several miles, he pulled off the highway and began following a dirt trail across a flat stretch of meadow that gradually began to climb into the hills. "As long as we have some time, I'll show you something."

He was relieved to see her relax and stare out the window with interest as they climbed past the tree line and came to a stop alongside a picturesque body of water that snaked its way from the higher elevations. It gradually narrowed as it meandered between stands of decaying trees.

Brand opened her door and took her hand as he led her toward a fallen log.

"This is Devil's Creek. Come August, it will be little more than mud. But right now, after all the rain and melted snow, it's nearly overflowing its banks." He helped her to sit before taking a seat beside her on a fallen log. "I always try to come here in springtime to think."

"Why springtime?"

He thought a moment before answering. "A fresh new season. A chance to assess what works and what needs improving. And I like watching the water spill over those boulders." He pointed to the swiftly flowing water streaming over and around giant rocks in the middle of the creek.

"How deep is it?"

He gave her a teasing smile. "Want to find out? You go first, and I'll follow."

"Thanks. You mean if I'm in over my head, you'll know enough to get out fast."

"Of course. I told you. There's danger everywhere. So we learn to be careful."

"Just for that, I'll let you go first."

He winked. "For the record, I'd never let you drown."

"My hero." She playfully punched his arm. "I've been meaning to ask you why your great-grandfather is called the Hammer."

Brand stretched out his long legs. "I suppose there are a lot of reasons for that nickname, but it probably began with his history. When Ham was twelve, he and his father were caught in a blizzard up in the hills. His father slipped and fell and was badly injured. They were forced to spend the entire winter in a cave, with Ham the only one able to hunt food, keep the fire going, and tend his father."

Caught up in the story, Avery's eyes went wide. "At twelve?"

"Yeah." Brand gave a short laugh. "Imagine that." He stared at the water spilling around the submerged rocks. "When spring thaw arrived in the Tetons, Ham fashioned a sled from a hollowed-out log and was able to bring his father down from the hills and to a country doctor, who did his best. Shortly after that his father died, but he let Ham know how grateful he was to spend his last days in his own bed. Alone in that one-room shack, Ham continued the work of his father, taming acres of wilderness into a sprawling, successful ranch. He met and married his Mandy when he was only seventeen. Together they raised Gramps Egan, while burying three more infants who didn't live more than a couple of months. And Ham continued working the land."

Brand sighed. "And now, at an age when most men

would be content to sit by the fire and relive their youth, Ham is still found most mornings mucking stalls before dawn."

Avery put her hands to her mouth to cover her gasp. "What an amazing story."

Brand smiled. "Yeah. Ham is an amazing man. And if you don't believe me, just ask him."

The two of them shared a laugh.

"You're starting to sound like Casey."

"My brother's a pain in the…"

"I love his sense of humor."

He broke into a smile. "I do, too, but don't ever tell him I said so."

She studied the fast-moving water. "You never said. Is it deep?"

"In the middle. My brothers and I have been swimming here since we were kids. It's the perfect summertime get-away from hot, sweaty chores until it dries up."

She leaned back against a thick knot in the log. "You're lucky to have brothers. I think it would be great to have a sibling to share things with."

"Like what?"

She shrugged. "When I just want somebody who"— she searched for the words—"somebody who shares my history. Or when I'm feeling troubled."

"What's troubling you, Avery?"

She looked away, staring into the distance.

Brand fell silent, wishing he hadn't pushed her. But then she started talking, catching him by surprise.

"It's funny. When we were up in the hills with the herd, you talked about both of us following in the family business. That had me thinking. From the time I was a little girl, I used to follow my father on his rounds whenever he permitted it. All I ever dreamed of was being a doctor. When I started med school, I aced my classes, and all my friends were convinced I would make a name for myself in the medical field. After all, I wanted to live up to my father's reputation."

"I thought you told us you aren't a doctor."

He saw her staring down at her hands, avoiding his eyes. "Like that stream, I changed course. Actually, it was an injury from a fall that changed everything. I was on my way to class on my bicycle and had a collision with a slow-moving car. At the time, it had seemed a simple enough spill. When my doctor recommended therapy, I accepted it so I could get back to the way things had been before the damage to my shoulder." While she spoke, she idly began massaging her shoulder, reminding Brand of the way he continually rubbed his injured leg.

"Those exercises the therapist put me through"—she glanced over, then away—"most of them simple, a few of them painful, taught me things about my body I hadn't thought of before. As a medical student, I knew of them, but until I was forced to really think about how to undo the damage done, I hadn't understood the connection between mind and body. By the time my mobility was fully restored, I'd become convinced that I wanted, more than anything, to pass along what I'd learned to others who were suffering with injury and pain." She shrugged. "So I dropped some classes, added others, and became a certified physical therapist"—her voice lowered—"much to my father's disgust."

Brand couldn't hide his surprise. "Why would your father be upset? You're still part of the medical profession. Don't most doctors consider physical therapy an accepted medical practice?"

"Alexander Avery Grant isn't most doctors. He has spent a lifetime becoming an expert in his field. He's considered one of the top cardiothoracic surgeons in the country. He expected his only child to follow in his footsteps and become a part of his exclusive team."

Brand's tone was reasonable. "I'm sure he'll come around."

Avery got to her feet, too restless to continue sitting. "He made it plain when I left that I was a great disappointment to him. Sorry." As she started toward the truck, she called over her shoulder, "I never meant to vent."

Brand caught up with her and put a hand on her arm to stop her.

She refused to meet his eyes.

His voice lowered. Softened. "Vent any time you need to. Sometimes life beats us up and we just need to get it all out. As you said, without siblings, you needed someone, and I'm glad I was available."

"It's not like me to share family trouble."

"I won't tell a soul. Besides, I'm betting by the time you get home, your father will be so happy to see you, he'll be ready to do whatever is necessary to make it up to you."

She gave him a wistful smile. "Thanks, Brand. But you don't know my father."

"You're right. I don't. But from the little I know about his daughter, there must be a lot of good in him." His hand moved along her arm and across her shoulder. "Because you're a really special person."

She felt a quick sexual tug and tried to make a joke to cover her feelings. "I'm sure you'll change your tune when I start pushing you through those routines I have in mind."

"Go ahead. Push me. I can take it."

His big hand cupped the back of her head, and she knew in that instant he was going to kiss her.

She gave a murmur of approval as he dipped his face to hers and covered her mouth with his.

The moment his mouth took hers, she was lost in a kiss so filled with heat and need, all she could do was sigh with pleasure.

Oh, his mouth felt so good, so right on hers. The man knew just how to play her, using absolutely no pressure as he lightly nibbled and tasted.

Without realizing it, her fingers curled into the rough plaid shirt and drew him fractionally closer, urging him to take more. And he did.

His arms wrapped around her, dragging her so close she could feel his heartbeat inside her own chest.

Fireworks exploded behind her closed eyelids. Her poor legs turned to rubber and her arms clung to his waist to keep from sliding boneless to the ground.

He changed the angle of the kiss and took it deeper. The kiss spun on and on, until her brain was spinning in lazy circles.

When at last he lifted his head, he surprised her yet again by brushing his hand over her cheek. Just the lightest of touches, but it caused a flutter deep inside.

He stared into her eyes, and she wondered how much he could read in them.

"I won't say I'm sorry." His voice was little more than a whisper. "I've been thinking about doing that all day."

Her breathing was strained. She knew her cheeks were flaming as he opened the passenger door and helped her up to the seat.

By the time he'd rounded the truck and turned

the key in the ignition, she'd managed to compose herself.

Instead of putting the vehicle in gear, he reached over and took her hand. "I hope you don't regret telling me about your father."

"I don't know what came over me. It's not something I'm comfortable sharing."

"Then I'm doubly glad you shared it with me."

She arched a brow. "Is that why you kissed me? To offer me comfort?"

His lips curved into a sexy grin that shot an arrow straight through her heart. "There's no way you can mistake that kiss for comfort. It was pure energy. In fact, it packed more of a punch than Nonie's firehouse chili."

That had them both laughing as he put the truck in gear and started back across the field.

Avery leaned back, feeling oddly lighthearted. Maybe, she thought, that little spot by Devil's Creek really was a good place to think. And other things.

CHAPTER FIFTEEN

As Avery descended the stairs, she paused, hearing the chorus of voices coming from the kitchen.

How odd, she thought, that just days ago she'd found herself among a crowd of strangers. And here she was, recognizing them by voice alone.

They were as distinctive to her now as they'd once been unfamiliar. And as different as they all were, she found each of them fascinating. And one more so than the others.

· Brand.

Though he sparred openly and often with his brothers, Avery could see his pride in them. Because of his tough-guy image, she found that tender side of him endearing.

Despite his initial reaction to her in the beginning, she could feel him warming to the thought of accepting physical therapy. She was determined to do all that she could to earn her pay and see that he was pain-free before her employment ended.

Who was she kidding?

Though that was true, her interest didn't end with his health. She was working very hard to remain detached, but the simple truth was...

She sighed. What was the truth? When he'd kissed her, her world had been rocked. But she couldn't afford to act on those feelings. She was here for one reason only. And when her time here was up, she would have to leave Brand and his fascinating family behind and start over with a new patient.

She swallowed back a little sigh and forced a smile to her lips before stepping into the kitchen.

Billy spotted her and pointed to the kitchen counter. "Hey, Avery. We've got ice water, lemonade, beer, and wine. Your choice."

"Thank you, Billy." She picked up a stem glass of pale wine and walked toward the family, clustered on one side of the room.

"Well look at you." Casey was the first to call her out on the new boots.

She put a hand on her hip and lifted her foot. "According to Sheila Mason, they're the best in her shop. Authentic Western boots."

"Worn by an authentic Midwesterner," Jonah drawled.

The others laughed.

Meg touched her arm. "Don't mind their teasing, Avery. I think you look great. Like you were born here."

"Thank you." She saw Brand watching her and felt the heat rise to her cheeks. Damn the man. All he had to do was look at her like that and she was remembering that kiss by the creek.

Hammond, frowning at this exchange, was seated in his favorite chair, sipping a cold beer. He said to no one in particular, "Did I see one of those delivery trucks leaving?"

Liz turned to her grandfather. "Mom helped me choose the photos for my showing in San Francisco. I finally had them ready for shipping today. I called Evelyn and told her when to expect them."

"You ought to be going with them for the showing, girl." Seeing that Liz was about to protest, the old man's voice lowered. "It would do you good to meet the people who buy your work. I'm sure they're curious about the artist who takes all those grand pictures."

Liz leaned close to press a kiss to his leathery cheek. "Thanks, Ham. For liking my photos, that is. I know you mean well, but you know there's no way I could ever go that far from home."

"I don't know about that, girl. There's a big world out there to see." He patted her arm.

"I'll go if you will."

He winked at Liz. "I can guaran-damn-tee you that will never happen. I have no interest in seeing California."

Watching the two of them, Avery was amazed at the transformation. Hammond's eyes and voice had gone all soft and soothing. And instead of taking offense at his words of reprimand, Liz reacted as though he'd just paid her the highest compliment. Despite the fact that they were both prickly, it was plain to see they shared a strong bond.

Avery was beginning to wonder if she would ever be able to figure out all the family dynamics.

Over dinner, she was content to watch and listen as the family members recounted their day.

In the middle of assuring his great-grandfather that there had been no signs of illness among the newest calves, Casey suddenly looked at the cook. "A perfect steak, Billy."

"Thanks. I knew you'd appreciate the marinade, Casey." Billy winked at Avery before explaining, "Our vet acquired a fondness for fancy sauces and marinades during his time spent studying far from home."

Avery lifted a brow. "Where did you study veterinary medicine?"

"Texas A and M."

"The College of Veterinary Medicine and Biomedical Sciences," Bo said proudly.

Casey grinned at his father before saying to Avery, "Pop thinks those fancy words make me sound smart. His genius son is now a doctor of biomedical sciences."

That had everyone smiling.

"I have to admit that I enjoyed my time in College Station, Texas."

"Where he got a taste for all things hot and spicy," Jonah added. "And I don't mean just food."

Casey merely grinned. "They do have some spicy women."

"That's probably why their daddies started carrying rifles whenever a certain cowboy came to call."

Even Hammond chuckled at that before saying, "I'm sure Egan can relate to that. I recall one time when he threatened to greet one young man with a gun if he ever darkened his daughter's door again."

Egan and Meg shared a laugh before Egan said, "Young Schmidt. I don't remember his first name."

"Kirby," Liz said. "I was sixteen, and he was my first big crush. And after the reception you gave him, he never tried to see me again."

"That's right. Kirby Schmidt. And we had good reason to scare him off. You were sixteen and he was twenty. Your mother and I knew he was too old for you." Egan shared a look with his wife, who nodded her agreement.

Liz grinned. "Actually, I was a little afraid of him. But I was flattered that an older guy found me attractive."

"Dangerous territory, Aunt Liz." Casey nudged her arm. "Aren't you glad your folks took charge?"

"Yes. But at the time I wasn't about to admit it."

"Older and wiser." Her mother smiled. "I guess that could be said for all of us." She looked over at Billy. "I think the evening is too pretty to pass up. Let's take our coffee and dessert on the porch."

Every member of the family complimented Billy on his chocolate four-layer cake, topped with rich fudge frosting and a big scoop of vanilla ice cream. Afterward they sipped coffee and watched as the sun slowly slid behind the peaks of the Tetons, leaving the sky layered in ribbons of red and pale pink and gold.

Billy loaded dishes onto a rolling cart, while Liz sat beside her grandfather, describing the photos she'd included in the shipment to her agent.

"I wasn't sure about sending along any of the black and white pictures until Avery raved about the ones I'd taken up in the Tetons during that deep freeze."

Hammond glanced over at Avery. "Liz showed you her photographs?"

Avery blushed. "I stumbled into her studio by accident."

The old man lifted a brow and turned to his grand-daughter. "I'm surprised you didn't throw a hissy fit and order her out."

It was Liz's turn to blush. "I did. But then I realized that Avery hadn't done it intentionally, so I chased after her and asked her to stay awhile."

Hammond gave her a long, calculating look before

turning to Avery. "I hope you realize you're one of the precious few."

"I do. And I'm grateful. It gave me a chance to see what a gifted artist Liz is. I admire all her work, but I especially loved those black and white photos she took in the Grand Tetons."

Liz turned to him. "You remember the ones, Ham."

Hammond nodded. "Those were some of my favorites." He stared at the mountains in the distance, his gaze taking on a faraway look. "I guess because they remind me of my boyhood up in those hills."

"You climbed the Tetons?"

At Avery's question, he turned and fixed her with a look. "I did. That was before all-terrain vehicles like we have now. At that time, all we had was our horse and our own resourcefulness. If a snowstorm blew in, a body either figured out a way to survive or it was all over."

Avery smiled at him. "Since you're still here, I guess you figured things out a time or two."

"Desperation will do that." He took on a pensive look. "I don't believe I've ever been as cold as I was that winter up in the hills, after my daddy took a really bad fall with a blizzard blowing in, and I realized we'd be trapped up there until spring."

"Brand told me a little about it. What did you do for shelter?"

"I found a cave. Thank heavens it wasn't inhabited by a bear." He grinned at his great-grandsons, who'd heard the tale too many times to count. "But I was desperate enough that I believe I'd have fought that bear for the cave, and won."

They all chuckled.

The old man had Avery's complete attention. She was

on the edge of her seat. "How did you get your dad to the cave?"

"I carried him."

"What about heat and food?"

"I spent every day hauling tree limbs to the cave and chopping them for firewood. As for food, we ate whatever I managed to trap. The day I bagged a deer, my daddy and I thought we'd died and gone to heaven. We had enough food to last us a month or more. And I hung the hide over the entrance to the cave to keep out the worst of the freezing wind."

"You really were resourceful. How old were you?"

He leaned back and stretched out his long legs. "Twelve." He paused, thinking. "I guess today we'd call that a boy. Considering the life-and-death situation I was in, I had to become a man whether I was ready or not."

"Indeed you were. Brand said that because of you, your father was able to die in his own bed. He had to be so proud of you."

He arched a brow and studied her with interest before he said softly, "I guess he was."

A short time later he called good night and made his way inside. Shortly after, the others followed, until only Brand and Avery remained on the porch.

When he was certain they'd all headed for their rooms, Brand said softly, "The Hammer is warming to you."

At his words Avery looked over. "How can you tell?"

"Well, first of all, he has a new audience for the wild stories of his youth. You're the only one here who hasn't heard everything."

"I loved hearing his story of survival."

"And he loved telling it. But you did something else tonight."

"I did?"

Brand chuckled. "Always before, whenever he recounted that story, he concentrated on how desperate the situation had been and how hard he'd worked to keep both himself and his father from starving or freezing. Tonight you pointed out something he'd never considered before."

When Avery merely stared at him, he added, "You suggested that he'd made his father proud. For a man like my great-grandfather, that's the highest compliment of all."

"I wasn't trying to flatter him. I meant it."

"And that touched him deeply. Or didn't you notice?"

She shrugged. "I saw him staring at me with that frown."

"That frown wasn't disapproval. It was concentration. In fact, it was discovery. You've given him something new to think about. Something that will warm his heart whenever he thinks about that time in the hills with his injured father."

Avery gave a long, deep sigh. "Then I'm glad I said it."

Brand reached over and took her hand in his. "Me, too, tenderfoot."

She felt the curl of heat along her arm and thought again how nice it was having someone hold her hand.

They sat together for the longest time, watching as the sky darkened, and the moon was just a small golden sliver hanging above the highest mountain peak.

"We'd better get inside." Brand kept her hand in his as he got to his feet. "Chores start early."

They stepped apart.

He held the door and Avery led the way inside.

Upstairs, he paused outside his door. "'Night, Avery."

"Good night." She climbed to the upper floor before looking back.

He was still standing where she'd left him, watching her. The look on his face sent a shiver along her spine. It felt as though, despite the distance between them, he was touching her.

She smiled at him before opening her door.

Once inside her room, she closed the door and leaned against it for a moment to catch her breath.

She'd hoped he would kiss her again. And was at the same moment relieved that he hadn't.

What in the world was wrong with her? She was feeling like a teen with her first crush.

Maybe he was, she thought suddenly. It seemed to her that all the guys she'd ever known were just distant memories, now that she'd met Brand Merrick.

CHAPTER SIXTEEN

Avery stepped into the greenhouse, a basket on her arm, a garden trowel in hand. She paused to breathe in the moist air, filled with the musky scent of damp earth.

She couldn't help smiling as she looked at the tidy rows of green, growing plants. Everything about this place delighted her. Maybe, she thought, it was because she'd never before had the chance to see so many vegetables at various stages of development, from tiny sprouts just peeking above the ground, to vines heavy with snap peas and red tomatoes.

She'd volunteered to pick the vegetables for tonight's dinner. Billy had given her a list of the greens he'd wanted for the salad and the carrots he planned on steaming.

She carefully picked the spinach, radishes, little green onions, and tomatoes. At a row of carrots, she knelt and began plucking them from the ground using the trowel, brushing loose dirt from each before placing them in the basket.

"Oh, just look at you." She held up a tiny carrot. "You're so perfect."

"I bet you say that to all the plants."

At the sound of Brand's voice, she looked over with

a smile of surprise. "I thought you were repairing a tractor."

"It's fixed and running like new."

"What are you doing here?"

"Looking for you. Billy said I'd find you in here." He ambled over to kneel beside her before pulling a carrot from the row. After wiping it on his sleeve, he whispered, "Another perfect carrot. Just right for my snack." He popped it in his mouth, chewing contentedly. "I finished my chores and thought this might be a great opportunity to take that therapeutic walk you suggested."

She arched a brow. "When I told you about walking on hilly ground, you didn't seem very enthusiastic."

He grinned. "I wasn't. But the more I thought about it, the more I realized you were onto something. It's one thing to correct my bad habits in a room, where the floor is level and I'm thinking about every step. It's quite another while walking outside. So"—he shrugged—"if you'd like to try something new, I'm ready."

She dropped the last of the carrots into the basket and got to her feet. "I'll just take these to Billy and we can get started."

He stood beside her. "I'll go with you."

As they stepped out of the greenhouse, Avery was smiling. "Billy told me this was his best gift ever."

Brand nodded. "He was really happy about it."

"I can see why. The minute I step inside, I can't stop smiling. It just lifts my spirits."

"I noticed." He tugged on a lock of her hair. "You have the same look in your eyes as Casey when he's delivering a calf. Like he's taking part in a miracle."

"You don't feel that way?"

He shrugged. "Sometimes calving gets so rushed,

and so messy, I forget about how amazing each one is. But Casey never forgets. He treats each new calf like his first."

"That's sweet."

"I agree. Just don't tell him I said so. His ego is already inflated."

They stepped into the kitchen, where Billy was busy stirring something on the stove.

He turned with a smile. "I see you found her."

"Yeah. Right where you said she'd be. Talking to the plants."

Avery laughed. "I wasn't talking to them."

"To yourself then."

"Okay. I admit it. I was talking to the carrots."

Billy chuckled. "Let Brand tease all he wants, Avery. Whenever I'm in the greenhouse, I talk to the plants, too."

"I guess it's okay," Brand said with a wink, "as long as the plants don't answer you."

With a laugh, Avery set the basket on the kitchen counter. "Want me to wash these?"

"I'll do it. Brand said he came back early for some therapy."

"Actually, a walk in the meadow. And soon, I hope, he'll be walking without a limp."

Brand was shaking his head and grinning. "So says our wise leader."

He reached into the refrigerator. Over his shoulder he called, "I'm grabbing a chilled bottle of water. Want one?"

"Yes, please."

He helped himself to two bottles and handed one to Avery.

"Okay." He led the way toward the back door. "Let the torture begin."

"Are you feeling the burn yet?"

"Yeah." Brand frowned. "Walking is a lot easier when I don't have to think about every step I'm taking."

"After a couple of weeks, you'll forget about it and it'll become routine."

"Promise?"

Avery nodded.

She found herself smiling as she and Brand circled the barns and began the ascent to the meadow. Along the way, they passed a fenced pasture where several mares and their foals were grazing.

Avery paused to lean on the fence and watch the antics of a coal-black foal racing alongside its mother, doing its best to keep up. When at last the mare paused to nibble grass, the foal ran in circles around and around. Every few minutes the mare would lift her head to keep an eye on her frisky child.

"I spent an hour or more here the other day, watching these mothers and their babies. They're just the sweetest things."

"Yeah." Brand paused beside her, enjoying the press of her hip on his. "That little guy has more energy than all the others put together."

"He's adorable."

They stood, watching and laughing as the foal began chasing a butterfly across the pasture, until he came up against the fence and was forced to halt, while the butterfly disappeared into a line of trees.

Brand leaned close, his warm breath tickling her ear. "Thank goodness for fences."

Avery shivered, enjoying the closeness of him. "Or that little guy would be long gone."

"Until his mother caught him and forced him to turn around. He may be frisky, but he's not going to argue with his mama."

They shared an intimate smile before drawing away and continuing their uphill climb until they reached the meadow, abloom with wildflowers. There they followed the trail Avery had followed days earlier.

"The minute I saw this, I thought of you, Brand. It's the perfect place to test how well you can walk, since we use different sets of muscles for uphill climbs and for descents."

"You're right." Brand was surprised and pleased at the fact that she'd thought of him during her walk. "Where to first?"

She pointed. "We'll climb to that tree line first. I know it won't seem natural at first, but I'd like you to really concentrate on using your damaged leg for the first step, then follow with your good leg."

They set off at a slow pace. Every so often Avery would drop back, allowing Brand to move ahead so she could observe his gait.

Halfway up, he paused. "Well? How am I doing?"

"Really good. But I bet you're feeling the strain."

He winced. "Oh yeah."

"I'm sorry, Brand." She closed a hand over his. "It's always harder to undo bad habits. Since your injury, you've been forcing your undamaged leg to do the bulk of the work. Now, with your injured leg completely healed, this is the only way to get back to the way things were. But you're making great progress. You're well on your way to being completely healed."

"I get it." When she released his hand, he rubbed the tender place on his right leg. "But knowing that doesn't make it any less painful."

Avery pointed to a low boulder. "Come on. We'll stop there and rest a bit."

As Brand lowered himself to the boulder, Avery heard the ping of an incoming text and lifted her phone from her shirt pocket.

The message was terse.

So far and yet so tantalizingly near.

Like the first, there was no identifying phone number.

Brand watched as all the color seemed to drain from her face. She stood, as still as a statue, her gaze fixed on her phone.

"Bad news?"

For a moment she didn't respond.

He got to his feet and reached a hand to her shoulder. "Hey. What's wrong?"

Before he had a chance to read the message over her shoulder, she touched a finger to the screen, closing it down.

She looked away, avoiding his questioning gaze. "It's nothing."

His hand tightened on her shoulder. "If something's bothering you, I'd like to help."

"Thanks, but I'm fine. Do you still want to climb to the tree line?"

He could see the way she'd closed up, shutting out any chance for him to question her further. "Yeah. Sure. Let's go."

He swung away and reminded himself to concentrate on putting as much pressure on his injured leg as he did on the left leg. He hoped the effort would keep him from wondering what had been in that text. Whatever it was, Avery had been really rattled. He'd never seen her look that pale. Whatever tender moments they'd shared had now taken second place to what appeared to be bad news.

Avery walked a few steps behind him, forcing herself to remember why she was here. It wasn't just an escape from reality. She was here as a therapist. Brand deserved all her attention.

"You're doing really..."

The sound of a horse's pounding hooves coming up fast behind them had the words dying on her lips.

Without thinking, she grabbed Brand's arm and cried out, "Watch out. Someone's..."

"Hey." Feeling her nails digging into his flesh, he spun around and closed a hand over hers.

Despite the heat of the day, her hand was cold as ice.

With a look of terror, she peered over her shoulder and lifted her other hand in a defensive gesture, as though braced for an attack.

"Hey, Brand." A wrangler reined in his mount inches from them, his horse's hooves spewing dust and dirt.

"You in a hurry, Brennan?"

"Yeah. Sorry." The wrangler touched a hand to his hat. "Ma'am." He turned to Brand. "Casey sent me to find you. He has a sick heifer on his hands and wonders if you could drive the stake truck up to the herd now."

"Sure thing. Tell him I'll be right behind you."

As the wrangler turned his mount, Brand continued holding Avery's hand while looking into her eyes. "Okay. What just happened here?"

"Nothing." Seeing his probing look, she ducked her head.

"Nothing?" He tugged on her hand, urging her to look at him. "Something spooked you."

She pulled her hand free of his touch. "I wasn't expecting anybody to come barreling after us like that."

"You looked like you were expecting to see the devil himself."

She couldn't quite meet his eyes. "I'm not used to the way things are done around here." She tucked her hands into her pockets to keep him from reaching for him. "I guess this is the end of the walk we'd planned. You'll have to hurry if you're going to drive up to the herd."

Still he held back. "Why don't you come along? It's a pretty drive."

She shook her head. "No thanks. I'll just...take my time heading back to the house."

"Okay. Suit yourself." He swung away and started down the path, so deep in thought he was no longer able to concentrate on avoiding the limp that had become routine.

All his thoughts were centered on Avery. On her pallor when she'd read that text. Whatever the message, it had left her visibly upset. And then there was the fear in her eyes when Brennan had come galloping toward her.

She could deny all she wanted. He knew what he'd seen. Something, or someone, had frightened her so badly that she'd been expecting the worst and was prepared to fight back. But who or what would she be fighting way out here?

Since she was new to Wyoming, whatever troubled her had to be baggage from home. And since her fear seemed to be related to that text, it would seem that someone from her recent past knew just what buttons to push to get her really riled up.

Or was he reading too much into all this?

He couldn't get the image of Avery, looking wild-eyed and terrified, out of his mind. *Running scared.* The phrase summed up what he'd just seen.

It begged the question: Why would someone from Michigan volunteer to come all the way to Wyoming? Had Avery Grant really come here just to tend a patient? Or had there been some other reason for volunteering to take a job so far from home?

CHAPTER SEVENTEEN

Avery was passing the barn when she heard voices. Pausing in the doorway, she could see activity in one of the stalls. She hurried over to lean on the railing as Casey and Brand took charge of a bawling heifer.

Casey held up a needle. "Hold her still."

"I've got her." Brand began cooing to the animal and cradling her head. "Hey now, little girl. This won't hurt a bit."

Avery went very still, absorbing a tiny thrill as she watched the unexpected tenderness in Brand as he held the animal and tried to comfort it.

Casey, too, was murmuring as he plunged the needle into the soft hide. "Steady now. There you go."

Caught up in the moment, seeing these tough cowboys willing to show their tender side with a helpless creature, Avery felt the same sort of strange emotions she experienced each time she entered the greenhouse. As though here in this place she was more in tune with nature than any place she'd ever been.

"Okay." Casey closed up his black bag and got to his feet. "We'll keep her quarantined in here for twenty-four hours and see how she's doing." He clapped a hand on Brand's shoulder. "Thanks for your help, bro."

"No problem." Brand stood. "I'll see she's fed and watered."

"Great." Casey turned and spotted Avery. "Hey. How long have you been here?"

"Just long enough to see you give that poor animal a shot."

"Antibiotic. It should do the trick. I expect she'll be ready to join the herd in no time." He grinned. "Welcome to my hospital."

She gave him a warm smile. "Thanks. I like the way you work." Her gaze settled on Brand. "I should say I like how both of you work together."

"That's us. A team." Brand slapped his brother on the arm. "His brains and my brawn."

Casey gave a quick shake of his head. "Don't let Brand kid you. When it comes to brainpower, he always seems to be two steps ahead of me. My big brother is the reason I decided to study veterinary medicine."

After Casey let himself out of the stall and walked away, Avery watched as Brand filled a trough with feed and another with water.

When he'd secured the door to the stall, he stood beside Avery to watch the heifer drink noisily from the trough.

Brand kept his gaze on the heifer. "I didn't see you when I drove down from the hills. Were you up in your room?"

She shook her head. "I kept on walking."

"Walking always helps me think."

She nodded. "I want to see as much as I can before I leave, so I can carry it in my mind. Pastures filled with horses. Hills swarming with cattle. And acres and acres of wildflowers. It's so pretty, it takes my breath away."

"Yeah." He'd gone very still, staring at her with that

directness that had the heat rushing to her cheeks. "Pretty things have a way of doing that to me, too." He lifted a hand to brush a strand of hair from her eyes and kept his hand against her cheek.

She felt the sexual jolt all the way to her toes.

His voice lowered to a seductive whisper. "Sometimes when I look at you, I lose my train of thought completely. Probably because all I can think of is…" He leaned toward her and brushed his mouth over hers. It was the merest touch of his lips, as though testing to see her reaction.

She absorbed the tug of desire and thought about stepping away from the heat, but his hands were already at her shoulders, drawing her against him as he kissed her with a thoroughness that had her heart hitching.

With a hum of pleasure, she wasn't even aware that her arms had encircled his waist as she offered him more.

He took, like a man starved for the taste of her.

She heard a strangled sigh and realized it was her voice.

He pressed her back against the door of the stall while his hands moved over her, causing fire and ice to collide along her spine.

His hands tangled in her hair as he rained hot kisses over her upturned face.

"Brand…"

"Shh." He nibbled the sensitive hollow between her neck and shoulder until she could feel her body's urgent response.

Her head was swimming from the unexpected feelings he unleashed. And though she knew things were moving too quickly, she couldn't deny she welcomed it. And wanted more. So much more.

Her breath was coming faster now, as her body absorbed the pleasure of those strong hands moving over her.

Even with her eyes nearly closed, she saw or felt a shadow looming over them.

"So how's the sick heifer?"

At Jonah's voice, their two heads came up sharply to stare at him.

Struggling for breath, Brand kept a hand on Avery's shoulder as they stepped apart.

She was grateful for the support. If not for that, she feared her trembling legs might fail her and she would sink into the straw at their feet.

Jonah studied the two of them before, with a sly grin, he turned and deliberately focused his attention on the heifer. "Looks like everything's just fine in here."

"Yeah." Brand kept his gaze on Avery. "I thought you stayed up in the hills with the herd."

Jonah arched a brow. "That was the plan, but I figured I may as well get back in time for supper. Billy's making beef tenderloin. You know I just can't pass up something that melts in my mouth like butter. Whether it's good food or pretty women, I guess I'm not the only Merrick with that weakness. It seems to run in the family."

"You're not amusing." Brand's voice was a low growl.

"Sorry you're not seeing the humor. I think it's funny how impeccable my timing is." Jonah reached around Brand and Avery and opened the stall door before stepping inside.

When he realized Jonah had no intention of leaving, Brand narrowed his eyes on him. "You smell like a trail bum. Before sitting down to supper, you'll want to head inside and grab a shower."

Recognizing his brother's impatience, Jonah smiled lazily. "There's plenty of time. I think I'll just stay out here with the two of you." After running a hand over the heifer's back, he stepped out of the stall and turned to Avery. "Did you get to see Casey in action as he played doctor?"

"I did." Avery was grateful she'd had a moment to compose herself. At least her voice didn't sound all strangled and breathy, even though that's how she felt. "And I have to admit, I was impressed."

"Yeah. When he's being the good doctor, he's really something. Of course"—he winked at her—"Big Brother Brand is pretty impressive, too. When he's not being obnoxious."

Brand's eyes narrowed. "It's time for you to get out of here."

"Yeah. I have to admit, it's been fun messing with you." Jonah offered his arm to Avery. "I'm heading up to the house. Want to go along?"

Laughing at the absurdity of the scene, she looped her arm through Jonah's, then tucked her other arm through Brand's. "I think it's time for all of us to get cleaned up for dinner."

Scowling, Brand moved along beside her. And while Jonah kept up a running conversation with Avery, Brand was cursing the rotten timing of everything that had happened this day. Nothing, it seemed, ever went as planned.

"You were right, Jonah. Best meal ever." Casey helped himself to another slice of tenderloin and another scoop of garlic mashed potatoes. "If I ever find a woman who can cook like you, Billy, I'm going to ask her to marry me."

Jonah gave a snort of laughter. "Any woman who can cook that good will have cowboys standing in line to marry her. Why would she settle for you?"

"She'll take one look at this handsome face and this perfect body, and all those other cowboys will be a distant memory." While the family burst into laughter, Casey dug into his food and sighed from the pure pleasure of it.

Egan nudged Bo. "As his father, you should have told him there's more to marriage than good looks and a full stomach."

Bo grinned at his sons. "There is?"

Meg patted her husband's arm. "Maybe you're the one who forgot to pass along that information to our son."

Bo winked at her. "Or maybe I've been alone so long, I've forgotten what you and Pops taught me."

"If you're feeling lonely, Dad, you may want to join us in town tonight." Casey devoured the last bite of steak and sat back with a pleased smile. "Nonie has just the cure for loneliness. And every time she sees us, she asks about you. You're quite the catch, you know."

Bo chuckled. "You make me sound like a lobster in some fisherman's trap."

"Not all women want to trap a man, boy."

At Hammond's gravelly voice, the entire family looked over at him before bursting into laughter.

Billy lifted a bottle of red wine. "A little more, Miss Meg?"

She shook her head. "No, thank you, Billy. A sip was all I wanted. It will have to keep for another time."

When dinner ended, Jonah pushed away from the table and turned to Brand. "Want to head to town with Casey and me?"

Brand shook his head. "Not tonight. But thanks for the offer."

Jonah turned to Casey. "As long as Brand isn't going

with us, maybe he could volunteer to check on that heifer before turning in tonight."

Casey nodded. "Good idea. You up for it, bro?"

Before Brand could respond, Jonah glanced from Brand to Avery with a knowing smile. "I'm sure our big brother won't mind some time in the barn. And, Avery, if you're okay with it, you could probably lend a hand." He paused for effect. "In case Brand needs help with . . . anything."

Avery could feel the heat stain her cheeks even as she was forced to answer his teasing question. "I'd be happy to help."

"I figured as much." Jonah gave an exaggerated smile to Brand. "You're welcome, bro. 'Night, Avery."

Seeing the frown on Brand's face, Casey punched Jonah's arm. "On the drive to town you'll have to fill me in on your little private joke."

"Happy to."

The two of them ambled away, heads bent, laughing together.

When they were gone, Avery turned to Brand. She couldn't stop the laughter that bubbled up.

He gave a shake of his head. "You realize we'll be the hot topic of the night at Nonie's. Those two can't be trusted to keep anything to themselves."

"I know." She tried, but failed, to bite back the grin that curved her mouth. "But I love all this silly teasing." She chuckled. "Maybe it's because I never had a brother."

"You can have mine." Brand's words lacked any anger, and she could tell he was already seeing the humor in the situation. "I'll gladly give you both of them. And good riddance. As for your . . . help in the barn, I can't wait."

*   *   *

Using the bands Avery indicated, Brand finished a dozen stretches on each leg. By the time he finished, he was sweating.

Avery handed him a towel. "Feeling the burn?"

He pressed the towel to his face. "Yeah. But it gets a little easier each day."

"If that's the case, I think it's time to add a half dozen more stretches to your routine."

"Now you're beginning to sound like that drill sergeant I was expecting when Gram Meg first told me she'd hired a physical therapist." He tossed aside the towel and hung the bands on a hook on the wall. "I could use a cold beer. Want to join me before we head out to the barn?"

She nodded and followed him down the stairs.

In the kitchen, they found Egan, Meg, and Hammond seated at the table.

"Ah." Egan lifted his coffee mug. "Join us. We're just having seconds of Billy's brownies."

"Sounds good." Brand turned to Avery. "Coffee and dessert, or beer?"

"I'm ready for seconds of Billy's brownies." She filled a mug and set a brownie on a plate.

Brand helped himself to a longneck from the refrigerator.

They looked up as Bo stepped in from the porch to join them.

"Coffee or beer?" Brand asked.

"I think I'll have what you're having."

Brand handed his father his beer and opened another for himself.

As they settled around the table, Hammond turned to his grandson. "What's new in town today, Bo?"

"Buster Mandel's wife took a fall and ended up in

surgery. Broken hip. Doc thinks she'll be using a walker for a while."

"Oh, poor Trudy." Meg put a hand over Egan's. "I wonder if her daughter can come up from Calgary to lend a hand."

"With three little ones?" Egan arched a brow at a sudden thought, before glancing at Avery. "I bet she'll need therapy."

Hammond's eyes narrowed. "Seems like everybody around these parts needs more and more doctoring. That's what comes of being soft."

Brand grinned at his great-grandfather. "Like me?"

Hammond was quick to defend his own. "You know there's nothing soft about you, boy. It's the doctors these days. Foisting all this extra care on folks. Why, we've been falling and getting up from the beginning of time. And nobody told my generation they needed to learn how to walk all over again."

Knowing how his grandfather could dominate a conversation with his theories, without a care about any hurt feelings, Bo cleared his throat, determined to change the subject. "While I was in town today, I heard that Luke Miller and C.C. are visiting her parents."

His words were greeted by a stunned silence.

Avery glanced from one to the other, wondering at the impact these names had on the people here. She'd never heard of them before. And she'd never before seen this family look so shattered.

Meg's voice took on an edge as she glared at her son. "I won't have you speak those names in this house. Do you hear?"

Just then Avery caught a slight movement in the doorway and realized that Liz was standing there. Instead of coming toward them, she looked frozen in place, a look of horror on her face.

As the others looked over, she turned and fled.

But not before Avery caught sight of the tears spilling down her cheeks.

"Now you've done it." Meg's brow furrowed with concern. "There'll be no living with her after that news. We'll have to tiptoe around for months. Or maybe, if she follows the usual pattern, years."

CHAPTER EIGHTEEN

After Billy left to head to his room for the night, Avery cleared the table and put the dishes in the dishwasher, while the family, clearly agitated, began drifting from the kitchen to their rooms.

Brand set aside his empty bottle. "I promised Casey I'd look in on the heifer." He turned to include Avery in his smile, hoping they could take up where they'd left off earlier.

Just then Bo got to his feet and put an arm around his shoulders. "I'll join you, son. We can talk out in the barn."

Bo shot a look of regret toward Avery. "Want to come along?"

Realizing Bo craved some private time with Brand, she shook her head. "It's been a long day. I think I'll head up to bed."

Brand mouthed the word *sorry* before following his dad from the room. Avery switched off the kitchen light and started down the hallway toward the stairs. As she passed the darkened great room, she heard a sound that had her backing up.

Peering through the darkness, she saw a shadow across

the room. As her eyes adjusted, she could make out Liz, seated in a wing chair by the fireplace, head bowed, sobbing into a handkerchief.

"Liz." As Avery approached, the young woman's head came up sharply and she blew her nose.

Avery dropped to her knees beside the chair. "Is there anything I can do to help?"

Liz shook her head. "Nobody can help me."

"I'd like to try."

"No." Liz lowered her head, refusing to look at her. "It's personal. And…humiliating. Just go."

"Okay. Sorry. I didn't mean to intrude." Avery got to her feet.

As she started out of the room, she heard muffled weeping and realized Liz was trying without success to cover up her cries.

Though she'd fully intended to go upstairs and give Liz the privacy she craved, she had a sudden thought.

Ignoring the stairs, she turned toward the kitchen. Minutes later she returned, carrying the bottle of wine left over from dinner, as well as two stem glasses.

Seeing that she'd come back, Liz glowered at her, and Avery was reminded of old Hammond. Liz and her grandfather had a great deal in common. Both could wither a person's resolve with a single dark look.

Without a word, Avery poured and handed Liz a glass, before filling a second one and setting the bottle on a side table.

Liz accepted the glass and sipped, turning her head to stare anywhere but at Avery.

Avery held her silence and lifted the glass to her lips.

Liz drank a bit more, then leaned back in the chair and looked over, meeting Avery's eyes for the first time. "I was just about to join the family when I overheard what my brother said. The mere mention of Luke Miller nearly stopped my heart."

"I didn't recognize the name." Though Avery had dozens of questions, she bit her tongue, hoping Liz would answer them in her own time, in her own way.

Liz sighed. "There was a time when Luke Miller was the love of my life. Maybe he still is. I thought the sun rose and set on him."

Avery sucked in a breath, her only reaction to this sudden, unexpected news. It was the last thing she'd expected to hear.

"Does he live around here?"

"His family owns a ranch on the far side of Devil's Door. I've known him since I was a kid, but I never really paid much attention to him until he asked me to a Founder's Day Dance. That's our annual summer festival in town. After that, we were inseparable."

"How old were you?"

"Eighteen. Luke was twenty."

"Did your family approve?"

Liz nodded. "They liked Luke. He was a good guy. Men enjoyed his friendship. Women flirted with him. And he took it all in stride. Everybody liked Luke Miller." She looked down into her glass. "Everybody, that is, except my best friend, C.C. Farmer. She told me she couldn't stand him. And that was hard, loving Luke and not being able to talk about my feelings with my best friend."

She sipped her wine and when Avery held up the bottle, she allowed her to pour some more. "When I look back, I realize I spent a whole lot of time defending Luke to C.C. But she would have none of it. We fought about him a lot. She told me right to my face that I'd regret loving him."

With moonlight spilling through the windows, Avery watched the play of emotions on Liz's face. "Is that why you broke it off?"

"What makes you think...?" Liz took another sip of wine and stared pensively into the glass. "On Christmas Eve, Luke asked me to marry him. I said yes, and we shared the news with our families. What a celebration it was. Mom and Dad wanted to give us the wedding they'd never had, and Luke's folks wanted to give us a piece of their land so we could share rangeland. Luke and I were just basking in all the love and happiness."

"Did you set a date?"

Liz nodded. "February first."

"That's pretty fast."

"I said that very thing, but Luke said if he could have his way, we'd elope and marry the next day. But after a talk with my dad, Luke agreed to be patient. So we reserved the church and agreed to hold the reception in the church hall in town, so it would be midway between his family's ranch and ours. By then C.C. wasn't speaking to me, even when I begged her to relent and be my maid of honor. So I asked that my folks and Luke's folks be our witnesses. The invitations went out, and Mom and I found the perfect gown. The night before the wedding, after the rehearsal supper here at the ranch, Luke told me that he would never love anyone but me until the day he died, and I was so happy, and so crazy in love, I cried like a baby."

Avery, caught up in the story, found herself almost weepy.

Liz drained her glass and set it aside. Her voice was

stronger now. Not the strangled breathy sound of tears but steady. Resigned. "The next day when I arrived at the church with my family, Reverend Dohlman told us that he'd had a strange phone call from Luke, saying he and C.C. were on their way to Jackson Hole to be married."

"Your best friend C.C.?"

Liz held out her empty glass and Avery poured more wine.

Liz took a long drink. "I guess you should call her my ex–best friend. I never heard from her or Luke. Not one word. And now..."

"That's..." Avery shook her head, struggling for words. "Oh, Liz, that's unforgivable. How could they do such a thing?"

Liz shrugged and took another long drink. "I guess I was blind to the fact that I wasn't the only one charmed by Luke. After all, he was handsome and so likeable. How could C.C. not fall for him?"

"But she told you she couldn't stand him."

"Maybe that was all a lie. Maybe what she couldn't stand was that he was attracted to me instead of her." She looked over at Avery. "C.C. had this perfect body, and she was so beautiful, she used to turn heads wherever we went. But Luke never seemed to notice her."

"Do you think that was a problem for her? Do you think she saw Luke as a challenge and decided to see if she could get his attention?"

Liz was silent for a long time. "Don't think I haven't asked myself all those questions and more. I've gone over every reason I could think of. But why would she need Luke? She could have any man she wanted. As for Luke, whenever I think about our last night together, I think about how sincere he sounded when he said I would be the only woman he would ever love. Is it possible for a man to lie that convincingly?"

Avery remained silent. Like Liz, she had no answers. Only more questions.

Liz drained her glass and held it out. "Would you pour me some more?"

Avery hesitated. "I hope you won't have a headache in the morning."

Liz gave a grunt of laughter. "It beats the heartache I've been carrying around for a lifetime. And it certainly loosened my tongue."

She nodded toward the bottle in Avery's hand. "Will you stay and help me finish it?"

"That's what friends are for." Avery chuckled. "I wouldn't want you to suffer all alone tomorrow."

For the first time, Liz managed a throaty chuckle. Feeling mellow, she tucked her legs under her and turned to stare at the darkened outline of the mountains in the distance. "As you can imagine, in a town the size of Devil's Door, after my public humiliation I became the object of gossip for miles around. It got so bad I refused to go along whenever anybody in the family headed to Devil's Door." She took a sip of wine. "The longer I stayed locked up here in my own little cave, the easier it got. And after a while I realized my whole life was centered around this ranch and those mountains. Thank heaven for my photography. It's become my salvation."

"You have a real gift, Liz. Of course, it goes without saying that even without all the pain, your talent would be recognized."

"I'm not so sure." She swirled the dark liquid around and around in the glass, staring into its depths as though it had all of life's answers.

She looked over at Avery. "While I was planning my wedding, it was my intention to put aside my hobby and pour all my energy into being a rancher's wife."

"Hobby?" Avery's voice went up a notch. "Liz, what you have is a rare talent. There's nothing wrong with wanting to be a good wife, but isn't it possible to be both? A devoted wife and a talented photographer? Would you have asked Luke to put aside his hobby of ranching to devote all his time to being your husband?"

At her words, Liz stared at her, eyes going wide. "I...never thought about it that way."

Avery could see the wheels turning.

Finally Liz nodded. "I've never heard it said aloud before. I guess I've been telling myself that I was just filling the empty hours by taking pictures."

"What about your agent? Your family? All those buyers eager to collect your work? Are they just being polite and humoring you? Or could it be they actually recognize talent when they see it?"

The smile came slowly to Liz's eyes and then her mouth. "I guess I should respect their judgment and listen to them."

"And listen to your heart. You have to know, in your heart, that your photographs are works of art, and worthy of the time and attention you put into them."

Seeing that Liz was mulling over her words, Avery took in a breath and said cautiously, "If I were you, I'd walk proudly through town every chance I got. And I'd let everyone see that whatever happened seventeen years ago has no power over me now."

Liz said softly, "You mean, 'Look at me. I'm still standing.'"

Avery nodded. "Exactly. Still standing, and standing tall and proud."

Maybe it was the wine. Maybe it was Avery's words. Laughter suddenly bubbled up in Liz, and she put a hand to her mouth as she giggled. "It might be fun to see their faces if I did walk through town. But why should I give them the satisfaction of more gossip?"

Avery paused a minute before saying, "I would think they have better things to talk about than something that happened all those years ago." She gave Liz a tentative smile. "By now they've all witnessed births and deaths. They've achieved success and suffered failure. They've moved on with their lives. Maybe you should, too. You were a girl then. Now you're a woman. A lovely, bright, and very talented woman."

Liz shrugged. "Maybe…" She sipped her wine. "Who knows? Maybe I'll just do that. Someday." She turned her attention to Avery. "What about you? Is there an important guy in your life?"

Avery shook her head and thought about Brand. "No." A lie, she thought, but a little white lie to cover her confusion.

"Has there ever been?"

Avery set aside her glass and leaned back on her elbows, staring into the fire. "For a little while there was a guy. A doctor."

"Ooh." Liz gave a dreamy smile. "I'm not surprised. You went to med school. Your father is a doctor. It stands to reason. What's his name?"

"Trace Martin." Suddenly restless, Avery sat up, wrapping her arms around her knees.

"Trace. A sexy name. So? Details. Handsome? Charming? Brilliant?"

"Yes, yes, and yes." Her tone hardened. "Also a fraud."

"He hurt you." Liz sat forward, putting a hand on Avery's.

"It barely hurt at all. But it caught me by surprise when I learned that he was only dating me to impress my father so he would be invited to join his surgical team. Once I knew the truth, I broke it off, but I wasn't really hurt because we were"—she paused—"just friends."

"How did Trace take that?"

Avery shrugged. "After his initial anger, he seemed fine with it."

"Does your father know Trace was using you?"

Avery looked away. "He does. He said he won't let personal feelings get in the way of his professional plans. Every report he had from fellow doctors regarding Trace reinforced his original assessment that Trace is a brilliant surgeon. He hoped I would agree that a single lapse in judgment shouldn't be allowed to destroy a man's entire future."

Liz caught both of Avery's hands in hers. "That has to hurt every bit as much as learning that Trace was just using you to get ahead."

Avery blinked hard. "In a way, it hurts more because I expected my dad to defend me."

Liz gathered her close. "Men. We can't live with 'em, can't live without 'em."

Choking back laughter, they drew apart.

Liz shared the last of the wine with Avery and held up her glass. "Here's to shared heartache."

Avery shook her head. "I'm done with heartache. Here's to two strong women."

Liz gave a sudden smile. "We are strong, aren't we?" She drained her glass, then looked at the empty bottle. "I can't believe we drank all that."

"I don't know about you," Avery said as she finished her wine, "but I'm going to pay tomorrow." She set aside her glass and got to her feet.

Liz did the same.

As the two women started out of the great room, Liz caught Avery's hand in hers. "Thanks for listening. I haven't talked about any of this since it happened."

"Not even to your family?"

"Especially to my family." Liz lifted eyes that were now free of tears. "I haven't had a best friend since Luke and C.C. betrayed me."

"I left all my friends behind when I came here."

"I'll be your friend here in Wyoming, Avery. Especially now that we've shared secrets."

"I only shared mine because of that wine."

Liz startled Avery by throwing her arms around her neck and hugging her fiercely. "I know. I'm tipsy, too. In fact, I believe I'm very drunk. But I don't care. You were the best listener ever. I'll never forget this."

"I'm glad I was able to be here for you. Good night, Liz."

"'Night, my friend. I wish…"

Avery paused. "What?"

She shrugged. "I wish you were going to be here longer than a few weeks."

"Me too. But we can still make the most of whatever time I have here." She stuck out her hand. "Deal?"

Liz grasped her hand. "Deal."

The two women turned away and headed in opposite directions to their rooms.

Later, as Avery lay in her bed, she thought about the strange twists and turns of the day. A menacing text. A chance to watch Brand interact with his brothers. That kiss in the barn. Despite the interruption, it had been intense, causing her to wonder just how it could have ended.

And Liz. Avery never would have imagined that the closed, wounded woman who had held her at arm's length since her arrival would open up to share something so painful and humiliating that it had colored her entire adult life.

She was glad now that she'd followed her instincts instead of rushing up the stairs. Thank heavens for a little wine.

CHAPTER NINETEEN

Avery woke to the sound of voices drifting up the stairs. A glance at the clock let her know she'd overslept. By now the men would be finishing their chores and ready for breakfast.

Breakfast. The thought of it had her letting out a little moan of protest as she slid out of bed and headed for the shower.

By the time she descended the stairs, she was fighting a pounding headache and thinking about going back to bed. But the need for caffeine was too great. She would drink a gallon of coffee, she promised herself, and then head back upstairs.

Added to her physical discomfort was the realization that this was all her fault. If she hadn't provided the wine, Liz would have had a good cry and then gone off to her room. By now the poor woman was probably furious that she'd opened up to a perfect stranger and laid bare the secrets of her heart.

Avery moaned out loud. How was she ever going to face Liz? She hoped and prayed she wouldn't have to see her for the rest of the day. The way her luck had been going, an ugly scene with Liz could be the final straw, causing the Merrick family to send her packing. It would certainly be a blot on her record and a roadblock in her career. Not to mention what her father would say when his only child failed miserably at her blatant attempt at independence.

And then there was Brand.

Of all the losses she would suffer, leaving Brand would be the most painful. Not because of any personal feelings she might have for him, she told herself as the thought formed, but only because she hadn't yet eliminated that painful limp of his.

Liar.

She stumbled on the stairs and had to pause a moment as the realization dawned. She hadn't meant for him to matter. But he did. She certainly hadn't taken the time to figure out just what he was to her, but in the brief time she'd been here, he'd become much more than just an injured patient in need of her healing touch.

Yes, Brand mattered. And what he thought of her mattered.

If the family decided that she'd meddled in something too painfully personal and dismissed her on the spot, she had no doubt she would feel the sting of Brand's anger. And that would hurt more than anything else.

"Billy, I think this omelet may be the best one you've ever—" Liz looked over as Avery walked into the kitchen. "Here you are. 'Morning, sleepyhead. I'm glad I'm not the only one who overslept."

"Good morning." Avery saw the way the family was looking from Liz to her and back again. She picked up a mug of steaming coffee from a tray on the counter and downed half of it before making her way to the table.

"I'm making ham and cheese omelets," Billy called from the stove.

"No, thank you, Billy. I'll just have coffee this morning."

Liz was shaking her head. "You have to taste Billy's omelets. They're wonderful."

"I couldn't. Oh." When the cook slid a plate in front of her, Avery prayed she wouldn't be sick in front of everybody. What was she going to do with all this food?

Seeing them watching her, she took a small bite. Chewed. Forced herself to swallow. And realized it was delicious. And she was suddenly ravenous. She simply had to enjoy this amazing breakfast, in case it was her last one here.

She looked over. "You're right, Liz. This is wonderful."

"Told you." Liz finished her own breakfast and sat back, sipping coffee before turning to the foreman. "How are the trails looking up in high country, Chet?"

Like the others, Chet had been watching her with a look of concern, waiting for her to break down and flee the room, as was her usual reaction to anything related to Luke and C.C. At her question, he blinked before glancing around at the family. "They're finally drying out from all that rain." He gave her a steady look. "You thinking about heading up-country?"

She nodded. "I'd like to take advantage of this sunshine before the next line of storms rolls in."

Around the table, the family appeared confused.

Hammond spread jam on his toast. "You thinking about going today, girl?"

"Yeah. Just a quick day trip."

Meg was shaking her head. "Sorry, honey. Today won't

work for me. I promised Buster I'd visit Trudy. But if you wouldn't mind waiting until tomorrow..."

Liz shrugged. "It's okay, Mom. Yesterday I heard you telling Buster you'd be by for a visit." She turned to Avery. "I was thinking you might like to drive up to the hills with me."

"I..." Avery knew her jaw had dropped. From the looks of the others, they were as surprised as she was by this completely out-of-the-blue invitation. She glanced helplessly at Brand. "I wouldn't like to miss a therapy session."

Liz turned to her nephew. "It looks like you get to call the shots, Brand. Are you willing to miss a session with your favorite therapist so she can go into the high country with me?"

Brand, like the rest of his family, was staring at his aunt with a mixture of confusion and relief. "I don't think one day will make a difference." He turned to Avery. "Is this something you'd like to do?"

She couldn't keep the smile from lighting up all her features. "I'd love to see a part of the country I've never seen before." She turned to Liz. "But I have to warn you. I don't know the first thing about survival in the wilderness."

There was a smattering of laughter around the table, and Liz joined in. "We're just driving up into the hills. We'll only be a few miles from the herd. It's far from any ranches, but not exactly primitive. Want to take a chance?"

Avery's smile grew. "When do we leave?"

"Right after you finish that omelet." Liz turned to the cook. "Billy, would you mind packing some food? We won't be back until dark."

At his nod of agreement, Liz shoved away from the table. "Thanks, Billy. Avery, you'll need some comfortable hiking boots. And bring a jacket and hat. I'll go pack up my cameras and gear."

"Wait." Avery ate the last bite of her breakfast and thanked Billy before rushing out of the room behind Liz.

As the door closed behind the women, the Merrick family sat perfectly still, looking at one another with matching looks of confusion.

It was Casey who broke the silence. "Who was that woman, and what has she done with Aunt Liz?"

It was all they needed to have them exploding with relief and laughter.

At a knock on her bedroom door, Avery hurried over to find Brand standing in the hallway.

She tried to read the look on his face but couldn't decide if he was angry or simply curious.

"If you're not okay with this, I'll understand. After all, I'm being paid to work with you, not go off into the hills on a day trip—"

Brand held up a hand to halt her apology. "I'm fine with it. And someday, when you have the time, I'd like to know just what you did to break through the impenetrable wall of misery that has dogged my aunt Liz, known around here as the loner of the county."

"I didn't do anything—"

He stopped her again. "Save the magic, or whatever you did, for another day. I just came up here to remind you to bring along a poncho, in case you get into some weather up there. I know Billy will stow some bedrolls.

Even though my aunt is calling it a day trip, it could turn into an all-nighter if the weather turns ugly."

Avery couldn't hide her alarm. "Should I be worried?"

"No." He put a hand on her arm. "Aunt Liz has spent a lifetime hiking these hills. I just want you to be prepared for anything. But right now, it looks like a perfect day for a trip to the high country."

She exhaled. "Okay." She couldn't hide her smile. "I'm so excited. I feel like a kid at Christmas. This is a chance to see the real Wyoming. What can I expect?"

"The unexpected," Brand said with a laugh. "If you're lucky, you'll see a herd or two of mustangs. Maybe some deer."

"Are there any big cats in those hills?"

He nodded. "There are. But they're hard to spot. They aren't fond of people."

"Good. I think my heart would stop if I saw a big cougar ready to pounce."

He couldn't help grinning. "Don't worry. Liz always carries a rifle."

"A rifle?" Her eyes widened. "You're kidding, right?"

"I'm not kidding. Nobody in their right mind would go into the high country without one." To soften his words, he took her hand. "Come on. Liz will be waiting. You're going to have a memorable day."

"Just so it's good memorable, and not scary memorable."

He was chuckling as he led the way down the stairs and out to the waiting truck, idling alongside the back porch. It had already been stocked with food and camera equipment.

With goodbyes to her family, Liz settled herself into

the driver's seat and waited while Avery climbed into the passenger seat.

Brand reached up and closed a big hand over Avery's. "Make memories."

"Only happy ones." She adjusted her sunglasses and turned to wave as Liz gunned the engine. They took off across the pasture behind the barn, then headed toward a line of trees at the top of the ridge.

"Do you have a map?"

At Avery's question, Liz gave a snort of laughter. "We're going on a photo adventure. For that, there are no maps or guideposts. We'll just follow the sun and see where it takes us."

"I guess if we get lost or in trouble, we can always call." Avery touched a hand to the fully charged cell phone in her pocket.

At that Liz turned to her with a smile. "They won't do us much good. There's hardly any service up in these hills."

Avery felt a quick moment of fear at what she'd signed on for. Then the moment passed as she reminded herself that she was about to have a real back-country adventure with a woman who, until last night, had largely ignored her. And she would get to watch Liz go about the work that was admired by people the world over.

And if she was lucky, the weather would hold, they would have a few laughs together, and she would see things she would never see back home in Rose Arbor, Michigan.

CHAPTER TWENTY

It was one of those perfect spring days. A few puffy clouds drifted across the bluest sky Avery had ever seen. With the windows of the truck open, a soft breeze kissed their cheeks.

Liz kept her eyes on the trail. "About last night..."

"I'm sorry, Liz. I had no right to come barging in like that."

Liz glanced over. "I want to thank you."

"Thank...me?"

"All the way to my room I kept thinking about what you'd told me. That what happened to me seventeen years ago has no power over me now." She returned her attention to the trail. "I barely took the time to undress before falling into bed. I suppose I could blame it on the wine, but I have the feeling it was more. It was the best, deepest sleep I've had in ages. And this morning when I woke up, I didn't want to think about the past. I just wanted this feeling of..." She struggled for the words. "I knew I wanted this feeling of optimism to stay with me. I don't want to go back to the old Liz, who held on to all the past hurts and wallowed in misery. I want to concentrate on my photography and enjoy my life here on the ranch." She looked over. "Am I being melodramatic?"

"Maybe just a little."

Liz burst into a fit of laughter. "Oh, Avery, that's what I love about you. You're so open and honest. You just can't fib, even to spare my feelings."

Avery joined in the laughter and realized she couldn't stop. Maybe it was the sense of relief, knowing Liz didn't hate her for sharing too much wine and too many secrets, while revealing a few of her own. Maybe it was hearing that her words had actually given a troubled woman some comfort. Most of all, it was the realization that Liz wasn't going to ask that she be dismissed. She still had some time to spend with Brand and his amazing family.

Their vehicle climbed through flower-strewn fields and dense woods, until at last they reached a high meadow green with waist-high grass. Here the Tetons looked close enough to touch, and Avery could see the snow on the upper peaks.

Liz parked the truck in a stand of evergreens and the two women stepped out.

From the back, Liz retrieved her camera and a backpack filled with accessories, before reaching for her rifle. She handed a second backpack to Avery. "This contains our lunch and bottles of water. Billy said he also included some protein snacks for the trail."

Avery slid her arms through the straps and adjusted the backpack to a comfortable position. "Am I carrying dinner, too?"

Liz shook her head. "We'll come back to the truck for that. We'll build a fire and grill the steaks Billy put in that cooler. By the way," she added, "he told me he noticed an empty wine bottle and two glasses on the hearth in the great room."

Avery looked alarmed. "Did he say anything else?"

"As a matter of fact, he did. He said next time you and I should try the pinot grigio."

"He knew it was us?"

Liz chuckled. "There isn't much that gets by Billy."

She stood a moment, assessing the sunlight. "Let's head up there. I think the light will be perfect for some shots."

As the two set off, Liz suddenly paused and touched a hand to Avery's arm. Without a word, she pointed and Avery followed the direction to see a herd of mustangs moving past them just ahead.

Avery was frozen to the spot, completely enthralled at the sight of the mares, many of them heavy with foals. Taking up the rear was a coal-black stallion, his head turning, eyes watching as the herd seemed to follow some invisible trail.

Even when they spotted the two women, the herd continued moving until they were within a hundred feet of them. The stallion halted, as though challenging the humans to make a move. Avery took her cue from Liz, remaining as still as a statue until the horses veered off into a wooded area. Within minutes they had completely blended into the foliage, until there was no trace of them.

Avery put a hand to her throat. "Oh, Liz, they're so beautiful."

"I know." Liz lowered her camera, and Avery realized she'd been clicking off photos the entire time. "I've been seeing herds of mustangs since I was a little girl. But no matter how many times I see them, it always feels magical." She sighed. "It would be a shame to eliminate these herds from the landscape."

"Is that possible?"

Liz gave her a gentle smile. "There are federal laws that allow the roundup and auction of mustangs to thin the herds."

"Yet, here they are. Living free. What about your family? Do they resent the wild horses?"

Liz put a hand on her arm. "The Merrick family lives by the live-and-let-live code." She turned away. "Come on. I want to take advantage of this light while it's so perfect."

They ate lunch on the banks of a stream. Using fallen logs for seats, they unwrapped thick club sandwiches and drank bottled water.

Avery chuckled as she devoured her sandwich. "I can't believe how hungry I am."

"Yeah. Hiking the high country has a way of draining the body even while it's nourishing the soul."

Avery sighed. "My soul is overflowing right now. I can't believe the things I've seen. A herd of mustangs almost close enough to touch. You called them magical. They're more than that. There's a mystical quality to them. I almost expected to see them sporting a single horn and turning into unicorns and flying across the sky."

Liz leaned back, stretching out her legs. "I see you've caught it."

"Caught what?" Avery looked over.

"I call it the high-country fever. Once you come up here and see the things you can never see anywhere else, you're infected with it. You have to come back, again and again, just to prove that your mind wasn't playing tricks on you the previous time. There really are animals living free. Not in zoos or parks, but in the wild, just as their ancestors lived hundreds of years ago."

Avery nodded toward the peaks of the Tetons, looming behind them. "What about up there? What would I see if I were to climb?"

Liz shrugged. "White, shaggy mountain goats. Birds

that thrive in cold and snow. Amazing frozen pools in winter that are crystal-clear in summer. When you're there, you feel you're in another world."

Avery gripped her hands together. "Oh, I want to see them."

Liz laughed. "Now I know you're in trouble. I don't think there's enough time for you to do all the things you'd like."

"I know." Avery drained her water and stowed the empty bottle in the backpack. "But a girl can dream."

"Speaking of dreaming…" Liz shot her a sideways glance. "I hope your experience with Trace hasn't soured you on all men."

"Why would you ask that?"

Liz arched a brow. "Because I want you to know my nephews are good and honorable men."

"I'm sure they are. But what's that to me?"

Liz merely smiled. "I've got eyes, Avery. And I see the way Brand looks at you when he thinks nobody's watching."

Avery felt her face flame.

"Hmm. I guess you've noticed it, too." As Liz finished her lunch, she pointed. "I think we'll climb up there, to that highest meadow, and grab what's left of the sunlight before heading back to the truck."

"Look." As they made their way down the hill, Avery pointed to the sky. "Not a cloud left. Just all that glorious blue."

"It won't be blue for long." Liz adjusted her camera. "The sun's already fading."

"But it lasted long enough for you to get some really great photos."

"And you saw a mountain goat. Well," Liz added, "not up close. But through the binoculars."

"Thanks to you. All I saw was a blur of movement until you handed me your binoculars. I think for a moment my heart stopped. It was just as you'd said. A shaggy white goat standing on that rock ledge." She dropped a hand on the woman's shoulder. "Liz, seeing that goat just made my day."

Liz laughed. "You said that about the mustangs. And about the deer in the woods. And the eagle."

"This whole day was more than I could have ever hoped for." She kept stride as they spotted the truck in the distance. "And now we get to grill steaks over an open fire."

"I suppose that's another first for you, city girl?"

"You bet. The closest I ever came to grilling was making s'mores at summer camp when I was eleven."

"Your education is sadly lacking."

"But I'm making up for lost time."

"You are. And you know what?"

When Avery looked over, Liz gave her a big smile. "You never once complained about hiking through brush, or the day being too hot or too cold or any number of things most first-time hikers complain about."

"I was too busy trying to keep up with you."

"Don't put yourself down, Avery. You did yourself proud today."

"Thanks. This day was like a bonus. One I never expected to get while working here."

When they reached the truck, the two women stowed their backpacks.

As Liz set her rifle down, Avery grinned. "Thankfully you didn't have to use that."

"That's always a good thing. But I'd never hike up here without it." The two women were sharing a laugh when they heard the sound of hoofbeats growing close.

Liz picked up the rifle and turned to face their intruder.

Seeing Chet astride his horse, Liz lowered the rifle before calling, "Hey, Chet. What are you doing way out here?"

"Just seeing how you two ladies are doing." He slid from the saddle and gave her an assessing look before tethering his horse to a tree.

"Can you·stay for supper?"

He nodded. "If you brought enough."

Liz arched a brow. "You know Billy. He always packs for an army. He sent steaks."

"Then I'm staying." He turned away, calling over his shoulder, "I'll collect enough wood for a fire."

As he sauntered away, Avery was smiling. "That's really sweet of him to check up on us."

"Yeah, that's Chet. Every time I come up here, he finds an excuse to check up on me."

"He cares about you."

Liz shrugged. "I think my mother is the one who worries and asks him to be my bodyguard. I'm sure Chet has better things to do than walk away from all his chores just for me."

Avery looked over as he came back into view, his arms laden with tree limbs that would stagger most men. "They grow them tall and strong in Wyoming. That is one handsome, rugged cowboy."

Liz followed the direction of her gaze and said nothing as she continued to stare at him until he'd deposited the wood in a pile. After adding kindling, he soon had a fire crackling.

He wiped his hands on his pants before turning away. "I'll get a few more logs."

He was no sooner gone than they heard the sound of more hoofbeats drawing near. They looked over to see Brand riding toward them. When he reached their camp, he dismounted and led Domino closer.

Liz put her hands on her hips. "What are you doing here?"

"Would you believe it if I said I was in the neighborhood and decided to stop by?"

"Not a chance." She laughed. "Now try the truth."

He merely grinned and stared beyond her to where Avery stood watching. "I wanted to make sure our tenderfoot was still standing."

"Standing and hiking like a native," Liz assured him. "Will you stay for supper?"

"If there's enough."

She laughed. "That's what Chet just said."

"Chet?" He spotted the foreman's horse tethered nearby. "Looks like we both had the same idea."

Liz removed a wire rack from the back of the truck and placed it over the fire before unwrapping the meat from the cooler. "Billy sent enough steaks to feed all of us."

"Good." Brand reached into the cooler and removed several longnecks, before opening them and handing them around.

As Chet returned with another log, Brand handed him a cold beer before slapping him on the shoulder. "Looks like we both had the same idea, and just in time for supper."

The two men grinned before taking over the grilling duties, giving the women time to unwrap all the other surprises Billy had packed for them. Tiny new carrots and asparagus wrapped in foil for grilling, along with a loaf of crusty sourdough bread, thick slices of mozzarella cheese, and sundried tomatoes.

Liz held up a bag of Billy's freshly baked chocolate chip cookies. "Sorry, Avery. No s'mores."

That had Brand and Chet looking over.

"Your little tenderfoot," Liz explained, "said her only camping experience was making s'mores at camp."

"I was eleven," Avery said proudly.

"And making gooey dessert was your only accomplishment?" Brand arched a brow.

"Well, come to think of it, I was the only girl in my troop who didn't go home with poison ivy."

Brand laughed. "Did you win a medal for that?"

"I should have." She handed him the packet of vegetables to place on the grill. "But I did win a medal in archery."

"You hit the bull's-eye?" Chet asked.

She shook her head. "My arrow landed in the target. Everybody else missed completely. There were arrows all over the grass."

"So you won by default?" Brand's remark had her joining in the laughter.

"I guess that's so. But I never questioned how or why I won. That medal became my camper's badge of honor. I wore it proudly for the entire summer."

Brand tugged on her hair. "I bet all your friends were jealous, tenderfoot."

At his touch, and his use of that silly nickname, she felt heat spiral all the way to her toes.

Suddenly, as they gathered around the fire, balancing plates heaped with food and tipping up bottles of chilled beer, the evening turned into a celebration, and their laughter drifted on the breeze.

CHAPTER TWENTY-ONE

I got the most amazing shots of that herd of mustangs that passes through here every spring." Liz was animated as she began describing their day to Chet and Brand, who were seated in the grass beside her and Avery.

She turned to Chet. "You know which herd I mean. The one led by that black stallion you call Gladiator."

Avery asked him, "Why do you call him Gladiator?"

"The name suits him." The foreman smiled, his eyes glinting in that tanned, handsome face. "He guards his herd like a Roman soldier, ready to fight anyone or anything that threatens them."

"Sort of the way you guard this ranch and everyone in it." Brand was grinning as he turned from Chet to his aunt, both looking more relaxed than they had in a long time.

Avery sighed. "My first glimpse of him with his herd took my breath away. Whatever you call him, he's beautiful."

"There's that word again. Beautiful." Liz gave a toss of her head. "Avery said that about every wild animal she saw today."

"I didn't."

Liz laughed. "You did. Not only Gladiator, but the deer, the eagle, the goat…"

"You climbed high enough to come across a mountain goat?" Brand looked at Avery in surprise.

"No." Liz was quick to explain. "I spotted a mountain goat on a rock shelf and loaned Avery my binoculars so she could see it up close."

"He was so beautiful." As soon as Avery said the word, she put a hand to her mouth. "Oops. I did it again."

"You see? Nothing but beautiful." At Liz's words, they all burst into laughter.

Avery joined them. "I guess I did overuse that word today. But it was so exciting to see all those wild animals living here, the way they're meant to be. The only way I've ever seen them until today was in pictures. Probably taken by Liz for all those wildlife magazines. But up close, they're all just so…beautiful."

Brand took her hand in his. "It sounds as though the two of you had a memorable day. Or should I say a 'beautiful' day?"

She absorbed the heat of his touch. "And I wasn't scared once."

At Liz's arched brow, she added, "Okay. Just once. When I stumbled on some stones and thought I was going to tumble right over a cliff."

Liz added dryly, "She would have landed about four feet if she'd actually taken a fall."

"But I didn't know that until you pointed it out to me. At first, I really thought I could tumble hundreds of feet and break some bones, which is why I grabbed hold of that tree limb to keep from falling over."

"You were holding on to it with such a death grip, I had to pry your fingers open."

The two women laughed.

Brand deadpanned, "And then we'd have to hire a physical therapist for our physical therapist."

"I wonder what Hammond would have to say about that?" Chet remarked.

"I can already hear him." Liz gave a mock shudder. "Now look what you've done, Margaret Mary Finnegan." As an afterthought, she added, "Ham always calls Mom by her full maiden name whenever she gets under his skin."

Laughing with her, Brand crossed to the fire and filled four mugs with coffee bubbling over the hot coals. As he passed them around, Chet opened the bag of cookies and helped himself to one before handing it around to the others.

They sat in companionable silence, enjoying their coffee and dessert and watching as the sun slid behind the high peaks of the Tetons, leaving behind a sky awash in hues of rose and pink and mauve.

"This never gets old," Brand remarked.

Avery gave a sigh. "I've never seen anything so beautiful."

At that, the other three burst into laughter. Realizing what she'd said, she joined them.

"All right. So this day, and everything I've seen so far, is beyond beautiful. There are no more words."

Brand looked at her with a silly grin. "I'll tell you what else is beautiful. Billy's steaks on the grill. These chocolate chip cookies." As Liz and Chet loudly agreed, he added in an aside, "And you, tenderfoot. You're the most beautiful of all."

Rendered speechless, she sat feeling such a glow that all she could do was give a dreamy smile.

Across from her, Liz watched with a knowing smile. "Tell Chet and Brand about your dream vacation."

Brand turned to her. "Where did you go?"

"Not where I went. Where I'd love to go." She pointed. "Oh, how I wish we could have climbed up there." As Avery pointed to the high peaks of the Tetons, Brand shot her an incredulous look. "Is the woman who was afraid of the wilderness the same one who'd actually enjoy climbing the mountain?"

"That's one of my dreams. But I guess I'll have to save that for another lifetime."

While Chet and Liz continued talking, Brand said in hushed tones, "You never cease to amaze me, tenderfoot."

While Brand and Chet raked the last of the fire's embers and doused it with sand, Liz and Avery rinsed the utensils in a stream and placed them in the back of the truck, along with the cooler.

When Chet untied his mount, Liz surprised him by saying, "I feel like riding." She turned to her nephew. "Would you mind if I took Domino, and you and Avery could ride back in the truck?"

Brand shrugged. "Suit yourself. It's a long way home."

"That's just what I crave. A long night ride." She turned with a laugh. "With my very own gladiator by my side."

Chet untied Brand's horse and held the reins as Liz pulled herself into the saddle, before mounting his horse alongside her.

Liz turned to call, "Enjoy your evening, you two. We'll see you back at the house."

As the two started off, Brand and Avery stood watching until they disappeared around a bend.

Brand caught Avery's hand and surprised her by lifting it to his lips. "Alone at last. I owe my aunt big-time."

"I don't think she planned this. I got the sense that she was suddenly enjoying a new sense of freedom."

"Whatever the reason..." He lifted his hands to her shoulders and drew her close before murmuring against her temple, "I'm just happy to have you all to myself. Finally."

She shivered at the warmth of his breath. "We're alone every day during our sessions."

"With the certain knowledge that half the household is apt to walk in on us." He moved his mouth lower, to her ear. "And they usually do."

"I don't mind. After all..."

"I mind." His lips hovered a fraction over hers. "There are times, when you're concentrating on an exercise, I can hardly keep from crushing you in my arms."

Her eyes went wide. "But you never—"

Whatever words she'd been about to say were cut off by a kiss so hungry it wiped all thought from her mind. All she could focus on was the way it felt being held in his arms.

Cherished.

The word played like a litany as his mouth moved on hers.

Oh, the man knew how to kiss. Whether nibbling the corner of her lips, or taking her fully into his heat, he did it all with such ease. She could get used to this. But just when she began to relax and enjoy the delicious tingles racing along her spine, he changed the angle of the kiss and she became aware of the subtle change in him. From casual flirtation to fierce, barely controlled passion seething just below the surface. From easygoing cowboy to a man struggling to rein in an all-consuming need.

He was holding her so firmly she could feel him in every part of her body. Those muscled arms that held her as carefully as though she were fragile glass. That wall of chest that had her blood flowing hotly all the way to her toes. His thighs molded to hers. His arousal, which only added to her own.

He ran nibbling kisses down her throat and she arched her neck on a sigh of pure pleasure, giving him easier access. He pressed his mouth to the little hollow between her neck and shoulder before moving lower, to the soft curve of her breast.

He made a sound of impatience before grabbing her T-shirt by the hem and pulling it over her head. Beneath it she wore a lacy bra that revealed more than it covered.

For a moment he merely stared at her with a smile of pure male appreciation. "You're so beautiful, you take my breath away."

"You're beautiful, too." She ran her hands up his chest, across his shoulders.

That had him laughing.

Her eyes widened. "Hasn't anyone ever told you that before?"

Still laughing, he shook his head. "Believe me. You're the first."

Her smile was quick and sexy. "I like being your first." She slid her hands up his arms and locked them around his neck before standing on tiptoe to kiss him.

He went as still as a statue, surprise and pleasure mingling in his eyes. Then he mirrored her actions, dipping his head to return her kiss while sliding his hands down her arms, then along the naked flesh of her back.

She absorbed the most delicious curls of pleasure as their kisses deepened and their breathing became ragged, their heartbeats thundering.

He lifted his head. His smile turned into a look of fierce concentration. "Unless you say otherwise, I'm not stopping this time."

In reply she reached for the buttons of his shirt. As she slid it from his shoulders, she leaned in to run a trail of kisses across his hair-roughened chest.

He gave a low moan of pleasure before backing her up until she was pressed against the door of the truck.

For a moment she welcomed the coolness of it against her heated flesh. Then all thoughts dissolved except one. She wanted this man with a desperation she'd never experienced before. Want, need, lust, love had been tangled up inside her for so long now, and she was helpless to fight this battle any longer.

Their breath was coming harder, faster as they dropped to the ground. Cushioned by the last of their clothes and the cool, lush grass, they gave in to the need to touch, to taste. To feast.

His hands moved over her at will, the rough, calloused fingers deeply arousing against her smooth skin.

She was free to run her hands over the muscles of his arms, the slope of his broad shoulders.

She lifted a hand to his hair, spilling over his forehead. He paused a moment to stare deeply into her eyes, and she could feel herself being drawn into him in a way that had her heart nearly stopping, before beginning a wild thundering in her chest.

"Avery." He spoke her name almost reverently, and she could swear the earth moved beneath her.

She couldn't speak above the pounding of her heart.

All she could do was clutch at him as he began exploring her body with his hands, his mouth, his tongue. Each touch sent fresh shock waves through her until her body was a mass of nerve endings.

The last of the sun's rays bled into the night sky, creating an otherworldly glow to the clouds. The full moon gilded the land and the two people locked in an embrace. On a distant hillside a coyote howled and another answered. A night bird cried to its mate. A breeze whispered in the towering trees. But the two lying together were unaware of anything except the needs inside them clawing to be free.

Avery felt as if she were melting into him. Into the touch, the taste, the sheer strength of him. She breathed him in, that dark, musky male scent that would always remind her of Brand, and the fresh smell of spring grass and earth, so unfamiliar and yet now locked into her memory for all time.

He was so strong he could easily snap her in two. Yet she could feel the way he exerted such control as he moved over her, as though determined to be gentle. That only made him all the more exciting.

He levered himself above her, and she lifted her arms to welcome him. But instead of giving her the release she sought, he began to trail hot, wet kisses down her body, taking her on a wild ride.

When he brought her to the first glorious peak, her body shuddered, and she called out his name. He gave her no time to recover as he took her up and over yet again, leaving her almost blind with need. Each time she thought she could take no more, he surprised her yet again, until, driven by a sort of madness, he could wait no longer.

When he entered her, she went very still, until, driven

to move with him, to climb with him, she experienced a wave of such raw energy that she could have climbed to the highest peak of the Tetons.

She was unaware of her nails digging into his flesh as she clung to him and climbed even higher.

"Avery." He spoke her name on a hoarse cry as, hearts pounding, bodies slick with sheen, he joined her in a shattering climax.

"Did I hurt you?" His words were whispered against her throat, sending fresh vibrations through her already jittery system.

She moved her head from side to side, though even that seemed too much effort.

"That was…" His words trailed off, as though anything he said would sound trivial after what they'd just shared.

"Yeah. I agree."

"With what?"

"It was…"

They both laughed at the same moment.

He leaned up to frame her face with his big hands. That was when he felt the moisture with his thumbs. "Wait. Are you crying?"

She sniffed. "I never cry."

"Okay. Good." He ran kisses over her face, tasting the salt of her tears. "So these…these not-tears have a meaning? Are you sorry this happened?"

"Brand, these are happy tears." She put her hands over his. "How could I be sorry for something as wonderful as this?"

"It was pretty amazing, wasn't it?"

"Umm." She gave a little cat smile. "Better than."

He pressed a kiss to the corner of her mouth. "I'll go one better. It was monumental."

"Oh. You want better?" She moved her face slightly, so her lips were fully locked on his. "How about earth-shattering?"

"Splendiferous." He spoke the word inside her mouth.

She chuckled. "That's not a word."

"Is too."

"Is not."

"I'll make it a word and use it in a sentence." He gave her a smug smile. "If you agree to stay up here for the night, you'll agree we're splendiferous together."

She sat up, dragging hair out of her eyes. "Stay the night? Here in the dark? In the hills with wild animals?"

"I'll keep you safe, little tenderfoot. And if you decide you don't like being outside in the dark, we can always sleep in the back of the truck."

"Are we going to sleep here in the grass?"

"You don't like grass?"

"I'll admit it's soft. And cool. Right now, I need cool."

"Yeah. I guess things really heated up." He smiled. "Billy packed sleeping bags, just in case."

"In case of what?"

"He was prepared for a storm. And in a way, that's what happened."

She brushed a quick kiss over Brand's mouth. "Yeah. It was definitely a storm." She looked around. "Will we make a fire?"

"Of course. And there's plenty of food left, in case we need to fortify ourselves for whatever activities we might like to try."

"Activities?" Her laughter bubbled up. "You sound like my old camp counselor."

"When you were eleven."

"Yes."

"And made s'mores over the fire."

"You're not going to forget that, are you?"

He couldn't hold back any longer. With a roar of laughter he wrapped his arms around her and gathered her close. "Avery, I see it as my solemn duty to give you a taste of real ranch life, in all its glory. And if, in a little while, we decide to try a few more earth-shattering moves, well, at least we'll do them in the comfort of a sleeping bag."

"Thanks, cowboy." She ran a hand down his side, then up again. "But for now, just give me another of those heart-stopping kisses."

"It would be my pleasure, tenderfoot."

As they came together, there were no more words as they lost themselves in their newly discovered passion.

CHAPTER TWENTY-TWO

Avery snuggled close to Brand.

Though Billy had packed two sleeping bags, they'd slept together in one, positioned beside a cozy fire.

With a smile, Avery traced a finger over his mouth. Throughout the night she'd come to know it well. The shape of it. The taste. The pure pleasure his mouth could bring her.

There had been little time for sleep. Caught up in the excitement of the moment, they couldn't seem to get enough of one another. At times their lovemaking had been as wild as a spring thunderstorm. At other times, they'd been like old lovers, with all the time in the world.

Throughout the long night, they had bared their souls to each other. Brand told her about the house fire that had taken his mother and the mark it had left on all of them.

"Liz said your father still checks all the fireplaces before going up to bed."

Brand nodded. "The smell of woodsmoke triggers too many memories for him."

"And he never remarried."

"Gramps says he's a Merrick through and through. Merrick men only give their hearts once, and it's the kind of love that lasts an eternity."

Avery sighed. "That's so beautiful."

"So are you, tenderfoot." He leaned close and pressed a kiss to her temple. "Now tell me about your family."

Her smile faded. "Not much to tell. My mom was my best friend. We did everything together. I know now that she was the glue that held us together. When she died, my dad and I had nothing in common except our love of medicine."

"That's a pretty strong bond."

"It was. But I can't be what he wants me to be. He made it clear that he wanted me on his surgical team, and I let him down."

Brand was shaking his head. "I find it hard to believe. What father wouldn't be happy to see his child following her heart?"

"Alexander Grant, that's who. He often boasts that his surgical team is his family. They spend more time together than most marriage partners. Both in the operating room and during their follow-up rounds. There are more team members single than married, and he likes it that way. I've heard that he gets very cranky when one of the team members asks for personal time off."

"Maybe that's what it takes to be at the top of your game."

"Maybe." Eager to change the subject, she said, "Now tell me about Liz and Chet."

He frowned. "What about Liz and Chet?"

"Are you saying you haven't noticed the way he looks after her?"

"That's not personal. It's just Chet's way. He considers

himself responsible for everyone and everything on our ranch. As for my aunt, she has always been...fragile."

"She told me about Luke and her best friend C.C."

He shot her a look of surprise. "She told you? When?"

"After everyone else went off to bed last night."

He leaned up on one elbow to stare down at her. "How did you work that little miracle?"

"I found her crying in the great room and was about to leave her alone. Then on a whim I remembered that bottle of red wine left over from dinner and figured maybe she'd like some company."

He gave a shake of his head. "You and that wine did what none of us have been able to do."

"Dumb luck," she muttered.

"Call it what you want, tenderfoot." He drew her close and covered her mouth with his. "I'm calling it a miracle."

"Sort of like this night."

"Oh, yeah. That's exactly what I'd call it. So which one of us is the miracle worker?"

"Both of us. Working together."

"You mean, loving together."

With soft words and tender sighs, they proceeded to work their own little miracle of loving.

When Avery returned from a quick wash in the stream, Brand filled two plates with the last of the steak and some fried potatoes.

They were both ravenous.

"Oh, this is heavenly."

"So, have you decided you like camping in the wild?"

She lay her hand over his. "I love it. I wish we could stay here."

"Me too. But I figure by now my brothers are cursing my name while they pick up my chores in the barn."

"You'd do the same for them."

"Yeah.. But I'd have a few choice names for them while I did it."

The two shared a laugh as they cleaned up the campfire and loaded the back of the truck. Brand held the passenger door for Avery before rounding the truck and settling into the driver's side. As they started away from their little slice of paradise, Avery turned for a last look, trying to commit everything to memory.

Bouncing across a high meadow, Avery felt the need to describe everything she'd seen on her remarkable day with Liz. She couldn't contain the excitement she felt over every new thing she'd experienced.

"Liz said the mares in that herd will have their foals way up here, far from civilization. That way they're safe from intruders. Have you ever come across the mares and their young?"

He nodded. "Once in a while. If I'm out searching for stray cattle. They're really savvy about slipping out of sight. That stallion knows every hidden canyon and valley for a hundred miles or more."

"I'm glad. I couldn't bear to think about those helpless foals or their mothers being harmed."

"They're not helpless as long as they have Gladiator. Liz said you saw lots of wild things."

"Herds of deer. The fawns so cute, racing along beside their mothers. And an eagle. Oh my, he passed so low over our heads, I could see his talons. And his eyes. He was so…" She stopped herself when Brand shot her a sideways glance.

"Did you think the mountain goat was beautiful, too?"

She heard the laughter in his voice. Instead of bristling, she found it endearing. "I did. That thick, shaggy white coat. Liz said he blends in so perfectly with the snow, he's almost impossible to spot. But I'm really glad she noticed him and let me watch through her binoculars."

Brand caught her hand and squeezed. "All in all, a grand adventure. And you made happy memories."

Oh, how she loved having her hand held in his big, rough palm. He was the only man who had ever held her hand, except for her father when she was little, and that didn't count. "Very happy memories."

He kept her hand in his as the truck moved down and down until the first of several barns loomed up.

The sound of a text on Avery's phone had her going very still.

Brand felt the way her fingers automatically gripped his tightly, before she pulled her hand away and lifted her phone from her shirt pocket.

He drove past the barns and pulled up alongside the back porch.

He climbed down and walked around to open her door. Her face, which moments before had been so filled with joy and animation, was now pale and drawn.

He offered her a hand. She accepted it and stepped from the truck. As she did, the phone fell to the ground.

Brand stooped and picked it up. He couldn't help reading the illuminated text.

Try ignoring this.

I warned you Wyoming isn't far enough.

"What the hell?" He looked from the words on her phone to her face. "What's going on, Avery?"

"Nothing." She held out her hand.

Instead of giving it to her, he shook his head. "I want to know what this is about."

"Please give me my phone."

"Who sent you this text?"

"I can't tell you."

"Can't? Or won't?"

"I can't tell you because I don't know for certain who's sending these."

"These?" His tone lowered with rough passion. "There were others?"

She nodded, afraid to meet his eyes.

"Avery." He put a hand against her cheek, trying to be tender, though an emotion closer to raw fury simmered inside. "Have you reported this to anyone?"

"Not these. But there were other things. The police in my hometown said that the evidence wasn't enough to point to a crime. In fact, they had their doubts about the entire thing. I won't go through that again."

"You need to. I don't know much about city police, but I'll call Noble Crain, our police chief. He'll listen, and he'll do whatever he can. He's a good guy."

"He may be a nice man, but what can he do? All I can tell him is that someone is sending me texts. They could be coming from anywhere."

"They could. But someone is going to a lot of trouble to threaten you. Whether Noble can help or not, you need to share this with him and let him advise you on how to deal with it going forward."

She met his gaze. "I thought if I ignored them, whoever was doing this would just give up and stop."

Brand held up her phone. "This doesn't sound like someone about to give up."

She sighed. "I know."

"Will you let me call Chief Crain?"

"I don't know." She began wringing her hands. "I just don't know."

"Doing nothing is not an option. Will you trust me?"

Reluctantly she nodded.

He handed her the phone. "Don't erase this. Do you have the other texts?"

"Yes."

"Good. Keep them and let Noble decide how to proceed."

"All right." She took in a breath. "I just don't want to make a big fuss. I'm here to work, Brand, not to cause trouble."

"You're not the cause of this. As for trouble, we'll leave that up to the chief. Okay?"

She nodded. "Okay. Thanks, Brand. I feel better knowing you know. I really needed another opinion about this."

"Ham likes to say that joy shared is double the joy. Trouble shared is half the trouble." He took her hand. "Let's get cleaned up and head to town. We can have lunch there."

They walked into the house. Finding the kitchen empty, they glanced out the window and could see the flutter of a chef's apron as Billy stepped into the greenhouse.

"No welcoming committee, I see." Brand smiled. "I'll leave a note and let the family know we're back and will see them at suppertime." He nodded toward the stairs. "Let's head up and grab showers before going to town."

As they climbed the stairs, he took her hand. "We could save water by showering together."

Avery chuckled. "Good line, cowboy."

"Can't blame a guy for trying." He paused outside his

door. "If you change your mind, just come on in. I'll leave the door open for you."

As she started away, he pulled her back, gathering her close. "I'm glad you had your day with Liz up in the hills."

"Me too."

"I'm even happier about the night we had together."

"Me too—" Her words were cut off with a long, slow kiss that had her heart rate speeding up even as her brain seemed to shut down.

The press of his body on hers had her aware of the fact that they fit together like the missing pieces of a puzzle.

He gave her a long, probing look. "After a quick shower I'll empty the truck and wait for you outside." He shot her a sexy grin that had her heart doing a crazy dance. "Unless you change your mind and join me under a hot spray. It could keep your mind off your troubles."

She managed a shuddering laugh. "That's really noble of you, cowboy."

He gave her another grin that jolted her heart. "I do my best, tenderfoot."

On shaky legs, she climbed to her room and stepped inside before leaning against the door and taking in several deep breaths.

Last night had been the most amazing night of her life. Ever since the time she was a little girl, she'd been expected to be calm and reasonable. Both her parents had frowned on anything spontaneous. But somehow, with a few kisses, everything had changed. Not only had she fallen for the guy she was supposed to be helping, but also he was now bent on helping her. And he had just sweet-talked her into believing she should share her most deeply held personal problems with the police chief of his little town.

The mere touch of Brand's mouth on hers had her befuddled. She knew she was in over her head. But for some strange reason, it didn't seem to matter. Nothing mattered, except Brand.

Wasn't she pathetic? Willing to give up all her hard-earned independence for a few weeks with a gorgeous cowboy, knowing when it was over she would have to head back to reality? And once there, she knew in the deepest recesses of her heart that no other man would ever measure up to Brand Merrick. She would rather spend the rest of her life alone than settle for second best.

Even knowing all this, she'd never felt so gloriously alive. As though she'd been sleepwalking through her life, and one kiss from this amazing cowboy had awakened her to all that was grand and beautiful in his world.

What she wouldn't give to trade her by-the-rules existence for a life of spontaneous freedom here in this beautiful paradise. With Brand.

CHAPTER TWENTY-THREE

Brand read a text on his phone and smiled. "Billy just found my message and is asking me to pick up some supplies while we're in town."

As the truck ate up the miles to town, Brand watched Avery clutch her hands tightly in her lap, as though holding herself together by a thread.

He reached over and put a hand on hers. "I'm glad I caught Chief Crain in his office. Have you thought about what you'll tell him?"

She shrugged. "The truth. But it's not much to tell."

Sensing her nerves, he kept his hand on hers. "Noble is a good man, Avery. His wife teaches part-time at the school. They have three little daughters. He's really easy to talk to."

"That's good." She turned to look out the side window, and he patted her hand before returning his attention to the road. It was obvious that she wanted to be alone with her thoughts.

"If you'd like me to leave while you talk to him, I can wait outside for you."

She shook her head. "I think I'd like you with me, Brand."

"Good." He breathed a sigh of relief. He hadn't really

wanted her to have to deal with this alone. He hoped whatever the chief's reaction was, it would ease both their minds.

"'Morning, Noble." Brand led the way into the chief's office and shook hands.

"'Morning, Brand. Miss Grant, may I call you Avery?"

At her nod, the chief indicated two chairs facing his desk. "Make yourselves comfortable. Would either of you like coffee?"

They both shook their heads, and the chief smiled. "Not that our coffee comes anywhere close to what Billy makes at your place, Brand. Next to his, ours tastes like mud."

His little attempt to put Avery at ease did the trick. She smiled in spite of her nerves.

The chief steepled his hands on his desktop. "Brand tells me you have something you'd like to report."

Avery swallowed. "Since coming here, I've received these texts." She brought up the three messages on her phone before handing it across the desk.

The police chief read the three texts, taking his time to record each one before handing the phone back to her.

"I see the sender is blocked. Do you know who's sending these?"

She paused, choosing her words carefully. "I think I know. But the problem is, I have no proof. And once I name him, it could impact his career."

"Is this a former lover?"

She arched a brow.

Noble Crain gave a small smile. "In my line of work, when a pretty woman is being harassed, it's most often by a man with a vested interest. Maybe he fears losing her.

Maybe he's already lost her. At any rate, he starts with veiled threats, which can often escalate into something more."

Seeing Avery's frown of concentration, he waited.

Silence filled the room, and Avery could hear the sound of her own breathing.

Her words were halting. "His name is Trace Martin. Doctor Trace Martin. First in his class in medical school. He's considered a brilliant surgeon and has been invited by several teaching hospitals to join their surgical teams. I didn't know all this when he asked me out. But I soon learned that he knew who I was."

"Who are you, Avery?"

Beside her, Brand turned to look at her.

"The daughter of Alexander Grant, one of the leading cardiothoracic surgeons in the country. What I didn't know was that Trace was among those hoping to be invited to join my father's surgical team. I was told that by dating the lead surgeon's daughter, he'd hoped to have the inside track."

"Who told you all this information about Trace Martin?"

"One of the nurses at our hospital, Renee Wilmot. When she learned Trace was seeing me, she warned me about what he was up to."

"After her warning, you stopped seeing him?"

"Yes."

"How did he take the news?"

"Not very well, which surprised me. When you meet him, Trace is the whole package. Handsome, charming, brilliant. But when I told him about what Renee had said to me, he became unglued. He called her a liar who couldn't be trusted and said I should ignore anything she told me."

"Did he give you any reason why she would lie?"

"No. In fact, he refused to say anything more. But it was obvious he was furious."

"What was your reaction?"

"I told him I didn't know who to believe, but it didn't matter. We'd had only casual dates. Nothing serious. But the mere suggestion that he could be using me to get noticed by my father was enough to make me step away. I told him I had no intention of seeing him again."

"Did you take this news to your father?"

"Not right away. I didn't want to be the one to jeopardize Trace's chances of making my father's surgical team, in the event that Renee was wrong about him. Not long after, my father asked me about a rumor that I was dating Trace. I told him that we'd gone out a few times, but that we were no longer seeing one another. He praised Trace as one of the most brilliant, bold surgeons he'd ever worked with. His choice for the next surgeon on his team had narrowed to Trace and one other young surgeon."

"Was your father aware of the texts?"

"No. These started after I left home to accept the job here in Wyoming. But he knew about the two previous incidents."

The chief held up a hand to stop her. "Incidents? Such as...?"

"My new car was keyed in the parking lot of the hospital."

"Were there any witnesses to it?"

"No."

"So it could have been anybody. Anything else?"

"One day after work I found a crude message on the door of my apartment, written in my own lipstick. A lipstick I'd lost in Trace's car weeks earlier."

"Did the local police investigate?"

"They answered my call and photographed the message. They asked the name of anyone I suspected, and I told them I'd lost that shade of lipstick in his car. When the detective assigned to the case confronted Trace, he had witnesses who could prove that he'd been in the hospital the entire day. He also admitted to the authorities that we'd dated briefly. When he gave the detective assigned to the case permission to search his car, my lipstick couldn't be found, and without that evidence, the detective admitted that anyone could have written the message, including me. Although he didn't actually accuse me, he suggested that sort of thing is often employed by a woman scorned."

The police chief winced. "Ouch. And your father?"

She sighed. "To his credit, he read the final police report, which stated that these acts could have been done by anybody. Again he expressed doubts about Trace being a party to this, and reminded me that a person is innocent until proven guilty. Why would a brilliant surgeon with his whole life ahead of him stoop to petty threats over a breakup, especially when neither of us had considered it a serious relationship? What could Trace possibly gain by this?"

"Those are logical questions. Did you agree?"

Avery nodded. "It just doesn't make sense for Trace to risk everything for something so petty."

The chief paused before asking, "So these texts began after you left town?"

"Yes."

He thought a moment. "Has your father made his choice for his surgical team?"

"Not that I'm aware of. I haven't heard from my father since I came here."

"Is that typical?"

She looked down at her hands. "My father has little

time for anything outside the hospital. When I'm home, even though our therapy office is on another floor of the hospital, he and I see each other only in passing. I'm sure, however, when he makes his choice of team member, he'll let me know of his decision."

Noble Crain let that pass without comment. "Have you been in contact with Trace Martin since you left home?"

She shook her head. "There's no reason to contact him."

"And yet, when you arrived in Wyoming, these texts began." The chief sat back, his brow furrowed. "What could Trace Martin gain by threatening you now? If he's caught, he has to know he'll lose everything he's worked for. Unless," he muttered, "he's unbalanced."

"That's what Renee hinted. That his brilliance was a curse."

He paused a moment before saying, "Sometimes a brilliant mind is one step away from insanity. Maybe the brilliant young surgeon can't focus on anything except the thing he can't have."

Avery gave a look of disgust. "You make me sound like a...a kid's toy."

"I'm sorry. But that's how a sick mind works." He reached into a drawer and retrieved some forms. "I'd like you to fill these out."

Avery was shaking her head. "I told Brand how I felt about making a report. I've already been through it once, and it made me feel small and petty for even mentioning Trace's name to the local police."

"Avery, these three texts are brief, but carefully written. Though they hint of a threat, it's veiled. Alone, these wouldn't hold up well in a court of law. But sometimes a veiled threat reveals a deeper danger. In any case, I intend to take them seriously." He shoved the forms toward her.

"I'd feel better if you would read these carefully and answer them the best you can."

Avery took her time and filled out the forms, before signing and dating them.

The chief looked them over. "If you have no objections, I'll copy these to the state police. They have the resources to dig much deeper than my understaffed office could."

"I have no objection."

"Good. It goes without saying, if you receive any more texts, or feel threatened in any way, please let me know immediately."

"I will." She stood and returned his handshake. "Thank you, Chief Crain."

The chief shook Brand's hand as well. "I'm glad you persuaded Avery to report this, Brand. It was the smart thing to do." He nodded to both of them. "I'll be in touch."

Brand caught Avery's hand and led her from the office. Outside, he continued holding her hand. "How do you feel?"

"Shaky. A little guilty, again for suggesting Trace could do such a thing. But relieved, too. Thank you for bringing me here, and for listening. And for not reacting." She smiled. "You're very cool, cowboy."

"Only on the outside. Inside I was seething. If that hotshot doctor was standing in front of me, I'd probably have my fist in his face before he had time to say hello."

"Then I'm glad he's thousands of miles away."

Brand wrapped an arm around her shoulders. "Hungry?"

"Yes. Now that my interview with the police chief is over, I'm famished."

He nodded at the people walking past, many of whom called and waved. "Bar food or Italian?"

"I've tasted Nonie's great chili. Maybe it's time for some pasta."

"You got it." He led the way toward a restaurant with a red and green awning.

Inside, the already crowded room smelled of garlic and bread baking. In a corner of the kitchen, two elderly women were making various pastas by hand. On the far side there was a glass showcase filled with pastries.

Avery breathed deeply. "I do love Italian."

They took a booth in the rear of the restaurant and enjoyed big plates of spaghetti and meatballs.

Their lunch was interrupted by Ben Harper, owner of the grain and feed store, who paused to chat.

"Afternoon, Brand." He whipped off his hat. "Avery. Nice to see you again. I hope you're enjoying the famous Merrick hospitality."

"I am. Thank you."

He turned to Brand. "Bo called in a list of supplies and said Billy told him you'd be by for them."

Brand nodded. "I'll stop by as soon as I pick up Billy's order."

"Good." The older man nodded and smiled at Avery. "I hope you'll come into our town again really soon."

"I'm sure I will."

Across the room they saw Chief Noble Crain having lunch with Wilson Tremont. Both men waved at Brand and Avery before bending close to talk.

"Noble is hoping Wilson will replace the locks on the cell doors. He was telling Ham that old Hal Huddle was sleeping off a drunk and wandered out of his cell before passing out in front of the jail, where half the town saw him in nothing but his torn, ratty underwear. Knowing it was Hal, most folks didn't mind, but Erna Banks made a fuss about it and told Noble she was issuing a formal complaint to the state police for allowing such gross indecency."

Avery coughed, nearly spitting out her coffee, before putting a hand over her mouth to cover her roar of laughter. "Thanks for that image. I'll never get it out of my mind. I hope old Hal isn't here today."

Brand looked around, then leaned across the table. "I don't see Hal, but don't look now. Erna is at the corner table. She's the one with the pinched face scolding the poor waitress, Bitsy. If Hal is the town drunk, Erna is the town grump."

That had Avery laughing harder.

When a shadow fell over their table, they looked up to find a short, squat man, red-haired and freckled, standing beside them.

"Buster." Brand got to his feet and offered a hand-shake, giving Avery time to swallow her giggles. "How's Trudy?"

"She's doing fine, Brand. Doc says her recovery will be slow, but she'll get there."

Brand handled the introductions. "Buster Mandel, this is Avery Grant."

"The physical therapist. How do, ma'am."

"Mr. Mandel."

"Just plain Buster," he corrected.

"Buster." Avery smiled at him. "I heard about your wife. I'm glad she's healing. I'm sure she'll need some therapy after such a nasty fall."

"That's what the doc is saying. And that'll mean a drive all the way to Blanton, about thirty miles from here."

"You know my family is ready to lend a hand with what-ever you need, Buster. Whether it's food, or driving Trudy wherever she needs to be, we're happy to help out."

"I know. Miss Meg already stopped by to tell me that very thing. I'm grateful, Brand. Say thanks to all your family." He nodded toward Avery. "Glad to meet you."

When he left, Avery watched him walk slowly through the room, stopping at nearly every table to exchange a few words. "It must be such a comfort to know everyone around will lend a hand when needed."

Brand nodded. "That's the good side of small-town living. Of course, the not-so-good side is that everybody knows everybody's business, whether we like it or not."

"From where I'm sitting, the good side outweighs the bad."

Brand paid their bill and they left the restaurant, but not before pausing at several tables to offer greetings and exchange small talk.

Once in the truck, they made several stops to pick up the supplies before Brand's cell phone rang. After the first few words, his smile disappeared, replaced by a look of alarm.

"Where is he now?"

He listened. "No. We're still in town. We'll be right there."

He dropped his phone in his shirt pocket. "That was Gram Meg. She and Gramps Egan are at the clinic with Ham."

"Is it something serious?"

"Ham took a fall in the barn. He was in enough pain that they decided to rush him straight here. Doc is taking X-rays now. They'll know by the time we get there just how serious this is."

CHAPTER TWENTY-FOUR

They drove the entire block in stunned silence.

At the clinic, they hurried inside and were led to an examining room where the entire family had gathered around the bed where Ham lay, looking as fierce as a wounded bear.

Brand leaned close to his grandfather. "What've you learned?"

Egan's voice was a hoarse whisper. "We're still waiting for Dr. Peterson."

Ham's voice boomed from the bed. "No need to tiptoe around, boy. I'm not dead yet."

Just then the doctor stepped into the room and strode toward the bed. "You got lucky, Ham."

"At the moment I'm not feeling very lucky."

The doctor smiled. "The reason I insisted on both an X-ray and MRI is because I usually see this sort of thing in a young athlete. I wanted to be certain you didn't tear any of the muscles. Thankfully, there were no tears and nothing is broken. But all that pain is natural when you suffer what, in layman's terms, we call a groin pull." He peered at the old man. "I'm betting you tried to stop the fall and ended up nearly doing the splits."

Ham nodded. "That's a fact. So, what's to be done for me?"

"It's going to take a little time for that pain to subside. First you'll follow what I call RICE. Rest. Ice. Compression. Elevation. And for the next day or so I'll recommend an anti-inflammatory drug."

"And then what? Surgery?"

Dr. Peterson shook his head. "The best cure for a groin pull is time and activity. You'll need to get up and moving."

Egan turned to the doctor with a look of alarm. "According to Ham, he can't put any weight on the leg at all."

"I understand. And that's the problem with an injury like this. The cure for the pain will cause more pain, but it has to be done." Dr. Peterson turned to Ham. "I've asked my assistant to bring in a walker."

The old man was already shaking his head and leaning up on one elbow. To his great-grandsons he called, "Get me out of here."

"Now hold on, Ham."

Hammond shrugged aside the doctor's words and motioned for Brand, Casey, and Jonah to come closer. "I don't care if you have to carry me—get me out of here now."

As usual, it was Miss Meg who took charge. "They'll do nothing of the sort, Hammond. You'll stay put and listen to the doctor."

The entire family turned to Dr. Peterson, who cleared his throat before saying, "Now, Ham, I'm afraid your old bones are going to take a beating for the next few weeks. But you'll just have to trust me when I say, after the inflammation is healed, the more you get moving, the

quicker the pain will start to disappear. At first, you'll
think you're doing more harm than good with every step,
but if you persevere, you'll be back to your old self in
no time."

Hammond glared at the doctor's assistant standing in
the doorway with a walker. "I'm not using that contraption."

"It's just for the short-term, Ham. And believe me,
you'll be glad you have it the first time you try to walk.
Without it, you could easily fall and do more damage.
The next fall could mean broken bones."

"I can hold on to the back of a chair, like I did fifty
years ago after a fall."

"You were fifty years younger and stronger, and could
have easily lifted a chair, a table, and a sofa."

That had the family nodding and laughing.

"Fifty years later, you'll soon learn a chair is heavy
and hard to move. A walker is lighter and will help with
your balance until the pain subsides. I promise you'll use
it no more than a couple of weeks, Ham."

Seeing his father's temper rising, Egan intervened.
"Can my father go home now?"

Dr. Peterson nodded.

A second assistant entered pushing a wheelchair.

Hammond's jaw clenched. "I'm not an invalid,
Peterson."

"All our patients leave in a wheelchair, Ham. Once
you're outside the clinic, feel free to use whatever mode
of transportation you choose. But while you're in here,
I get to call the shots." The doctor turned to Meg. "I've
written a prescription. He'll be in some pain for the next
few days. After that you'll need to get him up and moving.
The sooner the better." He nodded toward the walker.

"He'll walk with the help of that, until he's pain-free and steady on his feet."

He turned to Avery. "Since you're available, I'd like you to oversee a few therapy sessions for Ham. Maybe he and Brand could work out together."

Avery took one look at Hammond's face and could see that he was about to explode. Did Dr. Peterson have any idea how much fuel he'd just added to the old man's fiery temper? The good doctor had just handed her an impossible assignment. If convincing Brand to accept her help had been a tough hill to climb, convincing his great-grandfather would be like climbing a mountain.

Barefoot.

In the dead of winter.

As Hammond was wheeled from the room, with the others trailing behind, Casey paused beside Avery.

"You look worse than the old man. Not that I blame you. You've just been condemned to a fate worse than death."

She lifted her chin like a prizefighter. "Don't be silly. I haven't met a patient I can't handle."

Casey nudged Brand. "Tell her what it's like to crawl into a cave during a blizzard and discover you're in the den of a hungry cougar."

Her eyes widened. "That actually happened to you?"

He winked. "Yeah. I was lucky to escape with my life. But that cougar got in a few licks before I got away."

"More like swipes with those sharp claws," Casey added. "Not to mention those deadly teeth. But that's nothing to what you'll find if you think you can persuade Ham to accept physical therapy."

As Casey walked away, Brand took her hand in his. It

was cold as ice. "You don't have to take this on. Ham has already said he's having none of it."

"I know." Her eyes were troubled. "But he's hurting, Brand. And I have the ability to help him."

He shook his head as they began trailing behind the others.

He leaned close to whisper, "Just remember. Fools rush in..."

"I know. And I'm no angel."

"You are to me."

"Now that the worst of Hammond's pain has subsided, we'll need a strategy going forward." Meg smiled at Billy, who handed her a mug of coffee. She sipped, before looking at the family. All of them were there, including Avery.

They took their places around the table and listened as she began handing out assignments.

"I'll make this quick, before Hammond wakes from his nap. Thank heavens for that pain medicine Dr. Peterson gave him. For the first couple of days he was in quite a state." She took several swallows of caffeine. "Egan and I will continue to get him up in the mornings and get him ready for bed in the evenings. I'd like each of you to take a couple of hours throughout the night, in case he should wake and need anything." She turned to Avery. "Once Hammond is strong enough for therapy, we'll leave him in your capable hands."

"And good luck with that," Casey deadpanned.

Around the table the others merely smiled.

It was clear to Avery that the family was deeply troubled by this turn of events. Their beloved leader had fallen, and they were all collectively holding their breath.

She'd watched as Meg had calmly taken up nurse's duty, seeing to the old man's every need. Egan, Bo, and Liz followed Meg's directions without question. The three great-grandsons had handled the heavy lifting, carrying Hammond to the table, the few times he'd agreed to leave his room. But as the days dragged on, instead of suffering cabin fever, the old man had begun to enjoy being waited on like a dictator.

Avery decided to say what was on her mind. "Miss Meg, as the family nurse, you know how to tend to wounds of every kind."

With a smile, Meg nodded. "I've been doing it my whole life."

"But I'm not sure any of you were hearing what Dr. Peterson was saying. There are no broken bones. Ham is in pain, but it's natural after pulling a large muscle."

"He's ninety years old," Bo said sternly.

"And that means he may heal a little slower than you. But he needs to move, to flex that muscle, so it doesn't get a chance to tighten up and cause even more pain." She looked around the table. "If all of you continue pampering him, he's going to think there are things you're not telling him. He will start to believe there's a conspiracy of silence because he's more seriously injured than the doctor said."

Liz frowned. "We can't just pretend nothing happened. What if he tries to get up in the night and falls again?"

"I'm not suggesting we treat this lightly. I'm saying we follow the doctor's orders. It's our job to get him up and moving, even when it hurts."

Egan was shaking his head. "You don't know my father. He's never going to give in and use that walker."

"He will if he can't lean on any of you to get wherever he needs to go."

Brand, seated beside her, put a hand on hers. "You're saying we shouldn't give him a hand when he needs it?"

She sighed. "I'm saying that instead of lending a hand, you've all become enablers. Like most people who are injured, he's been going through stages. First there's anger. Then there's self-pity. And finally, hopefully, there's a determination to get through this and come out healed and whole. But that last stage has been stalled because he'd discovered that he likes all the attention."

"He's certainly been getting a lot of that." Egan wrapped an arm around his wife's shoulders. "Especially from my poor Meggie."

Meg leaned into him before saying, "Thank you. And thank you, Avery. I guess we all needed to hear that." She took in a deep breath. "All right. We'll stand back and see how much Hammond is capable of doing on his own. If he needs help, we'll give it, but until he asks, we'll let him figure things out for himself."

As she and Egan pushed away from the table and started to walk away, Meg paused beside Avery and touched a hand to her shoulder. "I'm so glad you're here."

When the others had left the room, Brand took Avery's hand and lifted it to his lips. "What Gram Meg said, tenderfoot. We're lucky to have you."

She couldn't help laughing. "Says the rough, tough cowboy who told me I was wasting my time and his."

He joined in her laughter.

Billy set two cups of coffee in front of them before getting out a roasting pan and several skillets in preparation for supper.

Brand looked thoughtful as he drank his coffee. "Isn't it amazing how quickly things can change? One minute we were having a lazy day in town. And now we're all tiptoeing around my great-grandfather and hoping he can come back from this."

Avery closed a hand over his. "You said yourself that Ham can climb any mountain. He'll climb this one, too."

"From your lips, tenderfoot." He leaned close, then remembering they had an audience of one, he finished his coffee in silence.

"Margaret Mary." Hammond's voice boomed from his bedroom.

Meg ambled into his room and stood at the foot of his big bed.

Ever since his return from the clinic, whenever he'd summoned her, she'd rushed in, breathless, to see to his request. Each time, he'd wanted another pillow, another glass of water, and once even asked her to fetch one of his great-grandsons to carry him to the bathroom.

Though she'd agreed with Avery's suggestion that they let him take care of his own needs, Meg's tender heart wouldn't allow her to say no to even the smallest request.

At her invitation, Avery had visited his room while he napped and had seen to a few helpful changes. Meg decided it was time to challenge her father-in-law.

"What do you need, Hammond?"

"I want to sit up. Give me a hand."

Meg didn't move. "See that length of rope tied to the end of the bed?"

He barely glanced at it, even though the other knotted end lay beside his hand. "I see it. What about it?"

"Avery has been giving me a few lessons in occupational therapy."

At the very mention of the word *therapy*, the old man glared at her, prepared to shut her down.

"Occupational therapy is about the business of every-day living. It helps us learn new tricks to old habits."

"I'm not interested—"

She held up a hand to silence him. "That rope, secured to the end of the bed, will allow you to do some things for yourself. Just take hold of it and pull yourself into a sitting position."

"Why can't you just help me, since you're standing right here?"

"I can't always be around when you need me, Hammond. And I need to know that when I'm not here, you can take care of your own needs. Why don't you give it a try?"

Though he muttered a few rich, ripe curses under his breath, he did as she suggested and was able to easily pull himself up.

He sat there a moment, before noticing that the hated walker was positioned directly beside the bed. "And I suppose your therapist wants me to walk myself to the bathroom?"

"That's what we all want, Hammond." Meg fought to keep her tone cheerful. "And I know that's what you want, too, so you can quickly regain not only your independence, but also your privacy."

With a grimace of pain, he managed to swing his legs over the edge of the bed. He grasped the handles of the hated walker and managed to pull himself into a standing position. Beads of sweat stood out on his forehead.

It took all of Meg's courage to stand back and watch, without offering to help. It simply wasn't in her tender nature to see her beloved father-in-law suffer so.

Egan, approaching the doorway, started forward to help his father.

Meg's hand shot out and she caught him by the wrist. He was forced to pause beside her, watching as Hammond took one halting step after another until he'd crossed the room to the doorway of the adjoining bathroom.

Minutes later he returned, leaning heavily on the walker. When he reached the side of the bed, he tumbled onto the mattress, his breath coming in short bursts.

When Egan ignored Meg's warning look and hurried over, Hammond turned to him in triumph. "See that? No damned fall is going to keep your old man down, boy."

Egan managed, barely, to hide his surprise before bursting into laughter. "You got that right. I certainly didn't expect any less from you, Pops."

Standing just outside the bedroom, Avery turned away quickly, wearing a little smile of victory.

CHAPTER TWENTY-FIVE

During Hammond's recovery period, the family was treated to Billy's extensive menu of the old man's favorite comfort foods. Fork-tender pot roast. Garlic mashed potatoes, swimming in beef gravy. Macaroni and cheese, with Billy's secret three-cheese topping. Chicken soup, with chunks of tender chicken, greenhouse potatoes, and carrots. And for dessert, Hammond's beloved creamy rice pudding, served warm and topped with a dollop of whipped cream and a dusting of cinnamon.

Every day, as Hammond pushed the walker into the kitchen, he couldn't hide his delight at the wonderful smells that perfumed the entire house. Though it wasn't like him to lavish praise, he couldn't help letting Billy know how much he was enjoying the special attention.

Dinner time had turned into a daily celebration. Avery found herself looking forward to not only the amazing menu, but also the spirit of warm camaraderie as Hammond regaled them with tales of his youthful exploits in the wilderness he'd tamed. Hearing his stories, she realized just what an adventurous spirit he possessed. A spirit he had passed down to his son Egan, grandson

Bo, and great-grandsons, Brand, Casey, and Jonah, who all adored him.

The women of this amazing family, Meg and her daughter Liz, were equally courageous, filling each day with work that brought them real satisfaction.

That had Avery thinking about her own life. She had spent way too much time worrying about pleasing her father and not enough time enjoying the fact that she'd found real purpose. Life could have been simpler if she had acceded to her father's wish to follow the course he'd charted, accepting a position on his surgical team. But she would have never had the opportunity to feel completely fulfilled while doing something that gave her so much pleasure.

And just today she'd heard from Chief Noble Crain. The state police, working with the Michigan authorities, had done an extensive investigation of Trace, his cell phone history, and a follow-up interview with those closest to him and could find no connection between Trace and the texts sent to Avery. Although they considered the case still open, they were willing to concede that they didn't have a shred of evidence to connect Dr. Trace Martin to these curious texts, or to the incidents that occurred before Avery left home.

With so much time and distance between them and this latest report, she had begun to believe that it was all behind her now.

Feeling Brand's hand close around hers under the table, she glanced over to see him wink before giving her that sexy smile that always touched her heart. Another reason to be grateful she'd followed her own path to take this job so far from home, she realized. If not for this chance to break free, she would have never met this cowboy who had completely captured her heart.

* * *

Brand stepped into the therapy room and stood a moment, watching Avery across the room.

She turned with a smile. "Right on time. After the number of chores you did today, I don't know how you can bear to think about doing more."

"This one isn't a chore. This is the only time I get to be alone with you."

She crossed the room and he gathered her close to press a kiss to her temple. "I've been missing you all day."

"Same goes, cowboy."

Hearing footsteps on the stairs, they both turned to see Hammond taking one halting step at a time, with Casey and Jonah on either side of him as he maneuvered the walker.

As they hastily stepped apart, Hammond looked sharp-eyed from one to the other.

As he stepped farther into the room, he looked around with interest, while Casey and Jonah stood back, allowing him to walk unaided.

"I haven't been up here in a long while now." He moved to the floor-to-ceiling windows and drank in the panoramic view of the hills spread out in all directions. "Has Brand told you that we own all this? As far as the eye can see, it's Merrick land."

"He told me. It's hard to believe." Avery stepped up beside him. "The first time I looked out this window, it took my breath away. You have to be so proud of what you've done here, Ham."

He kept his gaze fixed on the view. "It's not just the land. It's the life I've made here with my family. Four generations living and working here, and all of us loving what we do. My sweet Mandy loved all this as much as I. She was the reason I could work so hard to have my dream." He turned to study her. "I wish every man could have what I have, in life and in love."

Avery heard the passion in his tone.

He glanced at the bench, the chair, and the elastic bands hanging on a hook along the wall. "So this is your torture chamber."

That brought a round of laughter from the others.

"Speaking of torture, I don't believe you put yourself through that painful climb just to visit your old rooms."

"You're direct, girl. I like that." He glanced at his great-grandson and shocked all of them by saying, "I've seen how much better Brand's been walking since you started working with him. I thought maybe I'd try a little of your therapy, and see if it can get me where I was before the fall." He narrowed his gaze on her. "Is that something you can promise?"

"Everything depends on how hard you're willing to work to reach your goal. But if that's what you want, I'll help you get there."

"Now you're being careful with your words, instead of being direct. What you mean is, it's all up to me."

She gave him a bright smile. "That's what I'm saying."

"Smart, too. I like that in a woman." He shrugged. "Sorry. I meant to say, I like that in a person. My family has been reminding me that my words can be construed as sexist."

Behind his back, his great-grandsons looked at one another with astonishment.

"So." He turned to Avery. "Let's get started. You may have noticed I'm not a patient man."

With a grin, Avery led him toward the chair and invited him to sit.

"Step one. You'll pull yourself up to a standing position, using the walker, half a dozen times."

She watched as the old man struggled with each movement. When he'd finished, the first beads of sweat were glistening on his face.

"Step two. You'll stand, without the aid of the walker, four times. Now remember, without the walker for balance, you'll feel a little shaky at first. Do everything in slow motion to avoid a fall."

By the time he'd complied, his face was bathed in sweat and he reached out reflexively to the walker for balance.

Avery handed him a cool, damp cloth, which he held against his face for several long minutes, before accepting a dry towel.

He dropped them into a basket alongside the bench and looked up eagerly. "Okay, girl. Now what?"

"That's it for your first time."

He looked confused. "That's it?" His eyes narrowed. "Now you're coddling me, and you should know I don't want to be coddled like some old geezer."

Brand chuckled. "I said that very thing to her after my first session. I really thought I had to suffer before I'd see any improvement. But so far, there's been a lot less pain than I expected. And you said yourself you're seeing the improvement in me."

Hammond gave a grudging nod. "All right." He turned toward the door, where Casey and Jonah stood waiting and watching. "Now for the hard part. I have to make it down all those stairs without taking another tumble."

Avery walked beside him to the door. "Or, you could

change in the other room and end your session the way we've been ending most of ours. With a relaxing steam in the sauna."

The old man's eyes went wide. "That old sauna still works?"

When the others nodded, he gave a delighted laugh before turning to Casey. "Find my trunks, boyo."

Avery sat on a bamboo bench between Brand and Jonah. Across from them were Casey and Ham.

The old man was in rare good humor and had been regaling them with stories of his youth. Between the tall tales of adventure, the jokes, and the teasing, their laughter rang out.

Seeing Hammond stifle a yawn, Avery turned to his great-grandsons. "I think that's enough steam for tonight, Ham. I know you're supposed to walk as much as possible, but if you don't mind, I'd like Casey or Jonah to carry you down the stairs and to your bedroom."

He frowned. "Why?"

"Because your muscles are so relaxed, they'll feel like rubber. You could easily fall the minute you try to stand."

Brand nodded. "Listen to her, Ham. The first time I stepped out of the sauna, my legs were shaky, and I'm half your age."

"No need to remind me of that, boy." Hammond wrapped a bath towel around himself and allowed Casey to lift him.

At the top of the stairs, Ham looked over his great-grandson's shoulder with a twinkle in his eye. "I'm looking forward to another therapy session tomorrow, girl."

Avery couldn't hide her happy smile. "I'm looking forward to it, too, Ham."

When they descended the stairs, Jonah was shaking his head. "If I hadn't heard it with my own ears, I'd have never believed this one. Ham morphed from grumpy old man to therapy convert in the blink of an eye." He shot Avery a long look. "You may be the original miracle worker."

He turned away and followed his brother down the stairs and to Hammond's bedroom.

When they were alone, Brand grasped the ends of the towel Avery had tossed around her shoulders, drawing her close. "Jonah's right. Tonight I witnessed something I never would have believed. You had the old man eating out of your hand." Against her temple he murmured, "Not that I blame him. You've had the same effect on me since you walked through the door."

"Really?" With a laugh, she lifted a hand to his cheek. "As I recall, you stormed out of the kitchen like a wounded bear and I figured my time in Wyoming was over before it began."

"That was the old Brand. The BA."

"Bad Ass?"

He chuckled. "Before Avery."

He lowered his face to hers. With his hands in her hair, he kissed her with a sort of reverence, and she returned his kisses, wrapping her arms around his waist, loving the feel of his bare flesh against her palms.

Against her mouth he whispered, "I'm thinking about another kind of therapy. How about some sexual healing?"

"Mmmm, I'd like that."

They both looked up at the sound of footsteps on the stairs. Before they could step apart, they saw Casey and Jonah, still wearing their bathing trunks. Behind them were Bo and Liz and Chet.

Avery knew her cheeks were bright red, even though Brand didn't seem concerned about the fact that they'd just been caught in an intimate embrace.

Bo was grinning from ear to ear. "Ham was raving about the fact that the old sauna still works its magic with sore muscles."

Liz added, "After the day I've put in, I couldn't wait to join the others." She looked over at Brand and Avery with a sly smile. "I hope you haven't already turned off the heat."

Brand narrowed his gaze on her. "I'm sure it's a lot cooler now."

She slapped his arm. "I was talking about the sauna."

"Oh, that. It's still on high." He tossed her a bath towel. "Go on in and test it."

She grabbed the towel with one hand and led the way into the sauna, with Chet, Bo, Casey, and Jonah following behind.

Brand turned to Avery. "I wasn't expecting a flash mob. Looks like my little seduction will have to wait a while longer. Sorry."

She touched a hand to his arm. "Not nearly as sorry as I am, cowboy."

Hand in hand, they turned toward the sauna to join the crowd for another round of teasing and laughter.

CHAPTER TWENTY-SIX

As the family gathered around the kitchen, helping themselves to chilled longnecks, ice water, or freshly squeezed lemonade, Brand stepped up beside Avery.

He kept his voice low so the others wouldn't overhear. "I've missed you. Even our sessions aren't the same now that Ham has joined us."

"I know. But look how far he's come. You have to admit it's worth the loss of privacy just to see the way he's embraced physical therapy."

Their shoulders brushed, and she felt the heat of him, wishing they could slip away to another room.

He leaned close. "I took a break at lunchtime, hoping to see you, but you weren't here."

"Liz invited me to her studio. It's such a rare honor, I could hardly refuse."

His smile was back. "I'm glad you're becoming friends. She's been too long without anyone to talk and laugh with."

"We did a lot of that today. When she's relaxed, she's so much fun to be with."

He touched a hand to hers. "I just wish I could be alone with you. Between my ranch chores and my family taking up so much of your time, we never have any time to ourselves."

Meg looked over at the doorway and gave a little gasp of surprise.

Everyone turned to watch as Hammond, walking with the aid of a three-pronged cane, crossed the room.

Egan called, "What? No walker?"

"You can take that contraption back to Doc Peterson. Today Avery introduced me to this little device, and it's just fine, at least for the short-term. I'm thinking by next week I won't even need this."

"Oh, Hammond." Meg hurried over to loop her arm through his. "Just look at you."

"Now, then, Margaret Mary, let's not make a fuss." Despite his protest, the old man was beaming and enjoying every minute of the attention.

In the midst of the excitement, Avery heard the ping of a text. At once her smile faded. With a feeling of dread, she reached for her cell phone.

Beside her, Brand watched her reaction, his hand clenched at his side, anticipating the worst.

She read quickly, and her smile blossomed before she turned to him. "It's from my father. He just sent out a group text announcing his choice for his surgical team." She looked up at Brand. "He's chosen Trace."

"Which means, when you return, he'll be working in the same hospital as you. You'll be forced to see him all the time. Is that going to be a problem?"

"No. It won't matter." She was quick to put a hand on Brand's arm. "I have to be willing to trust my father's judgment. If Trace turns out to be all my father believes him to be, I'll be willing to put all this behind me."

Brand's eyes narrowed. "Are you sure?"

"Maybe we'll never be friends, but at least I can be civil when I see him. In fact, just to show him there are no hard feelings, I'll call the hospital service tonight and leave both my father and Trace a message of congratulations that their worries are over and a choice made. That will make my father happy, and hopefully it will ease any tensions between Trace and me."

Brand was shaking his head. "Or it could encourage him to do something worse."

"You said yourself the authorities haven't found a shred of evidence that Trace is involved in this. The cell phone can't be traced to him. He's been kept so busy at the hospital, he's barely had time to sleep. I still believe that a person is considered innocent until proven guilty. And the more distance I have between myself and Trace, the more I'm beginning to believe in him."

"What about when you get home and have to see him every day?"

"I'll worry about that when it happens. For now, let's just concentrate on celebrating the remarkable progress Ham is making."

Brand closed his hand over hers. "You're an amazing, forgiving woman. I'm just glad your father finally contacted you, although a phone call would have been more personal."

"It's all right." Her smile brightened. "At least he thought to add my name to the list of recipients. Knowing how much he has on his mind these days, I'm grateful for even that small gesture."

He leaned close to whisper, "Speaking of grateful. I'll be grateful if we can find some alone time later. In fact, if I have to, I may carry you off to the barn and climb to the hayloft." He wiggled his brows like a villain. "We could probably hide up there all night and nobody would be the wiser."

"Is that what they call a roll in the hay?"

"What I have in mind is a whole lot more than a simple roll, tenderfoot."

They shared a secret laugh.

Across the room, Hammond's gaze sharpened as he watched his great-grandson. His mouth softened into a smile before he turned to join in the conversation between Bo and Egan.

Just as Billy was inviting them to gather around the table, Liz and Chet walked in together.

Meg looked over at her daughter. "Where've you two been?"

"Riding." Liz's hair was windblown, her cheeks suffused with color.

She took a seat at the table, with Chet beside her. "Ever since I rode down from the hills after Avery and I had our little adventure, I realized how much I missed riding. I've been spending way too much time in my studio. So when I told Chet, he said he didn't want me riding alone and suggested we try to get a couple of rides in each week, after the chores are finished." She gave a long, deep sigh. "There's nothing quite like galloping across the fields after a day of work to chase away all the clouds."

"Unless," Casey deadpanned, "the clouds are so dark and heavy, the only way they can disappear is to unload all that rain on your head."

Liz joined in the laughter. "Don't you worry, Dr. Casey. A little rain couldn't dampen my spirits these days."

Casey and Jonah looked at each other and said in unison, "Just your clothes."

As the others laughed, Avery found herself thinking how sweet it was that Liz had regained so much joy. It was good to see her looking so relaxed and happy.

After a long, lazy supper and a therapy session that seemed to drag on forever, Hammond decided he was too tired to take advantage of the sauna.

He stifled a yawn. "I think I'll head downstairs and watch a little TV in my room."

As he turned away, Avery stopped him. "You forgot your cane."

He gave her a smile that reminded her of Brand's heart-tugging grin when he was about to tease her. "I was hoping you'd notice, girl. You can send that back to Doc Peterson to join that other hated contraption. I don't need either of them anymore."

While Avery and Brand watched wide-eyed, he took hold of the banister and descended the stairs.

She put a hand on Brand's arm. "That sly old sweetie. I'll bet he was planning this surprise all day."

Brand gave a shake of his head. "He pulled it off. I never saw it coming." He had a sudden thought. "That's why he didn't have Casey or Jonah with him. He wanted to prove he could handle the stairs by himself."

He looked around at the empty room. "Are we really alone?"

Avery heard the change in his tone. "We are. Think it will stay that way?"

"I can't be sure. Now that the family has discovered the joy of the sauna, they could already be changing into bathing suits. But I'm betting there's one place we could be alone." He put a finger to his lips and took her hand, leading her down the stairs and out the back door.

Seeing no one around, he kept her hand in his and started toward the barn. Once inside, he drew her close and pressed his lips to her temple. "Alone at last."

Avery felt the curl of heat spiral through her veins, all the way to her toes. With a little laugh she wrapped her arms around his neck, inviting his kiss. The heat between them grew, until they were both trembling.

"Avery." His lips moved on hers, adding to the heat. "You're all I think about. This is all I think about. Whether it's morning chores or riding in the hills, you're with me. Oh, baby, the need for you is like an ache."

Against his mouth she murmured, "I'm very good at healing aches. Right now, I have a few of my own." A small laugh escaped her throat. "Are we going for the hayloft?"

"I don't think I can make it that far." He backed her against the rough wall of a stall door, running his hands up and down her sides, his thumbs finding her already taut nipples.

The unlatched door suddenly opened inward and the two of them tumbled into the straw, hands groping, mouths fused, bodies heated. Undeterred, they continued their scorching kiss.

"I thought I heard something. Hey, you two."

At the sound of Casey's voice, they both jerked apart, like kids caught with their hands in the cookie jar.

Brand offered a hand to help Avery to her feet. Nearby, a stall door opened and Casey stood staring at the two of them.

It was Brand who found his voice. "What the hell are you doing here?"

"One of the foals has a limp. I've been treating him, and I like to check on him every night before I head inside." His smile grew in direct proportion to Brand's scowl. "I'm glad you're here. I need a hand, bro."

Brand's voice was a growl of frustration. "Find someone else. In case you haven't noticed, I'm a little busy."

"Oh, I noticed. Come on. It'll only take a minute. Then you and Avery can get back to that physical therapy you two are so passionate about."

Embarrassment gave way to the ridiculousness of their situation. Avery couldn't hold back her laughter any longer. Her laughter was contagious, and after another few moments, Brand joined her.

"Come on." She caught his hand. "Let's help your brother."

As they stepped into the stall beside Casey, he looked at the two of them more closely before grinning. "Hold this little guy while I administer an antibiotic."

Brand easily held the skittish foal and Casey plunged the syringe into its hindquarter. When he was finished, he soothed the frightened animal until its quivering stopped and it began munching hay.

As they stepped out of the stall, Brand turned to Casey. "You heading inside now?"

Thoroughly enjoying himself, Casey shrugged. "Depends. You and Avery thinking about staying out here? Or are you heading inside?"

Brand glared at his brother. "If you're staying, we're leaving."

Casey chuckled. "Suit yourself, bro. But if you're heading inside, you might want to pick the straw off your hair and backside before you go in."

With a little whistle he sauntered away.

Brand turned to Avery and caught sight of a piece of

straw clinging to her hair. She reached up and removed several more from his hair.

Laughing, they caught hands and walked back to the house.

He leaned close. "If it's okay with you, I'll slip upstairs to your room in a while."

She squeezed his hand. "More than okay. And if I'm asleep, you have my permission to wake me."

He paused on the back porch and drew her into his arms for a long, lazy kiss that had them both sighing with pent-up need.

Against her mouth he murmured, "Oh, you have my word on that, tenderfoot."

CHAPTER TWENTY-SEVEN

Dawn light was just coloring the sky when Brand awoke and studied the woman asleep in his arms.

What a night they'd shared. From a barely controlled passion that had them coming together in a storm, to low, whispered conversations baring their souls of secrets they'd never before shared with anyone. And in between the loving and the talking, there had been so much laughter between them.

Being with Avery transformed him. His heart was so overflowing with love that he wanted to shout with joy from the top of the mountain. If his family knew how wild and free he was feeling at this moment, they would think he'd lost his mind. Maybe he had. There was no doubt he'd lost his heart.

Trying not to wake her, Brand slipped out of bed and picked up his clothes, strewn about the floor of Avery's room, where he'd tossed them in haste the night before.

Avery sat up, shoving hair from her eyes. "You're leaving?"

"Chores." He leaned over to press a kiss to her lips. "Sorry. I wish I could stay."

"Mmm." She wrapped her arms around his neck and held him to her. "Me too."

He melted into her and took the kiss deeper. "I suppose I could stay a few more minutes."

Her mouth curved into a smile. "What I have in mind may take a bit longer."

"Yeah?" The clothes fell from his hands and landed on the floor unnoticed. He slid into bed beside her and gathered her close.

Against her mouth, he muttered thickly, "I guess Casey and Jonah can carry my share. They owe..." As he lost himself in her, the last of his words died on his lips.

"This time I'm really leaving." Brand stepped out of bed and began gathering the clothes he'd dropped.

"I'll miss you." Avery lay back against the pillow. "But there's always tonight."

"Or maybe even some time this afternoon, if I can get away."

"Promise?"

"Cross my heart." He kissed her again, long and slow and deep, before forcing himself to turn away. If he didn't move quickly, he'd be right back in bed with her. Leaving her was like a physical pain.

When the door closed behind him, Avery lay a moment, smiling at the thought that if she were a kitten, she'd be purring.

On a sigh, she slid out of bed and headed to the shower. Pulling on denims and a plaid shirt, she decided she would join Brand and his brothers in the barn.

"Good morning, Billy." She picked up a coffee from the tray on the kitchen counter.

"'Morning, Avery. Where are you off to?"

"Barn chores."

At his arched brow she laughed. "You should see your face."

He gave a shake of his head. "It's hard to imagine you cleaning stalls and forking up manure."

"It builds muscles. Not to mention character."

That had him laughing. "That's what Bo always told his three sons."

"I know. That's what they've said. And I figure it's a great morning workout."

"So, you're just doing this to keep that perfect figure?"

"Thanks for the compliment." She finished her coffee and set the mug in the sink. "I'm doing it because Brand, Casey, and Jonah keep me in stitches with their comedy routine the whole time they're working."

Billy grinned. "You're right. Those three make everything fun."

As she walked away, he stood a moment, lost in thought.

In the short time Avery had been here, there had been so many changes in the Merrick family. Some subtle, some dramatic. But everyone here had been touched in different ways by her presence. Liz had made a friend and, in the process, had started coming out of that shell she'd built around herself for so many years. It was plain to see that Miss Meg was enjoying the company of another female in the house. Old Hammond was still that stern, reserved elder of the clan, as was his son, Egan, and grandson Bo, but all had begun to trust this young woman and no longer saw her as an outsider. But the biggest change was Brand. He was still tough as nails. But the affection he had for Avery had softened all his hard edges.

Billy found himself wondering if he was the only one aware of the power of one small, determined female.

"Steak, asparagus, and macaroni and cheese." Bo rubbed his hands together as the family gathered around the table for their evening meal. "Now this is my kind of supper."

"You take after me, boyo." Ham took his place at the table and set aside the cane, which Avery had advised him to keep for several more days, just in case.

Avery smiled at him. "You weren't really leaning on that, Ham. In fact, it looked more like a theater prop."

The old man was grinning from ear to ear. "I wondered when you'd notice, girl. Now I'm certain you can send that back to Doc Peterson, just like that walker contraption. Don't need anything except my own two legs, thanks to you."

"Any pain at all?" Meg asked him.

He shook his head. "Not a one. It's like that fall never happened."

"Oh, Hammond." His daughter-in-law blinked away a tear. "I'm so glad." She looked over at Avery. "And I'm so glad you were here when we needed you."

"Not half as glad as I am." Brand looked around the table at his family. "In case none of you noticed, I'm walking better, too."

"Oh, I've noticed, bro." Casey nudged Jonah, and the two shared a grin. "About time you got rid of that limp so you can catch up with us. We were getting ready to whip your…" Seeing the way Hammond's eyes narrowed, Casey added lamely, "Hide."

"Any time you want to try," Brand growled.

"I don't know." Jonah winked at Casey before adding,

"We both think you're getting soft on"—he paused—"all this comfort food Billy's been dishing up."

"That's not the only thing he's gone soft on," Casey muttered, bringing another round of laughter.

Egan neatly turned the conversation to ranch-related topics by saying to Chet, "I heard there's an auction planned over at the old Mason ranch."

Chet nodded. "They're posting flyers all over the area. It's scheduled for next weekend. They already have a buyer for the cattle. But nobody's come forward for the land, buildings, or equipment yet, so it looks like the bank will be stuck with it."

"Which means it'll go for a third of its value," Hammond said glumly. "Old Charlie Mason must be turning over in his grave."

When dinner ended, Meg suggested they take their coffee and dessert on the back porch. While they watched a spectacular sunset, Billy pushed a wheeled trolley containing coffee and strawberry shortcake with strawberries grown in the greenhouse, real whipped cream, and scoops of vanilla and strawberry ice cream.

As Billy passed around his special dessert, everybody's mood lightened considerably.

Bo looked around at his family before giving a sigh of pleasure. "Life doesn't get much better'n this."

"Amen," Hammond muttered.

Meg turned to Avery. "You're looking relaxed and happy tonight. It must give you such a sense of satisfaction to see two of your patients doing so well."

Avery couldn't contain her smile. "It does. And the fact that I heard from my father just added to this pleasant day. He phoned me to say he's received my message of congratulations and was so pleased with his choice of

Trace. They've been spending hours working together, and he says the fit is a good one. After we talked for a while, he asked me how my work was going, and when I told him how comfortable I was here, we had a long and pleasant conversation."

Egan seemed perplexed. "Is this the first time you and your father have talked since you left home?"

Avery nodded.

"So, you two don't routinely talk on the phone?"

"Hardly ever. Because my father is so often tied up in surgery, he has a lot of messages to return. As you can imagine, he's not fond of spending all his time on the telephone. To him, it's just another intrusion on his work. But we arrange to get together over dinner every other week or so."

Casey turned to her. "You have to make an appointment to visit your own father?"

Avery winced when she saw the looks being exchanged among the others. She felt a sudden need to defend her father. "I know it sounds that way, but he prefers to call it our date night. With his busy schedule, it's the only thing that works."

As the others fell silent while lingering over coffee and dessert, Meg took pity on Avery and turned to Liz. "I saw a delivery truck here earlier. Did you manage to get that shipment of additional photos off to your agent?"

Liz nodded. "I'm so glad to have all the decisions finally out of the way. I sent Evelyn long texts with all the photos I wanted included in the show, along with my reasons, and then she asked for more, so I Skyped her to show her a dozen more that I'd planned on keeping. She loved all of them and asked me to send them along, too. Now the last of my babies are on their way to

San Francisco, and I can breathe a sigh of relief and concentrate on just doing what I love."

Chet gave her a resigned look. "I suppose that means another trip to high country soon?"

Liz laughed. "I certainly hope so." She turned to Avery. "Want to come with me?"

"If I have time, I'd love to. But I'll be heading home soon. My time here is almost up. And in case you haven't noticed, Brand no longer needs a physical therapist."

At her words, Brand's smile was wiped away.

"Oh, I've noticed." Liz felt a moment of pity for her nephew. He wasn't even aware that he was wearing his heart on his sleeve.

Suddenly Liz looked over at Avery. "Oh, I almost forgot."

At Avery's puzzled look, she added, "The driver had a delivery for you. A padded envelope." She looked over her shoulder. "Where did you put it, Billy?"

He pointed to the mudroom.

A minute later, Liz returned and handed the manila envelope to Avery.

"Thank you." She studied the neatly typed label that bore her name and the address of the ranch, and nothing more. "I wonder who sent this."

"No return address?" Billy handed her a letter opener bearing the ranch's logo.

"No." She shrugged. "It was mailed from Keeling, a little town in Michigan not far from Rose Arbor."

Everyone watched as she slit open the seal and handed the letter opener back to Billy.

She reached inside and drew out a mound of shredded paper. Half hidden in the midst of it was something small and soft.

Smiling, Avery parted the shredded paper and picked it up. "It looks like some sort of tiny stuffed animal. Now who...?"

She picked it up by its tail and found herself holding a blood-spattered dead mouse.

With a cry of distress, she flung it from her. It landed on the worn wooden boards of the porch.

The family gathered around with a collective gasp of horror.

The bloody little animal had been decapitated.

CHAPTER TWENTY-EIGHT

When Chief Noble Crain arrived, he found the Merrick family gathered in the kitchen, talking in low tones.

Avery, having time to regain her composure, sipped chamomile tea forced on her by Billy to soothe her frayed nerves.

"'Evening, folks. Avery." The chief accepted a mug of strong, hot coffee before taking a seat beside Avery. "Brand told me about the...surprise that was delivered. I'd like you to tell me again, in your own words."

After walking him through what had happened, she indicated the padded mailer residing on a sideboard. The shredded paper and the dead mouse lay on top of it.

Chief Crain walked over and studied it in silence before turning. "I'll send this along to our state police task force. The fact that it went through the mail could make it easier to trace." He crossed the room to place a hand on Avery's shoulder. "In his phone call, Brand said you'd left a message of congratulations for Dr. Trace Martin a couple of days ago."

He felt the little shiver that passed through her before she met his dark gaze. "I was trying to be fair to Trace. I thought I'd let him know that I was willing to put the past behind me. But…" She gave a shake of her head, wrestling with all the dark thoughts filling her mind. "But the fact that this was sent to me so soon after I left that message, I can't help but think it triggered something in him."

"Like what?" the chief asked.

She shrugged. "I wish I knew. Could it be hearing my name? My voice?" She brought her hands to her face, her words muffled. "But if he's innocent, why would he send me something so repulsive?"

"Could he want to get revenge for having been named by you as a suspect? Furthermore, did he know that you have an aversion to mice? Is it something you'd mentioned?"

"No. I never had a particular aversion to mice before this." She shuddered. "Doesn't everyone have an aversion to headless animals covered in blood? Do you know what it felt like to open that mailer and find that headless…?" She didn't bother to say the word.

"Have you given any more thought to an enemy you may have had in the past?"

"That's all I've done is think. I can't come up with anyone. My friends, my coworkers, the hospital staff. We all have really good, friendly relationships. There have been no arguments, no harsh words. Not even a hint of anger with anybody I can think of."

"Still, somebody sees you as an enemy or a threat."

She lifted her hands, palms up. "That's just it, Chief. I'm not in line to take anyone's job. I'm not in competition for any promotions. I can't think of a single person who would do something like this."

"Tell me about the message you left for Dr. Martin."

"It was a simple phone message congratulating him on

making my father's surgical team. It certainly couldn't be seen as any kind of threat to him. And for him to answer with…" She glanced at the mailer on the sideboard.

"I'd like you to tell me exactly what you said. Every word of that message."

"Word for word?" She took a moment to mull it over, reflecting on the night she'd left a message for her father and a second one for Trace.

She'd been so happy and relieved. And truly willing to start over.

"I believe I said 'Congratulations, Trace. My father just related your good news, and I want you to know I'm very happy for you. I'm sure you'll become a valuable member of his team.'"

Chief Crain gave a slight nod of his head. "Are you sure that's all you said?"

She shrugged. "I can't be sure, but it's as close as I can recall. Oh." She clapped a hand to her mouth. "I almost forgot. I also said, 'Once I'm back home, I'll be sure to congratulate you in person.'" She felt the need to explain. "Once I'm back at the hospital, I'll be running into him periodically, and I thought by saying that up front, he wouldn't feel uncomfortable the first time he saw me coming toward him. After naming him as a suspect in these incidents, I wanted him to know I was willing to put it behind me, and hoped he could do the same."

The chief considered all her words carefully. "You left this on his cell phone?"

She looked over at him. "No. With a father like mine, knowing how busy surgeons are, and how frustrating it is to deal with dozens of phone messages as soon as he gets out of surgery, I left the message on the hospital service number. That way, the surgeons can pick up all their messages at the end of a shift, or if they're tired, pick them up the following day when they're fresh."

"So this is available to all the hospital staff, and there will be a record of it in the log?"

Avery nodded. "Of course. In case there's any question about a message, either from a patient or any of the medical personnel, they can read the log for the time of the message and the location where it originated. Or they can replay the tape and hear the message again and again if it contains any kind of detailed instructions."

"Good." The chief gave her a reassuring smile. "As soon as I hear anything at all from the state police, I'll let you know. In the meantime"—he turned to include everybody in his remarks—"it's reassuring to know you're here with the Merrick family. Texts and packages can cause a certain amount of fear, but they can't physically harm you. I'd like to keep it that way."

"So would we." Egan spoke for all of them. "As long as Avery is our guest, we'll see to it that she's safe." He caught Brand's eye and asked the question that was on all their minds. "Avery's six weeks are up in a few days. Do you think she should consider extending her stay with us, Noble?"

The chief gave a shake of his head. "Sorry, Egan. That's not my call." He turned to Avery. "Have you been assigned to another case somewhere?"

"No. I won't be included in the rotation until I return to Michigan. But it wouldn't be right to delay my return. After all, I can't stay on here indefinitely. These good people shouldn't have to deal with all this."

Bo held up a hand. "Have you heard any complaints from us?"

"Of course not. You've all been so kind and welcoming. But this isn't your battle to fight."

Casey made a fist. "In case you haven't noticed, the Merricks are pretty good in a fight."

"Pretty good?" Ham surprised all of them by saying, "When it comes to a knock-down, drag-out fight, the Merrick family is the best there is, boy. And don't you forget it."

That brought a round of laughter to break the tension.

Chief Crain donned gloves before carefully bagging the padded mailer and its contents and heading for the door. "This will go to the state police lab for testing. As soon as I hear anything back from them, I'll be in touch."

When he left, the family took their places around the table. Billy filled mugs with coffee and set a plate of warm cinnamon buns in the middle of the table, along with small plates, cream, and sugar.

While they nibbled the pastry and drank their coffee, Avery refused any refreshment and sat with her hands gripped in her lap.

Brand said what they were all thinking. "I know the state police have an excellent team. But their investigation will take time." He turned to his grandfather. "Wasn't Newton Calder one of your best friends when he was with the state boys?"

Egan nodded. "He was their lead investigator for years until he retired."

"Do you think you could persuade him to take this on? Not as a member of the task force, but as a private investigator?"

Egan smiled. "I know he misses police work and does an occasional bit of work just to keep his hand in." He pushed away from the table. "I'll call him now."

He dug out his cell phone and stepped from the room. Minutes later he returned to the kitchen. "Newt said he'd be happy to do whatever he can. He said he prefers to work with the state police but is free to go off in any direction he chooses, as long as he shares all his information with them. Maybe, by adding Newt as another member, he'll bring something new to the mix."

Egan put a hand on Avery's arm. "Newt echoed what Chief Crain said. Sending something through the mail could make this a lot easier to trace. It's just a matter of time before they have some answers to all this."

"Thank you, Egan. I'll be happy to pay whatever your friend charges."

"We'll worry about that later." Egan squeezed her hand before wrapping an arm around his wife's shoulders.

Avery looked around at the others. "I'm so grateful to all of you. And again, I'm sorry for bringing all this trouble here."

"Not another word of apology, girl." Ham pushed away from the table. "While you're here, you're one of us. And your problems are ours. Don't you forget it."

The others began calling their good nights and drifting to their rooms.

Brand remained in the kitchen, wishing he could think of a way to ease the tension he could see in Avery. She was holding herself together and putting up a brave front, but he knew that bloody surprise had shocked her to her core.

As the hour grew late, they made their way upstairs. When Avery paused on the landing in front of his bedroom door to say good night, he took her hand and continued up the stairs to her room.

Once inside, before she could say a word, she looked

up into his eyes and saw the way he was devouring her. She melted into him and they came together in a storm of passion.

Throughout the long night, as Avery slept fitfully, Brand held her, willing her his strength to get through whatever fears were holding her in their grip, until they had the answer to this mystery that grew more puzzling, and more creepy, by the day.

CHAPTER TWENTY-NINE

Avery woke to find Brand fresh from the shower, a towel draped low on his hips, his hand on the doorknob.

She sat up. "You're leaving without a word?"

He hurried across the room and settled on the edge of the mattress. "You looked so peaceful I didn't have the heart to wake you."

She leaned up to press a kiss to his cheek. "Thank you for last night."

He quirked a brow before assuming a silly drawl. "Why, you're welcome, little lady. It was purely my pleasure."

She couldn't help laughing. "You see why I lov…" She quickly covered by saying, "Loved last night. It was just what I needed."

She saw him watching her a little too closely and could feel her face growing hot at that little slip of the tongue. She would have to guard her words carefully. "Okay. Go shovel manure. If I can move fast enough, I'll join you."

"There's no need. Take your time." He brushed a slow, heated kiss over her mouth before heading toward the door.

When he was gone, she lay a moment, thinking about the way Brand had treated her last night. With a rare sort of tenderness guaranteed to erase all her fears. It would be easy to believe he had the kind of feelings for her that she had for him.

Love. She'd almost said the word aloud. It could have been an awkward moment, catching him off guard like that.

She slid out of bed and walked to the shower, where she stood under the warm spray for long minutes. She had to work hard to put aside all the worrisome thoughts that crowded her mind now that she was alone.

That padded mailer and its contents had left an indelible image, one that would be hard to forget, even with all of Brand's tender ministrations.

The only solution for it was hard, physical work.

Dressed in jeans and a plaid shirt, she descended the stairs.

In the kitchen she could hear the low hum of voices. As soon as she stepped inside, the voices abruptly stopped. Though the family, huddled around the table, greeted her warmly, she had no doubt they'd been discussing her and her situation.

Billy handed her a mug of steaming coffee.

"Thank you." She sipped.

Liz crossed to her. "I was just telling everyone that I'd like to head up to the hills later today and spend a couple of days photographing whatever I find. I'm hoping you'll come with me."

Avery glanced toward Brand, who, like the others, seemed to be paying close attention.

She took a breath, determined to speak her mind.

"Look, if this is all an elaborate plan to keep my mind occupied, or to keep me safe…"

Liz put a hand on her arm. "It is. And it isn't." She huffed out a breath. "What I mean is, I was planning on going anyway and am inviting you along. You know you had a grand time in the highlands on our day trip, and you were such fun to be with. The others agree that it's the best place for you to be right now. Letters can't reach you up there. And there is rarely any phone service. We'll see enough wildlife to stir your soul. Best of all, Chet and Brand are looking forward to steaks over a fire, so we can count on them to drop by at least one of the evenings. What do you say? Are you up for another wilderness adventure?"

Avery looked into Liz's eyes and could read the honesty in them. With a sigh she nodded. "You're a sly one, Liz. You know I can't resist the lure of seeing another herd of horses, or an eagle, or…" She laughed. "Maybe this time we'll climb high enough to come face-to-face with that mountain goat. But what about Brand's physical therapy? That's why I'm here."

Brand winked. "I say you've already earned your keep as my therapist. I've been walking without a limp or even a hint of pain for at least a week."

Meg chimed in. "Amen to that. It certainly lets me off the hook for hiring a guy to hang out with my grandsons."

That had everyone laughing.

Liz stuck out a hand. "Deal?"

Avery took her hand and squeezed. "Okay. Deal."

"Great." Liz was already leading her toward the stairs. "While our guys are doing their morning chores, we should pack." She turned to Billy. "That ought to give you time to make one of your special breakfasts before we head out."

"How about steak and eggs, fried potatoes, and a side of pancakes? Will that fortify you ladies for the drive to the hills?"

"I don't know about them," Casey called as he started toward the door, "but it'll go a long way toward rewarding me for the filthy stalls I'm about to clean."

Both Liz and Avery were laughing as they followed the others out of the kitchen.

Avery dropped a backpack on loan from Liz in a corner of the kitchen just as Chet and Liz walked in.

Liz was laughing at something Chet said, and their joy was contagious. Avery felt her heart growing lighter as she thought about their planned trip. A wilderness filled with the wonders of nature. A final chance to experience this amazing countryside before returning to the routine of home and work.

"Most of the supplies are loaded," Liz called. "Except for Billy's food, which he's still assembling."

Billy looked over, while carefully turning steaks on the stove's grill top. "It's all packed and ready. I just have to finish in here before loading it."

"Just point me in the right direction," Chet said to him, "and I'll take care of loading it."

Billy showed him the filled containers and coolers, and Chet began hauling them out to the truck.

By the time the morning chores were finished, and the men had washed up in the mudroom, breakfast was ready and the family gathered around the big table.

"Now this is what I call a ranch breakfast." Casey speared a sizzling steak and cut off a bite before helping himself to scrambled eggs and potatoes fried with onions and peppers before passing along the platters to Jonah beside him.

At each place was a second plate, which they filled with a stack of pancakes swimming in maple syrup.

Soon they were all murmuring their approval as they dug into their amazing meal.

Midway through her breakfast, Avery sat back, sipping coffee. "I can't believe you can eat like this every day and never gain an ounce."

"Hard work," Casey said. "When a man works like a mule, he doesn't have to worry about his weight."

"And if he spends his days shoveling manure," Jonah added dryly, "his weight won't matter because the smell will keep everybody from coming anywhere near him."

Their laughter was interrupted by a loud knock on the back door.

While the others continued eating, Billy made his way through the mudroom to the door. When he opened it, a pretty woman greeted him with a sweet smile, her voice drifting into the kitchen.

"Hello. My GPS tells me I've reached my destination. Is this the Merrick ranch?"

Billy nodded. "It is."

"Oh. Thank goodness." She gave a throaty laugh. "I'm looking for Avery Grant."

Billy held the door wider. "She's in the kitchen. Follow me right this way."

As they stepped into the kitchen, the chorus of voices stilled as Billy called, "Avery, you have company."

"Company?" Avery, like the others, turned to stare at the guest.

Her eyes widened. "Renee?" She shoved away from the table and started across the room. "What in the world are you doing in Wyoming?"

"Looking for you." The young woman opened her arms.

Avery hesitated for a mere fraction before giving her a hug. "What's this about?"

Renee paused as though aware of their audience. "Maybe we should talk in private."

Avery put a hand to her elbow and steered her closer to the table. "Whatever you have to say can be said in front of everybody here. Renee, I'd like you to meet the Merrick family, who have been my gracious hosts for almost six weeks. Everybody, this is Renee Wilmot, a nurse at the Rose Arbor Hospital."

Billy was already setting an extra place at the table. "Come join us for breakfast."

The young woman shot him a grateful smile. "Oh my." She looked around at the platters of food. "Except for coffee, I haven't had anything since last night. This looks like a feast."

She smiled at Casey, holding a platter of steak, and accepted a small piece before helping herself to potatoes and eggs, all the while nodding as Avery introduced everyone by name.

"I didn't mean to intrude on your meal," she said, smiling at Billy as he offered her a mug of steaming coffee. "I drove through the night from Jackson Hole after landing. I was afraid I'd be so early I might wake the household."

"We're ranchers," Bo said with a trace of pride. "Our day starts before dawn."

"I should have known." Her cheeks colored sweetly as she lowered her gaze to her plate. "Being a nurse, I'm used to different shifts, from morning to midnight. I guess I forget that other people have crazy hours, too."

"We don't mind. It's as natural to us as"—Bo spread his hands—"as a feast like this before we start the next round of chores. Speaking of which"—he shoved away from the table—"I'm heading up to the herd with Chet. Casey? Brand? Jonah? You joining us?"

As they got to their feet, Chet turned to Liz. "Everything is packed and ready."

She stood and carried her plate to the sink. Behind Renee's back, she shot Avery a questioning look.

With a nod of understanding, Avery turned to Renee. "You haven't said why you came all this way."

Renee kept her voice low. "I wanted to warn you about something."

Instantly the others stopped in their tracks and started back toward the table.

Seeing Renee's startled look, Avery put a hand on her arm. "You can speak freely. Everyone here knows what's been happening."

"Oh." The word came out in a whoosh of relief. "Okay then. I came here to let you know that Trace has been acting strangely for the last couple of days."

Avery's eyes widened. "In what way?"

"I walked in on him going through your director's files. When he saw me there, he started swearing and then just stormed out of the office. Afterward, I realized he was searching for the name and location of the ranch where you're working. And there's something else. Even though he's just started on the surgical team, he asked for time off to take care of some personal business."

"Did my father grant his request?"

Renee nodded, adding, "I think this time he's gone off

the rails. I'm so worried about you, I decided to fly to Wyoming and find you before he could."

The Merrick men exchanged dark glances before Brand put a hand on Avery's shoulder. "We need to contact Chief Crain."

Avery nodded.

When he reached the police chief, he handed the phone to Avery, putting it on speaker so all could hear.

When she'd repeated what Renee had told her, the chief cleared his throat. "This just adds more fuel to the fire. I think that now, more than ever, you'll want to go with your plan to drive up to the hills with Liz. That way, you're a much more difficult target to find. You can see how easy it was for your friend to find you with the help of a GPS. Without a known destination, it will be impossible for Dr. Martin to find you in that wilderness."

Around the table, the family nodded their agreement.

When he disconnected, Brand said firmly, "Avery, I agree with the chief. I think you and Liz should leave now."

"Leave?" Renee glanced from Avery to Brand and back.

"Liz and I were just about to take a trip into the hills. Liz is a professional photographer and needs the time to take some photographs. I planned on accompanying her for a few days."

Renee's eyes lit with excitement. "A camping trip? Oh, that sounds like heaven."

Avery looked over at Liz to see her reaction. Knowing how private a person she was, Avery was pretty certain Liz wouldn't be happy spending time with this stranger.

Liz surprised her by saying, "Any friend of Avery's is welcome. After all, you came all this way. It would be a shame to just turn around and leave. Unless, of course, you need to get back to work."

Renee put a hand to her mouth before giving Liz a smile so bright it could light up an entire room. "Oh my goodness. I can't even imagine how lucky I am to be included in such an adventure. I certainly have the time. I took my personal days off. But are you sure you want me along?"

"I'm sure." Liz returned her smile. "I'll add another sleeping bag to the truck and throw in another hoodie and a parka in case the nights grow cold." She paused in the doorway. "We'll leave in half an hour."

As the others got ready to begin their chores for the day, Billy topped Renee's mug and began to clear the table.

Seeing Brand walking out with the others, Avery turned to Renee. "Excuse me. I'll be right back."

She caught up with him in the mudroom, where he was grabbing a wide-brimmed hat.

"Are you all right with me leaving the ranch with Liz?"

"Like Chief Crain said, it's safer than being here. If this nutcase comes looking for you, he'll have to go through all of us before he could ever hope to find you up in those hills."

She took in a deep breath.

Seeing it, he wrapped his arms around her and drew her close. Against her temple he muttered, "I like your friend. She seems really concerned about you. I think Liz will like her, too. I'll try to swing by your campsite tonight or tomorrow night. In the meantime, try to put all this out of your mind and just enjoy the wildlife."

"Oh, Brand." For a moment she clung to him before stepping back. "I know I'll have a great time, but I'll miss you."

"Good." He kissed the tip of her nose. "I like the fact that you'll miss me, since I know I'm going to miss you like crazy."

As he sauntered away, she watched until he joined his father and brothers in a convoy of trucks heading to high country.

Minutes later, she and Renee joined Liz outside, where the truck was loaded and idling.

With a wave to Meg and Egan, Hammond and Billy, the three women drove off for their much-anticipated adventure in the wilderness.

CHAPTER THIRTY

Renee, seated between Liz at the wheel and Avery by the passenger window, swiveled her head from one side to the other, drinking in the amazing view of meadows and forests, hills black with cattle, and paths barely visible carved through wilderness. "I can see why you call this area the high country. I think we've been climbing ever since we left your ranch."

Liz nodded. "The land around here mirrors the Grand Tetons." She pointed and both Renee and Avery turned to stare at the mountain peaks in the distance.

Avery said with a trace of awe, "Liz and her family have actually climbed the Tetons."

Renee shivered. "I don't think I'd like to try it. They look cold and forbidding."

Liz nodded. "They can be. Summer is brief, and once it's over, they're covered in snow and ice for most of the year. That's the challenge of climbing. As I told Avery, who's dying to climb, it can feel like summer at the base and be completely frozen at the summit."

"Liz showed me some of the photos she took while in the Tetons." Avery's tone was filled with admiration. "They're just so breathtakingly beautiful." Her eyes glowed. "Like being in a frozen ice palace. Water melting in the sun and freezing before it can reach the ground."

Liz chuckled. "I can tell that's your favorite."

"One of many. It would be impossible to choose a favorite from so many fantastic photographs." Avery turned to Renee. "Liz just sent a shipment of her photos to her agent for a showing in San Francisco."

Renee appeared suitably impressed. "So, does that mean you're famous? Should I know your work?"

"If you have to ask, I can't be famous."

"But people know your work?"

"Those who love all things Wyoming. It's what I most love to photograph. The mountains. The countryside. The wildlife. And portraits of Wyoming ranchers."

"The real West." Avery said the words almost reverently as Liz maneuvered the truck through a maze of evergreens in a wooded area. "And you and I are lucky enough to be here among people who actually know it and love it."

Liz shot Avery a sideways glance. "Sounds like you've learned to love it, too. Not just the land, but the people."

Avery felt her cheeks color just as Renee turned to her. "You said the Merrick family knows about Trace. Have you heard anything from him since you left Michigan?"

Reluctantly Avery told her, in as few words as possible, about the menacing texts and about the envelope and its contents. "It was a dead mouse."

Liz, listening in silence, was aware that Avery was trying to relate these things without the emotion that was surely churning inside her.

Renee seemed horrified. "Then I was right. Trace has really gone off the rails."

Avery gave a brief nod, her hands clenched in her lap. "It looks that way."

Renee's voice lowered. "It must have been horrible to open that envelope and find all that blood and gore."

Avery shivered. "Please. I'd rather not talk about—"

Liz interrupted her by pointing. "Look. Up ahead."

The two women stared through the front window to see a herd of mustangs just melting into the woods. Bringing up the rear was the coal-black stallion, his head turning this way and that until the last mare was safely hidden among the trees. In an instant he was gone as well, fading away as if he'd never been there.

Avery took in a breath before shooting Liz a smile. "Now that's a sight that can chase away every kind of trouble. How can I hold a dark thought when I'm seeing wild horses?"

"That's the plan." Liz reached across Renee to squeeze Avery's hand. "Let's make a pact. While we're up here, there's to be no mention of anything unpleasant. Let's agree to leave all that behind us."

Avery gave a deep sigh of gratitude. "Agreed." She smiled at Liz and felt a rare lightness around her heart. "It would be a shame to let anything spoil the beauty of this place."

"But…" Seeing the two women looking at her, waiting for her agreement to the pact, Renee was forced to give a quick nod, despite the dozen or more questions bubbling up, begging for answers.

Liz parked the truck beside a rock formation shaped like a turtle. When Avery commented on it, Liz laughed. "Good eye, Avery. Around here we call it Turtle Rock."

Avery joined in the laughter. "I should have known I wouldn't be the first to see the similarity."

"It's probably been called Turtle Rock for a hundred years or more. We'll have to ask Ham when we get home how it got its name. I swear my grandfather knows more history about this land than most of the state's historians. But at least our forebears gave it a name everyone can understand." Liz climbed from the truck and walked to the rear to remove her backpack loaded with her camera's accessories.

Avery stepped from the passenger side, followed by Renee.

At the back of the truck, Renee caught sight of Liz's rifle and halted in midstride.

Seeing the direction of her gaze, Liz smiled. "You don't like guns?"

Renee seemed to mentally shake herself before giving a shudder. "They have only one use. And that's to kill."

Liz gave her a gentle smile. "I should have known you had a tender heart. Actually this rifle has another use."

At Renee's arched brow she said, "Protection. Some of the animals living up here are afraid of man. Others are predators and see man as food. I'd rather not be a predator's dinner tonight. So this rifle goes wherever I go."

"I assume you know how to use it?" Renee was still staring at the rifle.

"You bet. I've been handling a rifle since I was old enough to understand the rules of handling a firearm. If you grow up on Merrick land, you grow up knowing how to take care of yourself in unexpectedly dangerous situations."

Renee stood back as Liz and Avery divided the supplies they would carry on their first day of the trip.

Liz hooked the rifle's carry strap across her chest before looping the cords of her two favorite cameras around her neck.

Avery pushed her arms through the straps of the backpack holding the camera accessories before adjusting it to a comfortable position.

Renee paused. "What can I carry?"

"This light backpack." Liz smiled. "It's the lunch Billy packed us. Since this is your first hike, I don't want you weighted down with anything too bulky, until you see how you feel after a few hours on the trail."

"Okay." Renee nodded her agreement and accepted the backpack.

As they started out, Liz took the lead, with Avery behind her. Renee trailed behind them, following in their footsteps.

By midmorning they had shed their jackets, tying them around their waists.

By noon they were high in the rugged hills before stopping beside an icy-cold stream to enjoy the lunch Billy had packed.

Renee dropped into the grass and set the backpack aside before removing her sunglasses to wipe a trickle of sweat inching down the bridge of her nose.

"How are you doing?" Avery set aside her backpack and looked at Renee, who was leaning back on her elbows and frowning at the sun.

"I'm fine."

"Not too tired?"

Renee shook her head. "I'm the first to admit I'm not much of an outdoor person, but I guess knowing I got here in time to warn you about Trace gave me a boost of energy." She put a hand on Avery's arm. "If you'd like to talk about him, I'm here for you."

Liz held up a hand. "Only pleasant talk. Remember?"

Avery gave her a grateful smile before crossing to the stream, where she took off her hiking boots and dipped her feet in the icy water.

Liz laid her rifle in the tall grass and positioned her two cameras alongside it before handing around wrapped sandwiches.

Avery stepped from the stream and hurried over to sit beside her, feet bare, toes wiggling.

When the three women unwrapped their sandwiches and began to eat, there were little murmurs of pure pleasure.

"Bless Billy," Avery said on a sigh as she bit into freshly baked cheese bread filled with thin slices of roast beef, along with lettuce, tomato, onion, and one of his homemade spreads that held a hint of mayo and the tang of wine vinegar.

Renee turned to Liz. "I can't believe you get to eat like this every day."

Liz shrugged. "I have to say, Billy's cooking is always a surprise. I'm not sure we've ever had the exact same meal twice. He always manages to add something that grabs our attention." She lifted her sandwich. "Like this dressing."

"Whatever it is, it's pure yummy." Avery nibbled a crumb from her finger.

After draining their water bottles, they filled them with the frigid water of the stream, lingering along its banks for nearly an hour, talking about the wildlife they'd spotted so far, and listing the animals they were still hoping to see.

Finally Liz got to her feet. "Are the two of you up for another hike?"

"Where to?" Avery was ready, hiking boots on, backpack adjusted.

"Up there." Liz pointed to the higher elevations, shrouded in woods. "Maybe, if we're lucky, we'll see that mountain goat today."

With their lunch eaten, Renee's backpack was empty and she was able to carry it easily slung on one shoulder, as she again took up the rear.

"Look." As they came through the woods and into a clearing, Liz pointed.

The other two followed her direction to see a herd of deer grazing in a meadow. When they spotted the humans, the deer began moving higher, toward a distant stand of trees.

Liz started out at a fast pace, clicking off photos, with Avery and Renee behind.

Suddenly Renee cried out and the other two paused. Seeing her in the grass, they hurried back.

Renee looked more contrite than hurt. "That was stupid of me. I must have stepped in a hole in the ground and I've twisted my ankle."

Liz knelt beside her. "Can you put any weight on it?"

Renee caught Avery's arm and started to haul herself up before crumpling back into the grass. "I may have sprained it. I think it's swelling."

Liz looked alarmed. "We'll get on either side of you and help you back to camp. We can have you at the clinic in Devil's Door by dark."

"No." Renee waved her away. "I'm not ready to put any weight on it. Let's give it some time. You go ahead and get those pictures before that herd gets away from you."

"I wouldn't think of it. I'm not about to put my photographs ahead of your safety."

Avery shook her head. "I agree with Renee. We've come so far, Liz. You go ahead and grab all the photos you want. I'll stay here with Renee. By the time you get back, maybe she'll be able to walk without pain. If not, we'll just move as slowly as necessary to get her back to the truck. But for now, go. Get the photographs you came here to get."

"You're both sure of this?"

Renee and Avery nodded.

Reluctantly, Liz turned away.

As she did, Renee called, "Wait. Are we safe here?"

"That's a fair question." Liz turned back and set her rifle in the grass. "Since you two can't move as quickly as I can, I'd feel better leaving this with you, just in case."

To Renee, she added, "I don't want you to be uncomfortable. It's loaded, but I have the safety on."

Renee managed a smile. "I'm sure we won't need it, but it's a comfort knowing we have it. And it certainly frees you with one less thing to carry."

With a nod, Liz turned and started in the direction of the herd, moving quickly to make up for lost time.

As Liz disappeared over a ridge, Avery deposited her backpack in the grass before bending to examine Renee's ankle.

With her head lowered, she asked, "On a scale of one to ten, how bad is the pain?"

"Not as bad as yours will be."

At the harsh, almost unrecognizable tone, Avery's head

came up at the same moment that she felt a sudden sharp pinprick of pain in her arm.

She gaped in surprise at her arm, then at Renee, whose smile had been wiped away. In its place was a tight, pinched look of anger. Her eyes were narrowed on Avery with pure hatred.

In her hand, sunlight glinted off the syringe in her hand, the tip dripping fluid.

"What...?" Avery's lips felt stiff, making it difficult to speak.

"Feeling a bit tipsy?" Renee gave her a look of smug satisfaction as she lifted the syringe. "Versed. Benzodiazepine. Just enough to slow your reflexes and make you lurch like a drunken sailor. Pretty soon you'll be seeing double, and your legs will feel like rubber."

Avery struggled to make her brain work, though all she could focus on was a sense of terror as she peered down at the grass, searching for Liz's rifle.

Two rifles swam in and out of her line of vision, while the ground below her seemed to dip and sway, causing bile to burn her throat as nausea rose up.

Seeing the direction of her gaze, Renee bent and picked up the rifle in one easy sweep of her hand.

Seeing the way Avery flinched, her smile returned. "Don't worry. I'm not going to shoot you. But I will if I have to. I've got much better weapons in my arsenal that will do the job quickly and silently. I simply wanted to make sure your friend didn't have this to use against me."

Renee let those words sink in before saying, "I measured every drug before coming here. From your files I learned your height and weight. I gave you just enough, in this first sedative, to keep you off-stride. You're too

drugged now to fight me, but still strong enough to walk."
She waved the rifle menacingly. "Now, let's go."

"Go?" Struggling against the dizziness, Avery tried to
form the words spinning around in her brain. "Go...?"
She licked her lips and tried again. "I don't understand.
What're you...?"

"Shut up and move." Renee gave her a rough shove,
sending her stumbling to her knees. "If we make good
time, your friend Liz can stay alive. By the time she gets
back here, we'll be long gone. But if you try to fight me,
I'll scream, and you can be sure Liz will come running.
And then you'll be responsible for what happens to the
famous photographer you seem to admire so much when
I'm forced to eliminate her."

She dragged Avery to her feet. "Right now, we're
heading down to the truck. I'll keep you in front of me,
so you can't try anything cute. If you do"—she patted her
pocket and produced a second syringe—"all those wild
animals you seem so crazy about will be feasting on your
dead body tonight."

CHAPTER THIRTY-ONE

At the ranch, Egan pressed a kiss to his wife's cheek.

She looked up from her reading. "What was that for?"

"Do I need a reason to kiss my beautiful bride?"

Meg chuckled. "Are you forgetting that I was a bride almost fifty years ago?"

"You're still that beautiful bride to me, Meggie." He sat beside her and took her hand in his. "I was thinking, since all the young ones are gone, maybe you and I could ask Pops and Billy if they'd like to go to town with us. We'll have lunch at Nonie's and walk around town eating ice cream like we did when Bo and Liz were kids."

She set aside her book. "Sounds like a fine plan. Do you think your dad's up to it?"

Egan nodded. "We'll ask him. He's been trapped in the house ever since that fall, and now that he's got that old spring back in his step, I think he'll enjoy getting out of here for a while."

They were both smiling as they started toward Hammond's room. Finding it empty, they checked in the kitchen.

"Here you are," Egan called.

Ham looked up from the table, where he was drinking coffee.

Billy was washing vegetables at the sink. "Ham and I picked all these in the greenhouse for our lunch."

"Speaking of lunch…" At the sound of his cell phone, Egan paused to answer it.

Hearing the deep voice of Noble Crain, Egan said, "Hey, Noble. Do you have some news for us?"

"I have." The chief's voice rang with urgency. "And it's important. Is your family there?"

"There's just Meg, Hammond, Billy, and me."

At a cue from Meg, Egan turned on the speaker, and the chief's voice bounced around the room. "Where's everybody else?"

Meg answered. "Our men are up with the herd. Liz drove Avery and her guest up into the hills for a few days."

At the chief's muttered oath, Egan remarked, "You sound troubled, Noble. What's wrong?"

Chief Crain huffed out an impatient breath. "I was hoping I wasn't too late to find everybody still there. Especially that guest you mentioned."

As the four exchanged puzzled looks, he explained. "Egan, you asked Newt Calder to join the state police team, and praise be, he came with a fresh viewpoint. Everyone seemed focused on Dr. Trace Martin, but he's been cleared of any involvement in sending those texts and that headless critter to Avery. That had Newt wondering who we could be overlooking. Someone nobody suspected of having a reason to threaten Avery Grant."

"And…?" Egan demanded.

"And when Newt started digging, he discovered that the nurse who first warned Avery about the doctor may have had some dark reasons for doing so. According to Trace Martin, that pretty young nurse pursued him like a dog with a bone until he agreed to take her out. He broke it off after only a couple of dates because she was, in his words, weird. In fact, he said she seemed determined to get her hooks in him."

Hammond scratched his head. "Can you put that in plain language, Noble?"

"It seems the nurse, Renee Wilmot, has a fatal attraction to the handsome young doctor and may want to eliminate anyone she perceives as her competition for his affection."

"Renee Wilmot." Meg looked at the three men as her voice rose in alarm. "Noble, she's up in the wilderness right now with Liz and Avery."

"How long have they been gone?"

Meg glanced at the kitchen clock. "They left right after breakfast. I'd say a good three or four hours ago."

Chief Crain muttered another oath before saying, "The state police are already on their way to your place, hoping to interview the nurse. I'll let them know they'll need backup." He paused before adding, "I know cell service is sparse in the hills, but you need to alert your men and the wranglers, since they're closer than we are. Ask them to fan out and give us a hand finding those three women as soon as possible. I'll have the state boys send up a chopper." He inhaled deeply. "I should warn you. The hospital found a supply of drugs missing."

Meg's frown deepened. "From my nursing training, I know that the same drugs used to heal can cause serious damage in the wrong hands. What is Renee Wilmot armed with, Noble?"

"So far they've listed a sedative—a benzodiazepine—

and insulin. There may be more. They're still doing an inventory. As far as the hospital can determine, she's armed with enough doses to render even the strongest person helpless. And enough, if she chooses, to be fatal."

As commanded, Avery walked a few steps in front of Renee. "Why?" It was the only word she could manage. And even that was an effort. Though her words were muddled, her mind was screaming a warning. She knew she was in extreme danger. If only she could make her body obey her commands "Why...doing this?"

"Shut up. I hate the sound of your voice." Renee had slung the rifle strap over her shoulder as she'd seen Liz do. She continued to hold the syringe in a menacing manner as she trailed close behind.

"...makes no sense. You...all happy and friendly, and suddenly...turn into...monster. Did Trace...ask you...hurt me?"

"Did Trace ask me to hurt you?" Renee's voice took on a whiny tone. "Do you hear yourself?"

Avery paused, and Renee gave her a rough shove. "I said keep moving."

"If...isn't for Trace, what...about?"

"Oh, it's about Trace. It's all about Trace. Always and forever. I knew, since our first meeting, it was him. My life has become all about Trace. He's the man of my dreams. My soul mate. He may not know it yet, but we're fated to be together forever."

Avery heard the words and let them circle around in her mind as she began to understand. "You're obsess..." She bit back the word. A woman who would go to such lengths as sending ugly texts and a dead mouse, and then come all this way for a confrontation wasn't just obsessed.

She was unhinged. There was a need to tread carefully here, even with her words. "You're in...love...Trace."

"And why wouldn't I be? He's everything a woman could ever want. Handsome. Charming. Brilliant. And absolutely mad about me, though he's too shy to admit it."

"I wish you...had told...If I'd known...I would have broken...off sooner."

Avery felt a blow to her back, sending her falling. As her face planted in the hard earth, Renee pressed her knee hard into her back, the syringe an inch from her neck. Her hand was actually trembling with the urge to plunge the needle. "Stop your lying. I know the truth."

Avery twisted her head, peering into eyes that had a look of madness. "What...truth?"

"I know all about women like you. It's all about the chase, isn't it? You agree to one date, and then make a man work for the next one, just to keep him dangling."

"Don't you...remember, Renee? You told me...only interested in earning a place...my father's surgical team. That was when...I broke...off. I wasn't...to be used like that."

"Liar!"

She felt the sting of Renee's nails raking across her cheek, leaving a trail of blood. But at least it wasn't another dose of drugs.

Renee's voice went up a notch. "I called Trace that very night you claimed to have broken it off and invited him over, and he said he was busy. I know who he was busy with, you slut." She stood over Avery menacingly. "Now get up and get moving, or I'll end this right here."

Avery got to her knees and shook her head to clear it. Then, as Renee yanked her to her feet, she forced herself to put one foot in front of the other, even though the ground beneath her continued to sway and tilt, making her head spin.

While she struggled to walk, her mind was circling ways to escape before they reached the truck. Once inside a vehicle, there was no way of knowing where Renee would take her. And she felt certain Renee would give her another, more lethal dose of drugs to control her.

At least here, though she was moving like a drunk, there was still the chance of staying alive.

Avery kept her eye on the line of trees up ahead. Once there, if she could distract Renee for even a moment, she could lose herself the way the deer and mustangs did, by melting into the woods and becoming invisible.

It was a very slim chance, considering her condition, but one she had to take. It was clear that Renee had come here with one thing in mind. To kill the woman she saw standing in the way of her happiness.

Avery's words may be muddled because of the drugs, but the seriousness of her situation had her mind growing sharper with every step she took. She realized now that she was in the presence of a madwoman completely out of control. A woman who had already decided there was only one way to eliminate the competition and win back the man of her fantasies.

Avery knew, with all her being, that her will to live had to be stronger than Renee's determination to kill her.

With that in mind, she forced herself to pay attention to every little thing around her. The flat meadow, abloom with range grass and wildflowers high enough for a body to hide in. Rocks along the ground that could be used as weapons. And up ahead, the looming woods, where an animal twice her size could slip away unnoticed.

If she couldn't outfight this predator, she had to out-smart her.

Egan snatched up a set of truck keys and raced to the barn. Before he could back out, Meg and Hammond had the door open and were climbing in the passenger side.

His head whipped around. "We agreed that you two would wait here."

Ham shot his son a stern look. "That's what you tried to order us to do. But we agreed to no such thing."

"I told you..." Egan drove the truck around to the back door and came to an abrupt stop. "There's danger up there. Get out. Both of you."

Hammond crossed his arms over his chest. "Now you listen to me, boy. There's a crazy woman trying to harm one of ours, and I'm not sitting back letting you shoulder it all."

"You know better than to argue with your father, Egan," Meg said. "We're wasting precious time."

Defeated, Egan put the truck in gear and gave his wife a sideways glance. "I suppose you put him up to this?"

"Hammond doesn't need me to tell him what to do. But I happen to agree with him. As long as Billy was willing to remain at the house and act as liaison between us and the authorities, I see it as my duty to go with you. Avery is in grave danger. Since I'm the one responsible for bringing her here, I have to do whatever I can to help now."

Hearing his wife's guilt in every word, Egan patted her hand before turning the wheel sharply and tearing along a rutted path to the hills. "Meggie, we're all responsible for Avery's safety. Now let's hope we make it in time."

"We will," Meg said almost to herself. "We simply

must keep that sweet young woman safe. I'll never forgive myself if anything happens to her."

Father and son exchanged glances over Meg's head, their faces tight with determination, their eyes as hard as flint.

Hammond drew an arm around his daughter-in-law. "We've been through tough times before, Margaret Mary Finnegan. We'll get through this one as well. You'll see. You just have to believe."

She allowed herself to lean in to him for just a moment before squaring her shoulders and whispering a prayer for Avery's safety. It wasn't only Avery who would suffer at the hands of this stranger. She'd seen the look in Brand's eyes whenever he thought no one was watching. It was a look she'd seen in Egan's eyes when they'd first met. And a look she'd seen in her son Bo's eyes when he'd met Leigh, the great love of his life.

No matter the time they were given on this earth, some people were simply destined to be together. She prayed her grandson and this lovely young woman were granted their time.

CHAPTER THIRTY-TWO

Brand and Chet were in high spirits. A day in the hills with the herd always had that effect on them. To add to the enjoyment of the day, they'd made plans to join Liz and Avery for steaks and beer around a campfire in a few hours.

Brand could see, in his mind's eye, an opportunity to slip away after the others were asleep and show Avery his favorite spot at the very top of the south meadow. In a field of wildflowers, under a starry sky, they would make slow, delicious love, after which he intended to declare his intentions.

Life didn't get much better.

When the ranch truck pulled up in a cloud of dust, the wranglers barely looked over as they tended the herd, but spotting his grandparents and great-grandfather, Brand touched a heel to Domino's side and the gelding turned neatly before trotting over.

Casey, Jonah, Bo, and Chet followed and remained in the saddle, while Brand dismounted and lifted his Stetson from his head, shaking it against his thigh.

"I knew it. The minute your therapist gave you the all clear to resume work, you just had to hurry up here. Want me to saddle you a horse, Ham?"

The old man put a hand on his great-grandson's shoulder, hoping to soften the blow. "We're here because we just heard from Noble Crain."

Brand's smile widened. "Great. Have they figured out who's stalking Avery?"

"They have." Hammond turned to Egan, who cleared his throat.

"Avery's in danger, Brand." Egan clasped Meg's hand as he delivered the news he knew would be a blow to his grandson. "The authorities are convinced the stalker is Renee Wilmot."

"Renee." The news was so unexpected that it took Brand and the others several moments of stunned silence to digest.

"I don't understand." Brand looked at his brothers. "That sweet little nurse who came all this way to warn Avery? She's the stalker? Why?"

"According to Chief Crain, she's crazy about Dr. Trace Martin." Egan gritted his teeth. "I mean actually crazy. They think she's here to get rid of her competition."

"Get rid of…" As the realization sank in, Brand's eyes narrowed. "You mean hurt Avery?"

"Or worse," Hammond said bluntly.

Brand looked up at his father, his brothers, and Chet astride their horses. All of them looked as shocked as he felt. "Does the chief know how she intends to do this?"

"Apparently a lot of drugs are missing from the hospital. Renee is a nurse. She would know exactly which ones can control a person and which ones could cause death."

With a vicious oath, Brand pulled himself into the saddle. "We have to stop her."

"Now listen, boy." Hammond caught hold of the reins.

"The state police are on their way. We've instructed Billy to tell them the approximate location we think Liz might travel, but we can't be certain exactly where the women are."

"We know the general area they'll be in." Brand motioned to the others. "If we go now, we can find their base camp and the truck before we fan out and cover more distance. Once the state police arrive, we'll be able to give them a clearer picture of where we've already looked."

Hammond continued clinging to the reins. "You don't want to go off half-cocked, boy. You need to take time to make some plans."

Brand was shaking his head. "My only plan is to stop this crazy woman and save Avery."

"I get it. I know how you're feeling, boy."

Brand's eyes narrowed. "I don't think you do, Ham. Avery has become much more to me than a physical therapist."

"You think I don't know that? I've seen the way you look at her, with your heart in your eyes, boy. And I know right now your heart is running ahead of your mind. But you have to be smart, Brand. And more than anything, you have to be careful."

Brand leaned down to squeeze the old man's shoulder. "Thanks, Ham. I will. But I need to go now. I have to be there."

He patted the rifle in the boot of his saddle, and the others did the same.

He turned his mount, and the rest fell into place behind him as they started across the high meadow.

It seemed incongruous to Brand that on such a perfect day, with the sun shining on vast fields of wildflowers bending in the slight breeze, someone could be planning the death of the woman he loved.

The woman he loved.

As his horse's hooves ate up the miles, the words played like a litany in his mind.

Why had he waited so long to tell Avery what he was feeling? Had he been too proud, too unsure, to risk baring his soul to her? He had arrogantly believed he had all the time in the world. Hadn't the sudden, wrenching loss of his mother at such an early age taught him anything at all about how precious time can be? Look at the price his father paid, choosing to live alone all these years rather than consider allowing another person into his heart. At this moment, Brand understood that so clearly.

Nobody was promised tomorrow. Nobody knew what the next hour, the next minute might bring. How many nights had he wasted, keeping silent about the feelings that were burning inside him? Here he'd been, fantasizing about the perfect night and the perfect moment to profess his undying love. And now, with the very real threat of harm hanging over Avery like a great, black cloud, he found himself wishing with all his might that he would be given another chance to speak the truth. He wouldn't need a special time or place. Just being with her was special enough.

Please, he thought as his horse's hooves raced across the hills, *keep her smart. Keep her strong.*

Keep the woman I love safe.

Liz moved out at a fast pace, eager to tell Avery about all the fantastic photos she'd taken, not only of the deer but also of the herd of mustangs she'd spotted in a clearing.

She loved the fact that Avery shared her reverence for

wild animals, especially horses. Ever since she'd been a little girl, she'd been over the moon at seeing the herds of mustangs running wild and free across their land. Once she'd learned to handle a camera, she'd had this tremendous need to show them to the rest of the world through her photographs. It gave her a rare sense of elation whenever she received a letter from someone who had bought her photographs of mustangs because those beautiful, mystical animals had touched a similar chord in their souls.

She was smiling as she came over the ridge to look down at the place where she'd left Avery and Renee.

When she didn't see them, she quickened her pace. Had Renee's ankle worsened? Had Avery taken it upon herself to help Renee back to camp?

As she came to the spot, she was startled to see the backpack with all her camera accessories still lying in the grass. Knowing how expensive they were and how important to her work, Avery would have never left them behind unless she'd been under tremendous pressure.

Was Renee's ankle broken? Was the swelling so severe Avery had to move out immediately? Was she strong enough to carry Renee on her back?

Lying a few feet away was the empty backpack that had held their lunch. Liz picked up both backpacks and looked around in the grass for her rifle. Seeing it gone, she felt an odd prickling along her scalp. Why would Avery leave the expensive camera supplies but take a rifle she had never fired?

Something was wrong here.

As she started across the high meadow, Liz's mind was working overtime.

Renee had reacted almost violently when she'd first

spotted the rifle in the back of the truck. Almost as though she saw it as a threat. And yet, it had been Renee's worry about being safe that had caused Liz to leave her rifle behind while she trailed the herd of deer.

At the time, Liz hadn't questioned her decision. It had seemed logical to put Avery's and Renee's safety ahead of her own. Besides, her mind had been completely focused on getting those photos before the herd disappeared.

Now, with time to mull, she found it strange that Renee, who professed a real distaste for rifles, had been so willing to have it right there, almost beside her in the grass.

Unless...

Liz stopped in her tracks.

She'd told Renee it would only be used in defense. What if Renee understood that and wanted to be certain she wouldn't have any defense?

Defense against what?

The thought flooding her mind had her dropping to her knees in the grass. It was Renee who had initiated the discussion of Trace Martin and what had happened. She'd seemed absolutely fascinated by hearing Avery talk about the texts and how they made her feel, and her reaction to the disgusting contents of the mailer. In fact, it had been Renee who had mentioned blood. Thinking back, Avery hadn't mentioned a bloody, headless mouse. She'd merely said a dead mouse.

The other details had been supplied by Renee.

Liz clapped a hand to her mouth as the horrible doubts began to reveal the ugly truth. Only the person who sent that mailer would have known about its contents. It was blindingly clear to Liz that Renee had more than a passing interest in Avery and Trace. Hadn't she taken personal time off work to fly all the way to Wyoming and drive through the night to the ranch, just to warn Avery?

She'd said that Trace had gone off the rails. Her words. But she'd brought no proof.

Instead of coming all this way, why hadn't Renee gone to the authorities with her concerns? Or at least to Avery's father?

Liz closed her eyes against a wave of terrible guilt. Why hadn't she asked these questions when Renee arrived?

Because this stranger had seemed so sweet and sincere. Apparently this smiling, pretty young woman had fooled not only Liz, but all of them as well.

Liz got to her feet and began running across the field, her mind in turmoil. On the one hand she prayed she was completely off course, and Avery and Renee had disappeared simply because of Renee's ankle.

On the other hand, she couldn't dismiss the very real fear that Renee Wilmot was not at all what she'd seemed, but was, in fact, the very essence of evil. And she'd come here to harm a young woman the entire Merrick family had learned to love.

CHAPTER THIRTY-THREE

Avery's mind was working every angle as she staggered through the tall grass. Seeing the woods ahead, she knew she had to make her move soon.

Since Renee had the advantage of being steady on her feet, Avery would need to come up with a distraction that would help her overcome the sluggishness brought on by the drugs. Her life depended on reaching the woods ahead of Renee and then melting into them.

As they neared the woods, a strange, fast-moving shadow fell over them. Both women looked up in alarm as an eagle swooped so low they were forced to duck their heads. The eagle landed a short distance ahead and caught a rabbit in its talons before lifting high in the air. The writhing little animal managed to slip free, and the great bird began a sudden descent, pouncing on the rabbit as it staggered and attempted to run.

Seeing that Renee was caught up in the life-and-death struggle, Avery made a dash toward the line of trees. Fighting through the haze of drugs, she dared not look back to see if Renee was following. Her only thought was reaching the blessed dim light of the forest up ahead.

She was vaguely aware of the death screech of the

poor rabbit as the eagle tore into its flesh. With her breath burning her lungs, she made it to the first line of trees and kept on moving as quickly as the dense undergrowth would allow.

With branches whipping her face and arms and snagging her hair, she forced herself to continue deeper into the woods. Brambles tore at her legs and she stumbled forward, grateful for the protection of her jeans and hiking boots.

She tripped over a fallen log completely covered with brush and leaves, and found herself falling through space as she went over a ravine. She landed with a grunt of pain and lay panting, her heart beating a thunderous tattoo in her chest.

As her breathing slowly returned to normal, she lay as still as death, listening for any sign of being followed.

"Damn you!" Renee's voice came from somewhere above her. "You're too drugged to get far. You can't hide. I'll find you, you slut."

Seeing a small outcropping of rock, Avery rolled beneath it, praying she wasn't visible from above.

"You won't get away," Renee shouted.

Her voice seemed to be moving. "I won't quit until I find you. And when I do, I promise you, this disgusting wilderness will be your grave."

As they reached the higher elevations, the five men on horseback fanned out, all eyes on the surrounding countryside.

When they spotted a figure emerging over a rise, all five spurred their horses into a run.

As they circled Liz, Bo dismounted and caught his sister in a bear hug.

Liz held on to him as she wheezed out a breath. "Thank heaven. I've been running at top speed ever since finding Avery and Renee gone."

"Gone?" Brand climbed from the saddle to place a hand on her shoulder. "Start at the beginning. How did you get separated, and where did you last see them?"

Her eyes narrowed. "What aren't you telling me?" She turned to Bo. "What's happened? Why are all of you here?"

As quickly as possible, he told her about the things the police chief had reported.

She clapped a hand to her mouth. "I was hoping I was wrong. But this confirms what I suspected." She then told them about finding the two women gone, along with the rifle, while leaving the backpack with her camera accessories behind. "I was hoping against hope that they were gone because of Renee's ankle. Now I know in my heart that twisted ankle was only a lie to separate us. And I know without a doubt Avery is with her, whether by choice or against her will. Oh, Brand. Renee has my rifle."

"That's not her only weapon. According to the hospital, she has an arsenal of drugs with her as well."

Liz closed her eyes against the fear that raced through her. "If Renee is as dangerous as the authorities believe, Avery's in terrible trouble."

Her words were another blow to his heart.

To keep from dwelling on the worst, Brand's mind was already leaping ahead. "Since you didn't spot them on your way down here, and we saw no sign of them on our way up, I have to believe they're either left of us, in the high meadow, or to the right of us, somewhere in the woods."

The others nodded their agreement.

"I say we split into two groups." Brand motioned toward their rifles. "We're all armed. Let's arrange a signal. Three shots in succession means they've been spotted."

At their words of agreement, Liz walked to Chet and lifted a hand to pull herself up behind him.

Seeing her intention, Bo's brotherly instincts kicked in. "Maybe you should keep on going to your truck, Liz, and let us handle this. This crazy woman is dangerous and won't care how many she hurts."

"All the more reason why I'm going with you." She caught Chet's hand and pulled herself up behind him, wrapping her arms around his waist. "This crazy woman," she said, tapping her own chest, "would like a few minutes alone with Renee Wilmot. Anybody who threatens one of us threatens all of us."

"Have I told you lately that I love you, Aunt Liz?" Brand saluted her before wheeling his mount, with the others fanning out.

Avery lay under the outcropping of rock, listening for anything that would alert her that Renee was nearby. A rustle of leaves. A snap of a twig. A sudden silence of birds or insects to indicate that someone had frightened them.

Hearing nothing, she decided she'd hidden here long enough. Despite the fear that clogged her throat and had her blood pumping, she had to risk moving. She planned on keeping to the shelter of the woods as she descended the hills, hoping, by the time she reached the lower meadow, that Renee would be lost somewhere in this maze.

She recalled what Billy had said on her first day here, when she'd wanted to walk around and explore her surroundings.

No matter how far you walk, this place is too big to miss.

Even from these hills, she would, once she was past the woods, find her way back to the ranch. With that comforting thought in mind, she inched her way from her hiding place and stood, feeling her head swim. Though the drugs were still in her system, the nausea had passed. She was still a little unsteady on her feet, but her mind was clear.

She stepped behind a tree and peered around in the gloom. Seeing no sign of Renee, she began to move stealthily from one clump of trees to another and, always heading downward, crept toward the ranch.

It was the thought of the Merrick homestead and Brand's sheltering arms that kept her going.

Brand, Chet, and Liz slipped silently into the forest, while Bo, Casey, and Jonah took to the high meadow.

Overhead they heard the sound of helicopters and knew the state police were circling.

Brand had sent out a text explaining where they were and where they had already searched, hoping it might get through to Ham and the others. With service in these hills being sketchy, there was no way of knowing, unless he should receive a response. In the meantime, he watched and listened, praying he would soon find Avery safe and sound.

Safe and sound. It was all he cared about now. It was what drove him. To keep her safe from a crazed woman bent on evil. A woman with a rifle and a pocket full of lethal drugs.

For a moment he closed his eyes, seeing Avery as she'd looked this morning, so happy and eager for this adventure in the hills. She was like a kid in a candy store just thinking about the wild creatures they might encounter. And now her grand adventure had turned into a nightmare.

To turn off such dark thoughts, he slid from the saddle and began to lead his mount through the dense woods.

Not far away, Chet and Liz followed suit, while a little more distant, his father and brothers were doing the same.

All of them fought to hold their tension at bay as they moved silently forward, praying for the best outcome while fearing the worst.

Avery had no way of knowing how long she'd been walking. Though it could have been less than an hour, it felt like an eternity as she tensed each time she heard anything out of the ordinary.

She'd seen deer pass. Had frozen in place as a snake slithered across her foot, though it had taken all of her discipline to keep from crying out. Her hair was snagged with twigs, her arms bleeding in half a dozen places from thorns and tree branches. Her vision was clearer now, and her gait steadier. The longer she forced herself to keep moving, the more her system worked off the drugs.

Hearing the sudden snap of a twig behind her, she turned, desperate to hide. Seeing a depression in the ground, she dropped into it and reached out to snag a dried tree branch, hoping it would cover her.

Close by she heard the hurried footfalls of someone moving quickly. She lay perfectly still, afraid to breathe for fear that slight movement could give her away.

Through the maze of leaves covering her face, she could make out a shadow moving over her, and she tensed, praying she was invisible.

She felt a slight bump against her hip and heard a muttered curse as Renee stumbled over her and fell, face-first, beside her.

Avery was on her feet first, but Renee quickly recovered and stood facing her, the syringe in her hand.

"I knew sooner or later I'd find you." Renee's eyes were wide and over-bright with madness. "This is the perfect place to get rid of you forever. If I'm lucky, those dangerous predators your photographer friend worried about will dispose of your body and there will be nothing left for anybody to identify."

"That photographer friend has a name. Liz Merrick. She's one of the people I've come to love here on this ranch. And I'm not going to let you hurt her because of me."

"You're not in a position to save even yourself, slut. Mark my words. You're going to die today in these woods, and if anybody tries to stop me, they'll join you in this unmarked grave forever."

CHAPTER THIRTY-FOUR

Brand paused, wondering what he'd just heard. Had it been a woman's voice? Or was he so desperate to find Avery that he was confusing a bird's call with something else?

He continued moving forward, ears straining for even a hint of a human.

Moments later he heard the unmistakable sound of Renee, her screams high-pitched in fury.

That was all he needed to throw caution to the wind and start racing toward the sounds of an all-out fight.

Renee flew at Avery, lifting the syringe in an arc toward her arm.

Avery sidestepped, and Renee missed her by inches.

Turning, she came at Avery a second time. This time Avery was ready. With feet planted, she caught Renee's outstretched arm and gave it a vicious twist.

With a cry of pain, Renee went down on one knee while the syringe dropped from her fingers, landing in the tall grass.

Avery fell on top of her and began pummeling her about the head.

Renee broke free and got to her feet. Grabbing a tree limb, she hit Avery with such force that it sent her crumpling to the ground.

Pain burst through Avery's head, white-hot sparks swimming in her line of vision.

She shook her head, but there was no time to recover as Renee lifted the heavy limb and hit her again.

Avery caught it, giving it a mighty tug, dragging Renee forward to her knees. As Avery stood poised to retaliate with the heavy branch, Renee grabbed her foot, causing her to land with such force she saw stars.

As she sat up, struggling to clear her head, Renee tossed a handful of dirt into her eyes.

With Avery momentarily blinded, Renee used that distraction to fumble around for the syringe. Realizing her intention, Avery grabbed at her hair, yanking Renee's head back viciously. As she did, she caught the glint of sunlight on the syringe, lying beside her foot.

Before she could reach for it, there was a deafening sound of three gunshots in quick succession.

Both women froze as Brand stood facing them, his rifle aimed and steady.

"Get up." He flicked the rifle at Renee, studying her through narrowed eyes. "Do as I say. Get up nice and easy."

As she pushed her way up, she turned slightly, and in that instant she managed to wrap an arm around Avery's neck while removing a second syringe, which she held against Avery's throat.

Brand could read the shock in Avery's eyes as Renee said, "Now you'll do as I say, cowboy, or you can watch this little slut die here and now." She motioned with her head. "Toss the rifle over here."

As he started to lower his weapon, Avery gave a cry. "Don't do it, Brand. She's mad. She'll kill you, too."

His voice was pure steel. "If you let Avery go, I'll willingly take her place and I give you my word, I won't fight you."

Renee smiled. "You first. Drop your rifle to show me you mean it."

Brand tossed the rifle toward Renee. "Now turn Avery loose."

As the weapon dropped at Renee's feet, her smile disappeared. "I see she has you fooled, too. I'm sorry you're willing to risk your life for someone so unworthy. You see, she has to die. It's the only way I can ever have true love."

Brand heard her words and realized that all pretense of normalcy had slipped away. The madness that had brought her to this moment was now front and center and was taking over any hint of humanity.

He studied the distance between himself and the two women and knew, without a doubt, that he could never make it in time. Even if he could span the space in a single leap, there wouldn't be enough time. That syringe was so close to Avery's neck, it would take but a second for Renee to plunge it into her tender flesh.

His voice lowered with urgency. "Avery. I need you to know something. I wish I'd told you sooner..."

Renee gave a hiss of annoyance. "Shut up. Not another word. She's nothing but a lying slut, unworthy of even a single thought. And since you can't see that, you have to die, too."

For the first time since her ordeal began, Avery felt tears sting her eyes. "Oh, Brand, I'm so sorry. I never dreamed I would bring something so horrible to you and your family."

They all looked up at the sound of voices calling and people racing through underbrush.

Renee's grip tightened on Avery's neck. "Looks like a whole lot of folks are going to die today. Fools. They just had to get in my way."

"You have no right. This isn't their fight, Renee."

"Stop your whining. This is all because of you."

Renee motioned toward Brand. "Stick out your hand."

When he shot her a questioning look, Avery cried, "Don't do it, Brand. She intends to inject you, to get you out of her way. She has a pocket filled with syringes."

Renee gave a smile of pure malice. "You said you were willing to take her place. Did you mean it, or were you just playing for time?"

His eyes narrowed as he gauged how much time he would have to disarm her after the sedative was in his system. All he needed was seconds to take her down and free Avery.

"I meant what I said." Brand stepped closer and held out his hand. "Go ahead. Stick me with that needle, but give me your word you'll let Avery go."

"Do you take me for a fool? Weren't you listening? You both have to die."

As she reached out with the syringe, Avery felt a wave of desperation.

With all the force she could muster, she brought her elbow backward into Renee's chest.

Caught by surprise, Renee's hand lowered as she gasped with pain, struggling for balance.

That was all Avery needed to wrestle the syringe from Renee and jab it directly into her arm.

For a moment, Renee recoiled as the sting of the needle shocked her. "No. This isn't how I'd planned..."

Then, as she realized what had happened, her eyes went wide and she looked about wildly as her legs began to fail her.

Brand reached out to wrap his arms around Avery, who was still holding the empty syringe. It dropped from her fingers as she clung to him.

"Oh, baby. That was the bravest thing I've ever seen."

"Not brave," she murmured against his throat. "I was desperate. I couldn't let her hurt you. I couldn't bear it."

As Renee dropped to the ground, the others, drawn by Brand's gunshots, gathered around to stare in wonder at the scene that greeted them.

Bo was the first to reach them. He hugged his son fiercely, then Avery, needing to feel them safe and warm and alive. Casey and Jonah did the same.

Liz was weeping. "I foolishly left my rifle with that woman."

"Shh." Avery found herself comforting Liz. "She fooled both of us. None of this was your fault. It was all mine. She came here because of me."

Hearing her, Brand turned Avery in his arms. "This woman's madness had nothing to do with you."

"It had everything to do with..." Avery looked up at the sound of helicopters, alerting them that the state police were landing in the meadow just beyond the woods.

When the troopers arrived, one man separated himself from the others and hurried over to grab Avery in a fierce embrace.

"Dad?" Her words were muffled against his shoulder as he held her so tightly she could hardly catch her breath.

"Avery. Oh, my darling. I was so afraid I'd be too

late. When I heard what had happened, I demanded to be allowed to fly here with our state troopers, who had joined the Wyoming police's team. They agreed that I had a personal interest in joining them on this mission."

He stared at Renee, who lay on the ground. "The police told me about Nurse Wilmot."

Avery turned to the medics who were kneeling on either side of Renee. "She's been shot with Versed."

The medics nodded, and one of them said, "Benzo. She'll be immobile for some time."

At his words, Renee's lips moved, and the two medics leaned close to listen.

One of the medics looked up at Avery. "I'll need the syringe you used, Ms. Grant."

She stared around before finding it on the ground.

The medic bagged it before saying, "According to the victim, this isn't a benzo."

Avery's eyes widened. "But I thought she said she'd given me a sedative. What is it?"

"According to her, this syringe held insulin. She measured out enough to kill half a dozen people so that you'd have no chance of recovery."

"She was going to use that on me? On all of us?"

"It appears so, ma'am."

Avery blanched. "I...sentenced her to death? I've killed her?"

"We may be able to mitigate the damage." One of the medics was already up and racing toward the helicopter for the supplies needed.

Seeing the horror in Avery's eyes, Brand stepped between her and her father. "You didn't know what was in that syringe. You thought you were merely sedating her.

She was the one hoping that the injection would be fatal. This is all on Renee."

"But I plunged that syringe into her arm, Brand."

"Oh, baby." He gathered her close. "She intended to plunge it into your neck. Remember that."

As she wept silently, the state police strapped Renee to a gurney and bagged the evidence, while the others gathered around Avery and Brand, trying their best to offer comfort.

When at last Avery had composed herself, her father took charge, wrapping an arm around her waist as he began drawing her away from the scene.

Brand and the others followed in somber silence.

While a group of wranglers arrived to retrieve the horses, the police provided trucks and SUVs for transport back to the ranch. It was a subdued group that finally descended the hills.

Inside the house, Billy moved about the kitchen, offering coffee to the state police detectives as they took Avery's statement.

Her father sat beside her, holding her hand, listening in silence, while the Merrick family listened as well.

"According to the Michigan state police, we believe the damage to your car at the hospital and the note written on your door were also the work of Nurse Wilmot. Dr. Trace Martin said she could have found your lipstick in his car and used it while you were at work."

Avery's father closed her hand in both of his. "And I made light of it, instead of having your back."

"Don't, Dad." Seeing the remorse in his eyes, she rested her head on his shoulder.

When the police had completed their report, they took

their leave, and the family spoke in low tones as Avery accepted a cup of tea from Billy.

Her father broke the silence. "The hospital is sending a plane for us. It's been cleared for landing at the fairgrounds in Devil's Door."

Avery's head came up. "We're leaving? Today?"

Her father nodded. "I...We need to get back home. I left my surgical team to cover for me."

"Of course. You need to be there."

"What I need is to be with you, Avery." He glanced around at the others, watching and listening. With a sigh, he added, "There's so much I need to tell you. So much I've left unsaid for too long."

Brand, standing apart from the others, looked from father to daughter, his face expressionless. But his family could see the effort he was making to keep his emotions hidden.

Ham broke the silence. "You must have some powerful friends, Dr. Grant. The only one I know of who was ever allowed to land at our fairgrounds is the governor."

That brought grateful smiles and nods from the others, hoping it might help break the ice that had settled over all of them.

Dr. Grant cleared his throat, a sign of his discomfort. "I wonder if I could have a few words alone with my daughter."

"Of course." At a signal from Meg, the others followed her from the kitchen, leaving Avery and her father alone.

Alexander Grant kept his voice deliberately low. "I have some things I need to tell you."

"All right." She sipped her tea and waited.

He took in a breath. "After you left, I requested some

time to talk with Dr. Beth Milgrim, a specialist in family counseling."

Avery's face registered her surprise. "A therapist? I wasn't expecting to hear this."

"I'm sure you weren't. In fact, I surprised myself. But since our meetings, I've been learning some things about myself that I'm not very proud of. I realize now that, after losing your mother, I sold the house because everywhere I looked I saw her, and it brought me fresh pain. But as Dr. Milgrim pointed out, I never considered what it did to you to lose that bridge to your past. While I was trying to move on, I was cutting you off from all that was dear to you."

Avery put a hand on his arm. "It forced me to move on, too."

"But that's just it. You were forced to move on, whether you were ready or not, because of me. And then I decided that I could keep you close by insisting that you follow in my footsteps. But when you changed course and dropped out of medical school, I couldn't hide my disapproval."

Avery managed a small smile. "Are you saying you now approve of my choice?"

"Avery, I'm learning so much about myself, and in the process, a lot about us." He put a hand on hers. "I'm sorry for pushing you so hard. When I was grieving, I pushed you away. When I was getting on with my life, I pushed you even more, insisting on my way or the highway. And then, when you needed me to believe that you were being threatened by someone, I brushed it aside. The conclusion of the authorities in Rose Arbor only strengthened my belief that you were making too much of it. Not that it's any excuse for my behavior. I should have been on your side, and instead, I pushed you away once again and immersed myself in my work. Thanks to Dr. Milgrim, I'm only now coming to terms with how badly I've treated you and how forgiving you've been through it all."

"There's nothing to forgive, Dad." She brushed a kiss over his cheek. "But I'm glad you turned to Dr. Milgrim for some help."

"She's made me see so much that I'd overlooked. I want to learn to balance my work and my life. I want to see you succeed at whatever you do. I want to enjoy your friendship, as well as your love. I hope, when we get back to Rose Arbor, we can start fresh."

Avery squeezed his hand. "I want that, too."

At a tap on the door, Avery called, "Please come in."

Meg looked in on them. "Am I interrupting?"

"No." Avery pushed away from the table and crossed to her. "Dad and I are fine now." She looked past Meg to see the entire family waiting just beyond the door. "Please come in. This is your space."

As the others filed past, Meg took Avery's hands in hers and realized they were cold. "Honey, if your dad can spare you, why don't you go upstairs and take a nice hot shower."

Avery glanced down at herself, noting for the first time her filthy clothes, her arms scratched and bloody, and gave a weary nod.

When she was gone, Brand turned away and left the room.

In an aside, Casey muttered, "What the hell's going on with my big brother? I don't think I've ever seen Brand this quiet."

"I'd say," Bo remarked softly, "my boy has a lot on his mind."

*   *   *

Brand paused outside Avery's door, hand lifted to knock, when he heard the sound of water running.

He debated letting himself in but then turned and descended the stairs to the landing.

In his room he undressed and stepped under the shower spray, wishing he could as easily wash away the fear and desperation he'd felt while searching for Avery.

He'd always thought of himself as fearless, but the thought of losing Avery to that madwoman had sheer panic clogging his throat. Seeing Avery, bruised and bloody, with that syringe at her neck had torn at his heart. He had meant what he'd said to Renee. He would have given anything, even his life, to keep Avery safe.

He had his wish.

As he toweled himself dry and dressed in clean clothes, he couldn't stop thinking about the irony of their situation. Avery was safe. How could he wish for more?

But he did.

He wanted her here. And that wish wasn't going to be granted. Her father had every right to want to take his daughter back home where he could keep her safe. Wasn't that what every father wanted? Time for her to recover from this terrifying ordeal. Time to rebuild their relationship.

Time.

All Brand wanted was the time to make up for the way he'd treated her when she'd first arrived. Time to let her know how much she'd come to mean to him. Time to show her, in every way, how much he loved her.

What would he do when she left? All the time in the world wouldn't be enough to fill the empty place in his heart without her. But what right did he have to ask her to stay? She deserved to have this time with her often-absent father. To feel loved and cherished by him.

Hadn't Dr. Grant said he wanted to make up for the past?

Brand stepped out of his room and descended the stairs, his teeth clenched, jaw rigid, as he faced the painful truth.

If he truly loved Avery, he had to do the right thing, the noble thing, and keep his feelings to himself so that she could leave here with no hesitation.

He just prayed he could get through this without doing something foolish. Like breaking down and begging.

CHAPTER THIRTY-FIVE

Brand descended the stairs and followed the sound of voices to the back porch, where everyone had gathered, talking in low tones.

As soon as he stepped outside, Avery's father separated himself from the others and hurried forward. "Avery has been telling me how you offered yourself to Nurse Wilmot in Avery's place." He stuck out his hand. "I can't thank you enough. That was really heroic."

Brand accepted his handshake. "Anybody would have done the same."

"I doubt that." Dr. Grant studied him carefully. "I owe you big-time. I'll never forget this, Brand."

At the sound of the doctor's cell phone, he answered before turning to Avery. "The plane has landed, honey. By the time we get to the fairgrounds, they'll have finished refueling and be ready to take off. We'll need a ride to town."

"I have a rental car." Avery looked past her father toward Brand, who forced himself to meet her look with no emotion.

Meg, watching the strained interaction between her grandson and Avery, spoke gently. "Brand, maybe you could drive them to the fairgrounds and then turn in the car in town. Casey and Jonah, why don't you two follow along so you can drive Brand back here?"

With an effort, Brand nodded and held out his hand for the key.

Without a word, Avery handed it over, and he made his way to the vehicle barn to retrieve her rental car.

As he drove up, the family gathered around to hug and kiss Avery. After the Merrick family said their goodbyes, Dr. Grant opened the back door of the car and stowed Avery's bag before helping her inside. He settled himself in the front passenger seat and they all waved as Brand put the car in gear and they began moving along the curving driveway.

Brand glanced in the rearview mirror to see the ranch truck following behind.

Though he wasn't aware of it, his gaze softened as he caught sight of Avery staring at him with a look of sadness.

"So, Brand." Dr. Grant struggled to engage Brand in small talk to fill the strained silence he sensed between his daughter and this stranger. "Was my daughter able to help you?"

"Help me?" Brand kept his attention on the road as they turned onto the highway leading to town.

"With physical therapy. I'm afraid I never asked Avery what your health problem was."

"A limp from a fall."

"Oh. Well, she must have had success. I haven't noticed you limping."

"Not anymore. Your daughter corrected the problem."

"Well, that's good news. Would you say she's good at her job?"

"Of course."

The doctor turned to smile at Avery. "Maybe Brand will go online and give a recommendation. Enough of those will go a long way in moving you up the ladder to a position of authority."

"I like what I'm doing, Dad."

"Of course. And you're good at it. But everybody wants to move up. I wouldn't be surprised if the hospital board is already keeping their eye on you. The director of the physical therapy program is nearing retirement." He took in a breath. "We have a lot to catch up on, honey. I've been way too busy lately, and I want to make it up to you."

Brand watched Avery in his rearview mirror. Though she was pale and the scratches on her face from Renee's nails stood out in sharp relief, it was her silence that worried him more.

Was she wishing, as he did, that they'd had more time?

He dismissed that thought out of hand. Her pallor told him she was in shock. This horrible incident was simply too much to process in so little time. But her father was a doctor. She was going back to a hospital, where medical people trained in trauma would be there to treat her properly.

Whatever selfish wish he harbored for himself needed to be put aside for her welfare. It didn't matter if his heart was already breaking at the thought of losing her. What mattered was Avery. Only Avery.

As they neared the fairgrounds, they could see the small, sleek plane shining in the waning light. Workers moved around it, running through their checklist before takeoff.

Brand had a sudden urge to stop the car and ask Avery

to walk with him. There was so much he wanted to say to her. So many things he was feeling that needed to be expressed.

"Right up there will be fine," Dr. Grant said.

Brand clenched his jaw and pulled up beside the plane.

Dr. Grant stepped out and held the door for Avery, while Brand reached in and removed her suitcase.

It was so light. So little to show for the time they'd spent together.

Dr. Grant put his arm around his daughter and moved with her toward the steps of the plane.

A man in uniform greeted them, while a second uniformed man accepted the bag from Brand's hand.

When her father indicated that she should precede him, Avery held back. "I need a minute, Dad."

Turning to Brand, she realized he'd already stepped away.

She crossed the distance and stopped. "This has all happened so fast."

"Yeah." It was the only word he could manage. *Say something. Say you want her to stay.*

"I wish..." *Say something. Ask me to stay.*

She put a hand on his and saw him flinch.

Flinch? Because of her touch?

She was so hurt by his reaction she lowered her hand to her side and took a step back as though slapped. "I wish we hadn't been so rushed..."

He held up a hand to interrupt. "I don't blame your father. The sooner he can get you home, the sooner he can be assured that his little girl is okay. That's what dads do."

"Is that what your dad would do?"

"No need to ask. Look how we all fretted over Liz.

And now, thanks to you, she's coming out of that cave she'd been hiding in."

He took another step back, as though easing himself into their final goodbye.

"Well…" She folded her hands together to keep from reaching out to him. "My time with you…your family was special. I'll never forget you…any of you. Please thank them for everything."

He nodded.

She bit her lip before saying, "Goodbye, Brand."

Her father called from the top of the steps.

She continued standing there until she felt tears welling up.

Ashamed to embarrass herself in front of Brand, she turned away and started toward the plane.

"Avery."

Hearing Brand's voice, she looked over her shoulder.

He was standing beside the rental car. He'd slipped on his sunglasses, making it impossible to see his eyes.

Please, Brand, say something.

She paused and heard only the drone of the plane's engines.

Lifting her head, she strode to the stairs and climbed aboard.

Casey and Jonah had stepped out of the truck and began walking toward their brother.

Casey was saying something, but Brand was unable to hear anything except his own voice shouting, "Wait."

He was running, though he couldn't feel his legs. With a final burst of speed, he reached the plane's steps before they could be lifted.

Avery was seated in a high-backed leather chair that

faced a similar seat across the narrow aisle where her father was just strapping in.

Through a mist of tears, Avery saw that familiar tall, rangy figure coming toward her. Was he real, or had the sheen of tears blurred her vision?

He was wearing faded jeans and scuffed Western boots. In his hand was a wide-brimmed hat. His dark hair was in need of a trim, curling around the collar of his plaid shirt. And he looked as he had the first time she'd seen him. Stern and ready to do battle.

"Brand." His name was torn from her lips.

"I thought I could let you go. I want you to know I really tried."

She sat perfectly still, wanting to fling herself into his arms and hold on forever but unable to move.

Neither of them seemed aware of the two pilots who were looking from Avery to Brand and back again, nor her father, who did the same.

Brand dropped to his knees, kneeling before her and threading his fingers with hers. "Back there in the woods, when I didn't know if we would have any more time, I thought about all the things I should have told you. All the pretty words a guy says to the woman who matters more to him than anything in this world."

She was shaking her head, staring down at their hands. "I don't need pretty words."

He touched a hand to her face, forcing her to meet his eyes. "But you deserve them. You came here when I was at a low point, and I was a jerk who treated you like an intruder. You could have walked away, but you stayed and fought for me, and believed in me, and changed my life."

"That's my job."

"Maybe. But then you did something more that isn't in your job description. You touched my heart in a way I never thought possible." His tone gentled, as did his eyes. "I fell. Hard. And I was so surprised, I didn't know how to tell you. I denied. I hedged my bet, thinking it was just"—he shrugged and gave her one of those sexy smiles that always tugged at her heart—"that old devil lust. But now I know better. This is the real thing, tenderfoot. There's no denying any longer. I love you."

She was staring into his eyes with a mixture of shock and tenderness. "After all this? You love me?"

"This, as you call it, spoiled all my plans. I'd hoped to steal you away after our bonfire and declare my intentions, but…"

Her eyes went wide. "Declare your intentions?"

When he merely smiled, she felt her heart tumble in her chest. "And just what are your intentions, cowboy?"

"To ask you to…No. Let me start over. To *beg* you to marry me and let me love you forever."

"Oh, Brand."

Those hated tears started fresh, and she was helpless to stop them.

He wiped her tears with his thumbs and looked at her with those piercing eyes that she'd come to love as much as everything else about him. "I know it isn't fair to ask you to give up everything you've worked for in Michigan just to spend a lifetime with me here in Wyoming, but I can't imagine my life here without you. You mean more to me than my own life." His voice was a husky plea. "Please, Avery, stay here and save me."

She bit back a smile. "Save you? Are you saying you need more therapy?"

"A lot more. A lifetime of it. Please say you love me, too."

"Yes." She leaned close and wrapped her arms around his neck. "Yes. Yes. Yes."

He lifted her off her feet and swung her around before kissing her soundly.

The plane was filled with shouts as the two pilots, the doctor, and Brand's two brothers cheered wildly.

Both Avery and Brand looked around, noticing for the first time that they had an audience.

Brand set her on her feet and offered his hand to her father. "I hope you'll give your approval, Dr. Grant."

Alexander Grant was smiling broadly. "Just when I'm learning how we can be a family again, I learn I'm losing my daughter."

"You'll never lose me, Dad." She looked at Brand, whose smile rivaled the sun. "But right now, I have to be with Brand."

Alexander extended his hand. Brand grasped it in a firm handshake as the plane erupted in more cheers.

Brand caught Avery's hand and the two, laughing like children, walked from the plane, with Casey and Jonah trailing behind.

Both brothers hugged Brand and Avery before starting toward their truck.

Casey turned back. "You two coming?"

Brand smiled at Avery. "We'll follow in the rental car. But don't wait up for us."

Laughing, the two gave him a thumbs-up before climbing into the truck and driving away.

Brand and Avery stood together, waving as the plane taxied down the runway, turned, and lifted into the air.

When they were alone at last, Brand gathered her close

and buried his face in her hair. "Oh, baby, I don't know what I would have done if you hadn't said yes."

"And I don't know what I'd have done if you'd let me leave." She offered her lips for his kiss. "Oh, Brand, I love you so much."

"Not half as much as I love you, tenderfoot. Come on." He grabbed her hand and led her toward the car. "There's this perfect meadow up in the hills where I'd planned on making slow, delicious love with you before declaring my intentions."

"Sounds like heaven."

He leaned close to thoroughly kiss her, feeling his heart begin to slowly settle. "Anyplace with you is heaven, tenderfoot."

EPILOGUE

The late summer sky was so blue it hurt to look at it. The waist-high grass of the hills waved in a light breeze.

The Merrick ranch looked festive, with a long table the length of the big back porch covered with lace and crystal, as Billy worked his magic on a wedding feast.

There were two tall urns at the foot of the porch steps, filled with wildflowers and vines. Billy's special four-tiered wedding cake sat on a side table, along with fancy plates and an ice bucket holding several bottles of champagne.

Upstairs, Avery stepped from her bedroom and did a slow turn, earning approving murmurs from Meg and Liz as the sleek column of ivory silk swirled around her ankles.

On her feet were heeled sandals. In her hair, worn long and loose, was a spray of wildflowers Brand had picked an hour ago.

"Oh, honey." Meg put a hand to her heart. "You're the prettiest bride ever."

Liz gave a laugh. "When my nephew sees you in that, he's going to fall in love all over again."

Avery produced a small white handled bag and handed it to Meg.

Meg looked up. "What's this for?"

"For being my mother and grandmother when I had none."

"Oh, Avery." Meg opened the lid to find a silver chain on which dangled a cameo locket. The woman's profile, carved in mother-of-pearl, looked exactly like Meg.

Avery fastened it around Meg's neck. Seeing her reflection, the older woman wiped away a tear as she wrapped her arms around Avery and hugged her fiercely. "I love it. And I'll wear it always."

Avery handed Liz a similar bag. "For my maid of honor."

With a laugh, Liz opened the small box inside and gasped at the pearl and ruby pin showing a camera. "Push this tiny button," Avery said.

When Liz touched it, the camera revealed an image in the viewfinder of a rearing black horse.

"How in the world did you find something so perfect?" Liz asked as she pinned it to her pale blush gown.

"I found it online. And I couldn't resist."

"Thank you." Liz kissed her cheek, and the two young women hugged. "I'm so glad to have another female in the family." She turned to her mother, who nodded her agreement.

Brand's voice, outside the door, called, "Reverend Lawson is here, and that crowd downstairs is eager for a wedding."

Liz opened the door and she and Meg walked out, leaving Avery alone.

Brand stood perfectly still, staring at her with a look that was nearly blinding in its intensity.

He started toward her, shaking his head. "You're so beautiful. You take my breath away."

"Good. I hope I always have that effect on you, cowboy."

"Count on it." He brushed a kiss over her cheek before pulling his hand from behind his back. He handed her a bouquet of wildflowers and trailing ivy.

She buried her face in it and inhaled the perfume. "Thank you."

"Thank you, tenderfoot, for saving my poor heart." He took her hand. "Are you ready to take a leap of faith?"

"I've never been more ready." She absorbed the warmth of his hand holding hers. "How about you?"

"I said I'd walk through fire for you, baby. And with all those nosy neighbors outside, I feel like I'm about to."

Laughing, they walked down the stairs and paused in the great room where the family was waiting.

Avery's father stood beside Ham and Egan, looking so proud and happy in his dark suit and tie.

Casey, wearing a crisp white shirt and string tie, his old scuffed boots polished to a high shine, clapped a hand on his big brother's shoulder before hugging Avery. "I can't believe you could love a grumpy guy like Brand."

"When he's not grumpy, he's pretty amazing. You should have seen him up in the hills . . ."

Casey covered his ears. "Too much information."

Jonah shook his brother's hand and kissed Avery's cheek. "You've got the healing touch, Avery. Or maybe it's the magic touch. Whatever you've got, I hope it keeps working on Brand. I've never seen my big brother this mellow."

Bo hugged his son and then hugged Avery. "After three sons, I'm finally gaining a daughter."

Egan was all smiles as he hugged and kissed both Brand and Avery.

Hammond waited until everyone else had congratulated the happy couple before stepping forward.

He looked his great-grandson in the eye and said sternly, "I always knew you were smart."

"I get that from you, Ham. I guess this means you approve of my choice of bride?"

"I knew she was right for you before you did, boy. I was just afraid you'd let her get away." The two shared a knowing smile.

The old man gathered Avery into his arms. Against her cheek he whispered, "I'm so glad you're staying. You're a fine addition to the family, girl."

Avery felt a mist of tears and blinked hard. She wanted nothing to mar this occasion. "Thank you, Ham."

"Come on," Dr. Grant called. "I can't wait to walk with my daughter on her wedding day."

All their friends and neighbors had gathered on the porch, delighted to be invited to witness the marriage of another generation of Merricks.

The family stepped out the door and took their places as Avery and her father walked toward Brand, standing tall and straight as an oak beside old Reverend Lawson.

Afterward, they feasted on Billy's beef tenderloin and garlic mashed potatoes, along with marinated vegetables fresh from the greenhouse.

After many champagne toasts, they cut the cake, topped by figures of a cowboy, in jeans and a Stetson, and a dark-haired woman wearing a lab coat and carrying a medical bag.

As day faded into evening, the bride and groom slipped away to change into jeans and boots before waving to friends and family and climbing into one of the ranch trucks that had been loaded with enough supplies for a week.

After waving goodbye to the others, they veered off the road and started up toward a distant meadow.

Brand caught Avery's hand in his and brought it to his lips. "A week in the wilderness. Just the two of us."

"And deer and mustangs, and maybe that mountain goat."

"As long as they don't interrupt what I have in mind, tenderfoot."

"Dr. Peterson already has half a dozen patients lined up for me. I may have to hire a team of physical therapists."

"If you want, you can have an entire clinic at your disposal. Just as long as you come home to me every night, for my very own therapy."

"I promise."

As the truck climbed higher, they caught sight of a herd of mustangs, and Brand watched the way Avery's eyes lit with pleasure. Who would have ever believed that one woman, armed with patience and determination and a sense of wonder, could change his life so completely?

"Are we there yet?"

He closed a hand over hers. "Yeah, babe. We're right where we should be. Together forever."

BILLY'S STRAWBERRY SHORTCAKE

Ingredients:
2 pounds strawberries, washed, stemmed, and quartered
9 tablespoons sugar

Shortcake:
2 cups all-purpose flour
2 teaspoons baking powder
¼ teaspoon baking soda
2 tablespoons sugar
¾ teaspoon salt
1½ cups heavy cream

Whipped Cream:
2 cups heavy cream, ice cold
3 tablespoons sugar
1½ teaspoons vanilla extract
1 teaspoon freshly grated lemon zest (optional)

Directions:
Mix strawberries with 7 tablespoons sugar and re-
frigerate for an hour to allow juices to gather.

Preheat oven to 400°F.

Sift together the flour, baking powder, baking soda,
remaining 2 tablespoons sugar, and salt in a medium
bowl. Add heavy cream and mix until just combined.
Place mixture in an ungreased pan or a pan lined with
parchment and bake until golden, 18 to 20 minutes.

Remove cake from pan and place on a rack to cool
slightly. Cut into pieces and split each piece in half.

Spoon some of the strawberries with their juice onto
each shortcake bottom. Top with a generous dollop of

whipped cream or ice cream and then the shortcake top. Spoon more strawberries over the top and serve.

Whipped Cream:

Using a mixer, beat the heavy, very cold cream until soft peaks form, about 1½ to 2 minutes, gradually adding the sugar, vanilla, and (optional) lemon zest.

A perfect ending to a perfect meal, especially if it is enjoyed on the porch while watching a glorious sunset over the Grand Tetons in Wyoming.

ABOUT THE AUTHOR

New York Times bestselling author R. C. Ryan has written more than a hundred novels, both contemporary and historical. Quite an accomplishment for someone who, after her fifth child started school, gave herself the gift of an hour a day to follow her dream to become a writer.

In a career spanning more than thirty years, Ms. Ryan has given dozens of radio, television, and print interviews across the country and Canada, and has been quoted in such diverse publications as the *Wall Street Journal* and *Cosmopolitan*. She has also appeared on CNN News and *Good Morning America*.

You can learn more about R. C. Ryan—and her alter ego Ruth Ryan Langan—at:

RyanLangan.com
Twitter @RuthRyanLangan
Facebook.com

For a bonus story from another author that you'll love, please turn the page to read *Cowboy Rebel* by Carolyn Brown.

Ever since losing his best friend in a motorcycle accident, Taggart Baker wants to make every moment count. No dare is too dangerous, no adventure too crazy for this cowboy. But after one bad brush with the law, he realizes it's time to ditch his hooligan friends and grow up. But just as Tag seems ready to settle down for good, his troubled past comes calling—and this time he won't be able to walk away so easily.

FOREVER

To my cousins
Marthanna Goshorn and Brenda Long,
who love cowboys as much as I do!!

Dear Readers,

As I finish *Cowboy Rebel*, fall is arriving in Sunset, Texas, where the Longhorn Canyon Ranch is located. Y'all will be reading it just as summer is starting, so grab a glass of sweet tea, curl up on a porch swing, and enjoy the story. I was privileged to get to see the cover for this book before I even began to write it. Tag Baker was exactly as I'd pictured him in my mind— blue eyed, hair just a little too long, a slight cleft in his chin, and a swagger to his walk. That last part I couldn't actually see in the picture, but my imagination is very good when it comes to cowboys!

As always, I have a bushel basket of thanks to pass out today. The first one goes to all my fantastic fans who continue to support me by not only buying my books, but also by recommending them to their friends, talking about them at book clubs, writing reviews, and sending notes and messages to me personally. Please know that each and every one of you is precious and appreciated more than you'll ever know.

If my thanks were medals instead of heartfelt gratitude, Leah Hultenschmidt would get a gold one for everything she does to help me take a rough idea and turn it into an emotionally charged book. And my team at Grand Central/Forever, who do everything from copyedits to covers, promotions to sales, would have medals hanging around their necks for all their hard work behind the scenes.

As always, there are no words to truly say how much I appreciate my agent, Erin Niumata, and the staff at Folio Literary Management. Y'all are simply the best and deserve a bushel basket of thanks all of your own.

Last, but never least—thank you to my husband of fifty-two years, Mr. B. He's stood beside me through the thick and the thin of this writing career and continues to be my biggest supporter.

Keep your reading glasses close by after you finish *Cowboy Rebel*, because there's more on the way. Maverick tells me that he's feeling the magic of Christmas in the air, and Paxton and Hud are trying to convince me that they're not ever going to fall in love. Shhhh...don't tell anyone, but I know better.

Until next time, happy reading!
Carolyn Brown

Cowboy Rebel

Chapter One

W hat can I get you, cowboy?" The cute blonde whipped a towel from her hip pocket and wiped down the bar in front of him.

He tipped his cowboy hat back just a little so he could see her better. "A double shot of Knob Creek. Where's Joe tonight?"

"He works Saturday. I get Thursday and Friday," she answered. "Haven't seen you before."

"I only moved here a couple of months ago. My brother and I usually come in on Saturday nights. But we might change our days." He winked.

"Oh, and why's that?" She set his whiskey in front of him.

"You're prettier than Joe."

"I've heard that line before." She moved down the bar to draw up another beer for the woman sitting at the far end and then worked her way back down to him, her ponytail flipping back and forth as she went from customer to customer.

"Ready for another?" she asked when she was in front of him.

"Not yet. This stuff is sippin' whiskey, so I enjoy it a little at a time."

The folks between him and the woman down on the end were quick to leave the bar when Jake Owen's "Down to the Honkytonk" started playing on the jukebox. They soon formed a line dance, and the noise of their boots on the wood floor competed with the loud song.

He motioned for the bartender to bring him another drink and had just taken the first sip when a big, burly man burst into the bar and stormed across the floor with his hands knotted into fists the size of Christmas hams.

"I knew I'd find you here," the guy yelled above the music and dancers when he reached Tag.

The man bumped Tag on the shoulder when he passed by him. Tag spilled the rest of his whiskey down the front of his shirt. In Tag's way of thinking, it was a shame to waste even a drop of good Knob Creek.

He spun around on the barstool. "Hey, now."

"I'm not talkin' to you, so turn around and shut up. I'm talkin' to my woman down there." He pointed to the other end of the bar. "When she gets mad at me, she always shows up here."

"Well, you spilled my drink, so you should buy me another one," Tag said.

"I ain't buyin' you jack shit." The guy took a few steps and grabbed the woman by the arm. "Come on, Scarlett, we're goin' home."

She slid off the stool, shook off his hand, and got right up nose to nose with him. "I'm not going anywhere with you. If you want a woman, go get Ramona. I'm goin' to finish my drink and then have another one or two."

"I told you that she was a mistake. I broke up with her weeks ago, so don't give me that old shit." He drew back his hand as if to slap her, but instead grabbed a handful of her hair and jerked her to his chest. "I said you're coming home. I made a mistake but so did you. I wasn't the only one cheatin', and I damn sure wasn't the first one."

A bouncer who looked more like a strutting little banty rooster hurried across the room, got between them, and demanded that the guy leave. Tag could see from the fire in the bigger man's eyes that he wasn't going anywhere. And the stance that the bouncer had taken said he wasn't backing down either. It wasn't one bit of Tag's business, but the man had caused him to spill whiskey on his favorite shirt. While he slid off the stool, the jukebox began to blast out Trace Adkins singing "Whoop a Man's Ass." Now, that was an omen to Tag's way of thinking, especially when the words said something about cussin' and roughin' up a lady.

He took a few long strides and stood beside the bouncer. "The lady says that she's not going home with you," Tag said. "It'd be wise if you just scooted on out of here."

The big fellow put his hands on Tag's chest and pushed. Tag grabbed for anything that would keep him from falling and got a handful of a shirt. The bouncer fell into the woman and they fell into a pile. Before Tag could get out of the tangle of arms and legs and find his hat, Scarlett kicked the man in the knee about a half dozen times. He went down like a big oak tree, landing to one side of the pile.

"You bitch," he growled as he popped up to a sitting position and grabbed a beer bottle from a nearby table, slammed it on the floor, shattering the bottom half into a million pieces. "You know that's my bum knee." He drew back the bottle to hit her with it, but she ducked.

The bottle slashed right across Tag's chiseled jawline.

Tag had always considered himself a lover, not a fighter, but there was something about his own blood dripping on his new Western shirt that brought out the anger. Then he noticed that his best cowboy hat was now ruined with beer splatter and cast-off blood drops. He popped up on his feet, hands clenched in fists, ready to fight, but the bouncer had brought out an equalizer in the form of a Taser. A picture of David in the Bible came to Tag's mind as the man dropped to the floor and began to quiver. Amazing what a rock and a slingshot or a little jolt of electricity in today's world could do to a giant.

"You've killed my husband! He's got a bad heart," Scarlett screamed. "I'll sue the whole damn lot of you! Call an ambulance!"

"No!" the big man yelled from the floor, where he was still twitching. "Take me home. Cops will haul me into jail for assault on that cowboy."

Through a red haze of anger and pain, Tag could see that the bartender was already on the phone. He picked up his hat, settled it on his head, and slipped out of the bar before anyone could rope him into testifying or giving his story.

"Glad I didn't drive my motorcycle tonight," he grumbled as he got into his black Silverado.

He removed his plaid shirt and held pressure on the cut with one hand while he started the truck engine with the other. The hospital emergency room was the first place he'd checked out when he'd moved to Montague County the previous month. That information was pretty damned important when he lived by the words of his two bumper stickers. One said ONCE A REBEL, ALWAYS A REBEL. The other was the title of Tim McGraw's country song LIVE LIKE YOU WERE DYING.

He'd barely gotten out on the highway when blood started

to seep through his fingertips and drip onto his snowy white T-shirt. He hoped that the doctor would throw some super-glue and bandages on it and that it would heal up without too much of a scar.

The only parking place he could find was all the way across the lot. By the time he made it to the door in the heat, he was getting more than a little woozy. The walls of the empty emergency room did a couple of wavy spins when he stepped inside. A nurse looked up from the desk and yelled something, but it sounded like it was coming through a barrel full of water.

Then suddenly someone shoved him into a wheelchair, took him into a curtained examination area, helped him up onto a narrow bed, and turned on a bright light above his head. He expected to see his whole life begin to flash before his eyes any minute, but instead Nikki Grady, his sister's best friend, took the shirt from his hand.

"Want me to call Emily?" she asked.

"Hell no! Call Hud. His number is on the speed dial on my phone. It's in my hip pocket," he muttered.

"What happened?" she asked. "Looks like you were the only one at a knife fight without a knife."

"Beer bottle." Tag tried to grin but it hurt like hell. "Just glue me up. Give it a kiss to help it heal and call my brother Hud."

"Honey, with this much blood loss and the fact that I'm lookin' at your bone, it's goin' to take more than glue and a kiss," Nikki said.

*   *   *

Taggart, or Tag as the family called him, was one of those men who turned every woman's eye when he walked into a place—even a hospital emergency room. The nurses, old and young alike, were buzzing about him before Nikki even got him into the cubicle. With that chiseled face, those piercing blue eyes, a cowboy swagger, and a smile that would make a religious woman want to drink whiskey and do the two-step, it's a wonder he hadn't already put one of those "take a number and wait" machines on the front porch post of his house.

"The doctor is on his way. He just finished stitchin' up a patient with a knife wound. From the looks of you, I'd think you'd been in on that fight." Nikki applied pressure to the cut with a wad of gauze.

The curtain between the cubicles flew to one side, and a white-coated guy came over to the bed. "What have we got here? I'm Dr. Richards." He gently lifted the edge of the gauze. "Knife?"

"Beer bottle," Tag said.

"Well, the first thing we have to do is shave off that scruff. Deaden it up and then shave off the area around it, Nikki. I'll take care of the kid who thought he could ride his skateboard down a slide, and I'll be right back," Dr. Richards said.

"Yes, sir." Nikki nodded.

The doctor had been instrumental in getting Nikki her first job as a registered nurse, and she really admired him. An older man with a white rim of hair around an otherwise bald head covered in freckles, he was the best when it came to stitches, in Nikki's opinion. Tag was a lucky cowboy that Dr. Richards was on call that night. It could have been an intern doing the embroidery on his face, and it would be such a shame to leave a scar on something that sexy.

"You still going to go out with me even though I'm clean shaven and got a scar?" Tag asked her as she prepared to shave part of his face.

"If I don't work, I don't eat, and I'm real fond of cheese-burgers," she answered.

"What's that supposed to mean?" He winced when she picked up a needle to start the local anesthetic.

"That I don't have time to take a number and wait in line behind all those other women wanting to get a chance at taming you," she answered.

He wrapped his hand around her wrist before she started. "I'd move you to the front of the line, darlin'."

"Well, ain't that sweet." She patted his hand and ignored the heat between them. "But, honey, you're way too fast for this little country girl. Now be still and let me get this ready for Dr. Richards."

Without blinking, he focused on her face as she sank the needle into several places to deaden the two-inch cut. Whispers of other conversations penetrated the curtains on either side of Tag's cubicle, but heavy silence filled the space while Nikki put in the last shot.

"That all?" he finally asked, but his piercing blue eyes didn't leave her face.

"Except for cleaning up around it," she answered. "And you were a good boy. I'll tell Dr. Richards to give you a lollipop before you leave."

"It ain't my first rodeo," he said. "Did you call Hud?"

"Not yet," she said.

"Then don't."

"With the amount of blood you've lost and the shot Doc will probably give you for pain, you'll need a driver or you won't be released," she said. "So it's Hud or Emily. Take your choice."

"You're a hard woman, Nikki," he said.

"And you're a hardheaded man," she shot back as she carefully shaved the scruff from around the wound.

"We ready to fix this cowboy up?" Dr. Richards threw back the curtain. "What'd the other guy look like?"

"Not a scratch on him, but he was limpin'. His woman tried to kick his kneecap halfway to Georgia," Tag answered.

Dr. Richards chuckled. "And I bet you were defendin' her in some way."

Tag grimaced when he tried to smile. "Just helpin' out the bouncer a little. Seemed like the thing to do since 'Whoop a Man's Ass' was playin' on the jukebox."

"Well, looks like you was the one who got the whuppin'." Dr. Richards chuckled and turned to Nikki. "Good job there, Nikki. Now it's my turn. We could try glue and strips, but as deep as this is, stitches will do a better job."

"You're the doctor," Tag answered.

"It's up to you whether you shave your face clean when you get home, but if you don't, you're going to look a little like a mangy dog."

"Looked worse before," Tag drawled. "And probably will again."

A lady in pink scrubs poked her head between the curtains.

"What do you need, Rosemary?" Dr. Richards asked the nurse.

"Sue Ann just arrived. Nikki handles her better than any of us. Would you mind if I help out here and she takes that job?"

"Go on," Dr. Richards said. "I've got this."

"Where is she?" Nikki asked as she pushed back the curtain. Rosemary had fast become her friend since they both worked the weekend shift. The woman was average in every way—brown hair, brown eyes, but her sense of humor and smile were infectious.

"I'll show you and then get right back in there with Doc."
Rosemary led the way. "Lord have mercy." She laid one
hand over her heart and fanned her face with the other one.
"That cowboy could melt my panties with those blue eyes."

"Sue Ann strung out or drunk?" Nikki liked Rosemary,
loved working with her, but she was always teasing Nikki
about settling down and getting married.

"Maybe both. Did I hear you turn that man down when
he asked you for a date? Are you bat crap crazy?" Rosemary
asked.

"You're married and have four kids," Nikki said.

"And I'm on a diet, too, but that don't mean I can't
stare in the window at the candy store." Rosemary laughed.
"Oh, there's another good-lookin' cowboy out in the waiting room who says he's here for Tag. Want me to let him
come on back?"

"I'll get him if you'll keep Sue Ann pacified for another
minute." Nikki made a quick right turn.

Tag's twin brother, Hudson, stood up when he saw her.
"How bad is it this time?"

She motioned for him to follow her. "Stitches on his jaw.
The cut was deep. Doc's takin' care of him right now."

Nikki had had no trouble seeing that the Baker brothers
shared DNA from the first time she met them. The cleft
in Tag's chin was more pronounced, and he wore his hair
longer than Hud did, but those crystal clear blue eyes were
the same. Even with those similarities, there were enough
differences between them that she could hardly believe they
were twins. However, they were pretty true to what she'd
heard about it taking two personalities to make one when
it came to twins. Tag was the wild and crazy one. Hud, the
more grounded brother with a funny streak and a big heart.

"Right here." Nikki eased aside the curtain to Tag's cubicle.

"What'd you do now?" Hud asked.

"Had a little run-in with a beer bottle," Tag answered.

Nikki hurried away to take care of Sue Ann, their regular weekend patient in the Bowie emergency room. Some folks were happy drunks, but not Sue Ann. When she had too much liquor or snorted too much white stuff up her nose, she became the poster child for hypochondria.

"Oh, Nikki, darlin'." Sue Ann slurred her words. "Just take me on into surgery and take out my stomach. It's got an alien in it that's trying to eat its way out through my belly button."

"I need a list of all the medicine you've taken since you were here last week, and whatever you've ingested in the way of alcohol or drugs in the past twelve hours— no, make that twenty-four hours—before we can do that, honey." Nikki pulled a stylus from the pocket of her scrubs and was ready to write before she realized she didn't have her tablet. "You think about what you've had, Sue Ann. Things are hectic here tonight. I'll be right back."

"All done," Dr. Richards said as Nikki slipped inside to get her tablet. "You see to it that you call my office tomorrow and make an appointment for next Friday so I can check this. If you start running a fever, call me. I think Nikki did a good job of cleaning it up, but one never knows when it comes to bar floors and beer bottles."

"I'm riding a bull at a rodeo on Friday night," Tag said.

"We'll see about that." Doc turned to Hud. "Make your brother behave this week."

"That's an impossible job." Hud grinned.

"Then I'll admit him for a week. We've got restraints that we can use to keep him in the bed, and the nurses will love taking care of his catheter." Doc winked at Hud.

"I'll be good," Tag growled. "But I don't have to like it."

"Give me your truck keys. Paxton is out in the waiting room. He's going to drive it home, and I'm taking you," Hud said.

"I'll call if I need you," Nikki said as she picked up her tablet. When she reached Sue Ann's cubicle, the woman was sitting up in the bed. She was as pale as the sheet she tucked around her thin body. One hand was over her mouth and the other was pointing toward the bathroom. Nikki dropped her tablet on the table and barely got a disposable bag to Sue Ann in time.

When she finished emptying her stomach, Sue Ann handed the bag to Nikki and said, "I had a little drop of tequila at the Rusty Spur tonight."

"How big of a drop?" Nikki picked up her tablet and stylus. "Tell me the truth. If we have to do surgery, it'll make a difference in how much anesthetic we give you. You wouldn't want to wake up before we got done, would you?"

"Five shots. No, six, and then maybe four"—she lowered her voice to a whisper—"of those pills."

"What pills?" Nikki asked.

"The ones I bought from that cowboy who was dancin' with the pretty girl. That damned alien got in my stomach. They told me it was just the worm in the bottle of tequila when I ate it with a little lime and salt, but I know better. It looked like a baby alien, and I just swallowed it whole. Then my stomach started to burn and hurt. I saw that cowboy passing some pills to a lady, so I bought some from him."

Nikki thought she'd seen and heard everything when she worked at the nursing home in town, but this would be a story she'd have to share with her best friend, Emily. "Okay, then several shots of tequila and pills of some kind. I think we can kill the alien and fix you right up without surgery."

Sue Ann fell back on the bed with a sigh. "I don't know about that. Don't you need to do one of them TSA things?"

Nikki bit back a giggle. "You mean an MRI?"

"That too. Do all the tests you need to. I want this thing out of me." Sue Ann put a hand on her stomach.

"I'll talk to the doctor and be right back. Are you still taking..." Nikki read off a whole page of prescription drugs. "You do realize that you're not supposed to drink with about half of these or take street drugs with them?"

"I know my body better than you do," Sue Ann declared. "My grandma drank every day of her life and she lived to be ninety-eight."

"Yes, ma'am," Nikki said. "I'll go talk to the doctor and be right back."

She stepped out of the cubicle, tablet in hand this time, and stopped so fast that her rubber-soled shoes squeaked on the tile floor. One more step and she would have collided with Tag.

"It's just not my night." He smiled down at her. "I get in trouble for taking up for a woman, and now one almost falls into my arms but doesn't."

"It might be a sign that you need to peel those stickers off your truck and begin to reform a little," Nikki told him.

"Never." Tag grinned.

Chapter Two

If the next door neighbor's dogs hadn't set up a barking chorus with the landlady's mutts, Nikki might have slept until dark on Monday. That would have been disastrous since her mother expected her to answer the phone at exactly seven o'clock. If she didn't answer, then her mother would call the police station and the hospitals. Any other day of the week, it didn't matter if Nikki was lying in a ditch half dead, but no one had better mess with Wilma Grady's schedule.

"Thank God for barking dogs," Nikki said as she crawled out of bed. She had an hour until her mother called, so she took a quick shower and got dressed. She sat down on the sofa in her tiny three-room garage apartment and called her mother's number.

"It's not seven. My show isn't over, but there's a commercial, so what's wrong?" Wilma said curtly.

"Nothing's wrong. I thought maybe we'd go out, or I'd

bring a pizza or some fried chicken over for supper and we could visit in person," Nikki said.

"I eat at four thirty so I can take my medicine. I don't eat fried foods or spicy pizza. You know that, Nikki. The commercial is over. I'll call you at seven and we'll visit." And just like that she was gone.

Nikki was hungry, and she'd figured out that she didn't have to be in her apartment to talk to her mother on Monday nights at seven o'clock on the dot. She could talk to her anywhere, especially when Nikki's part of the conversation was nothing more than muttering, "Well, that's too bad," or "Bless her heart," now and then. She could do that in a booth at the Mexican place or sitting in the park while she ate a hamburger. With her purse and keys in hand, she locked the apartment door behind her. She made up her mind as she started the car engine that chicken enchiladas sounded really good that evening.

The hair on the back of her neck prickled when she walked into the restaurant. At first she attributed it to leaving the sweltering night air and coming into a cool building. Then she heard her name and turned to see Tag and Hud sitting in a booth, waving at her to join them.

It would be rude not to sit with them. They were, after all, her best friend's brothers. Besides, the place was full and there were no more seats available. She threw up a hand in a wave and started that way. When she got close enough, Tag slid over to the far side of the booth to allow room for her to sit beside him.

"How's the jaw? I see you opted to look like a mangy dog, rather than go clean shaven for a few days," she said.

"Sore as the devil, but it'll get well. Maybe you'll take pity on a poor old hungry dog and go out with him?" Tag cocked his head to one side and whimpered like a puppy.

Nikki grabbed a menu and propped it up in front of her. "You don't look like you're starving to me."

"You've met your match, Tag. You might as well admit defeat." Hud grinned.

"Why's it so important for me to go out with you anyway?" Nikki asked.

"Because he's never been rejected, not one time in his whole life," Hud answered.

Nikki reached up and gently patted him on the cheek. "Poor baby."

He grabbed her hand, brought her knuckles to his lips, and kissed each one. Sparks flitted around her like Fourth of July fireworks. It had been that way since the first time she met him, and then again a month ago at Emily's wedding to Justin Maguire. She'd served as maid of honor. Tag and Hud had both been groomsmen, and Tag had glued himself to her side all evening. As much as Nikki would have liked to be the maid of honor who went to bed with one of the groomsmen like in the movies, she wasn't interested in a one-night stand—not even with the supersexy Taggart Baker. And any kind of fleeting relationship she might have with Tag could complicate her friendship with Emily. No way on the great green earth would she ever do that—Emily meant too much to her.

"Why do you just keep breaking my little cowboy heart?" Tag's blue eyes begged for an answer.

"Darlin', you are way too wild for me." She told him the same thing every time he asked.

The waitress finally made it to their table and took their orders, then promptly returned with their drinks, individual bowls of salsa, queso, and a basket of warm chips. "Orders will be along in a few minutes," she said, and then hurried off to clean a table so another group could be seated.

Nikki's phone rang before Tag could come back with one of his famous pickup lines. She dug her cell out of her purse and checked the clock on the wall. It was five minutes until seven, so she was surprised to see her mother's number pop up. Evidently her mother's clock wasn't in sync with the one in the restaurant.

"Hello, Mama." Nikki would have to talk to Wilma or the world would come to an end for sure. She was about to tell the Baker brothers that she had to take the call and motion to the waitress to make her order to go. Then she would sit on the park bench outside until it was ready. But a long sigh preceded a whisper. "Mrs. Thomas from next door came over with a plate of chocolate chip cookies and asked me to make coffee so we can have a visit. I don't know what she's thinkin'. We visit on Tuesday evening at six, never at seven on Monday. She's getting senile and can't remember anything."

"Where is she now?" Nikki asked.

"In the bathroom washing her hands. I'll have to clean the room when she leaves because she always makes a mess, and all she does is gripe about how her kids never come to see her. I wouldn't go in that house either. She's a hoarder. I bet there's roaches in them boxes she's got stacked everywhere."

"Then you want me to call later?" Nikki asked.

"Lord, no, you can't call later. She'll stay until nine and you know that's when I have to get my medicine and then get ready for bed. We'll just have to talk next week," Wilma said. "She's coming out of the bathroom right now." A long sigh and then the screen went dark.

"You need to take your order to go?" Hud asked.

Nikki dropped the phone back into her purse. "No, Mama has company, so I'll talk to her later. We usually have a catchin' up visit on Monday nights."

"Only once a week?" Tag said.

"The first week we were on our ranch, Mama called twice, sometimes three times a day," Hud said.

Tag winced when he grinned. "Mama missed her pretty babies."

Hud chuckled. "Yeah, right. She's just afraid that you'll kill your fool self. From the look of your jawbone, she came close to being right. I told her this morning that you wouldn't be riding bulls on Friday night."

"Well, if a bull comes through named Fumanchu, you can bet your country ass I'll ride him, even if I've got stitches, a broken arm, and a busted up leg."

"You're crazy," Nikki said.

That was another reason she wasn't starting something with this cowboy—not even a first date. When Nikki fell in love, she fell hard, and the way Tag lived, well, he'd never see his first gray hair. She'd never knowingly put herself in that kind of situation.

"Maybe so, but when I check out of this life, I'll be able to say that I lived every single minute," Tag said.

The waitress brought their food, reminded them that the plates were very hot, and then asked, "Need more chips or dip?"

"I'm good," Nikki said.

"Prove it." Tag nudged her shoulder.

Heat popped out in her cheeks in the form of two bright red circles. "You have got to be the biggest flirt I've ever known."

"Thank you. I do my best," Tag said.

*   *   *

Tag and Hud settled their sweat-stained straw hats on their heads as they stepped out of the cool restaurant into the hot night air. Hud's truck was parked down the block with the windows rolled up. When Tag opened the passenger door, it felt like a blast from an oven hit him in the face.

"Hurry up and get this thing started so it will cool down," he said as he got inside.

Hud nodded, started the engine, and turned the A/C as high as it would go. He pulled away from the curb and headed back toward the ranch that he and his brother had bought. It adjoined the huge Longhorn Canyon Ranch, owned by the Maguire family. Their sister, Emily, had married the younger Maguire brother, Justin, and they were about to get their new house ready to move into.

Hud drove west out of town. "We really should name our ranch and get a brand registered."

"I was thinkin' the same thing." Tag smiled and then frowned. "Dammit! This thing hurts like hell when I grin."

"Serves you right for stepping into another couple's fight," Hud told him. "And you weren't really thinkin' about a name for our place. Your mind was still on Nikki Grady. What is it about her that makes you keep going back for more rejections?"

"It's just a game we play. A man would have to be blind or dead not to be attracted to those big brown eyes. But the truth is that in the long haul, we both know she deserves someone who's grounded and stable, not an old rebel like me," Tag answered.

"Do you feel more for her than, say, you did for all the other women you've sweet-talked into takin' their clothes off?" Hud took the road heading south toward Sunset.

Tag shrugged. "Maybe. Why are you askin'? Interested in her yourself?"

Hud shook his head slowly. "Not me. She's sweet and has a firecracker sense of humor, but there's no sparks between us. Got to admit, though, I see some serious electricity when y'all are flirtin'."

"She's fun, and I like her sass. That's as far as it goes or will go. Like I said, Nikki is one of them good girls who someone with my background don't have a right to." Tag adjusted the vents so the cool air blew right on his face. "This thing burns when I sweat."

Hud made a hard right onto a section line road off Highway 101. "Should teach you a lesson to stay out of other people's fights." Another right hand turn down the ranch lane and Hud pointed ahead. "Looks like we got company."

"Halle-damn-lujah! Maverick and Paxton have arrived. We've got help." Tag was out of the truck the minute Hud parked. He met the two Callahan brothers, distant cousins of his and Tag's, on the porch in a three-way bear hug instead of handshakes. When Hud arrived, it turned into a back-thumping event that looked like football players congratulating the quarterback on an eighty-yard run for a touchdown.

"We're here a day early," Maverick said. "Mam talked about having a going-away party for us. The plans fell through when our sister had to go on a business trip, and our parents had to go to a funeral."

"Well, we're glad y'all are finally here," Tag said. "Y'all had supper? Want a beer?"

"Had supper on the way," Paxton said. "But we're Irish. We'd never turn down a beer. Where are we bunkin'? I'll grab some of our gear and bring it inside."

Hud unlocked the door and swung it open. "House only has two bedrooms, so we set up twin beds in both of them. It's a little crowded but better than bunk beds. Me and Tag got one room. Y'all can have the second one. I hate that y'all missed your grandma's party, but we're sure glad you're here."

"I ain't sleepin' in the same room with my brother," Paxton said. "His snores rattle the windows. I got no problem sleeping on the sofa."

Maverick took a long look around the sparsely furnished house and turned back to Tag. "It'll do just fine. Slept in bunkhouses smaller than this many times. Matter of fact, one winter me and Paxton had to stay in an old line cabin and the whole thing wasn't any bigger than this room right here."

"I was ready to pour honey on him and stake him out in the snow for the fire ants to eat." Paxton grinned.

At just over six feet, both Maverick and Paxton had dark brown hair. Maverick was the oldest by three years, but they looked more like twins than Tag and Hud did. About the only difference was that Paxton's face was slightly rounder and his eyes a lighter shade of green. Their grandmother and the Baker boys' granny were cousins. They always had trouble figuring out if they were fourth or fifth or twice removed, or what the actual kinship was, so they just told everyone that they were cousins.

"So how is your grandma?" Tag asked.

"Mam is feisty as ever. Says if we don't behave out here, she'll get in her truck and come straighten us out," Paxton said as he tossed a duffel bag through the door.

"And she means it," Maverick assured them. "Now, about those beers?"

"Tag, you pop the tops on four beers. I'll help Paxton bring in the rest of their stuff," Hud said.

"Appreciate it." Paxton nodded. "My brother packed everything but the splinters from the boards on the corral."

"You might find those in my bags, so be gentle."

Maverick's drawl was a mixture of West Texas and Irish. His grandmother had come over from Ireland, but she hadn't totally lost her accent, and the brothers had spent a lot of time with her. "So the place don't look as bad as I thought it might. From what I can see from the drive onto the property, the fences are shabby. It's a wonder your cattle haven't broken through and gone visitin' the neighbors before now. I guess doin' some proper fencin' is the first order of business this summer?"

"And plowin' and plantin'." Hud heard the last of the comment as he came inside with a huge duffel bag on his shoulders. "Then we've been workin' with Emily's new husband, Justin, on a design for a bunkhouse so we won't be all crowded up in this little place. We might have the ranch lookin' pretty good in five years and be ready to expand if the neighbors down the road ever want to sell."

Maverick pointed toward a bag that Hud brought inside. "That one can go out to the barn to put in storage. Don't need what's in it until winter."

Paxton came in behind Hud with another load. "Guess this one can too. Where's the barn?"

Hud turned around and headed outside. "Y'all might as well come on and go with us. We still got enough daylight left to show off our new ranch while we drink our beers."

"Just barely." Tag grinned and then flinched. "Ouch!"

"Noticed that you've already been in trouble," Maverick said. "What happened?"

"It's a long story." Tag brought up the rear as they all paraded out of the house.

"That ends in the emergency room with Nikki Grady," Hud teased.

"I remember her." Paxton tossed the bag he'd brought back from the house over into the bed of the truck. "A cute little dark-haired woman with the biggest brown eyes. Emily's friend who was in the wedding last month, right? Seems I remember you hangin' around her a lot at the wedding reception."

Paxton and Hud slid into the backseat, leaving the front passenger seat for Tag.

Maverick got behind the wheel. "I'll drive. You tell me where to go, Tag. You talked that pretty girl into a night out with you yet?"

"No, he hasn't," Hud spoke up. "I think he might have lost his mojo."

"Surely not," Paxton chuckled. "All of us hit a dry spell every now and then, but it will rain again someday."

"I'm beginnin' to wonder," Tag said.

Chapter Three

Nikki was always on duty during the weekend, but sometimes if the staff got in a bind, she'd pull another twenty-four-hour shift through the week. When her phone pinged that morning, she figured it was the hospital calling. She was already headed to the kitchen to jerk her scrubs from the clothes dryer when she answered.

"Nikki, I need help. This is overwhelming me." Emily's voice sounded like she might cry, and that was so unlike her friend, who usually took any bull by the horns, spit in its eye, and then wrestled it to the ground.

"I'm on my way," Nikki said. "Want to stay on the phone while I drive out to the ranch? And am I going to the cabin or to the new house?"

"Cabin and I'll be fine until you get here." Emily sounded relieved.

Nikki slung her purse over her shoulder, slipped a pair of flip-flops on her feet, and locked the door behind her as she started down the stairs to her car. "Should I pick up maple iced doughnuts or ice cream?"

"Doughnuts would be great. I'll put on a pot of coffee. See you in a few," Emily said.

Nikki's pulse settled down a little after she heard that. Ice cream was reserved for big problems, so this wasn't too huge. Most likely, Emily was ready to throw things at Tag for getting into a fight that wasn't any of his business. They'd eat half a dozen doughnuts, drink several cups of coffee, and talk it out. Then everything would be fine.

Even after stopping at the doughnut place's drive-through, Nikki made it all the way to the back side of the Longhorn Canyon Ranch in record time. Emily was sitting on the porch when she parked. Two big mugs of steaming coffee sat on a small table between two white rocking chairs.

"You're smiling," Nikki called out as she opened the car door and grabbed the bag of doughnuts from the passenger seat. "I drove like a bat out of hell because you were crying."

"Yep, but when you said you'd come help me, I knew everything would be fine." Emily motioned to the other rocking chair and then held out her hand for the bag. "There's so many decisions about the house that need to be made, and it overwhelmed me. And my brothers living on the next ranch over doesn't help either. Mama calls me every day for a report on them." She took a doughnut from the bag and dipped it in the coffee. "And last night, the two hired hands from back home arrived, so now it's like having four brothers over there. You remember Maverick and Paxton?" She handed the bag to Nikki and tucked a strand of red hair back behind her ear.

"Oh, yes." Nikki sat down in the chair. "Two tall good-looking cowboys with a little bit of an Irish lilt in their Texas drawl. I didn't know they were going to be part of your brother's ranch. Did you give Tag a dressin' down for those stitches?"

Emily's chair stopped rocking and she sat forward, her blue eyes as big as saucers. "What stitches? What has he done now?"

Nikki wouldn't want to be Tag when his sister found out about his barroom brawl. Emily was a tall woman—plus-size they called it these days—and her temper knew no bounds when she was angry.

"I shouldn't have said anything." Nikki sipped her coffee. "That's his story to tell."

Tag chose that moment to step around the end of the cabin and sit down on the porch steps. "And I'll tell it, but first I'd sure like one of them doughnuts. Been a while since breakfast."

Nikki handed the bag toward him, but Emily reached out and snagged it.

"Talk first and then we'll see if you can have one. Good Lord, Tag! How many stitches are in your jaw and when did this happen?" Emily asked.

"Didn't count 'em and it happened on Saturday night or maybe it was after midnight and Sunday morning. I haven't been around because I knew you'd pitch a fit," Tag answered.

"Keep talking." She set the bag in her lap.

He explained pretty much the same way he'd told the doctor about what happened to get him cut open. "Now can I have a doughnut?"

She handed the bag over to him. "Are you pressing charges?"

"Nope. I shouldn't have meddled in it," he answered. "Maple is my favorite kind. Is there coffee left in the pot?"

Emily started to get up.

"Keep your seat, sis. I'll get it."

Tag's arm brushed against Nikki's shoulder as he went inside. That there were sparks didn't surprise her one bit. She needed to get back into the dating game—just not with him.

"What makes him so wild?" she whispered.

"That's his story too," Emily said. "You'll have to get him to tell you all about his teenage years sometime."

"Okay, then let's talk about what's got you upset this morning," Nikki said. "Are you doubting your decision to leave the retirement center?"

"No, that was a solid choice. I don't regret it one bit," Emily answered.

"What was a choice?" Tag asked as he carried a mug of coffee out in one hand and the pot in the other. "Thought I'd top off y'all's cups."

Nikki held hers up. "Thank you."

"You're just bein' nice so I won't tell Mama," Emily said.

He refilled her cup after he finished with Nikki's. "You want to be the cause of her worryin'?"

"Me? I didn't nearly get my throat slashed," Emily protested.

"Aww, come on, now. My jaw is a long way from my throat," he slung over his shoulder as he took the coffeepot back inside the cabin.

Nikki was jealous of the cabin, maybe even more so than the two-story house Emily and Justin were building on the other side of the ranch. The old cabin was peaceful and calm. Only the noise of an occasional truck or car driving past on the dirt road beyond the trees could be heard, or maybe a cow lowing off in the distance. According to what Emily had learned about the dwelling, it had been there for years and years. One big room housed the bedroom, living area, and small kitchen. The bathroom was tiny and had the world's smallest shower, but Emily, even at her size, loved every square foot of the place.

"Raising my own kids won't be as much trouble as Tag and Hud," Emily growled.

"Are you tellin' me that you're pregnant?" Nikki teased.

"Tell Mama that instead of about my unfortunate accident." Tag grinned as he joined them again. "She'll be so excited about a grandbaby that I won't matter anymore."

"I'm not pregnant." Emily glared at him.

Tag sat back down on the porch and reached into the bag for another doughnut. "What I came over here for is to ask if we might beg, borrow, or rent the cabin after you move into your house? We're findin' that our place is too little for four grown men, and we ain't even got to a weekend yet." He wiggled his dark brows. "It'll be the end of the summer before we can begin to build onto the house or put up a bunkhouse, and we need more room."

"Weekend?" Emily frowned. "What's that got to do with anything?"

"How are four big old cowboys going to bring home a girl if they get lucky on Saturday night?" Nikki answered.

"Well, well," Emily giggled. "I guess you'll have to shell out the money for a motel or else take turns using the tack room out in the barn."

"Come on, sis," Tag begged. "Will you just ask Justin? There'd only be two of us living in it anyway."

"There's one bed, Tag. Who'd sleep on the sofa?" Emily asked.

"Okay, then just one of us. I'll volunteer even though I can't turn around in that shower. Don't know how you do it." Tag touched his wounded jaw and looked at her with sad eyes.

"I'm not going to feel sorry for you, so don't play that wounded hero card with me," Emily declared. "However, if Justin wants to rent the cabin to you, that's between y'all. If he does let you move in, you could always turn the living room over at your ranch house into a bedroom and then the other three could have a little privacy."

"Thank you." Tag finished off the doughnut and took a sip of coffee. "I never thought of that. You're a genius, sis. I'll leave you ladies to whatever you were talking about when I got here. I'm going to see Justin and offer to help any way I can to get y'all out of this cabin and into your new house."

With that, he disappeared around the end of the cabin, and in a little while they heard the faint roar of a four-wheeler somewhere over to the east.

"Must've rode up close to the fence and then walked on over here." Emily sighed.

"I didn't hear anything before," Nikki said.

"Me neither. I imagine the sound of your car kind of masked the noise. But now to my problem, Justin's mama is driving me crazy," Emily said. "She calls every day to see how things are going with the house and wants to add her two cents to every decision. She thinks we shouldn't have carpet. The new thing is vinyl plank that looks like hardwood. And she keeps sending me pictures of crystal punch bowls and candlesticks. I don't like all that stuff!"

"Tell her that you don't," Nikki advised, and finished off her coffee.

"She's only trying to help, I'm sure, but I've got different tastes than she does." Emily sighed. "I don't want to hurt her feelings just when we're beginning to get along."

"Sounds like you're between one of those rocks and a hard place," Nikki said.

"Okay, let's turn this thing around. You've met my mama," Emily said.

Nikki wasn't sure she liked where this might be headed, but she nodded. "Of course I have. I stayed at the ranch out there in West Texas for a week before the wedding and a day afterwards."

"Okay, let's say that you fell in love with Hud." Emily pulled the last doughnut from the bag and took a bite.

"Why Hud? Why not Tag or Matthew?" Nikki asked.

"Tag is too wild for you, and Matthew is too uppity. Anyway, let's say that you fell in love with Hud, and y'all got married. You were building a house just the way you wanted it, and my mama got all up in your business. You know how bossy and tough she is, so think about it." Emily was about to take another bite when Beau, the ranch dog, ran up to her side. She pinched off a big chunk of the doughnut and held it out to him.

Nikki could have sworn that the dog, a mix between a blue tick hound and a Catahoula, smiled at Emily when he'd devoured the doughnut. He wagged his tail and laid a paw on her lap.

"You're worse than my brothers." Emily broke off another piece and gave it to him, and then turned to Nikki. "Well, what would you do?"

"Your mama likes me," Nikki answered.

"It's true Gloria and I didn't get off on the best foot. I want to stay on her good side without having to give in all the time." Emily gave Beau the last of the doughnut. "That's all of it. So all the begging won't do you a bit of good."

Nikki hated confrontation. Always had. Probably always would. "I understand where you're comin' from, and it would be tough on me to stand up to your mama and tell her to butt out. But I'd do it."

"Then you're tougher than you look because I'm not sure I'd tell my mama to butt out if she told me how to furnish my new house," Emily laughed. "But today, I've got to make the decision about where to use tile or carpet. Justin says that he doesn't care as long as it's soft on his bare feet. Will you go with me over to Wichita Falls and help me?"

"Of course," Nikki agreed. "Let's get nachos on our way through Nocona."

"Sounds great." Emily stood up. "I'll get my purse."

"I'll make a dash through the bathroom before we leave." Nikki headed into the bathroom and stood in front of the small mirror above the wall sink. She stared at her reflection and thought about what Emily had said about her being married to Hud. She didn't feel a thing for him. Why, oh, why did she always have to be attracted to the wrong cowboy? Hud was a sweetheart—funny, kind, and almost as sexy as Tag.

Almost, she thought, *only counts in horseshoes and hand grenades.*

*   *   *

Tag found Justin throwing small hay bales onto a trailer over in the north part of the Longhorn Canyon. Chris Stapleton's "Tennessee Whiskey" was blasting from the truck radio. A vision of Nikki flashed through his mind as Tag pulled his gloves from the hip pocket of his jeans and shoved his hands down into them. He picked up a bale and threw it up to Levi, who was stacking the bales on the trailer.

"You ain't got enough work over on your place?" Justin asked. "Not that I'm complainin' one bit. I'll take all the help I can get."

"Got a favor to ask and I ain't one to stand by if there's

work to be done." Tag matched Justin, bale for bale. They were about the same height and weight, and both had blue eyes, but that's where the similarities ended. Justin's eyes were that steely blue that could look as cold as ice. Tag's were the color of the summer sky.

"Hey, remember there's only one of me and two of y'all," Levi said.

"Favor?" Justin asked.

"How much longer until you and my sister move into the house?" Tag asked.

"A week. Ten days at the most. You want to help us move in?"

"Don't mind a bit, but I was wonderin' if I could rent the cabin when y'all do. Maverick and Paxton are over on our place. Man, it's crowded," Tag answered.

"I'd tell you to move your help into our bunkhouses, but the kids will be here in a few weeks. Still, if you need the space until they get here, you're welcome." Justin stopped, took bottles of water from a cooler, and tossed one each to Levi and Tag. "Let's take a break. Trailer is full, so we'll need to take it to the barn."

"Thanks." Tag twisted the top off his bottle and took a long draw.

All three of them sat down on the ground on the shady side of the truck. Levi removed his straw hat and wiped sweat from his angular face with the tail of his T-shirt. His brown hair was plastered to his head. Even his eyelashes had droplets of sweat on them.

"I'll be glad to get this all in the barn. It's supposed to rain tomorrow. Looks like we only got one more trailer full after this." Levi downed half his bottle of water before he came up for air.

"I appreciate the offer of the bunkhouses, but we'd just

as soon stay over on our place. The cabin isn't far from the fence separating the Longhorn Canyon from our ranch, so I thought I could make a gate and"—Tag hesitated and took another drink before he went on—"and kind of go back and forth that way if you was willin' to rent to me. I'd be the only one livin' there and it wouldn't be for long, just until we can get a bunkhouse thrown up over on..." Another pause. "Dammit! We really need to get a brand and a name to the place."

"I can't rent to family. Wouldn't be right," Justin said. "But you're welcome to use the cabin as long as you want. Soon as we get moved out, consider it yours. I can't imagine being cooped up with three other grown cowboys in that little house. And if you want to put in a gate or a stile, just go right ahead."

"Thank you." Tag held out his hand.

Justin shook with him. "Remember, now, that bathroom is tiny."

"I can live with it," Tag said.

"You got any ideas for your ranch name?" Levi asked.

"A few but none we like. We're Longhorn fans, but y'all already got the Longhorn Canyon brand," Tag answered.

"Canyon Creek runs through your property as well as ours," Levi said.

"I like that. Has a nice ring. Canyon Creek Ranch," Tag said. "I'll have to talk to Hud about it and get Maverick and Paxton's thoughts. But I sure like it. Let's get this trailer taken to the barn, and I'll help y'all stack it before I get back to my fencin' business."

Justin stood up. "Thank you. Three of us can get the job done quicker than two. We got our hired help out workin' on fences and doin' some plowin'."

"Ranchin' ain't for sissies," Levi chuckled as he got to

his feet and dusted off the seat of his jeans. "But it gets into the blood and nothing else satisfies a cowboy."

"You got that right," Tag agreed.

After they'd unloaded and stacked the hay, Tag drove his four-wheeler back over to his ranch. He stopped at the entrance, where a wooden sign with JOHNSON RANCH emblazoned on it used to hang, and imagined one with Canyon Creek up there. The brand could be two Cs, back-to-back with a wavy line under them for the creek that snaked through his property. He liked it, but now he'd have to convince Hud, and dammit, his brother had to mull over everything for days before he made a decision.

Hud barely glanced up from driving T-posts when Tag hopped off the vehicle. "Where'd you disappear to?"

"Went over to face the music with Emily." He picked up a post and stepped off eight feet.

"How'd she take it? Is she goin' to tattle to Mama?" Hud chuckled.

"I'm not sure. Nikki had already told her," Tag answered. "I talked to Justin and he said whichever one of us wants to can use the cabin when they move out. It's not that far."

"I'm not living over there," Hud said. "Have you been in that bathroom? You have to practically take a shower on your knees. Besides, me and the guys have been talkin' this mornin'. We think we should turn the house into a bunkhouse until we can get one built. We can use the living room as another bedroom."

Tag drove the metal post into the ground. "Emily suggested the same thing, and I'm willing to move into the cabin."

"All it's got is that little window air conditioner. Remember how hot it got when we went over there for supper with Emily and Justin?"

"I'll take the living room," Paxton said from twenty feet ahead, where he was taking down the old wooden fence posts and rolling up the rusty barbed wire. "But only if I can have the tack room in the barn when I get lucky on Saturday night."

"What makes you so sure you'll get lucky?" Hud asked.

"Just feel it in my bones." Paxton grinned.

"No A/C out there. I guess old Eli Johnson never got frisky in the barn," Hud said.

"I'll be glad to have a bedroom to myself. I'll get rid of those twin beds and put in a king." Maverick stretched new barbed wire between the posts. "And y'all are gettin' too far ahead of me."

Tag finished with the post he was driving and went back to help Maverick. "Guess you are stringing five wires to our every one post."

"Can we store the twin beds in the barn?" Paxton asked. "I'd like to buy a bigger one too. Hey, I just thought of something. You're not doing us a big favor by moving to the cabin. You'll have it all to yourself. Talk about a chick magnet."

Tag's mind flashed on Nikki again, and in this picture, a heart-shaped magnet was glued to her scrubs. When he crooked his finger, it pulled her straight into his arms.

Yeah, right, he thought. *Like she said, I'd have to change my ways. You can't teach an old dog like me new tricks, especially when they mean changing a whole lifestyle.*

Chapter Four

Nikki drove between the concrete pillars on either side of the arched wrought-iron sign for Hogeye-Celeste Cemetery. She always made the trip out east of town to visit her brother's grave on his birthday, September 30; at Christmas; and on May 8, the day he died. She parked on the gravel road closest to his grave and reached over into the backseat for the gerbera daisies she'd gotten at the florist that morning. Flowers for a twelve-year-old boy hardly seemed appropriate, but daisies were better than roses—at least in her way of thinking.

She sat down in front of the small headstone and laid the flowers at the base. She traced his name, Quint Grady, with her fingertip and then the birth and death dates. Not much to say about a little guy who'd fought so hard to live. She could tell stories about his humor, even when everyone finally accepted the fact that even if by a miracle a bone marrow donor did show up with a match, his body wasn't strong enough for the transplant.

She pulled a few weeds, wiped tears away with the back of her hand, and said, "I'm sorry. I promised I wouldn't cry for you when you were gone, but I still miss you." She pulled up the tail of her T-shirt and dried her face. "Let's try this again. You always made me laugh, Quint. We had to stick together to survive all that tension in the house between Mama and Daddy. I missed you when you left us. Daddy left that next week after your funeral and Mama went to bed. For a whole year, Quint, and I was only fourteen. The cooking, paying bills, shopping for food, and all that fell on me. I used to spend hours in your bedroom unloading my problems on you."

The crunch of car tires on gravel caused her to look over her shoulder. It wasn't her mother's fifteen-year-old vehicle, but then Nikki wouldn't expect it to be. She'd never known Wilma to visit Quint's grave even once after the day of the funeral. Wilma was so wrapped up in her own ailments, real or imaginary, that she had little time for anyone else. Looking back, Nikki realized that's the way it had always been. Wilma was always sick or dying with something. When Quint died, she'd convinced herself that she was coming down with leukemia. She'd taken to her bed and only got out of it at meal time and when she had to go to the bathroom. A year later, she declared that she was in remission. Nikki didn't have the heart or energy to tell her that wasn't the way things worked. She was just glad that her mother was willing to take over some of the cooking and the housework again, even if it did mean that they ate at exactly the same time every day and the house had to be spotlessly clean at all times.

The vehicle stopped and the window came down partway. A man wearing a baseball cap and mirrored sunglasses stared her way for a few minutes before he moved on. Most likely he was looking for a specific grave site, she thought, and it wasn't in that area. She moved around behind the tombstone to take care of the weeds back there.

"There now," she said when she finished and stood up. "I've got you all prettied up for another few months. I miss you, Quint. Even yet, I miss you." She wiped a tear from her cheek and blew a kiss toward the big white fluffy clouds in the sky.

When she got into her car and drove away from the cemetery, the same vehicle that had been looking for a grave pulled in behind her. It followed her to the snow cone stand, where she ordered a rainbow with cherry, grape, and orange—Quint's favorite and her own little tradition on the anniversary of his death. On his birthday she bought a cupcake, put a candle on it, and sang the birthday song. At Christmas, she made iced sugar cookies and ate the Santa one in his memory.

She handed the girl behind the window two dollars when she handed her the snow cone and told her to keep the change. Then she drove straight to the park where she and Quint had spent so much time before he got sick. Sitting on the bench under a shade tree, she could picture him over there on the slide. He'd always been small for his age, but he had a big heart and a smile to match it.

Eating the snow cone, she noticed that same car from the cemetery passing slowly on the far side of the park. Had it been a pickup, she would have figured it was Tag, pretending to stalk her as a joke. But it was a fairly new shiny black sedan. Maybe a Lincoln or a Caddy—all cars looked alike to Nikki these days. The window rolled down but only for a moment; then the car slowly moved back out onto the road and disappeared.

Nikki looked up at the pale blue sky and sent up a short prayer. *You could send me a friend today, Lord. I could sure use one.*

*   *   *

Tag was on his way back to the ranch from Bowie with a trailer loaded with fence posts and rolls of barbed wire. They'd run out of both in the middle of the afternoon, and he'd been sent to get more while the other three guys began to clean out the barn. In a couple of weeks, the east pasture would be ready to cut and bale, and Tag would sure like to have new fences up on one side of the ranch by then.

The radio was blaring and he was keeping time to the music on the steering wheel with his thumbs and singing along to Clay Hollis's song "Can't Let a Good Thing Get Away." Listening to the words, he wondered how many good things he'd let get away from him somewhere along the bumpy road his life had been on for more than a decade.

He grinned and didn't even wince when it hurt. The next song was "Live Like You Were Dying." That told him that no matter how many good women might have slipped through his fingers, he'd sown lots of wild oats for both him and his friend Duke Fields, who'd died in a motorcycle crash when they were both only seventeen.

He was singing along with the lyrics about riding a bull named Fumanchu when his phone rang. He turned the volume down and answered, "Hey, Billy Tom, what's up?"

"Lots of good things. Want in on some fun and make some money at the same time?" Billy Tom slurred his words.

Tag glanced at the clock on the dashboard. "Little early to be hittin' the bottle on a weekday, ain't it, Billy Tom?"

"Man, I ain't drunk. I'm high," Billy Tom said. "And me and the old boys are back in town, ready to romp and stomp. You with us?"

"Sorry, man, I've left the panhandle. I'm out here in"—

Tag hesitated—"another part of the state tryin' to turn a ragged-ass ranch into something profitable."

Billy Tom chuckled. "The boys will be real sad if you don't join us. We're ready to ride again. Meet us at the old stompin' grounds on Saturday night. Surely you can take a weekend off and hear our proposition. It'll only cost you a thousand dollars. We just need to rent a truck. It'll be a..."

He paused so long that Tag thought he'd lost the connection.

"You still there or did that weed knock you on your ass?" Tag asked.

"Nah, man, where was I? Oh, we need a little investment. We got a new guy who can turn a thousand into ten thousand," Billy Tom said.

"No thanks. That buys a lot of fence posts and barbed wire. I'll pass. Y'all go on and have a good time," Tag said.

"Your loss, man, but just in case you change your mind, I'm going to tell the gang that you're with us. Just think of what a rush it'd be to have some fun like the old days when Duke was still with us."

Tag heard the roar of a motorcycle coming to life and then the call ended. He'd cut ties with Billy Tom and those guys more than five years ago. Tag lived close to the edge, but those guys went beyond that. They'd ride their motorcycles off a virtual cliff into the water thinking they could go so fast that they'd never sink. They were downright crazy and sometimes even illegal in their stunts, and Tag was glad he hadn't told Billy Tom exactly where he'd moved.

He turned up the radio to an old song from Vince Gill, "Go Rest High on That Mountain." He took the next right and found himself in a small parking lot at the city park. He pulled into a space, turned off the engine, removed his sunglasses, put his head on the steering wheel, and let the tears flow. What he was feeling was as fresh and raw as what he'd felt the day they'd lowered his best friend's casket into that deep hole while that same song echoed through the flat country of West Texas.

In spite of being named for John Wayne, Duke had been a small kid until they were juniors in high school. At the beginning of the school year, he'd barely reached Tag's shoulder. By the end of that same year, he'd outweighed Tag by thirty pounds and was an inch taller. That summer, the two of them used a big chunk of their savings from hauling hay to buy motorcycles. And that's when they got tangled up with Billy Tom and his posse of four other guys who all owned motorcycles.

Tag finally raised his head, dried his eyes, and put his sunglasses back on. That's when he realized that Nikki was sitting out there on a park bench eating a snow cone. He picked up his hat from the passenger seat, settled it on his head, and started the engine. But another song on the radio caught his attention and he stopped to listen to Vince Gill sing "Whenever You Come Around."

"I get it, Duke, I get it," he whispered as he shut off the engine, got out of the truck, and headed toward Nikki. She waved at him and smiled. That was a good sign, wasn't it?

*　　　*　　　*

Lord, this was not who I was thinkin' about, Nikki thought as Tag made his way across the playground toward her. *But, hey, if this is all you can do on short notice, I'll try not to bitch.*

Tag sat down beside her on the bench and she offered her snow cone. "Not much left, but it's cold and tastes pretty good on a hot day like this."

He took it and ate several bites before handing it back to

her. "I left a little so you could have the last of it. What're you doin' out here?"

"I might ask you the same thing." She finished off the last bite and tossed the empty cup at a nearby trash can.

"Missed that shot," he said as he stood and picked up the cup and trashed it.

"Thank you," she said.

"It wasn't a three-pointer, but at least I made the basket." He sat back down.

A full foot of space separated them, but the temperature rose by ten degrees. She wiped sweat from her forehead with the back of her hand. "Hot, ain't it?"

"It's Texas. We have four seasons. Hot, Hotter, Hottest, and Hot as Hell. We're just now to Hotter, but Hot as Hell is comin'," he chuckled.

"What in the world are you doing here, Tag?"

"It's a long story, but the truth is that a song on the radio brought back some tough memories. I couldn't drive with tears in my eyes," he said.

Nikki reached up and removed his sunglasses. His eyes were red and faint streaks were still visible down his cheeks. "Did the tears burn when they hit the stitches?"

"Little bit." He took his glasses from her fingers and put them back on.

"What was the song?" she asked.

"Vince was singing 'Go Rest High on That Mountain.' It gets me every time," he answered.

A lump the size of a grapefruit formed in her throat. They'd played that song at Quint's funeral, and even the guitar and piano lead-in made her cry. She quickly wiped at her eyes.

"Gets you, too, does it?" Tag asked.

She tried to swallow down the lump, but it wouldn't

budge. A vision of her precious little brother lying in that blue casket flashed before her eyes as the song played in her head. "Yes, it does," she whispered.

"My best friend and I bought our first motorcycles between our junior and senior years of high school. It wasn't a gang, but it was a rough bunch that we got tangled up with. They'd robbed a convenience store and were speeding out of town on their cycles. I learned later that they were going to an old cabin that Billy Tom's great-grandpa had used to run moonshine out of years before."

Another tear ran down his cheek, but he didn't even flinch when it pooled up in the stitches. "I've never told anyone this before. Don't know why I'm doin' it now. Guess after all these years, I just need to get it off my chest. You won't tell Emily, will you?"

"Not if you ask me not to." Nikki's mind flashed on another picture of her brother the first time he had gotten a nosebleed at the park.

"Don't tell Mama," he'd begged. "She won't let us come back if you do. She'll think I've got something horrible that she'll catch."

He was only seven that year, and yet the two of them already knew their mother's problems too well. At that age, kids shouldn't have even been at the park alone, much less worried about their mother's reaction to a bloody nose. But Wilma hadn't cared where they went or how long they were gone.

"I'm asking you not to, then." Tag's voice caught in his throat. "My friend Duke and I were riding our cycles out on the dirt road and being reckless when we saw the other guys. They came down the road five abreast, riding so fast that they were a blur with a cloud of dust behind them. We pulled off to the side to let them pass."

"Did the cops catch you?"

He shook his head. "Evidently the guys had lost them when they turned off on the dirt road, but we'd been wild and crazy with those guys all summer, so we wanted to see what they were into that night. Billy Tom motioned for us to follow, so we did. We didn't know about the big tree limb that had fallen over the road to the old cabin since the last time we were there. The first five split and went around it, but Duke never even saw it coming."

"Oh. My. God!" Nikki's hand shot up to cover her mouth.

Tag removed his sunglasses and leaned his head back against the bench. "My tire was about six inches from that tree when I came to a stop. Billy Tom and the others didn't even know Duke was hurt. I called 911 and held him in my arms until they got there, but he breathed his last on the way to the hospital. They played Vince Gill's song at his funeral, and every time I hear it, it tears my heart out."

She laid her hand on his shoulder. "I'm so sorry, Tag."

"Me too, Nikki. I got even wilder after that. I'm pretty sure Hud got his first motorcycle just to keep me out of trouble." He covered her hand with his. "Thanks for listening."

"That explains one of the stickers on your truck. What about the other one? The one with Tim McGraw's song on it?" She slipped her hand free.

"First time I heard 'Live Like You Were Dying' it seemed like Duke was speakin' to me right from the grave," he answered. "So I've lived every day with that in mind."

"Ever get any other messages from him, like it's time to put that song in your past and move on?" she asked.

"If I do, I don't pay much attention to them," Tag answered. "I still haven't ridden a bull named Fumanchu, and I haven't been skydiving."

Neither have you. Quint's voice was real in her head.

And I don't intend to do either one, she argued.

"Well, darlin'." Tag's blue eyes scanned her body from her toes to the top of her head. "Now you know my darkest secret. Will you go out with me now?"

"Not until you ride that bull and go skydiving. If you live through those two, then we might talk about it," she answered.

He picked up her hand and kissed the knuckles. "I'll have to get that done in the near future."

"I'll be waiting in the ER when you do." She smiled up at him.

Chapter Five

Tag glared at his reflection in the bathroom mirror. The stitches were still there, a blatant reminder that he wasn't going to ride a bull or a bronc that night at the rodeo. If Emily hadn't been going, he might have paid the fee for a late entry and ignored what Dr. Richards said. But the whole family had plans to attend, and besides, she'd insisted on going with him for his appointment.

"You goin' to stay in there all evenin' primpin' like a little girl?" Maverick yelled through the door.

Tag unlocked the door, picked up his toiletry kit, and stepped out into the hallway. "All yours," he said, vowing to himself that he wouldn't complain one time about the tiny bathroom in the cabin. At least he wouldn't have to share it with three other smart-mouthed cowboys.

When Tag reached the living room, Hud looked up from the shabby sofa and grinned. "All dressed up and no bull to ride. I can't remember the last time you had to sit in the stands at a rodeo."

"Me neither, and I don't like it," Tag growled.

"Then don't get hit in the face with a beer bottle," Hud said. "Too bad Nikki is working tonight so you won't even have anyone to flirt with."

"There are other women in this part of the state." Tag moved Hud's gear bag from the old wooden rocking chair in the corner and sat down.

"We've been here a whole month, and you haven't gone home with one of those 'other women.'" Hud made finger quotes around the last two words. "Or brought them home with you either."

"My mojo's in a slump," Tag said.

Paxton came through the front door. "You girls gonna sit here discussin' your feelin's all day, or are we goin' to go hang on to a bronc for eight seconds?"

Maverick joined them from the hallway. "Hey, I might want to talk about my feelin's, too, if I had the chance at a girl like Nikki Grady."

Tag whipped around and shot an accusatory glare at his brother.

Hud held up both palms defensively. "I didn't say a word."

"But Emily did," Maverick said. "When we were over there last night helping her move a few boxes, she told us you've been flirtin' up a storm with her friend Nikki."

Hud grinned. "Just think, if Tag got serious about her, he'd have his own personal nurse to put him back together when he gets into his crazy rebel mode."

"Sounds like a win-win to me."

Tag rolled his eyes. "We've got a rodeo waiting for us. Let's get this show on the road."

Paxton led the way outside, and Tag broke away from the group and headed toward his truck. "I'll be rootin' for all y'all, but don't wait up for me. I might not be home tonight."

*   *   *

Nikki hadn't planned on going to the rodeo, but Emily had begged her to be there for moral support to help handle Justin's mom, Gloria. Even though she'd have to go from the rodeo to the hospital for her shift, she couldn't say no to a friend in need.

The parking lot was full when Nikki arrived, but she finally nosed into a spot not too far from the stands. She adjusted the rearview mirror so she could see her reflection and reapplied bright red lipstick. Then she picked up her hat from the passenger seat, got out of the car, and settled it on her head. Wearing skinny jeans with rhinestones on the hip pockets, a Western shirt that hugged her body, and a big blinged-out belt, she pretty much blended in with the crowd.

It wasn't difficult to find Emily, not when the last of the day's sunrays lit up her red hair like a beacon. Then she waved, stood up, and pointed to the spot she'd saved beside her. Nikki held up a hand and started in that direction, but she almost came to a screeching halt when she got close enough to see that she'd be sitting between Emily and Tag.

"Well, hello." She tried to keep her voice cheerful as she sat down. "I thought you'd be riding some bull named Fumanchu tonight."

"Dr. Richards said no," Emily answered for Tag.

"Poor baby." Nikki patted him on the knee that was pressed against hers.

"Higher, darlin'." He winked.

"Poor baby," she said in a high, squeaky voice.

"Looks like you've met your match," Emily laughed. "I hope you can cheer him up, Nikki. He's been in a pout all day."

"I don't pout," he protested. "I'm just disappointed. I haven't got to ride a bull since we got here."

Justin's brother and sister-in-law, Cade and Retta, were sitting right behind Tag. Cade patted him on the shoulder and said, "There'll be ranch rodeos all summer. You'll get your chance. What's this about Fumanchu? Don't think I've ever heard of that bull."

"Two point seven seconds on a bull named Fumanchu," Retta reminded him of the line in the song. "It's part of that song from years ago that Tim McGraw sang about living like you were dying."

"You got it," Tag said.

"Y'all've come a long way this week," Cade said. "The fence is sure lookin' good over at your place."

"Thanks," Tag said.

"I knew he'd feel better once he got here. He's been an old bear because he can't ride tonight," Emily whispered in Nikki's right ear. "And thank you so much for coming. Gloria has been nice since she got here, but I can tell she's not happy about the carpet."

"It's your house," Nikki said out the side of her mouth.

"Amen," Emily agreed.

Retta leaned over her very pregnant stomach and whispered, "It'll get better, but you have to stand your ground."

"Oh. My. Lord," Emily gasped. "Did you hear what we..."

Retta shook her head. "But I can sure imagine what you

were talking about. Claire and I both had to come to terms
with her."

"Claire too?" Emily frowned.

"Levi might not be a blood brother to Justin and Cade,
but Gloria tried to put her two cents in on everything they
were doin' with their house too," Retta said. "I'm glad Cade
and I got the ranch house and didn't have to start from
scratch. Shhh..."

Justin and Cade's parents, Gloria and Vernon, joined
them, sitting down at the end of the row. Then Levi and
Claire took the seats that had been reserved for them right in
front of Tag and Nikki. Claire wasn't any taller than Nikki,
and she owned a little quilt shop in Sunset. Levi, the foreman at the Longhorn Canyon Ranch, kept her hand in his
when they sat down.

"Hey, son." Gloria smiled up at Justin. "Is the carpet all
in now? Is it time to move in?"

"Got it done today," he answered. "Surprised me and
Emily. We figured it'd take a week or more, but they had
it in stock and they didn't have a big job starting until
Monday, so they sent a crew over this morning. We've put
some boxes in the kitchen already. Tomorrow we'll get the
big stuff in."

"We thought we'd have Sunday dinner at our place,"
Emily said. "Everyone is invited."

"That sounds great. I'll bring the dessert," Gloria offered.

"Thank you," Emily said.

"Are y'all ready to get this rodeo going?" the announcer
asked from the press box above them. The whole area rever-
berated when the crowd clapped, whistled, rang cow bells,
and stomped their feet on the wooden stands.

"Lively bunch tonight, aren't they?" Tag asked.

"I'd say so." She nodded.

"First bull rider tonight is Maverick Callahan. He's a newcomer to this area, but he's got ten years under his belt from around the Tulia and Happy, Texas, area. Let's give Maverick a big hand as he gets into position on Blue Devil, one of the meanest bulls in the business," the announcer said.

The chute opened and the bull came out bucking. Maverick managed to hang on for five seconds before he landed in the dirt. He got up, brushed off the seat of his pants, removed his cowboy hat, and bowed to the crowd. Women threw kisses at him and the applause was deafening.

"Guess he's got a fan base up there in the stands," the announcer said. "Watch the number two chute for our next contestant, Riley Tate."

"You sure look pretty tonight." Tag leaned toward Nikki until their shoulders were touching. "I'd ask you to dance if we were at a bar."

"This is not my first rodeo, Tag, and I'm not a virgin to the Rusty Spur either," she said.

"So you'd dance with me?"

She shrugged. "It would depend on how many other sexy cowboys were lined up askin' me to dance."

"So you think I'm sexy?" He smiled, showing off perfect white teeth.

"Of course. I'm not blind," she told him.

"And yet, you won't go out with me?"

"That's right," she answered. "Most sexy cowboys are only interested in the sprint and not the marathon."

"Oh, honey, I like to take my time and do the job right no matter what I'm doing." His eyelid slid shut in a slow, sexy wink.

"You are impossible," Nikki said.

"Yes, he is," Emily agreed from her other side. "And he

loves to argue. The only way to get him to shut up is to ignore him. Want to change places with me?"

"No, I can handle him."

"Be gentle with me. My heart is fragile." Tag picked up her hand and laid it on his chest.

Nikki quickly pulled her hand free, but she couldn't stop the blush creeping up to her cheeks or the image of her hand on other parts of his body.

"And now we have another newcomer to our area. This young man and his brother, Tag, bought a ranch over around Sunset. Give it up for Hud Baker, folks. If he stays on Mister Salty for eight seconds, he'll be tonight's winner," the announcer said.

Glad to have something to focus on, Nikki kept her eyes on Hud when he came out of the chute. Mister Salty's hind legs pointed at the moon, and his nose smelled the dirt. At three seconds people jumped to their feet and started screaming Hud's name. At six, they were stomping the wooden bleachers again. At eight, the noise could've been heard all the way to the hospital. A rescue rider rode out and helped him get loose from the bull. When Hud's feet were firmly on the ground, he removed his straw hat and threw it like a Frisbee into the crowd. A teenage girl grabbed it and shoved it down on her head.

Emily leaned around Nikki and poked Tag on the arm. "Hud just stole your hat move."

"He deserves it. That rascal was a mean critter," Tag said. "I hope that girl gets him to sign the hat for her when the rodeo is over."

"Or sooner." Nikki motioned to the arena.

Hud jumped over the fence and the girl tried to give him back the hat, but he shook his head, pulled a pen from his pocket, and signed the brim. She and all her teenage friends blew kisses at him, and the crowd roared as he made his way back across the dirt toward the chutes.

"Nice move," Nikki said. "Have you given away many hats?"

"Quite a few over the years," Tag answered. "When I throw the next one, I'll make sure I sling it your way."

"Honey, I could never use your hat. Your head is way bigger than mine."

"You could just hang it above your bed and dream about me," he suggested.

I don't need a hat to do that, she thought.

When it was time for her to leave, she gave Emily a quick hug and stood up. "I have to work on Sunday, but I'll see you on Tuesday. If you don't have everything moved in and arranged by then, I'll be glad to help."

She was easing past Tag when he stood up. In the crowded stands, that put them chest to chest.

"Don't I get a hug too?" he asked.

"I don't think so. Nearly everyone in these stands knows me, Tag. And as much as the ladies have been salivating over you all evening, they'd never move in on what they thought was my territory. So if you ever want to get lucky again, then you better just shake my hand," she said.

His blue eyes were twinkling when he tipped up her chin and kissed her right on the mouth. The sweet kiss rocked her all the way to her toes and made her knees weak. She was surprised that she was still standing when it ended.

"That's all the gettin' lucky I need," he whispered so close to her ear that his warm breath caressed that sensitive spot on her neck. "Good night, Nikki. I'm sure I'll see you around."

"Good night, Tag," she said. "I hope it's not in the ER this weekend."

Her legs were still shaky when she reached the hospital a few minutes later. Rosemary met her in the waiting room and whistled through her teeth. "Where have you been?"

"That ranch rodeo." Nikki kept walking through the doors and down the hall to the tiny on-call room. She locked the door, slid down the back of it, and put her head on her knees. If a relatively chaste kiss could affect her this way, she couldn't help but wonder what a night in bed with Tag would be like.

She got her bearings enough to rise up, get changed into her scrubs, and grab her tablet from her locker. When she opened the door, Rosemary was standing right beside it. "Was that good-lookin' cowboy from last weekend riding tonight?"

"No, he wasn't." Nikki headed toward the break room for the briefing.

Rosemary followed behind her. "Was he there?"

"Yep," Nikki said.

Rosemary dug deep into the pocket of her scrub pants when her phone rang. "Hello," she answered as she kept pace with Nikki. "Is that so? Not half an hour ago?"

"Everything okay?" Nikki held the break room door open for Rosemary to enter first.

"Just fine," Rosemary said. "But after we get done with our briefing, I want to know all about that kiss you got right out there in public from that cowboy. Have you been holding something back from me?"

*   *   *

Tag glanced over at Nikki's cowgirl hat, which was sitting beside him in the truck. He should've just let Emily take it home with her, but truth was that he wanted to see Nikki again that night. Her lips on his had stirred something inside him that he thought had died years ago—a feeling of hope in life.

It was well past midnight when he marched into the ER waiting room. The place was as quiet as a tomb. Evidently no fights had broken out, no kid had shoved a bean up his nose, and no poor old cowboy had taken a blow to his jaw-bone. Surprisingly enough, there wasn't even a cowboy with a sprained ankle or a busted-up wrist from the rodeo that night. Hat with a feather stuck in a pink band in his hand, he went straight to the desk where folks checked in.

"Fill out this form, and I'll get someone to take a look at you as quick as possible," the lady said.

"I'm not here because I'm sick. I just need to see Nikki Grady. I'm returning something of hers." Tag held up the hat.

The lady looked up at him and her eyes widened in surprise. "You're that cowboy who came in last week with lots of blood."

"That would be me," he said.

"Wait right here, and I'll get Nikki. We're not very busy, so she should be right here soon," she said as she hurried through a door.

Nikki's expression was one of pure shock when she ran into the waiting room. She stopped so quickly that the soles of her shoes made a squeaking noise. "Where are you hurt this time?"

He held up the hat. "Not hurt. Just bringing your hat to you. You left it behind."

"Thanks. You didn't have to do that." She took it from him.

"It only meant driving a couple more blocks. Little quieter here tonight than it was last week at this time." He didn't want to just turn and walk away.

"Give it a couple of hours. The place gets to hoppin' about the time the bars close down." She smiled up at him.

He had to either get out of there or else he was going to kiss her again, and unless he was dead wrong, all those faces peering through the window in front of him were her coworkers. He might not mind the gossip that would spread like wildfire, but he didn't want to put her job at risk in any way.

"Okay, then, see you around," he said bluntly, and left without looking back.

When he reached his truck, he started the engine and turned on the radio. Leaning his head back, he thought about the night his best friend Duke had died. The two of them had been badass—and look where it had gotten them both. Duke was dead and here he was about to turn thirty before long.

"Give me something," he said to the DJ who was talking about the weather. "I don't care if it's going to rain or storm. I want a song to help me like Tim McGraw's has all these years."

Grow up and move on. Duke's high voice popped into his head. For a big guy, he sounded like a girl most of the time. But then his tone did have advantages—he could mimic Vince Gill so well that it was downright uncanny.

"And now we've got an hour of slow country classics comin' your way," the DJ said. "And we'll be playing five for five. Keep track and be the fifth caller. Tell me the song and the artist, and you'll win two tickets to Six Flags Over Texas."

The music started and Tag sighed. "That's Vince Gill and Patty Loveless singin' 'My Kind of Woman, My Kind of Man.' I'm not sure I'd ever be the kind of man any woman could trust, not with my past."

His phone rang just as that song ended. Hoping it was Nikki, his hands trembled as he dragged it out of his hip pocket. But it was Billy Tom.

"What's up?" he asked.

"You out on some old dirt road listenin' to country music with a woman?" Billy Tom chuckled.

"I'm in the emergency room parking lot listenin' to music all by myself," Tag answered. "Was there something you wanted?"

"Well, the boys and I have a little plan."

"I don't want any part of your little plans anymore," Tag answered coldly.

"Aw, c'mon. You used to be fun. Besides, all we're asking is to borrow your truck for a little bit. Hell, you should come too—for old times' sake."

"Is what you're about to do one hundred percent, guaran-damn-teed legal?" Tag asked.

"Hell no!" Billy Tom answered.

"Then my answer is hell no. I've got too much tied up in my ranch to be gettin' in trouble with the law again."

"You've gotten soft and old," Billy Tom complained. "When I come to see you on a brand-spankin'-new Harley, you'll be sorry you didn't buy into our venture."

"Maybe so, but when I come to see you in jail, you'll be sorry you didn't grow up," Tag told him.

Billy Tom ended the call without another word.

Tag turned the radio louder, put the pickup in gear, and backed out of the parking lot. His thumbs kept time on the steering wheel as he listened to Bebe Rexha singing "Meant to Be." When the song ended, he shut off the engine, got out of the truck, and walked across the yard. He wasn't ready to go inside yet, so he sat down on the porch. A redbone coonhound puppy settled in beside him.

"Where'd you come from?" Tag scratched the pup's ears and it crawled right up into his lap.

"Are you lost or did someone dump you?"

The dog whimpered and looked up at him with begging eyes.

"Hungry?"

"I thought I heard someone talking out here." Hud came out of the house and joined him. "Guess you didn't get lucky since you're home before daylight. See you've met our new hired hand. He's promised to protect the cattle if we feed him and scratch his ears every now and then."

"Where'd he come from?" Tag asked.

"Lady at the rodeo brought a litter in the back of her truck. She was giving them away. This was the last one and we felt sorry for him. We haven't named him yet. Thought we'd make that decision together." Hud sat down in a lawn chair on the porch. "Tomorrow evening we're going to decide for sure that we're going to name the ranch Canyon Creek or something else and we'll name this dog."

"Guess we're really puttin' down roots, aren't we?"

"It's time," Hud said.

"What's meant to be will be, and what's not meant to be might be anyway," he muttered.

"Granny says that all the time. What made you think of that when we're talkin' about roots?" Hud asked.

"Just a song I heard on the radio." Tag wondered if that statement his grandmother said about "what's not meant to be might be" could ever involve someone like Nikki.

Chapter Six

Nikki yawned as she got into her vehicle Monday morning at 1:00 a.m. Stars twinkled around the quarter moon, which looked like it was hanging right in the middle of her windshield. It had been the worst kind of weekend—slow and steady. The cubicles were never filled to capacity, and yet there was at least one patient all the time. The shifts went by faster when she was hopping busy and tired to the bone when she dropped to sleep.

She rolled the kinks from her neck and stuck the key in the ignition. Just as she put the car in reverse, her phone rang and startled her into hitting the brakes so hard that she flew backward against the seat with a thud. Her heart was thumping around in her chest like a bass drum when she finally found her phone in the bottom of her purse.

"Hello," she said.

"Someone is trying to break into my house," her mother whispered.

"Did you call the police?" Nikki whipped the car around and headed toward her mother's house on the other side of town.

"No, I called you," Wilma answered. "They're cutting the screen door. I can hear them."

"Is it locked?"

"Of course. Both locks on the screen door and four on the big door," she answered.

"Where are you?"

"Hiding in the bedroom closet. I've got a quilt over my head so whoever it is can't find me."

Nikki jacked it up another five miles per hour. "I'm on my way. Stay where you are. You call the police. They should be there by the time I am."

"If I'd wanted the police, I would've called them, not you. And turn off your lights and kind of coast into the driveway. If Mrs. Thomas sees or hears you, she'll come runnin' over here. She stays up all hours of the night and watches television. She's really fat, so you know she's eating the whole time," Wilma whispered.

"Hang up, Mama, and call 911," Nikki almost shouted.

"I will not!" Wilma yelled right back at her.

Nikki called the number herself, and the patrol car must've been in the area because a policeman was already there when she parked her car. She met him halfway between her car and the house. Her phone rang, but she ignored it.

"It was just a raccoon. He ran when I started up on the porch," the policeman said. "I walked all around the house but didn't see any signs. I think everything is all right."

"Thank you," Nikki told him as her phone rang again.

"Call if you need us. Better to be safe than sorry." He headed back to the patrol car.

"Yes, sir," Nikki said as she answered the phone.

"I told you not to call the police," Wilma said. "Thank God Mrs. Thomas didn't see the police car."

Nikki rolled her eyes and plopped down on the ladder-back chair beside the door. Why it was there had always been a mystery because Wilma never went outside to sit in it. "It was a raccoon scratching at the door, not a person. He's gone now. Open the door and let me in."

"I'd have to undo all the locks and put my dentures back in and my hair is a mess. I can't let you in or Mrs. Thomas might still see the lights and come over here. Weren't you listening when I told you that she's up all night watching television? You just go on home and get some sleep. We'll talk tonight at seven like we always do," Wilma said. "I'll get this quilt folded and put back on the shelf, and take one of my anxiety pills before I go back to bed. Now go away before Mrs. Thomas realizes you're here."

Nikki shook her head slowly and added paranoia to the list of her mother's disorders. "Four locks on the door. If she dies in that house, we'll have to break the door down."

She made her way from the house to her car and tried to close the door as quietly as possible so Mrs. Thomas wouldn't come rushing out of her house. Then she drove straight to her apartment. Once she was inside, she left a trail of clothing across the living room floor and was naked by the time she reached the bathroom. A three-minute shower took the smell of the hospital off her body. She dried off and didn't even bother with underpants or a nightshirt, just curled up between the cool sheets naked and was asleep the second her head hit the pillow.

The digital clock beside her bed rolled over to six-fifteen just as she opened her eyes, but she wasn't sure if it was a.m. or p.m. Surely she hadn't slept over fourteen hours!

Light peeking through the mini-blinds made her realize she'd done just that. Her mother would call in less than an hour, and there was no way she could talk to Wilma without a cup or two of coffee. She pulled on some pajama pants and a tank top, plodded barefoot to the kitchen, and put a pot on the stove. While the water dripped through the grounds, she gathered up her dirty scrubs from last night, shoved them into the washing machine with two other sets from her suitcase, started the cycle, and then checked her phone.

There were two messages from Emily: Got tied up. Moving in Monday night.

The second one read: Please come after you talk to your mama.

The third one was from Rosemary: Can you take an eight-hour on Wednesday? Four to midnight?

She hurriedly sent one to Emily: Be there at eight.

Then one to Rosemary: Of course.

She ate an energy bar and a banana while she waited on the coffee and was on her second cup when the phone rang. "Hello, Mama. Did you sleep well after we got rid of the intruder last night?"

"Don't you make light of that, young lady," Wilma scolded. "My heart was racin' worse than it does when I mop the kitchen. I swear if that woman you hired would do a better job of cleanin' this place, it would be nice. You should fire her and hire someone else. I liked that first lady. She did things right."

Nikki bit her tongue to keep from reminding Wilma that she'd hated the first lady and complained about her constantly. "Mama, I'm not firing Sharon. She does a fine job. Besides, what would Mrs. Thomas say if Sharon didn't show up every Friday? You want gossip going all over your neighborhood about you?" Nikki put the phone on speaker and brushed her teeth while her mother ranted about Mrs. Thomas being so nosy.

"When did you have four locks put on your door?" Nikki asked when she could get a word in edgewise.

"If you'd come over here to see me more often, then you'd know when. An old woman like me livin' alone needs to be protected."

Nikki got fully dressed and pulled her hair up in a ponytail while Wilma went on and on about a newspaper article she'd read where a ninety-year-old woman's house was broken into.

"She shot the man right in the leg and held him at gunpoint until the police came," Wilma said.

"You want a gun?" Nikki asked.

"Good Lord, no. I believe in Jesus and He'll protect me." *So why all the locks?* Nikki thought.

"Speakin' of Jesus," her mother was saying. "You missed a good sermon at church yesterday. I just wish our new pastor would get married. Folks are goin' to talk about the way he's so friendly with the single women," Wilma said. "And those brothers of Emily's were there too. That one they call Tag is pure trouble. You can tell by his eyes, and I heard that he kissed you at a rodeo. I hope that's all he's done. You stay away from that boy, Nikki. You set your cap on the preacher. If I was a healthier woman, I'd invite him and you to lunch so you could meet him. I wouldn't mind you marryin' a preacher."

Yeah, right, Nikki thought. *I might not be ready for a rebel like Tag Baker, but I'll never be preacher's wife material—and there's another line that goes right behind it that says I don't want to be, either.*

"Mama, you are only sixty-one years old, and Dr. Richards told you that you're very healthy for someone your age," Nikki said.

"What does he know? He's not even a real doctor. He just works in the emergency room like you do, and he only runs the clinic two days a week. It takes forever to get an appointment, and I need him to check my blood again. I've been taking calcium and a whole bunch of other supplements, but I think I might need something to keep my hair from falling out."

So let's see, Nikki thought, *we've covered the preacher and Mama's hair. We still have the phone service and her newspaper not arriving on time, and then I'll try to set up a supper and she will give me some absurd reason why she can't go.*

Nikki picked up her purse and phone, made sure she had her keys, and locked the door behind her.

"Have you called the news office about my paper?" her mother asked, but she didn't wait for an answer. "It's gettin' here later and later, and that boy who delivers it *knows* he's supposed to lay it on the chair, but he just throws it from the road and hits my door." She stopped for a breath. "I want it laid on the chair at three thirty so I have an hour to go through it before I have supper."

"You call and tell them. I've got a job, too, Mama," Nikki said.

"I never thought a child of mine would talk to me the way you do," Wilma pouted. "I don't ask that much of you, and you won't even call the newspaper for me."

No guilt trips today, Mama, Nikki thought. *I've been on too many as it is.*

"How about I pick you up for supper tomorrow night? We'll go to the Mexican place." She got into the car and hurriedly started the engine so she could turn on the air conditioner.

"I hear a car motor. Are you coming over here? You

know the last show I watch comes on at eight. This is a bad time for you to visit." Wilma's voice was so high-pitched that it was squeaky.

"Then tomorrow evening?" Nikki backed up and headed toward the ranch.

"You know very well I can't eat that kind of food. My stomach is too delicate, and besides, you always want to eat later than four thirty, and if I don't take my meds on time, then I don't feel good the next day. We'll have to do it another day. It's eight o'clock. Good night, Nikki," Wilma said.

"Good night, Mama." The only way Nikki could actually visit her mother was to drop in unexpectedly somewhere between one and four, and even then it upset Wilma's schedule. It had been a while since she'd seen her mother in person so she made a mental note to go see her that week.

She turned on the radio and scanned through the stations until she found the one out of Dallas that she liked. "Here's an old one for y'all this evening," the DJ said. "Trent Tomlinson singing 'One Wing in the Fire.'"

Nikki smiled as she drove through Sunset and turned to head east. The lyrics talked about a man's father being an angel with no halo and one wing in the fire. That made her think of Tag and hope that he was at Emily's that evening. He certainly didn't have a halo, and there was no doubt that one of his wings smelled a lot like smoke, but still she liked the way easy banter between them lifted her spirits. After listening to her mother, for what seemed like eternity, she needed it, or maybe a shot of Jack Daniel's—or better yet, both.

*   *   *

The prickly feeling on the back of Tag's neck told him that Nikki had arrived. No other woman had ever affected him like that, but all his senses heightened whenever she was near. He and Hud were moving an old upright piano into Justin and Emily's place that had come all the way from Tulia when the movers brought Emily's things. It was the last big piece of furniture, and it weighed as much as a baby elephant.

"You're going to owe me"—Tag stopped to catch his breath—"a chocolate cake when this is done." He and Hud set the piano down where Emily wanted it. He glanced around the room, and he couldn't locate Nikki, but she had to be somewhere. His neck hairs did not lie.

"And Granny said to tell you that it will definitely need to be tuned after it's been hauled around like this." Hud pulled a bandana from his hip pocket and wiped sweat from his brow.

"There's a chocolate cake already made and on the kitchen counter," Emily said. "And I've got a piano man coming this week to tune it. I thought we'd have way too much stuff, but I was wrong. This is one big house."

Justin wrapped his arms around her waist from behind and buried his face in her hair. "We'll pick out one antique a year on our anniversary. How's that sound?"

She turned around and hugged him tightly. "That's so romantic. I love it."

A streak of pure jealousy shot through Tag, something he'd never felt before, not even as a child when he had to share everything with a twin brother. But right then, he wanted someone to look at him the way Emily looked at Justin.

Holy crap! What's happening to me? He raised his hand to his forehead. *There must be something in the water that's causing my brain to deteriorate.*

Then there was Nikki. She came out of the bathroom at the end of the hall. Wearing jeans, a cute little off-the-shoulder cotton top, and flip-flops, she looked fantastic.

"Looks like you big strong men have been workin' hard today." She smiled.

Dammit! Why did the clouds part when she grinned? She wasn't the most beautiful woman he'd ever set his eyes on, so what was it about her that jacked his pulse up several notches?

How many women have ever turned you down? His granny's voice was clear in his head. *Go on, count them.*

He dropped his hand and thought about the question, but he couldn't hold up a single finger. So what to do about this sudden attraction? Maybe do his best to get her to spend a night in his bed? Surely that would get her out of his system, and then he could go back to being his normal self.

Jackass! His grandmother's voice was very plain. *If you treat that girl like one of your one-night stands, I'm going to kick your ass myself. She deserves better than that.*

When he turned back around, Nikki was nowhere to be seen.

"She's in the kitchen," Hud whispered. "She's helpin' Emily put things in the cabinets."

"What makes you think I was lookin' for her?" Tag asked.

"I'm your twin, remember. I know what you're thinkin' all the time." Hud fell back on the sofa. "I'm worn out. Bring me a piece of chocolate cake. That'll give you a good reason to be in there with the women folks. Oh, and I'd like a cold beer too."

Tag sat down beside him. "I was thinkin' you might bring me cake and beer since I lifted more than you did today."

"Hey, now," Maverick said from across the room. "I believe I outdid you both, and me and Paxton ain't even family, so maybe y'all ought to tote beers to us."

"I'll settle this argument." Nikki brought in a tray laden with five thick wedges of double-layer fudge cake on plates and five bottles of beer. She put it in the middle of the coffee table. "You'll have to feed yourselves, no matter how tired you are."

"Be a sport and at least feed me the first bite so I can get enough energy to lift the fork," Tag teased.

"I don't think so, cowboy. That would be eating your cake and having it too—now, wouldn't it?"

"I tell you, Tag, this place has sucked the mojo right out of you." Maverick leaned forward and picked up a piece of cake and a fork. "Do you want a full-fledged funeral when you die or just a graveside service?"

"Darlin', please don't die. I'd be obligated to go to the funeral to console Emily and my black suit is too small," Nikki teased.

Tag shivered at the thought of death and then reached for the last piece of cake. "With friends like y'all, who needs enemies?" For some insane and unknown reason, Billy Tom's smiling face came to mind. Had he always been an enemy or at one point had he been the friend that Tag thought he was?

"Praise the Lord!" Nikki raised a hand as high as it would go. "He's eaten two bites. I think he's goin' to live. I'll let Emily know so she won't ruin her makeup with tears." She disappeared out of the room.

"You should marry that woman," Maverick said.

"The M-word scares me worse than that smartass remark about death." Tag grabbed a beer and tipped it up.

"Amen, brother." Paxton nodded. "We're all still young."

"And we've got wild oats to sow," Maverick agreed.

"You're preachin' to the choir," Tag chuckled.

"He's lyin' to us, guys," Hud said. "He's been thinkin' about settlin' down ever since we got here. I can see it in his eyes."

"For being my twin, you don't know me at all." Tag was tempted to call Billy Tom and ask him exactly what kind of trouble he and the boys were about to get into, just to prove his point.

*   *   *

The kitchen was put together by nine thirty, and the guys had all left except for Justin. He'd fallen asleep in a recliner in the living room. Emily poured two glasses of white wine and handed one to Nikki, and motioned to the two stools shoved up under the bar.

"Thank you for coming tonight. Gloria was here this afternoon and thought she could arrange everything. I gave her a hug and told her that I wanted to do things my way since this was my dream house. She decided that she needed to make a trip to town to get her nails done if she couldn't 'help.'" Emily put finger quotes around the last word. "I am too tired to put up with the guilt trip that she'd send me on if she came back tonight, so I'm glad she didn't. I just want to go to bed with Justin this first night in our own home and have him hold me until we both fall asleep."

"Talk about a guilt trip." Nikki told Emily about talking on the phone with her mother. "I tell myself every week that I won't let her affect me like this, but I always do."

"Yep." Emily took a sip of wine. "I'll fight a forest fire with only a cup of water most of the time, so why do I let Gloria get my goat?"

"You want her to like you since she's Justin's mama. I want my mama to love me, and maybe she does as much as she's capable to love anyone other than herself. You and I make quite the pair, don't we?" Nikki downed her wine and put a hand over the top of her glass when Emily started to refill it.

"That's enough for me. I've got to drive home," she said. "And I should be going just in case you and Justin have enough energy to christen this first night in your new home." She slid off the barstool and gave Emily a sideways hug. "I love the house. Someday I hope to have what you've got here."

"I want that for you too." Emily pushed her stool back and followed Nikki to the door. "Call me. Tomorrow is going to be like the day after Christmas. We were busy with the wedding, and the house, and now it's all done. Until the kids come out to the ranch for summer camp in a few weeks, I'll have free time."

"Will do. And if you get bored, just come on over to my place. We'll break out the ice cream." Nikki waved over her shoulder on her way to her car.

She sensed that someone was behind her and noticed that black Lincoln she'd seen a few days ago. She whipped around to confront whoever it might be and ran right into Tag's chest.

"Hey, I didn't mean to spook you." He caught her in his arms to keep them both from falling. "I forgot to get the key to the cabin from Emily. I'm moving in there tomorrow."

Her first instinct was to take a step backward, but his hold felt almost comforting. She looked up to find his gaze glued to her face.

His forefinger traced her cheek, then cupped her jaw, and then he bent enough that his lips covered hers in a scalding hot kiss. He picked her up and set her on the hood of her car. The tip of his tongue touched her lips, and she opened enough to let him inside, and she discovered that the taste of chocolate and beer together was pretty damned amazing.

"I've wanted to do that since the wedding," he whispered when the kiss ended, and their foreheads were pressed together as they both tried to catch their breath.

If she were to be perfectly honest, she had wanted him to kiss her, too, but she couldn't make herself say the words. Then of all the crazy things to come out of her mouth, she heard herself ask, "Want some help moving in tomorrow? I don't have to work again until Wednesday at four."

Did I really say that out loud?

The expression on Tag's face told her that she had, and she couldn't very well take them back.

"That would be great. I've got to work until dusk. We've got to get the fences bull tight so we can turn our cattle out of the corral. We've got good grass," he said. "And I'm talking too much. If you'll give me your address, I'll pick you up at your place at seven, and maybe we can start with some grocery shopping."

"I'll be ready," she said.

He brushed a sweet kiss across her forehead and disappeared into the darkness. With trembling legs, she slid off the hood and got into her car. When she turned the key to start the engine, the radio was on and the Pistol Annies were singing "I Feel a Sin Comin' On." It seemed like every single word had been written just for her that evening, especially when Miranda Lambert said that she had a shiver all the way down to the bone.

Chapter Seven

Tag stood in the middle of the cabin floor and did a slow 360-degree turn. For the first time in his life, he wouldn't be living in the same house with his twin brother. Had he made the right decision volunteering to take the cabin?

"Hey," Emily yelled as she entered the cabin. "I had half an hour, so thought I'd stop by and see how things are going."

Her red ponytail stuck out the hole in the back of a baseball hat and her face was bright red from heat and sweat. Hay stuck to her long-sleeved chambray shirt and her faded jeans.

"Glad to see you, sis. Can I get you a glass of sweet tea or a root beer? That and water is all you left for me in the fridge."

"Water is good," she said as she sat down on the sofa. "We're haulin' hay between this place and our new house. I really stopped by to talk to you more than anything."

He took two bottles of water from the small refrigerator, uncapped them, and handed one to her. "Am I in trouble?" Had she somehow found out about Billy Tom calling him?

"Should you be?" She gave him the evil sister eye.

The old wooden rocking chair groaned when he sat down. "Sounds like this thing needs some tightening up."

"Now that the house is built, I want to be part of the ranchin' business—outside of course. Retta can have that book work in the ranch house. I'm not sure Justin wants me to be in the field." She paused and tipped up the water bottle for a long drink. "I'm more than willing to go help Retta however I can if she needs me when the baby comes. But I want to do more than cook and be a housewife."

Tag chuckled.

"It's not funny. I'm confused."

"Justin has a new beautiful wife. If I were him, I'd have misgivings about you being in the field too. All those hired hands are lookin' at you. And you can bet they're layin' wagers as to who can throw more bales or stack them quicker than you. That makes you the person they're talkin' about," Tag said. "I'm surprised you're talkin' to me about this instead of Nikki."

"I need a man's viewpoint," she said. "Speakin' of Nikki, I hear that she's volunteered to help you do some shoppin' tonight. Tag, I know you and I know Nikki. She's my best friend. Promise me you won't have a fling with her and then break her heart."

"I promise," he agreed.

"That was quick. Where's my real brother, Tag? What have you done with him?"

He managed a weak smile. "I'm not sure, but I think I left him out in West Texas, and to be honest, I don't know what to do with this new critter inside me."

"I'm your sister. You can talk to me," Emily said.

"I'm twenty-nine years old, and I've sown so many wild oats that we'd have a silo full if we harvested them all. But I'm not ready to settle down or to live by myself. Do you realize that I've never lived away from Hud? That we've lived in the same house all of our lives, most of the time right across the hall from each other since the day we were born?"

"Of course I do," Emily said. "I think the old Tag is worrying about all these changes. He doesn't like them at all. He loved being the bad boy. But now the new Tag has the responsibilities of a ranch, two hired hands, and a dream to make it prosperous. The new one is fighting with the old one."

"Which one will win?" Tag asked.

"The one you feed. If you continue in your wild ways, then you're feedin' that one. The ranch will survive. Hud and the Callahan cowboys will see to that, so don't worry about being a failure there. If you feed this new responsible Tag, the old wild boy will gradually slink off to be nothing but a memory. It's up to you what you want to do with your life, little brother," she said.

"You sound like Granny. What if I don't know which one I want to feed?"

"I'll take that as a compliment, and, honey, another bit of her advice is that you can't ride two horses with one ass, especially across a raging river. When you go to sleep tonight, lie there in bed for ten minutes and think about going to the Rusty Spur this weekend, picking up a woman, and going home with her for a one-night stand. Then put that all away and think about settling down and coming home every night to a woman who will be there with you forever. Whichever one brings you peace, feed that one. Now, I've got to go. Enjoy the cabin." She stood up and tossed the empty water bottle across the room to the trash can.

"That was a three-pointer for sure." Tag hurled his bottle that way. It bounced off the wall, missed the mark, and rolled under the bed.

"Yep, and one more thing—if I find out you've brought one of your bar bunnies to this cabin, I'll kick you out, and that's a fact." Emily started for the door. "You can pony up the money for a hotel or go home with her."

When she was gone, Tag did another turn, taking in the whole one-room cabin again. A coffee table that had seen lots of boots propped on it sat in front of a well-worn sofa that faced a fireplace that wouldn't be used for many months. Behind the sofa was a table with four mismatched chairs. Two steps away in the back right corner there was a tiny kitchen area with an apartment-size stove and refrigerator, maybe five feet of cabinets, and a closet with a hot water tank. To the left was a nice king-size bed—he forgot to thank his sister for leaving the sheets and quilt—and a window air-conditioning unit. He'd always envisioned the first place he lived in on his own would look more like a bachelor pad and less like a home.

You've outgrown a damn bachelor pad, his granny's voice said sternly in his head. *It's time for you to grow up and settle down.*

*   *   *

Nikki didn't know whether she trusted herself enough to allow Tag to knock and invite him into her apartment, or if she should just wait on the steps for him to arrive. After the kiss from the night before, she finally decided that she'd better be sitting on the stairs when he drove up. She picked up her purse, locked the door behind her, and was halfway down when she heard a truck door slam. When she reached the bottom, he was opening the door for her.

"You're right on time," she said as she slid into the passenger seat.

"One of my many good qualities." His gaze held her spellbound.

"Well, I appreciate it." She blinked and looked away, but her heart was still racing. "Did you bring a list?" She took a deep breath and started down toward him.

He leaned on the door a moment. "I know for sure I need some towels and toilet paper."

"Have you ever lived on your own before? Not even in college?" she asked.

"Didn't go. All me and Hud wanted to be was ranchers, so we graduated high school and went on the full-time payroll the next Monday morning." When he started the truck, the radio was on the same country music station that she liked, but he quickly turned it off. "I love music. How about you?"

"Love country music and if I'm in a really funky mood, a little jazz, but only in small doses," she answered. "The cabin is really your first home away from home?"

"I guess the ranch house over on Canyon Creek is the first one, but Hud was with me there, and then Maverick and Paxton. The cabin is my first time to have a place all to myself."

"Do you even know how to do laundry, or cook or clean?" she asked.

"Oh, yes, ma'am. Mama lived by the goose and gander law. That meant that us boys had to learn all the stuff that Emily did, and she had to learn all the stuff we did on the ranch. I'm particular about laundry, and I can clean a house good enough to pass military inspection. And I can make the meanest ham and cheese sandwich and chili cheese nachos in the state," he said. "I'll be glad to make either one for you anytime you want to come by the cabin. Or if that doesn't sound good, I know how to nuke a bean burrito and open a bottle of beer."

"Sounds good to me," she said. "Take the next left."

"Thanks. I've never driven from this side of town before." He flipped on the turn signal.

"Canyon Creek? Is that what y'all decided to name the place?"

"Yep," he answered as he circled the parking lot in search of a spot. "Now we're trying to come up with a brand that we like. And we named the dog too."

"Dog?" She raised an eyebrow.

"Ranch has to have a dog. We're goin' to do our best to train him to be a cattle dog, but a redbone is really a coonhound. We named him Ol' Red, but we're just callin' him Red."

"For Blake Shelton's song, right?" she asked.

"You got it." Tag pulled into a parking space.

"Was he a stray?" Nikki asked as she got out of the truck and started toward the store.

"Nope. Some woman was giving them away at the rodeo. Hud snagged the last one." He fell in beside her. "You like dogs?"

"Love them and cats too. I'd get a cat, but I'm gone from Friday night at midnight until Sunday night for work. I'd feel guilty about leaving it alone that long," she said.

"Ever had pets when you were a kid?"

"Oh, no!"

"That was pretty definite." The store's automatic doors opened, and he pulled a cart out from the line. "You want to push?"

"Make it easier if I do. Then you can have both hands free to load it up. And it was definite. You'd have to know my mother to understand." She pushed the cart inside and made a right to go to the housewares side of the store to look at towels.

"Does she live in that apartment with you?" he asked.

"Good Lord no!"

"Another definite answer." He pointed up to a sign that said towels were down that aisle. "How long have you lived alone?"

"Since the day I was eighteen. That was right after high school graduation. I've lived in the same apartment for over ten years now," she answered.

A cart bumped into hers when she turned the corner. "I'm so sorry," she started.

"I've told you a million times to watch where you're going," her mother scolded.

"Mama, what are you doing here at this time of night?" Nikki was totally in shock.

Wilma wore a trench coat buttoned up the neck and white dress gloves. Her dark brown hair was shoved up under a plastic shower cap. Red and white polka dotted rain boots peeked out from under the hem of her coat.

"I'm tired of Mrs. Thomas coming over on Tuesdays, so I decided to get out and do some shopping. I was out of calcium and my morning stomach pills, and since you refuse to shop for me anymore, I have to do it myself." She sighed.

"We've been over this, Mama. If I keep doing everything for you, you'll never get off the recliner or out of the house," Nikki said.

Wilma held up a gloved hand. "Don't sass me, but you can tell me what you're doin' with this hoodlum. My preacher is never going to marry you if you get a reputation with this..." She eyed Tag up and down with an evil look.

"Mama, this is Tag Baker. Tag, my mother, Wilma Grady." Nikki made introductions in a tone so cold that it would have put a fresh layer of ice over the North Pole.

"Pleasure to meet you, ma'am." Tag tipped his hat toward her.

Wilma gave him another disgusted look and turned back to Nikki. "I've got things to do. I have to be home by eight to see my show."

Nikki reached out and laid a hand on Wilma's shoulder. "Mama, it's hot outside. Why are you dressed like this?"

"Germs." Wilma shrugged off her hand. "You never know what you'll catch in a place like this. I'll take a shower when I get home and use that bacteria-killin' soap to be sure. It'll get rid of anything that I might pick up in here. Woman in my condition don't need to take chances with germs. I'll talk to you on Monday." Her rubber boots made a squeaky sound on the tile as she hurried toward the checkout counter.

"I'm sorry," Nikki said to Tag.

"No need to apologize for something you have no control over," he said. "But now I see why you couldn't have pets."

"And that's just the tip of the iceberg," Nikki said. "Let's go buy towels and try to put what just happened behind us."

"Yes, ma'am." He began to study the colors, thickness, and size of each stack of towels.

She watched him and hoped that tomorrow morning she didn't find an email with a dozen new shots of people who go to Walmart in weird outfits with her mother among them. In some ways she felt sorry for Wilma. In other ways, she wished that she'd been born into a different family.

"Need a hamper?" she asked when he put a set of bath towels into the basket.

"Nope, brought that when we moved into the house, but

I do need soap of all kinds. Dish, laundry, and shower," he answered.

When they'd finished his shopping, they were lucky enough not to have to stand in line long and got everything loaded into his truck.

"You had supper?" he asked.

"I had a sandwich."

"I haven't eaten yet. Barely had time to get a shower after fencing and cutting hay all day. Want to join me for a burger or maybe a pizza?"

"I'd rather have some of those chili cheese nachos you were bragging about," she answered.

It might not be a good idea to be alone with Tag, but he'd met Wilma, and this was probably the last time he'd ever ask her out. After all, she had the same DNA and there was a possibility she could grow up to be just like her mother. Who was it that said if you wanted to know what a girl would look like when she got older, just take a look at her mother?

Besides, she'd been in the cabin many, many times in the past few months since Emily had moved into it with Justin. It had a homey feel to it, not a one-night-stand kind of aura.

"That can be arranged. Nachos and beer and ice cream afterwards," he said.

"Sounds good," she agreed. "But are you sure you want to be alone with me now that you've met my mother?"

"We all have skeletons in our closets, Nikki," he said. "In our part of the world, we don't hide our crazy relatives. We put them on the front porch with a glass of sweet tea and let them wave at all the cars that go by."

She giggled and then laughed and then snorted. "I'm picturing my mother on the porch with one of those beekeeper hats on her head."

His laughter was as deep as his drawl. "Why a bee bonnet?"

The laughter ended as quickly as it had started. "Because she's afraid to go out without protection for fear she'll get malaria."

"I understand." He gently laid a hand on her shoulder.

Was this Tag really the same playboy who'd tried to sweet-talk her into bed the night of Emily and Justin's wedding? Or was this just a new tactic with hopes that it would lead to a different result?

She was still pondering the questions when they reached the cabin, but not a single answer had fallen from the sky. "I'll help unload if you'll hand the sacks to me. I'm too short to reach over the truck bed."

A puppy barked a couple of times from the porch and then ran out to meet them. He found his way to Nikki first and wiggled all over. She stooped down to pet him and got a lick across her face for her efforts.

"You might as well go on and get a Catahoula now. This isn't ever going to be anything but a pet." She picked him up, and he fell over to lie in her arms like a baby.

"You pet him and I'll unload all this stuff," Tag said. "Might as well bring him on in the house and rock him. That'll keep him out from under my feet." He set two bags on the porch beside the door.

His phone rang, and he fished it out of his hip pocket and opened the door for her at the same time.

"He was waiting on the porch for us, and, no, I won't spoil him by letting him start staying in the house."

A long pause while he listened to whoever was on the other end of the line.

"It's not like that."

Another pause as she sat down in the rocking chair.

"I'll bring him back over in the morning. See y'all bright and early, and yes, I'll be there in time for breakfast," he said before he shoved the phone in his pocket.

He·tossed the bags on the bed and went back outside, returning this time with three in each hand. They must've been heavier than the first ones because his biceps strained the fabric of the light blue knit shirt he wore. Nikki couldn't tear her eyes away from him and wondered how it would feel to wake up with Tag's strong arms around her.

"One more load," he said. "And then I'll make nachos while you take care of the baby."

"You got a deal," she told him.

He put away the groceries and then opened a can of chili and added several kinds of spices to it. Then he arranged chips on a platter that he'd bought that night and topped them with the chili and grated cheese. He nuked it all to melt the cheese and heat the chili, then added diced tomatoes and jalapeno pepper slices.

"Onions or not?" he asked.

"Not for me," she answered.

"Leaving the onions off," he said. "I'm not a big fan of them either." He put the platter in the middle of the table and opened two bottles of beer. "Dinner is ready, Your Highness. Red can nap on the sofa or go outside. His choice."

"But what about coyotes? Or hawks? Don't you worry that they'll kill him?" she asked.

"Not a redbone hound. He'll set up a howl and chase a coyote. That's his nature. And he's way too big for a hawk to carry off. I'd guess him at two to three months old," Tag said.

She set the dog on the floor, and he ran to the door. "That makes me feel better about him going outside. Give me time to wash my hands."

While Tag let the animal out, she went to the bathroom and washed the puppy smell from her hands and arms. She tiptoed to see her reflection in the mirror, and there was the same Nikki that she'd seen a month ago staring back at her. But this one had more questions in her eyes than the previous one—like even though the chemistry between her and Tag was undeniable, did she really want to take the next step with him? Was she setting herself up for heartbreak? And the biggest question of all was would it make things awkward with Emily?

She dried her hands and left the bathroom to find him holding a chair for her. "My first guest in my new home. Thank you for all your help and for coming over. It would be a sin to have to eat alone this first night."

"Well, when you get to the pearly gates, you be sure to let them know that I was the one who kept you from sinnin' tonight," she said.

"Well, dammit! I was hoping that since we broke bread—as in nachos together—it would wipe out the sin that will come after we get through supper." He grinned.

They were sure back on familiar ground now. "In your dreams, cowboy. Besides, Emily told me that she'd kick you out of your little piece of heaven here if you brought a woman home for the night. Last time I checked, I am a female."

"Yes, you definitely are, darlin'. I'll make a mental note to never attempt to date one of my sister's friends again, no matter how sexy and funny they are, because best friends share everything," he said. "Now, while we eat, tell me about yourself."

"Hasn't Emily already told you the Nikki Grady story? God, these nachos are fabulous. Better than any I've ever had at a Mexican restaurant," she said as she picked up another chip.

Tag shook his head. "All Emily's told me is that y'all worked together for a long time, and then you passed your RN test and went to work at the hospital. That was about the time that her Fab Five elderly buddies left the retirement center, right?"

The nachos were addictive. Like that commercial on television about potato chips, there was no way to eat just one. "Pretty much. That was when Emily decided to move to the ranch too. We all made a big change."

"I met those old folks at the wedding, and I've seen them at church the past couple of weeks, but I'd love to get to know them better. Emily says they're a hoot," he said.

She was sure that Bess, Patsy, and Sarah, the three elderly ladies from the retirement center, had already been swooning over him. That, and the fact that dogs loved him, too, had to be good signs, right?

"Have y'all adjusted to the change of not seeing those senior citizens every day?" he asked.

"Pretty much. Emily and I stop by the house the Fab Five bought together every couple of weeks and catch up on all their shenanigans. And, of course, she and I talk every day, except weekends when I'm working. How are you adapting to this big change in your life, Tag?"

"What did Emily tell you?"

"About?"

"Our talk this morning." He narrowed his eyes.

"Nothing except that you had one and that she forbade you to use this place as a brothel," she answered. "Let me tell you something, Tag Baker. Your sister would take a bullet to the head before she would betray a confidence. She told me what she said about you not bringing women here, but whatever else you told her is between y'all."

"Thank you." A smile covered his face. "And this cabin

is not a brothel. You have to pay for sex in those places. I've never charged."

She blushed at the idea of putting money on the bedside table as she left.

"As far as changes, darlin'." He leaned forward and his drawl got deeper. "Buying a ranch has been the biggest responsibility I've ever faced. I've never worked so hard or been as happy with the results or had dreams this big. Sometimes it overwhelms me."

She was almost as shocked by his admission as she'd been by her mother's appearance earlier that evening. "I thought you were ten feet tall and bulletproof, like Travis Tritt sings about. I didn't think anything would ever be an obstacle for you."

"Keep thinkin' that, darlin'."

It was after ten when he took her home and held her hand as they climbed the stairs side by side. She unlocked the door and turned to find him staring right into her eyes.

"I had a good time tonight, Tag," she said.

"Me too. When can I pick you up for a second date?"

"This wasn't a date," she told him. "It was a friend helping a friend move into his cabin and then having supper with him."

His hands cupped her face, thumbs brushing her cheeks. His palm felt like feathers dancing across the sensitive place on her neck. He leaned in for the kiss, and Nikki went up on her tiptoes.

She had been kissed before. She'd had long-term relationships. She'd had her heart broken more than once since she'd lived on her own. She'd made mistakes and learned from them. But nothing prepared her for the way she felt whenever Tag's lips met hers. The whole world disappeared in a flash, leaving only the two of them standing on a small upstairs porch with the moon and stars above them.

When the kiss ended, Tag took a step back and braced himself on the railing. "If that affected you the way it did me, then, darlin', this was definitely a date. Good night, Nikki."

He turned and walked away without looking back.

Normally she would have called Emily and confided in her about her evening, about the kiss and how it left her wanting more. But she couldn't tell Emily all that when she'd be talking about her brother. She threw herself on the sofa and finally called Patsy.

"Hello, Nikki. Are you all right? Do I need to get the other four up?" Patsy asked.

"I'm fine. I shouldn't be callin' this late, but I had to talk to someone," Nikki said.

"Darlin', I'm a night owl. You know that, and I'm here for you anytime you need me. So talk." Patsy was part of the Fab Five, as the five friends had dubbed themselves, and she was possibly the wildest one of the lot. She was a twin sister to Bess, and Sarah was their friend, right along with Otis and Larry. They were more like parents or grandparents to Nikki and Emily than just mere friends.

"I kissed Tag Baker tonight, and I liked it, and I can't talk to Emily about it. I can't like him, Patsy. I'm twenty-nine years old and ready to settle down. He's wild and never wants to be any other way, I'm afraid. Why am I attracted to the bad boys?"

Patsy giggled. "Because where's the fun in taming a sweet little preacher-type boy? You come on up here to Sunset and us girls will have a real face-to-face talk about this. And you're right, Emily would freak out, so don't tell her. Can you come tomorrow?"

"Have to work tomorrow. How about Thursday?" Nikki asked.

"That's even better. We'll send Otis and Larry to the store so we can have some time by ourselves. And, honey, if you liked that kiss, just imagine how he'd make you feel in the bedroom." She giggled again. "Or the hayloft."

"Patsy!" Nikki gasped.

"It's okay to dream, and thanks for callin'. It's been kind of dull around here since Emily and Justin got married. See you on Thursday at one o'clock. Don't eat a big lunch. We'll have snacks."

"Thanks, Patsy."

"Oh, no, baby girl. Thank you!"

The call ended and Nikki threw herself back on the sofa. Why couldn't Wilma invite her to have cookies and coffee or lemonade and treat her like a daughter instead of a liability?

*　　*　　*

When he got back to the cabin, Tag did what his sister had told him. He stretched out on the king-size bed and imagined always being that wild child he'd been since he and Duke got their first motorcycles. He closed his eyes and thought of the wind in his face, the dust boiling up behind him, and the thrill of going ninety miles an hour down a dirt road. He even thought about calling Billy Tom and asking if they could meet in Dallas some Saturday night so they could hit some biker bars.

Then he turned over in bed, pulled an extra pillow up next to his body, and put all those thoughts aside. He opened his eyes, looked at the ceiling; then he closed them again. He imagined that the pillow was someone he loved dearly, a woman like Nikki who'd be there waiting for him at the end of a long day on the ranch. Who would listen to his fears and share in his joys when the first new calf was born on the ranch, and at a later date when they could add more acreage to Canyon Creek. Who would cuddle with him before they went to sleep each night. The image was so real that his hand reached to stroke her long, dark hair before he remembered that what he was holding was just a pillow.

His eyes snapped open and he threw the pillow across the room. "Why is this so hard?" he asked himself.

No answer came.

Chapter Eight

By the time Nikki reached the ER waiting room that evening, she was wiping sweat from her forehead with the back of her hand. Once inside the cool room, she grabbed a fistful of tissues from the admitting clerk's desk and did a proper number on her face. Then she hit the hand sanitizer pump on her way back into the ER.

"Well, look at you," Rosemary said. "Is that twinkle in your eye because you've spent time with the sexy blue-eyed cowboy you were seen with last night at the store?"

"If anyone thinks they can hide anything in Bowie, Texas, they'd better think again. And what are you doin' here?"

"Same thing you are. The hospital is short staffed, so we both got called in. Let's hope we don't get it before we get our hours in," Rosemary said, and then whispered, "Is he as delicious as he looks?"

A deep crimson filled both of Nikki's cheeks. Good

Lord! She hadn't blushed this often in her whole life combined.

"Aha, he is, isn't he?"

"I wouldn't know, and we've got to get to reports." She whipped around and made a beeline for the break room.

The first name that popped up on her tablet was Sue Ann. Nikki covered her eyes and sighed. Talk about a buzzkill.

"She just got here a few minutes ago. I tried to assess her, but she told me to get the hell out and get you, Nikki. She's floating around and seeing spiders on the ceiling," the nurse who'd been on the eight-to-four shift said. "I hope you can do something with her."

"I'll do my best," Nikki said.

"There's a little boy from Nocona in number four. Leukemia in its last stages," the nurse said. "Dr. Richards said to give him whatever he needs to make him comfortable and ask his mother again if she wants to admit him. If she takes him home later tonight, then we should call hospice."

"I'll take that one," Rosemary said. "I can't do anything with Sue Ann."

Tears welled up in Nikki's eyes at the thought of a child dying. She knew this day would come someday, but she'd hoped that she'd have a harder heart when it did arrive.

"That's all we've got, ladies," the second nurse said. "Hopefully it'll be as slow for you as it has been for us. A heads-up—you'll probably be asked to pull a double, so get ready for it." They were both yawning when they left.

Rosemary touched Nikki on the shoulder. "You okay, kiddo?"

"Fine, just hurts me to hear about a child who's...well, you know," she said honestly.

"It's the job, darlin'. We do our best, especially with the

young ones. Now, let's get to it. You ready for a double and then the weekend too?"

Nikki nodded. "We'll have Thursday and Friday to catch up on sleep. Or at least I will. You've got kids and a husband."

"I won't bitch a single minute when I take my paycheck to the bank, though." Rosemary smiled. "Let me know if Sue Ann starts crawlin' the walls. I'll bring the restraints."

Nikki picked up her tablet, took a deep breath, and eased between the curtains into the cubicle with Sue Ann. "Hello, I'm kind of surprised to see you here so soon, and it's not even a weekend."

"It's devils," Sue Ann whispered. "I went to church Sunday after I was in here. I've got devils in me, and I took some pills to get rid of them."

"What did you take?" Nikki pulled up Sue Ann's chart.

"I don't know. Whatever was in the cabinet. Top shelf." She pointed to the ceiling. "That's where we kept Mama's pills."

"Sue Ann, your mama has been dead for ten years," Nikki said.

"Pills are still good, though, ain't they? Mama was a churchgoin' woman, so I figured her pills would get rid of the devils in my soul. Mama talks to me sometimes. I just have to be real quiet to hear her. She tells me to go to church and get right with the Lord," Sue Ann said.

Nikki stepped out of the cubicle and called the intern on duty. He was familiar with Sue Ann and told her to induce vomiting and call the psych ward. She went back into the cubicle with a dose of ipecac in her hand and thinking that compared to Sue Ann, her mother was the sanest person in the whole state of Texas.

"This is going to get the devil out of your soul, but you

have to drink it all," she told Sue Ann. "Don't sip it. Just throw it back like a tequila shot."

"You sure this will work? Don't you need to do one of the STI things where you put jelly on my stomach?" Sue Ann asked.

"No, Dr. Tillery said this is the very thing you need," Nikki assured her.

Sue Ann drew her eyebrows down into a solid line. "He's that good-lookin' new doctor, right? I like him. If Dr. Richards said to take it, then I'd throw it at the wall. I don't like that man. He don't believe I'm sick."

"Well, Dr. Tillery believes you. You take this to get rid of the devil and then we're going to admit you. How many of your mama's pills did you take?"

"Three bottles. Mama said that if I took them all that the devils would be gone and I'd be with her in heaven," Sue Ann whimpered.

"Well, honey, we're goin' to get rid of those mean things for you. Just take this," Nikki said.

Ten minutes later, Sue Ann had brought up dozens of undigested pills and was on her way up to the psych ward, where hopefully she would get some much-needed help. Unless, of course, history repeated itself and she checked herself out and went right back to the Rusty Spur. There was a very real possibility that she would be right back in the same cubicle with another devil or alien in her body come Saturday night or next Sunday morning.

Since they were short staffed, Nikki cleaned up the area and got it ready for the next patient. Then she slipped down the row and peeked into the room where the young boy was lying. His shaggy blond hair hung to his collar, and his eyes were sunken into his thin face. Frail hands held a computer game, but he finally dropped it and closed his eyes. She held her breath until his chest moved up and down a few times.

Other than the hair color, he reminded her so much of Quint those last days. If only she'd been a bone marrow donor, he'd be alive and well today. Or if they could have found a match for him before it was too late.

"We just got a call. Wreck out south of town and they're sending them here for first evaluations," Dr. Tillery said as he came out of his office. He peeked over Nikki's shoulder. "I hate it when they're kids."

"There's no way to find a bone marrow donor?" she asked.

"Too far along for that now. He's an only child, and from what I read in his charts, it would've taken a miracle to find a match," he said. "Better get ready for a rush. I understand there were six people hurt in the wreck, and I'm already going to ask you to work a double. You up for that?"

"Sure thing," she said.

*   *   *

Nikki was so bone tired when she left the hospital the next morning around eight thirty that all she wanted was a shower and a bed for at least twelve hours. Then she remembered that she'd told the ladies she would come to Sunset right after lunch.

"Oh well," she muttered. "That'll give me four hours of sleep."

She dragged her tired body up the steps and tried to wash away the smell of near death, blood, and tears in the shower. She forgot to turn off her phone when she fell facedown on her bed and wrapped the comforter around her. When she heard the ping, she glanced at it with bleary eyes. The text was from Patsy—she had forgotten that the Fab Five had promised to have dinner with Emily that day so they could see her new house. Could they postpone their time with Nikki until tomorrow? She sent a short message back that said: Sure thing. No problem.

While her eyes were semiopen, she read another one from Emily inviting her to the dinner. She sent one to her: Double shift. Need sleep. Rain check.

The last one was from Tag: Pick you up at eight on Thursday night. Have surprise for you.

I'll be ready, she replied.

Then she set her alarm clock for six, turned off her phone, and closed her eyes. The last thing she saw as she drifted off to sleep was Tag tipping his black hat toward her the first time she met him out in Tulia, Texas.

Chapter Nine

The apartment was straightened up, and Nikki was ready fifteen minutes early that evening. At first she thought she'd meet Tag on the steps like last time, but he said he had a surprise. If it was something that needed to be brought inside the apartment, then that would be awkward. After all, she'd been in his cabin—even shared nachos with him at his kitchen table, and talked about everything and nothing for a while. Not inviting him into her place would be downright rude.

She checked her reflection in the full-length mirror on the back of the bedroom door. She'd curled her hair, put on makeup, and chosen a brown-and-white-checkered sundress for the evening. Her brown cowboy boots matched it perfectly, but maybe she should have chosen sandals? Was she overdressed? Or worse, underdressed? Whatever, she didn't have time to change now.

After his comment about being on time, she expected

him to knock on the door at exactly eight o'clock. She was not disappointed, but the knock still startled her. She scanned the living room one more time to be sure everything was tidy before she opened the door.

Tag had a brown paper bag in his arms and a smile on his face. "You look gorgeous this evening. I'd thought we'd go for pizza, but since you're so dressed up, maybe we'll go somewhere nicer."

"Pizza sounds great." She couldn't keep her eyes off the bag. "I'm sorry. Please come in."

"Nice little place you got here." His eyes scanned the living room before he set the sack on the kitchen table. He removed a big round clear glass bowl first and carried it to the kitchen sink. Bright colored rocks were the first thing he added to the bowl before he filled it about halfway with water.

"I didn't know what your favorite color was, so I got the multicolored package," he said.

"What are you doing?" she asked.

"Fixin' up your surprise." He looked around again and set the bowl of water on an end table. Then he pulled out a small yellow container and set it beside the bowl.

"What is that?" she asked.

The last thing he brought out was a plastic bag with a goldfish in it. "This is your new pet. She can stay all by herself over the weekend. You only have to clean up after her about once a week and feed her every day. Maybe a little extra on Friday since she'll be all by herself all weekend. She told me that country music is her favorite, so you might want to leave the radio on while you're gone so it don't get lonesome."

For the first time in a very long while, Nikki was speechless.

"If you don't like it, I'll take it to the cabin." His eyes went to the floor, reminding her of her brother when their mother yelled at them about tracking dead leaves into the house or some other minor infraction that upset her perfect world.

"I love it. I'll tell her bedtime stories and let her listen to country music so she won't get lonely. Thank you, Tag." She took two steps forward and hugged him. "But how do you know it's a girl?"

He raised his head and his smile lit up the room. "It seemed like a good idea last night, but now it's kind of silly, isn't it? And it's a girl because she's so pretty."

"Tag, it's just about the sweetest thing anyone has ever done for me. Does she have a name?" she asked.

"You get to give her a name," he said. "And you get to welcome her home by dumping her out into the fishbowl. And there's a little booklet on how to clean the bowl in the bag too."

"I'll have to think about it for a few days to come up with the right name. Can I open the bag and set her free now?" She backed away from him.

"Yep, and then you can feed her. Look on the back of the can of fish food there to find out how much and how often," Tag said. "And once she's fed, we can go have our supper."

She picked up the can and read it, and then she opened the bag and set the goldfish free. Big bubble eyes stared at her through the side of the bowl, and then she made a couple of circles to check out the new housing. Nikki carefully pinched a little food between her finger and thumb and dropped it on top of the water. It floated for a few seconds and then began to sink. The fish gobbled down every sliver before it could hit the rocks.

"Is she still hungry?" she asked.

"The booklet says to just feed it twice a day, and the ideal thing is for it to eat all the food so that it doesn't pollute the water."

"Did you ever have one of these?" She popped the lid back on the food can.

"Nope. I thought about bringing you a turtle or maybe a lizard, but this seemed to be what would require the least upkeep. I'm glad you like it."

"I do. I really do," Nikki said. "Thank you one more time."

He pulled her back into his arms. "Nikki, I'm not good at this, so bear with me."

"Now that's a load of bull crap," she giggled.

"No, really, I'm not. I can sweet-talk someone I meet in a bar into bed in a heartbeat. I'm an expert at that, but anything more—well, I start to stutter and I'm all thumbs," he said honestly. "I don't know where this chemistry between us might lead, but I know for it to even take the first step outside this door, I have to be honest. So there it is."

He sounded sincere. There was definitely chemistry between them. But chemistry, vibes, sparks, electricity—whatever word was used for physical attraction—did not inspire trust, did it? She'd proven that when she'd given her heart to her last boyfriend, only to find out that he was married.

One date doesn't mean you're going to marry the man. Quint's voice was plain in her head.

"Surely you've had at least one long-term relationship," she said as she picked up her purse.

Tag shook his head. "I've lived like I was dying since I was seventeen. That doesn't leave room for anything except family."

"Didn't you ever want something more permanent?" She bent down and put a fingertip on the fishbowl. "You hold the place down, Goldie, until I get home."

"Nope." He opened the door for her and then waited on the porch while she locked it. "Truth is, I didn't think I'd ever want one."

"And now?" She started down the stairs ahead of him.

"Truthfully, I'm not sure what I want," he answered.

"Fair enough." She nodded. "Whatever it is that we're feelin'—let's take it real slow. And now changing the subject because I'm hungry. There's a Thursday night all-you-can-eat bar at the pizza place. Let's go get our money's worth."

The place was less than five minutes from her apartment. When they arrived, Tag escorted her inside with his hand on the small of her back. She was past being surprised at the electricity flowing through her body at his slightest touch. Like he'd said earlier, there was chemistry between them. To deny it would be lying.

He paid the lady at the counter for two buffet dinners. She handed them each a plate, bowl, and glass and said, "Silverware is over by the soft drink machine. Help yourselves. Place is a little crowded, but I see a booth in the back corner."

"If you'll take the plates and claim that table, I'll be the bartender." Tag handed her his plates and took her glass. "What're you drinkin' tonight, ma'am?"

"I'm not picky as long as it's diet," she answered.

She made her way to the back of the place, set the plates down, and slid into the booth to wait for him. Positioned just so she could see his every move, she got a full view of the way he filled out those jeans, and his swagger. Of course, nearly every woman in the place was watching him from the corner of their eyes as well.

He carefully carried two full glasses plus the silverware and napkins to the table. She took her glass from him, set it

down, and together they went to the buffet to fill their bowls
with salad and load up their plates with pizza.

She was back to the booth first, and a movement out the
window caught her attention. Four motorcycles had parked,
and the guys were wearing no helmets. The sleeves were
gone from their denim jackets, leaving ragged edges. Evidently it was to show off the matching tattoos on their upper
arms. Crossed swords with some kind of insignia in the
middle. One of them had a gold chain from his earlobes to a
ring in his nose. The swooping chains looked like they were
holding up his bulldog cheeks. Didn't the fool know that in
any fight someone could jerk on that and give him a world
of pain?

Tag slid into the booth next to her and shook his head.
"Girl, I thought you said you were hungry?"

"This is just the appetizer. I'll go for the main course
after this and then finish up with a plate of dessert pizza,"
she said. "I might be small, but, honey, I love food."

"Well, damn it to hell," Tag muttered.

"You don't like women who enjoy their food?" Nikki
asked.

"That *damn* wasn't for you," he whispered as the four
bikers with dusty jeans headed straight for them.

"Well, well, lookit what we've found, boys. Pretty little
lady with an ugly old cowboy. Let's whup his ass and show
her what real men are." The one with the chains leered at her.

Nikki's blood ran cold as she slowly unzipped the side
pocket of her purse and brought out a pink .38 pistol. She
aimed it right at Mr. Chain's crotch and said, "Boys, I only
got five shots, but I think I can take two of you out with
one bullet so I don't waste ammunition. Now get your sorry
asses back out there on those ratty bikes and leave before
you get hurt."

Tag held up a hand. "It's okay. They're teasing. What are you doin' in Bowie, Texas, Billy Tom?"

"You know these people?" Nikki slid the safety back on the pistol and slipped it inside her purse, but she kept her hand on it—just in case.

Billy Tom slid into the booth and threw his big beefy arm around Tag's shoulders. He grabbed the top piece of pepperoni pizza from Tag's stack and took a bite. "We're on our way over to Tyler to do that little business I talked to you about. Thought we'd stop in here for some food and maybe call you to get directions to your ranch. Maybe talk you into changing your mind about the deal I offered you."

One of the other bikers reached for a piece of Nikki's pizza. She slapped his hand as hard as she could. "I don't share my food, and I'm not real good about sharing a date."

"Whoo-eee!" Billy Tom laughed with food in his mouth. "You done got yourself a piece of work there, Tag."

"She's a helluva bodyguard." Tag grinned. "Y'all best go on up to the counter and pay for your dinner. Sign over there says that sharin' ain't permitted."

"Bet she guards your body real good." Billy Tom gave her another lewd look.

She took her gun from her purse, again, and wondered if she could tangle those chains up in her fork. "What business are you talkin' about?"

"Just a little venture that we need Tag's help with," Billy Tom answered.

"No, thank you," Tag said. "I told you already, I'm done with that stuff. Now you've interrupted date night with me and my lady, and I'd appreciate it if you got on with your business and let us have a nice quiet meal."

"Sure thing, buddy, but remember, once a rebel, always a rebel. You can run but you can't hide from what's in your heart." Billy Tom stood up, grabbed another piece of pizza, and walked out with his posse behind him. The three of them got on their motorcycles and just sat there for a full five minutes waiting until Billy Tom came around the corner of the building and gave them a thumbs-up. When he had mounted his motorcycle, he and the others made a big show of revving them up. Through the window, Billy Tom flipped Tag off before he popped a wheelie and roared out of town.

"Guess they decided not to have pizza tonight." Nikki picked up the shaker with red pepper in it and shook it over a slice of sausage.

"I'm so, so sorry about that," Tag said.

"What're they into?"

"Who knows? It could be some get-rich-quick scheme or else some kind of crazy crap. How they stay out of jail is beyond me," he said.

"So that's the Billy Tom you told me about. Somehow I didn't picture him that big or that brazen," she said.

"Somehow I didn't picture you with a gun in your hand. Is that thing real?" he asked.

"Yes, and I have a license to carry it, both concealed and open. Last time I was at the range, I drilled five holes in a target that you could have covered with a half dollar. So as your bodyguard, I can take damn good care of you, Mr. Taggart Baker. Anything else you'd like to know about what's in my purse?" she asked.

"Hand grenades?" He wiggled his dark brows.

"I left those at home tonight, along with the sawed-off shotgun. I only bring them out when I carry my big purse," she answered. "Remember how I told you that I moved out on my own at eighteen? Well, honey, it didn't take me long to realize that a woman of my size needs a little backup companion sometimes. So now you've met my mama and my backup, and I've met your past. Guess we're even," she said.

"I think we just might be. Now let's talk about us. I started to buy you flowers tonight, but I didn't know your favorite color or if you like roses or orchids or what. Then I remembered that you'd never had a pet." He picked up a slice of pizza and bit into it.

"I like gerbera daisies in all colors. My favorite color is sunshine yellow, and I've never been fancy enough for roses or orchids. And I like Goldie better than flowers," she said. "Now my turn. What's your favorite color?"

"Blue, but I could stare into your brown eyes all night and never get bored," he said.

"That's a pretty good pickup line," she teased.

"It's the truth, not a line, but since we're bein' honest, I have used that one before. Would you fall for it?"

She shook her head and glanced out the window in time to see a black Lincoln parking not ten feet away. "I wouldn't fall for that one. Give me another one."

"Is it hot in here, or is it just you?" he said.

"Nope, not that one either. Do you know who's in that black car out there?"

Tag turned and cocked his head to one side and then the other, studying the vehicle. "Have no idea. Why are you asking?"

"For one thing, I've seen it several times and even felt like it was following me. For another, whoever it is isn't getting out of the car. Why go to the pizza place and just sit there?"

"I'll take care of this." Tag eased out of the booth and started that way with Nikki right behind him. But only the taillights of the vehicle were visible when they got outside.

"Did you get a look at whoever it was?" she asked.

He shook his head. "But this has surely been one crazy date. Next time we go out, I'm taking you out of town. Let's go back in and finish our dinner."

"Got to admit it hasn't been boring." She looped her arm in his and together they went inside and to their booth.

*   *   *

After sleeping all day and then the adrenaline rush of the evening, there was no way Nikki was going to bed when Tag walked her to the door and left her there a little before eleven. She kicked off her boots and slouched down on the end of the sofa.

"Well, Goldie, this has been a helluva night," she said.

The fish wiggled her big fan tail and did a couple of laps around the bowl. Nikki started to ask her if she was hungry, but her phone pinged. She dragged it out of her purse to find a text from Emily: Call me.

She hit Emily's number on speed dial and the phone scarcely finished the first ring before she heard, "We need to talk. What's this about you calling Patsy because you thought it would upset me that you kissed Tag? You should know none of them can keep a secret, especially when they're worried about you."

"I'm sorry, but if you want the whole story—"

"I already know y'all were together at the pizza place tonight and that he bought you a goldfish," Emily said. "I can't believe that my little brother is going out with my best friend."

"Are you going to yell at me and tell me that I have horrible taste in men? Especially after the last boyfriend?"

"No, but I might yell at *him* and tell him not to break

your heart or I'll break his neck," Emily said. "A goldfish? Why?"

"Because I told him that I'd never had a pet. She's a beauty. I named her Goldie. Did whoever tattled on us tell you about Billy Tom and his gang of wannabe thugs showing up?"

"Good God! I thought when he bought the ranch out here that he'd finally grown up and left that part of his life behind. What did they want?" Emily sighed.

"Something about a business deal that they needed Tag for," she said. "That's all I know except that he turned them down."

"Well, thank God for that," Emily said. "I hear you're going to visit the Fab Five tomorrow afternoon. I'll be there, too, so we can talk more then. My sexy husband and I are about to take a long shower together."

"Don't let me hold up that kind of thing," Nikki laughed. "See you tomorrow."

She ended the call and tossed her phone on the end of the sofa. "Well, Goldie, it's just you and me and late-night television. What do you want to watch, girl?"

She picked up the remote and surfed through the channels until she landed on reruns of *Justified*. The main character, Raylan Givens, didn't look a thing like Tag Baker, but they'd be a close match if attitudes could be measured by DNA. She fluffed up a throw pillow and stretched out on the sofa.

"I agree, Miz Goldie, this is just what we need tonight," she said.

Sometime near the fourth episode of the all-night marathon, she fell asleep only to dream of Tag. They were riding down a dirty road on his motorcycle. Her arms were around his chest, and his heart beat fast against her palms.

Her ponytail flew out behind her like a victory flag, and the wind rushed past her face. Then red and blue lights flashed behind them, and sirens started to scream. She yelled at him to pull over, but he just went faster and faster, until they hit a hole in the road. They were floating in slow motion from somewhere up high down to the ground when she awoke with a start.

"It was just a dream," she told herself as she went to get a glass of water. But she imagined that she could still taste the dust from the dream, and her heart thumped so loud that it hurt her ears. Was fate telling her that Billy Tom was right: once a rebel, always a rebel?

Chapter Ten

Nikki hadn't been to church since she'd taken the job at the hospital, but she considered going when she got off work that Sunday morning at eight. There was still plenty of time for her to get dressed and get there before service started. When she got home, she flipped through the hangers in her closet and chose a pink cotton dress with buttons down the front and a thin white belt. She slipped her feet into a pair of white sandals, picked up her purse, and told Goldie that she'd be back in a little while.

The congregation was standing, singing "Put Your Hand in the Hand" when she slipped in the back door. That definitely had to be an omen. She saw Wilma sitting on the pew behind Emily, but there wasn't room for another person there, so Nikki took a place in a pew right beside Emily and picked up a hymnal. Emily smiled and pointed at the page number in the book that she and Justin shared.

They were beginning the second verse when Tag tapped

her on the shoulder and stepped in beside her. She held her hymn book over toward him, and he took hold of one side. His deep voice sounded like it was made for gospel hymns, but then she imagined it would sound pretty danged good singing something like "Your Man" by Josh Turner. When they'd finished singing and everyone had sat down, she and Tag were shoulder to shoulder, thigh to thigh, and the temperature in the church felt like it had risen twenty degrees.

The preacher, a young man probably in his midtwenties, took the pulpit, opened his Bible, and read some verses about Jesus being the light of the world. That's as much as Nikki heard before her mind started to wander. She knew that Tag had been a daredevil, but if he'd ever been like Billy Tom and that group of crazy bikers, then he'd already changed a lot. Emily nudged her on the elbow and tilted her head slightly toward the pew behind them.

Nikki glanced back to see her mother's eyes boring holes into her. There wasn't a drop of Jesus' light in that condemning look. Hoping that maybe she'd turn Wilma's negativity to something positive, she decided that she'd take her mother out to eat. She tried to focus on that idea, but it was impossible with Tag sitting that close to her. Finally, after what seemed like two hours instead of thirty minutes, the preacher asked Otis to deliver the benediction.

The moment the last amen was said and folks began to get to their feet, Wilma tapped Nikki on the shoulder. "What are you doing here?"

"I thought you'd be happy to see me in church," Nikki answered.

Wilma was wearing white gloves, but she wasn't dressed in her boots and a trench coat today.

"I am," she said. "But you should be at work."

"Got the day off since I worked Wednesday. Want to go to dinner with me down at the café?" Nikki asked.

"You know very well my delicate stomach won't take that kind of food. Besides, I'm already fifteen minutes late for taking my midday medicine. I left my sandwich ready to eat. We can talk tomorrow night," Wilma answered.

"How about I get a sandwich and bring it to your house?" Nikki asked.

"Sunday afternoons are when I have my weekly nap." Wilma glanced down at her daughter's legs. "And you really should wear hose to church, Nikki."

"I see you aren't wearing your Walmart garb," Nikki said.

"The blood of Jesus cleanses us in the Lord's house," Wilma said through clenched teeth.

There was no way Tag couldn't have heard the whole conversation. He was close enough behind Nikki that she could feel his breath on her neck. But it shocked her when he draped an arm around her shoulders. "Well, since you've got the day off and nowhere to go for dinner, you can come to Emily's for pot roast. Afterwards, I was thinking about going down to the creek and doing some fishing. Want to go with me?"

Emily turned around and smiled. "And we've got blackberry cobbler and ice cream for dessert. It's a pretty small group today. Just Claire and Levi, Retta and Cade and us. If you come, Tag won't be a third wheel."

"More like a seventh wheel," Nikki said. "But thank you, and yes, I'd love to join y'all. Do you need me to stop and pick up anything on the way?"

"Not a thing. We've got it covered," Emily answered. "But if you're going fishin' you might want to make a stop by your apartment and grab some different clothes and shoes."

Nikki gave her a thumbs-up and then glanced down to

see Wilma giving her a dirty look. "Want to skip that nap and go fishin' with us, Mama?"

"I hate fish and mosquitoes and being outside where God knows what infection I might get." Wilma stuck her nose in the air and blended in with the crowd heading for the front door.

"You can't fix it," Emily whispered.

"I know, but I keep hoping for a miracle." Nikki managed a weak smile.

"Fix what?" Tag asked.

"Mothers," Nikki answered.

*   *   *

The area just outside the yard fence looked like a used car lot when Tag nosed his truck into the line right beside Hud's. He frowned as he got out of his vehicle, shook the legs of his jeans down over his boots, and headed into the house. Hud, Paxton, and Maverick were already in the dining room setting the table.

"Emily, darlin', these three lazy bums didn't go to church this morning, so they don't deserve a good Sunday dinner," Tag said as he hung his hat on the rack in the foyer beside six others.

"We'll pray for their souls," Emily told him. "We can't deny our brethren bread on a Sunday."

"Then give them a slice of store-bought bread and send them home." Tag nudged Hud on the shoulder. "Move over. You're not doin' it right. Knife and spoon on the right. Fork on the left. Mama would kick your butt."

"So will I," Emily said from the kitchen.

"Get out of here. It don't take a fourth man to set a table." Hud pushed him toward the kitchen.

"And we can use some help in here," Emily said. "You can fill the glasses with ice, Tag."

Retta was sitting at the table tearing lettuce for a salad. She looked up and grinned at him. "They, and I mean the whole bunch of them, think I don't need to be on my feet."

"And I agree." Tag washed his hands at the kitchen sink and then lined up eleven tea glasses on the cabinet. As he filled them with ice cubes, a picture of Nikki wearing a maternity dress came to his mind. He shook his head to get it out—he wasn't even ready to think about the M-word. Children were a thing of the far distant future. "Have you come up with a name for the baby yet?"

Retta laid a hand on her stomach and shook her head. "We've narrowed it down to about a dozen. I told Cade that when we see her, we'll know immediately which name fits her."

"Hey, hey, everyone." Nikki came through the kitchen door. She stopped in the mudroom and kicked off a pair of grungy cowboy boots. She'd changed from that cute little dress into a pair of denim shorts and a loose-fitting chambray shirt that buttoned down the front. "I thought this was going to be a small group. What can I do to help?"

"It grew on the way home. Hud called and said he was starving. I can't let my brother go hungry," Emily said with a sideways glance at Tag. "And we'll take all the help we can get. You can fill the glasses with tea, and then you and Tag can take them to the table."

They'd just gotten the last of the tea on the table when Cade, Levi, and Justin began to bring in bowls and platters of food. A feeling of homesickness hit Tag right in the heart—so many Sundays at the Rocking B Ranch where he'd grown up, Sunday dinners were just like this. Everyone pitching in to help, and then family gathering around the table. He was glad that his sister lived close so they could continue the traditions.

"Next Sunday is at our place," Claire said as they all took seats. "If you're off work then, too, Nikki, you're welcome to join us."

"Thanks, but I doubt that will happen again for a while," Nikki answered.

"Justin, please say grace for us," Emily said.

Tag's hand closed around Nikki's. That's what married and dating couples did at the dinner table in his world, and he was glad that she didn't pull it away.

Justin said a short prayer of thanks and then everyone started talking at once. Paxton and Maverick thanked Emily for including them in the invitation for dinner. Justin picked up the meat platter and started it around the table. Emily did the same with the bread basket.

"You ever made Sunday dinner for this many?" Tag asked Nikki.

"Nope," she said. "When I was growing up, we usually had hot dogs, boxed macaroni and cheese, and pork and beans right out of the can for dinner after church. It's what I could fix. Mama always said that she had to have a nap because getting dressed and sitting through church exhausted her, so I fixed dinner for me and Quint and Daddy. Then Quint died and Daddy left, but I always fixed the same thing, kind of in their memory until I moved into my own apartment."

"If you had to make a family dinner, what would you make?" Tag passed the green beans to her.

"A family dinner would mean two people in my world." Nikki helped herself to two spoonfuls of beans and passed the bowl on to Hud, who was sitting on the other side of her. "And Mama has a strict schedule for what and when she eats, so that's a tough question."

"What if someday you have a big family of kids?" Tag asked.

Nikki's smile lit up the whole room. "Now that would be a miracle, wouldn't it?"

"Why's that?" Tag frowned.

"It takes two people to make babies. You've met my mother. Who would ever want that for a mother-in-law?" she said. "And besides, you know what my crazy hospital schedule is like. That makes it even tougher for a relationship."

"Hey, what are y'all whispering about over there?" Emily asked.

"Our favorite Sunday dinners," Tag said. "I love pot roast. What's y'all's?"

That sparked conversations all around the table. Tag lifted a forkful of corn casserole to his mouth and listened with only one ear. He had a bad reputation. Nikki had a crazy mother and an even more demanding work schedule. He could sure look past her issues if she could see past his.

Chapter Eleven

The bubbling sound of water flowing over a few scattered rocks reached Nikki's ears before they were in sight of the creek that hot Sunday afternoon. She carried a quilt. Tag had the rods and reels in one hand and a cooler with water and beer in the other. Although it had been years since she'd been to the clearing, she wasn't surprised to see that it was still free of willow and mesquite saplings.

Many years had passed since she'd gone fishing, but it had been at this very place, and it was only a couple of weeks before Quint died. Even though Wilma had thrown a hissy about her son going outside when he was so sick, her dad, Don Grady, had stood up to her. If Quint and Nikki wanted to go fishing, then that's what they would do. Quint had slept on a quilt they had brought along for most of the time. She remembered the sun rays coming through the trees and putting a halo around his bald head. Looking back, she knew that was the day she had finally given up hope and realized her brother wouldn't be with them much longer.

"Evidently Mr. Johnson liked to fish," Tag said. "I found this place a couple of weeks ago when I was walking the fence line to see if there was even one stretch that was worth saving."

"We used to have parties over on the other side of this creek when I was in high school." She flipped the quilt and it fell in front of a fallen tree.

"Why on that side?" Tag removed a plastic container of worms from the cooler. "From the looks of this old log, Mr. Johnson spent a lot of time down here, time he could have used to put up a decent fence and repair the barn roof."

Nikki sat down with her back to the log, took a worm from the container, and baited her hook. "We stayed over there because we knew Eli Johnson wouldn't come across the water to fuss at us. And if he did, it's only about a hundred yards from the creek to the road back there, so we could outrun him."

"Why'd you come here?"

"The water is spring fed, so it's always cold. We'd cross the Red River to Terral, Oklahoma, where they grow lots of watermelons. We'd steal three or four, bring them here, and put them in the water to chill. Then we would split them open and have a feast." She tossed the line out into the water.

"I can't believe you stole watermelons," he chuckled.

"Don't tell my mama, but I drank beer on those nights too." She wiggled around until she was comfortable but kept a firm hold on the rod. "Some of us actually fished and if anyone caught anything, we'd build a fire up next to the edge of the water and cook it."

"I should've known you'd fished before, the way you baited that hook."

Nikki's red and white bobber danced out there on top of the water. She took a deep breath. "My dad knew Eli Johnson, and I used to come here with Daddy to fish when I was a little girl, back before Quint got sick. Last time we were here was just before my brother died. Guess it kind of brings back memories."

"I'm sorry, maybe we could load up and go up to the Red River," he said.

"No, they're good memories. It's just that when we were in high school, I was still struggling with everything," she said. "I'm pretty much past that now."

"Want to talk about it?" Tag laced his hook with two worms and tossed it out a few feet from hers.

"Nothing to talk about, really. Mama was always sick with something, supposedly, and Daddy was gone much of the time. He drove a truck out of Dallas through the week, but he got to come home every Friday night. Saturday, he'd try to do something with me and Quint. Fishing when the weather was good. Hiking sometimes in the fall, but it was always away from the house and Mama's constant nagging. Then Sunday morning we'd go to church, and afterwards I'd make our dinner and he'd have to go back to Dallas for his next run."

Tag sat down beside her. "I think Eli used the log for a bench, but it makes a better backrest. I can't imagine not having a dad around all the time."

"It was a way of life for us. We couldn't wait until Friday nights. When he left on Sunday, Quint and I cried. But not where he or Mama could see it. It would make him sad, and Mama would think we were sick and want to give us some kind of awful medicine. So we'd go to my room and cry together."

Tag leaned over slightly and touched her shoulder with his. "Anyone ever tell you that you had a dysfunctional family?"

"Oh, yeah, I knew that the first time I brought a friend home with me after school and Mama told me we'd have to stay outside until her mama came to get her."

"That's harsh," Tag said.

"I didn't ever do it again." Watching the bobber was mesmerizing.

They were silent for a while and then she said, "Daddy came home for a whole week when Quint got bad and died. Then he left on Friday, as usual, and never came back. Mama got divorce papers in the mail the next month, and I haven't seen him since the funeral. But I got to give him a little credit. He set up an account for her, and money goes into it every month. She lives as comfortably as when he used to come home every weekend."

"Wow, that must've been a lot for you to process—losing your brother and dad at the same time."

She turned to answer him and could see genuine care in his blue eyes. Just that much was a comfort. "I've never told anyone that before, not even Emily."

"Why?"

She couldn't tear her eyes from his. "It sounds like I'm a victim, and I don't want to be like my mother. Even though he'd had all he could probably stand and left me to fend for myself with her, I wanted to be like him. That sounds crazy, doesn't it?"

"Not to me," Tag answered.

"She told me I was like him when I moved out of the house right after graduation. I thanked her and then closed the door behind me as I took out the last load of my things," Nikki said. "I took her words to mean I was strong enough to leave and if I had that much strength, I could make it on my own."

Tag scooted toward her, laid his fishing pole down, and cupped her face in his hands. His lips found hers in a sweet kiss of understanding and appreciation. When it ended, he picked up the rod again and stared out into the water.

If all that didn't run him off, Nikki thought, then he was one determined cowboy.

*   *   *

After hearing her story, Tag realized what a safe and love-filled environment he'd had the privilege of growing up in. No wonder Nikki was so independent and untrusting. He suddenly felt the need to call his mama and dad and thank them for all they'd done for him. He had been such a wild child, and he regretted all the nights when his mother probably lay awake wondering where he was.

"I guess I'll have to pay for my raising someday," he muttered.

"What was that?" Nikki asked.

"Just thinking of my own family and how I can't expect to have an easy life of parenthood. Everyone has to pay for their raising," he said.

"Your poor babies," she giggled. "Speaking of which. How's the jaw since the stitches came out?"

"Little tender yet. Dr. Richards said it'll still take a while to heal since the cut was so deep. And I do get to ride again. 'Course, the next ranch rodeo isn't for two weeks. Last day of this month to exact. You going to be there to see me ride?"

"Probably, unless Emily needs me over at Longhorn Canyon. That's the day before the kids come in for the summer. I told her I'd help out with whatever she needs since it's her first time to be a bunkhouse supervisor," Nikki answered. "I don't think there's a fish in this creek anymore. We haven't even had a nibble since we got here."

"We need a beer. Can't expect to catch anything if you aren't drinking a beer. Fish come around when they catch the wonderful smell of cold beer," he teased as he opened the cooler and brought out two bottles. He twisted the lid off both of them and handed one to her. He took a sip, then set it to the side and reeled in his line.

"Givin' up?" she asked.

"Nope, just sharin'." He held the top of the hook with one hand and poured beer over the worms with the other. "Give the fish a little taste of something good instead of plain old worms."

"You're crazy," Nikki laughed.

There'd been so much sadness in her eyes when she talked about her family, and now one silly stunt with a few drops of beer made her eyes glitter again. Tag was suddenly floating on air for doing that for her.

"Been told that lots of times," he chuckled. "Can't deny it. Won't admit it."

"That old Fifth Amendment thing, huh?"

"Yep." He tossed the line back into the water, and immediately the bobber sank. "See, crazy works." He got so excited that he knocked his bottle of beer over.

She grabbed it before it spilled even a single drop. "Don't waste beer just because you've got Moby Dick on the line."

"Thanks," he said as he brought in a nice-size catfish. "A couple more of these and we'll have us a fish fry. You're invited even if you don't catch anything."

"Well, thank you for that, but my bobber is doing a cute little two-step out there." She motioned out to the creek with her bottle and then took a long draw. "That'll give me the strength to get it in. Want to bet who's got the biggest fish?"

"Sure. Loser has to kiss the winner."

She hauled in a bass about half the size of his catfish. Tag removed the fish from her hook and put it on the stringer with his. Then he took it to the edge of the creek and staked it in the soft mud and rinsed his hands. When he returned, she was in the process of baiting a hook and pouring a little of his beer on it.

"Hey, now, you got to use your own beer." He plopped down on the quilt beside her. "It don't work if you use someone else's."

"Bull crap," she said.

"Before you throw that line in the water, you owe me a kiss. Mine was bigger."

She laid the rod and reel down, threw a leg over his body so that she was sitting in his lap, and removed his old straw hat. Then she drew his face to hers and kissed him—long, hard, and with so much passion that he was panting when it ended.

"Damn, lady, I hope that all my fish are bigger than yours today," he said between short breaths.

"After that kiss, you're calling me a lady. What constitutes a lady?" She shifted her body until she was back at her original spot. She tossed her line out in the water and took a sip of beer.

"You do, Nikki," he said. "If you look up the word 'lady' in the dictionary, I'm sure you'll find your picture beside it."

"And where would I find your picture?" she asked.

"Beside the word 'rebel,' but I think it's beginning to fade." He smiled.

"And how does that affect you?"

"Some days I'm good with it. Some days not so much. Guess I'm still on the fence."

She watched her bobber go down and reeled in a catfish, not as big as his, but a good size. "A barbed-wire fence can get pretty uncomfortable."

He took the fish off and put it on the stringer. "I know it all too well. The barbed wire is biting into my butt pretty good."

"You deserve it," she told him as she put another worm on her hook and slung it out to the middle of the creek.

"You are a tough lady," he said as he poured some of his beer over the worms on his hook and then finished it off.

"Had to be to survive. Don't know how to be any other way now."

He watched both bobbers as they moved down the creek in the current, not touching but close to each other. Remembering what his granny had told him when he was making a difficult decision about not being able to ride two horses with one ass, he began to imagine himself crawling off the barbed-wire fence.

"But which side am I on?" he muttered.

"You're talkin' to yourself again," she said. "Look at that. It's like there's a magnet in our bobbers drawing them close together."

"I know the feelin'," he said, giving her a meaningful look. "How about you?"

"Little bit, but to be honest, I had a bad experience with a relationship last spring. It was getting pretty serious when I found out he was married, and his wife was pregnant," she said.

"And he's still alive?" Tag chuckled. "Did you have that pistol back then?"

"Oh, yeah, but I couldn't take a daddy from a baby, even if he was a sorry daddy," she said. "Just thought you should know before we take this any further. I'm not sure why I feel like I can talk to you like this, Tag. It doesn't have anything to do with chemistry, but more friendship."

"It's because we're both troubled souls," he whispered.

"Maybe so. I need closure, and you do too," she said.

"You got it, darlin'. I've never talked to anyone about serious things like I have you, so thank you for that," he said. "And anytime you need to talk about anything, my door is open."

"Thank you. Mine too," she said.

*   *   *

Later that night, Nikki sat on the end of the sofa next to Goldie and replayed the whole afternoon in her head. That song about living like you were dying came to her mind.

"Well, Goldie, he's been fishin'. Now all he has to do is stay on a bull named Fumanchu for at least three seconds and go skydiving, then maybe he'll have the rebelliousness out of his blood," she said.

Telling Tag about her early years and about Quint brought back the emotions of those last hours with him there in the hospital. Quint knew he wasn't going to get better, and he accepted it. But not Nikki—she had held out hope for a miracle right up until the moment when he breathed his last. She was holding his frail hand when that happened, and she sobbed into her father's shoulder. When the undertaker came for his body, the two of them had gone home to tell Wilma that Quint's race was finished.

Nikki closed her eyes at the painful memory. Wilma had yelled at them for letting the undertaker take him to be embalmed. She'd wanted him cremated so that all those germs would be destroyed forever, and she wouldn't get leukemia.

Why do you trust that cowboy enough to talk to him about our family? The past should be buried and forgotten, not hung out on the line like underpants for the whole world to see. Wilma's voice was very real in her head.

Exactly what was it in the past that her mother wanted to bury? The whole town knew that she had problems. Simply seeing her in the Walmart store in her outlandish garb was proof of that. A heavy feeling settled in Nikki's chest, and she knew that she had to talk to her mother, face-to-face.

Well, are you going to answer me or just sit there like your father and ignore me when I talk to you? Wilma had said that many, many times to both her children.

"Tag might be a renegade like you say, but he listens to me and tries to make me feel better," she said out loud. She wiped a tear from her cheek and put a finger on the gold-fish bowl. The fish swam right to it as if she understood that Nikki was having a tough time. "Goldie, I'm going to Mama's tomorrow evening. It's time we had a serious talk that has nothing to do with her medicine or her schedule."

She could have sworn that the goldfish smiled at her.

Chapter Twelve

Nikki awoke on Monday to a text from Tag: Want to get a burger tonight?

She sent one back: Have plans. When's the fish fry?

The next one said: Friday night. Interested?

She sent back a smiley face, crawled out of bed, and spent the day doing housework, laundry, and grocery shopping—and worrying about how her mother would react when she showed up at her house just before seven o'clock.

By late afternoon, her stomach was in knots, so she only had a bowl of chicken noodle soup for supper. She picked up her purse and locked the door before she lost her nerve. When she got to her mother's place, she sat in the car for a full five minutes. Maybe she should just take Wilma's call like usual. She could sit right there in her car and say what she was supposed to, couldn't she? For real closure, she had to have some real answers. She needed to know things that had never been talked about before.

She inhaled deeply, got out of the car, and marched up to the house with determination. The sound of her phone ringing in her purse came right before she hit the doorbell with her thumb. She heard the sound of all the locks clicking and then the door opened.

"What are you doing here?" Wilma asked through the storm door. "We're supposed to be talking on the phone right now."

"We're going to be talking face-to-face tonight. Are you going to let me in?"

"I suppose." Wilma's expression said that she wasn't happy. "Why did you come?" She went back to her recliner and took a sip of her seven o'clock glass of sweet tea.

"Are you going to invite me to sit or offer me something to drink?" Nikki asked.

"I didn't plan on you being here, and there's only enough tea to last me until I go shopping, and if you want to sit, then sit. I'm not keeping you from it," Wilma said.

Nikki kicked off her flip-flops, sat down on the sofa, and drew her legs up under her, which got her a dirty look from her mother. People did not put their feet on the furniture, and if they did, then it had to be sprayed with disinfectant.

"I want to know about when you and Daddy got married," Nikki said.

"That's old news," Wilma said. "I don't want to talk about it."

"I'm not leaving until I get some answers," Nikki said. "I can sit here all night if I need to."

Wilma gave her the old stink eye. "I was working at a café downtown. He drove a truck through here on Friday nights on his way to Dallas. He'd stop by for a piece of pie and we got to talking. I was almost thirty and had no intentions of getting married. After all, I've never been healthy, and I didn't want children."

"So why did you marry him?" Nikki asked.

"I was tired of working at the café, and he said he loved me. No one had ever told me that before. So we got married and before we could even discuss kids, I was pregnant with you. It was horrible. I was sick the whole time, and when you were born, you had the colic, and Don was gone all week on the truck. I thought I was getting a good man who'd take care of me. All I got was two squalling kids I didn't want."

Nikki's blood ran cold in her veins. What if she turned out to be like her mother when she had children? Would she feel like they were a burden too?

No, I will not. Her kind of problems are not inherited, and besides, I'd refuse to be like that, she thought.

What if you're like your father and get tired of a bad marriage and just walk out? asked that pesky voice in her head.

"Hush," she muttered.

"Don't tell me to shut up," Wilma said. "You asked, so I'm telling you."

"I'm sorry," Nikki said. "I wasn't talking to you. Go on."

"Then Quint got sick and I had to take care of him. I did my duty by y'all as best I could, but you got to realize just how sick I've always been. I should never have married or had children," Wilma whined.

"Did Daddy ever get in touch with you after he left?"

Wilma looked past Nikki at the picture of Jesus on the far wall. "Not with me," she answered. "He sent those divorce papers, and it said right there in them that he'd put money in my bank account every month, so I signed them. It was a relief. We hadn't..." She blushed.

Nikki had never seen her mother's cheeks turn that red and could count on the fingers of one hand the times she'd seen her smile. "Hadn't what?" she pressed for more.

"You know." Wilma blinked several times. "My mama was past forty when I was born and Daddy was fifty. Daddy was gone before I got married. Mama had the same problems I do. She didn't come from healthy stock either. She didn't want me to get married, told me how awful things would be...you know, in the bedroom. She was right, so after Quint was born, I told Don he'd have to sleep in a different room."

"You mean for twelve years y'all didn't have sex?" Nikki gasped.

"I didn't. I don't know what he did when he wasn't home, and I didn't care." Wilma's cheeks went scarlet again. "I was glad when he would come to Celeste so he could help with you kids. I loved you as much as I could, but taking care of you was just too much of a burden for me. Don was five years younger than me and his health was good."

Nikki understood more of her mother's background right then than ever before, and she felt so sorry that Wilma had never known what a real, loving relationship should be. She wanted to hug her mother and tell her that life didn't have to be like hers had been, but that would be going too far. The last time she'd even put her arm around her mother's shoulders was at Quint's funeral, and then she'd shrugged it off.

It's not her fault. Her dad's words came back to her mind. They'd been fishing out at Canyon Creek when she complained about her mother's coldness. *You have to understand why she is the way she is. I thought I could fix her, baby girl, but some things you just can't fix.*

There were no more questions. She could understand now why her father left and a little bit about why Wilma was the way she was. Knowing left an empty hole in her heart, and she wanted so badly to fix her mother, to help her know joy and happiness. But she knew her father had been right. Some things can't be fixed.

Wilma glanced at the clock sitting on the end table and got that blank stare in her eyes again as she gazed over Nikki's shoulder. "I guess Jesus is telling me to give you what's rightfully yours. It's in Quint's room. I used to hide it in my bedroom, but when you left, I didn't want to look at it."

She hurried to her brother's room, but it took several minutes for her to build up the courage to open the door. All of his things had been given away before his funeral because Wilma was convinced that the germs from his ailment were hiding in his toys, his pillow, even his furniture. Nikki had salvaged a teddy bear and kept it hidden in her closet until she moved out. It was part of that last load of things she had taken out of the house.

She finally eased the door open and peeked inside. The room was empty. Over there against the wall, she imagined Quint's bed. He was curled up on it with a book in his hands. Her eyes traveled around the room to imagine his dresser with a globe on it. They'd spin it and put a finger on the places where they wanted to travel someday, and then he'd check out books at the library and study about the places.

She didn't see anything that would be called hers in the empty room until she opened the door all the way. Just inside, so that Wilma wouldn't have to go inside to reach it, was a box with all kinds of mail in it. She picked it up and carried it to the living room.

"What is this?" she asked.

"Stuff that's been comin' for you for the last fifteen years. I'd like for you to get it out of here," she said. "And it's almost eight o'clock. You should be going now."

"Do you tell Mrs. Thomas to leave when she comes to visit?" Nikki asked.

"That would be rude, but I do sometimes pretend to fall asleep," she said.

"Good night, Mama," Nikki said.

"You stay on the porch until I get all the locks done up. I'll flash the porch light when I'm done." Wilma followed her across the floor.

Nikki did what she was told and then carried the box to the car. She drove home trying to figure out whether she was angry or sad for her mother, and glad that she'd broken the curse that must've run through the family for more than a generation.

She parked the car, picked the box up from the passenger seat, slung her purse over her shoulder, and headed for the Dumpster. A brisk wind whipped her dark hair into her face, and she set the box on the bottom step to tuck the strands behind her ears. The hot breeze had blown one of the envelopes back toward the car. She chased it down and realized that it had never been opened.

"Now that's downright rude," she said as she returned it to the box. About to toss it along with the others, she noticed that the handwriting wasn't hers. A cold chill chased down her back, and she stood there in the fading sunlight and recognized her name on the card written in her father's hand. She flipped several more pieces over and they were all the same.

She dug her phone from her purse and called her mother.

"Hello, Nikki."

"Why didn't you give me these when they came? Why did you hold them back from me?"

"Because your dad should have taken you with him, not left me with a teenage girl to raise. It wasn't fair," Wilma said. "You can do whatever you want with them. Good night, Nikki."

The call ended. Nikki picked up the box and took it upstairs. She set the box on the bed and began to sort the envelopes by the dates they were mailed. The first one had come the week after Quint had died. It took two hours to read through more than twenty letters, fifteen birthday cards, Christmas cards that had at least a hundred dollars in each one with a note telling her to buy herself something nice, a graduation from high school card with money in it, and one for when she'd graduated from nursing school only a few months ago.

When she finished, the front of her shirt was tear stained. "Oh, Daddy," she said as she picked up the first letter and scanned it again. He tried to explain that he couldn't live with Wilma any longer, and he should have never married her. She'd seemed like a shy, sweet woman when he met her and fell in love with her, he said. It wasn't until they were married that he realized what he'd gotten himself into. If she ever couldn't stand living there, she was welcome in his new home. It was the same address that was written in the upper left hand corner of every single piece of mail.

She paced the floor from one end of her living room to the other and looked up at the clock. She couldn't call Emily at ten o'clock at night, but Tag had said his door was open if she ever needed to talk.

She fed Goldie and walked out of the apartment.

Chapter Thirteen

Tag had just left the ranch house not thirty minutes ago, so the sound of an approaching truck wouldn't be one of the guys. Emily wouldn't be out at that time of night unless it was an emergency, and then she'd probably call on her way. The hair on his neck prickled—his sister wouldn't use the phone if his granny had died or if his parents or older brother was injured. She'd bring the news to him in person, but then he realized that in that case, someone would probably call him first. He'd be the one on the way to comfort her.

He stood up and focused on the noise. Two headlights shone through the darkness, but they weren't high enough to be from a pickup or low enough to be on the front of Emily's Mustang. When it got close enough, he recognized the little silver car as Nikki's. Before she turned off the engine, he'd crossed the yard and opened the door for her. From the dim light in the car, he could see that she'd been crying.

"What's wrong?" he asked.

"You said your door was open. I need to talk." Her words came out one at a time, as if she had trouble getting them past a lump in her throat.

He held out a hand. "Come right in. I'll put on a pot of coffee."

She put her hand in his. "Got anything stronger?"

"Part of a jar of apple pie moonshine and half a bottle of what's probably stale blackberry wine that Emily left in the refrigerator." He closed the car door and led her into the cabin with Red at his heels.

"Moonshine will be great."

She sank onto the sofa and kicked off her flip-flops. Red hopped up beside her and laid his head in her lap. Tag went to the cabinet and took down a quart jar of apple pie moonshine and a glass. He carried it to the coffee table and set them down.

"Double shot," she said as he twisted the cap off the jar. "No, make that a triple."

"It's pretty strong, Nikki. You sure?" Tag started to pour.

"Positive." She waited until the glass he held looked like three fingers before she reached out and picked it up. "I've never had this before, but it smells wonderful."

"How well do you hold your liquor?" He was genuinely worried, a new feeling for him. Before he met Nikki, he didn't care how much a woman drank.

"Not so well, but tonight I don't care. I want to be numb." She took the first sip. "Now this is some good stuff."

He sat down on the other end of the sofa. "You said you wanted to talk?"

"No, I said I needed to talk. There's a difference. If I was just lonely and wanted to talk, I'd call you. But I need to get a lot of crap off my mind, and to tell the truth I don't even know where to begin."

"Then give me a minute." He went back to the cabinet and got down another glass. "If it's going to be a long story, then I'll join you in a drink. But only one for me in case I have to drive you home."

Something about this budding friendship seemed comfortable and right. No, it was more than that. After the kisses they'd shared, it was definitely a relationship. With his past, it might be at a standstill for a very long time and then fizzle and he could accept that. He deserved it. But right now it was nice to be needed, not just wanted, in any capacity.

He sat back down and said, "Okay, shoot."

"It all started with me thinking back over our fishing trip yesterday and how I opened up to you. Don't know why I did that since..." She took another sip.

"I'm a damn good listener," he said.

"Probably gets more women in your bed than all those pickup lines you've got up your sleeve." She finally smiled.

"Hey, now. I've worked hard on those lines for a long time and sometimes they work, so don't go knockin' 'em," he argued.

"But not as well as when you look deep into a woman's soul with those sexy blue eyes and listen to what she has to say," Nikki told him.

"What does your soul want to say to me?" Tag asked.

She set the empty glass on the table. "I'm comfortable with you, Tag. The only other person I've ever been able to talk to is Emily. Don't know if I like you because you're like a brother, but no, that can't be it, because I wouldn't dream of kissing my brother. Anyway, to get on with it. After we talked, I was thinking about it, and Mama's voice got in my head... You ever have that happen to you?"

He nodded. "All the time. Most of the time it's my granny's voice. What did your mama say?"

"She asked me why I'd tell family secrets to a cowboy," she answered honestly.

"Why not?" he asked.

"She thinks you are too wild for me, but I'm not listening to her, not even when she gets in my head." She went on to tell him everything her mother had said.

Red jumped off the sofa, scooted across the floor, and stopped at the door. Tag let him outside and returned to sit close enough to Nikki to hug her. "I'm so sorry. That had to be tough, to know that you weren't ever wanted by one parent and to have the other one desert you."

"Oh, darlin', the story isn't finished yet." Tears streamed down her cheeks.

Tag jerked a blue bandana from his hip pocket and wiped them away. "It breaks my heart to see you weep like this."

Between sobs, she told him about the letters and cards and all the money. "He must think that I didn't want to live with him, and I did, Tag. I would have."

And if you had, I would have never met you, he thought.

"Where does he live?"

"Just outside Dallas in McKinney, not far from here."

"Let's go see him," Tag said.

"It's been fifteen years, more than half my life. What would I even say to him?"

"'Hello, Daddy' would be a good start," Tag suggested.

"I work weekends and he works through the week." She yawned.

Poor girl was mentally exhausted and probably just as tired physically since she'd worked a forty-eight-hour shift.

"If you really want to see him, you'll make it happen." Tag went to the bed and got a pillow. "You should stay here tonight. You can have the bed. I'll take the sofa."

"No!" she protested. "That moonshine is hitting me hard.

I'll just stretch out here until it all metabolizes." She took the pillow from him and laid her head on it and was asleep in seconds.

He covered her with the quilt that was draped over the back of the sofa and pulled the rocking chair up close to the coffee table so he could stare as long as he wanted. She looked lighter now that she'd shed that burden she brought with her that evening. And what a load it was. His heart went out to her, and he was amazed at how strong she was, given everything she'd had to deal with in her family.

Dark lashes rested on her cheeks. Equally dark hair fell over one side of her face. One hand rested under the pillow. The other was tucked under the quilt. She looked so damned vulnerable that he wanted to wake her with a kiss and carry her to his bed. Not to have sex but to simply hold her and melt away all that pain.

And that isn't a bit like you, Taggart Baker, his grandmother said.

He nodded in agreement.

*   *   *

Nikki woke with a start the next morning and saw a note lying next to the jar of moonshine. She reached for it and read: *There's milk in the fridge and cereal in the cabinet. Coffee is already made.* It was simply signed with a *T*.

She sat up and stretched, then padded across the floor in her bare feet to the cabinets. After she'd poured a bowl of Cheerios and added milk, she sat down at the table to eat. She'd just finished when someone knocked on the door. Figuring it was Tag since she hadn't heard a vehicle approaching, she hurried across the floor and swung the door open.

Cold fear ran through her veins when she looked up into Billy Tom's menacing eyes. "What are you doing here? Where's your motorcycle?" She hoped she sounded a lot meaner than she felt.

"Where's Tag?"

"He's taking a shower," she lied. "How did you find this place?"

"I talked to a guy in town, asked where Tag and Hud Baker's ranch was, and he gave me the directions, then told me that Tag was staying in this place." He pushed his way into the house, scanned the whole cabin with one look, and then pushed open the bathroom door. His eyes drew down until his dark brows were one solid line, and then he jerked a pistol from his belt and leered at her. "I hate liars. Can't trust 'em."

She glared at him, determined not to show fear.

"Not so mouthy now that I'm the one with the gun, are you? Since Tag ain't here to do what I tell him, I'll just take his woman. Is that your car out there?"

"No, it's my mama's," she said.

"Well, it'll do anyway. You've got the keys, don't you?"

She shook her head and he pressed the end of the gun to her temple. "Remember I hate liars."

"The keys are in the car. Take it." She stared him right in the eyes without blinking.

"Oh, no, darlin', me and you, we're going for a little ride in your mama's car. If you make a sound or try to warn someone, you are dead. Understand?"

She nodded. Her purse and her pistol were in the passenger seat. If she could get to it, she'd show the big overgrown smartass just how mouthy she could get.

His left hand shot out and he grabbed her arm so tight that it hurt. "A hostage will come in real handy. Besides, it's been a while since I had a woman to keep my bed warm at night." He pulled her out the door, leaving it wide open.

"Can't I at least get my shoes?" she asked. "If I get caught driving barefoot, the police will ask questions."

"Get them," Billy Tom said through gritted teeth. "You can get behind that wheel and drive us out of here. And, darlin', I'll be right behind you. I can't miss your heart if I shoot through the backseat."

"Where are we going?" Nikki reached for her purse the second she was in the car, but Billy Tom grabbed it from her and flung it out the window. "No driver's license. You're askin' for trouble."

"Don't get stopped. Not one mile above or below the speed limit. Drive north to Nocona and catch Highway 82 going west," he said. "We'll have us a nice little road trip. Maybe if you do what I say, I'll even tell you stories about Tag and the good old days."

There was a very good possibility that she'd never see her father if she didn't do what he said. Life wasn't fair. She should at least get a chance to explain what had happened to his mail. She started the engine, turned the car around, and then braked. "The gas tank is nearly empty. If you don't let me get my debit card from my purse, we won't be going very far. I've got less than a quarter tank of gas."

"Get out and get it." He stepped out of the car and pointed the gun at her. "If you run, I'll put a bullet in your back. I can always drive myself if I have to."

She slowly walked back to where her purse was located, picked it up, and started to unzip the end pocket that held her pistol, but he grabbed it from her. "I'm not stupid, woman. I remember that you keep a gun in your purse."

He fumbled inside with one hand, brought out her wallet,

and then threw the purse on the ground. "Now go back to the car."

"Can I take my phone?"

"Nope," he said.

"Can I move my purse so I don't run over it when we drive off?"

"I'm watching you," he said.

She picked it up by the strap and carried it off to the side, where she deliberately pretended to stumble and fall over a rock. While she was setting her purse out of the way, she reached inside, grabbed her phone, and since Tag was the last person she'd called, she hit redial. Then she stood up and marched back to the car, yelling the whole way. "Thanks so much for being a jackass, Billy Tom. Where are we going?"

"Don't you scream at me, woman, or I'll put you in the trunk and drive myself," he threatened her again.

"I'd rather ride in there than smell you the whole way," she shot back.

He chuckled as he got into the backseat again. "I'll tell you when to make turns. You just obey me like a good little woman until we get there; then maybe I'll show you what a real rebel is, and it ain't Tag Baker, honey."

Nikki gritted her teeth and turned toward Sunset when she left the ranch. Hopefully Tag would get the call and know when she didn't answer that she was in trouble. It was a crazy world when her first thought in the face of danger was to reach out to Tag rather than hitting her mother's number.

"Not one mile over the speed limit." Billy Tom reached around the seat and pulled back her hair with the barrel of the gun. "Tag must've meant it when he said he was through with our way of life, fallin' for your type like he's done. So I bet he'll do exactly what we tell him to get you back."

Nikki held on to the steering wheel with a death grip to keep her hands from shaking. If she got out of this alive and unhurt, she would enroll in a self-defense class as soon as she got home to Bowie. When she reached Nocona, she turned west on Highway 82, just like he said.

She pointed to the left. "We should get some gas if we're going more than twenty miles. All right if we stop at that station right there?"

"That's fine, but don't you try anything funny. I'm hungry. We'll get some road food while we're here too."

She pulled up to the gas pump, picked up her wallet, and slipped her debit card into the slot. When she had filled the tank, Billy Tom got out, slung an arm around her shoulders, and walked her into the station. Either Billy Tom was stupid and didn't realize that the police could track her payments with the card, or the whole ordeal would be over before they even knew she was gone.

Her skin crawled at his touch and her nose twitched at the rancid odor coming from him. She wanted to kick him in the shins and run, but she could feel the barrel of the gun against her ribs.

"We'll go to the bathroom while we're here. If you crawl out a window or run while I'm in the men's room, when I come out I'll shoot everyone in the place. That's a promise, not a threat," he whispered as he pushed the door open.

"Can I help you?" the young pregnant clerk asked.

"Just need to use the restrooms and get some food," Nikki said sweetly.

"That's good," Billy Tom said from the side of his mouth. "Real good. Be a shame for a mama and baby both to die today."

She went to the ladies' room and used the facilities. Then she removed her library card and a pen from her wallet. She wrote *West on 82* on the back of the card and stuck it in the corner of the mirror. When she went back out into the store, Billy Tom was covering the counter with potato chips, cookies, fried pies, and a six-pack of beer.

"Y'all must be taking quite a road trip," the lady said.

"Yep, our very first one together," Nikki said.

Billy Tom gave her a dirty look. "We'll have half a dozen of them burritos in your hot food case, too, and half a dozen of them sausage biscuits."

"Yes, sir." She got it all out and bagged up. "Anything else?"

"What do you think, darlin'? You want some milk?" Billy Tom kissed her on the cheek.

She fought the desire to wipe her face. "Root beer, please. Bottles not cans. If you'll get it for me, all this should be rung up by the time you get back."

"You go get it," Billy Tom said. "I'll wait right here for you."

That squashed the idea that she might get a word with the clerk, but there were ways to slow the trip down. She picked up two six-packs of root beer and set them on top of a case of water.

"My little woman is sure strong." Billy Tom beamed to the clerk. "And looks like she's real thirsty too."

"That apple pie moonshine from last night makes a girl want water." Nikki set everything on the counter and took out her credit card.

"I'll need to see your ID if you're paying for the beer," the clerk said.

"That's sweet but I'm twenty-nine years old," Nikki told her, and flipped her wallet around so the lady could see her ID.

"Nikita Colleen. What a pretty name. Irish?" the woman asked.

"That's what my mama Wilma tells me." Nikki nodded. "As far as I know, we don't have any Irish in us. Go figure why people name their kids what they do."

"My mama got my name Jenny from a character in a book," she said. "If you'll sign this, you can be on your way, Miz Nikita."

Nikki signed her name with a flourish on the receipt. Billy Tom had picked up the water, so she wrote HELP below her name and nodded at Jenny as she picked up the two bags he'd left behind.

Of all the times for the convenience store's phone to ring—Jenny shoved the sales slip into the cash register without even looking at it. Nikki couldn't catch a break.

In her car and back on the road, Billy Tom kept the gun in one hand and twisted the cap off a bottle of beer with his teeth. When he spit it on the floor of her car, she grimaced. She was proud of her car. She'd worked hard to save up to buy a decent vehicle and she kept it in pristine condition. She was tempted to slam on the brakes when he tipped up the beer, gulped down half of it, and then burped loudly.

"Want one?" he asked.

"Want me to get drunk and pulled over for speeding? I'm sure the cops would love to get their hands on you, so, yes, hand me a beer," she answered. "What'd you do anyway?"

"I stole a white pickup and put the license plate I pinched from Tag's truck on it. Y'all were so much in love you didn't even suspect that I switched it at the pizzeria. That was a stroke of luck for sure, finding y'all in there like that. I used the truck to steal a load of ephedrine headed for a little meth lab over in East Texas. Then I sold the goods to another meth cooker. Now everyone is going to be looking for your precious Tag. He wouldn't join us, so we figured he could take the blame for driving the getaway truck." Billy Tom tossed four bottles of water over into the passenger seat.

"How'd you get to the cabin?" she asked.

His phone rang and he put it on speaker. "Hello, y'all at the hideout?"

"We're here. Where are you? You should've beat us here," a man answered.

"Stole me another car. Damn one I was driving ran out of gas a mile from the ranch, so I had to walk. All I wanted was for Tag to give me a ride to Mesquite to get my bike and maybe a hundred dollars to get me to my little hideout, but he wasn't there."

"Is this damn phone on speaker? I hear road noise."

Billy Tom burped loudly. "Hell, yeah. I've got a gun in one hand and a bottle of beer in the other. Tag's woman is driving. I figure he'll buy her back from us."

"We don't need that shit. We can divvy up the money we already stole and then lie low for a few months."

"Tag needs to pay for not goin' with us," Billy Tom said.

"You're crazy." A different voice laughed. "But I like it. Reckon he'll cough up five grand?"

"I'm thinkin' ten might get me a good used motorcycle, and I'll just leave mine out in Mesquite where I stole the car. Y'all get that money counted out. We'll be there in a few hours."

"We already got it in stacks. Damn driver of that ephedrine haul didn't even know what hit him," a third guy said. "We'll see you soon."

He ended the call, patted her on the shoulder, and then dug into the bag for the sausage biscuits. "Want a biscuit?"

"No, thank you. I'll just drink water," she answered. "And, Billy Tom, just so you know, I'm not Tag's woman."

"Then what the hell were you doin' in his cabin this mornin' or out on a date with him the other night?" He burped again.

Chapter Fourteen

T ag had just flipped two large pancakes on his plate when someone knocked on the door. Hud raised an eyebrow and started across the kitchen when they heard Maverick say, "Good mornin', Officer. What can we do for you?"

Tag set his plate on the table and followed Hud to the living room.

"May I come inside? I'm Deputy Davis. I'm looking for Taggart Baker."

Tag stepped around his brother and nodded. "Yes, come on in. I'm Tag."

"I'm here about your white pickup truck. Where were you last night between eight and midnight?" the officer asked.

"I was here until ten with these guys, and then I walked about a quarter mile over to Longhorn Canyon Ranch, where I stay in a cabin," Tag said.

"So how did your truck come to be in a robbery over

around Mesquite? I got a note this morning from the sheriff over there saying the plates match that truck out there in the driveway. One that was reported stolen."

"I have no idea," Tag said, and then groaned. "Billy Tom."

"You're runnin' with him again?!" Hud's voice bounced off the walls.

"No, I'm not." Tag wiped a hand across his forehead. "You'd better sit down, Deputy, sir. Billy Tom, that would be William Thomas if you want to look up his rap sheet, has been after me to give him money for some deal he had going. I wouldn't do it and he was in the pizza place in Bowie the other night when I was there." Tag went on to tell the whole story. "I've seen him switch plates on vehicles lots of times."

"So you do know him? How do I know that you didn't switch the plates yourself after you helped with the robbery? If you're his friend, you might do that, right?"

"I didn't do it." He didn't want to get Nikki involved in this or smear her reputation, but there didn't seem to be another way out. "A lady I've been seeing, Nikki Grady, can vouch for me." He slipped his phone from his hip pocket, just as it started to vibrate. "This is Nikki right now. Let me put it on speaker and you can ask her yourself."

."Hello?" he said. "Would you…"

"I'll tell you when to make turns. You just obey me like a good little woman until we get there. Then maybe I'll show you what a real rebel is, and it ain't Tag Baker, honey."

There was the sound of a car engine that faded as it got farther and farther away.

Tag tensed and balled his hands into fists. "That's Billy Tom's voice. He's got Nikki. I can almost guarantee it, and I know where they're headed."

"It's Billy Tom's voice, sir," Hud agreed as he got up to let in the dog scratching at the door.

Red came trotting in, dragging a handbag behind him. Tag took it from the puppy. "This is Nikki's purse. Red must've been there when they left. They don't have a very long lead. We might catch them if we head out now."

Davis headed for the door. "If you really want to help, tell me where they're going."

"They usually hole up at an old run-down cabin over near Tulia in Swisher County. I can draw you a map if it'll help. It's about five hours from here. The place belonged to his grandpa, but the old guy's been gone for years."

"Okay, son, I'll alert the local authorities, and they can check it out."

"Make sure you talk to Sheriff Lester Roberts," Tag advised as he followed Davis out of the house.

"You know him?" Davis asked.

"My parents own the Rocking B Ranch," he said. "And my brother Matthew is a volunteer deputy out there."

"With a family like that, how in the hell did you get in with someone like Billy Tom?"

"Bad decisions."

"Well, I hope you learned that every choice has consequences," Deputy Davis admonished.

"I have, sir, and I'm doin' my best to get past the bad choices," Tag said.

Davis nodded and got back into his patrol car. Tag was watching him leave when Hud yelled at him from the porch. "If you take your motorcycle, you might be able to catch them. I packed you some clothes and other things just in case," Hud said. "You go get it while I pack a bag, and then I'll call Matthew and give him the scoop while you're on your way."

He started out the back door toward the barn where his cycle was stored.

"Call when you get there and give Mama a hug for me," Hud yelled.

Tag held up a hand in acknowledgment. Choices, bad decisions, consequences, fate, and karma—he had a good thing started with Nikki and now he'd lost it for sure.

*   *   *

Nikki had drunk all four bottles of water by the time they reached Wichita Falls. "We're going to have to make a pit stop. I can't go much farther."

"Once you're on Highway 287, you can stop at the next station you see. I'll go in with you and the same rules apply. You run or turn me in and I start shooting everyone I see," he said.

"I understand," she said.

She whipped into a service station and hurried inside, glad that she had on flip flops, because the sign said NO SHIRT, NO SHOES, NO SERVICE. She pushed into the bathroom, praying there would be another woman in there, but no luck, so she removed a grocery store rewards card from her wallet and wrote *Help me. I've been kidnapped.* She wrote Tag's phone number on the back and laid the card on the vanity.

Once she'd finished, she slowly washed her hands and checked her reflection in the mirror above the sink. Lord have mercy! She looked horrible. Her hair was a tangled mess since she hadn't had time to brush it before Billy Tom knocked on the door. There were black mascara streaks down her face from all the tears she'd shed, and bags under her eyes. She took time to wash her face and then pulled her hair up into a ponytail with a rubber band she took from her wallet.

When she opened the door, Billy Tom was right there blocking her way with a hand on each side. "What took you so damn long?" he hissed.

"If you'll notice, I washed my face and tried to do something with my hair," she said.

"Gettin' pretty for me, were you?" He grinned.

"No, just trying to look less like someone you kidnapped so you won't cause a scene. Can we go now?"

"I want another six-pack," he told her. "Get it and pay for it."

She saluted smartly and walked under his arm. "Anything else?"

"Nah, we got enough food to last until we get to the hideout," he said. "We've wasted enough time. The guys are waiting for us."

"When are you calling Tag to ask for ransom money? It'll take him five or six hours to bring it to you. You willing to sit still that long and wait?"

Billy Tom glared at her. "He's got rich relatives. His brother Matthew can get it to us in less than thirty minutes, and after the money is in my hands, I'll tell him where he can find you."

"Am I going to be dead or alive? You've been letting me use my debit card everywhere. You do know they can track me with that?" she asked.

"I don't give a shit. This'll be over before they find you anyway. And dead or alive depends on whether you make me mad..."

She shot him the evilest look she could muster and marched straight up to the beer cooler, got out a six-pack, and went to the counter to pay for it. The old gray-haired fellow asked for her ID, and she gladly gave it to him, hoping that when someone came to find them, he'd remember the name Nikita Grady.

"Good girl," Billy Tom said. "You even remembered the brand I like."

"If I hadn't been afraid you'd shoot some kid's grandpa, I'd have bought you arsenic," she said as she started the engine. "I need more water."

He flipped four more bottles up on the passenger seat. "Sure you don't want something to eat? I've got burritos and one sausage biscuit left."

"You ate five biscuits?" She wrinkled her nose at the sight of him in the rearview.

"Didn't eat all day yesterday," he sneered back at her.

"Tag is going to kill you," she muttered.

"Tag is probably trying to talk his way out of a jail cell right now," Billy Tom laughed.

"Well, genius, did you remember to get the tag off that truck in Mesquite and put it back on his truck, or were you in such a hurry to kidnap me that you forgot?" she asked. "I don't remember us taking a detour by the ranch for you to take care of that."

He slapped himself on the head with the gun. "Don't you worry, darlin'. By the time the cops figure out my tag-switchin' business, it'll be too late. I'll just wait and call Tag when we get to the hideout. It won't take Matthew long to get the money."

Billy Tom's attempts at intimidation weren't working. For the last three hours, his tactics just made her that much more determined to go against the oath she'd taken as a nurse to help heal people. At some point, she'd take that gun away from him and enjoy giving him a reason to beg her to call an ambulance.

"Ain't got nothing to say to that, do you?" Billy Tom talked with food in his mouth.

There was so much tension in the car she thought for

a minute that Billy Tom would tell her to pull over to the side of the road, shoot her, and take her car on to wherever his hideout was located. But a glance in the rearview let her know real quick why he had slumped down in the seat. There was a police car coming up on them pretty fast from the rear.

She sent up a silent prayer asking that the lights would begin to flash and the sirens would blare.

"You better hope we don't get stopped, or I'll shoot the cop the minute he walks up to the car," Billy Tom threatened.

"I'm sure someone has missed me and put out my tag number," she said.

"Honey, your tag changed while you were in the bathroom at that first gas station. I switched it with a car the same color as yours in the parking lot of that convenience store." Billy Tom slouched down farther.

As if in answer to her prayer, the lights on the police car came on and the noise of the siren filled the air. Then the police car whipped around them and sped down the road until it was nothing but a dot in the distance.

"Now ain't this that policeman's lucky day?" Billy Tom sat up straight and took a bean burrito from the sack. "Riding makes me hungry. Want one?"

Nikki's stomach knotted up at even the thought of food. "No, I don't want food, but I need to go to the bathroom."

"Good God, woman, you got a bladder the size of a thimble. It ain't been thirty minutes since we stopped. Stop up here at Estelline, but this is the last time. Once you get done, we'll get on Highway 86 and in an hour and a half, we'll be at the end of the road," he said. "Remember the rules when we're in the gas station. You might as well fill up with gas while we're there. Once me and the guys divide up the money, I'm going to use this car to go back to Mesquite to get my motorcycle."

"I thought you were going to use the ransom money for a new bike." She pulled up next to one of the two gas pumps.

"We'll all split five ways and won't see each other for a month until this all dies down. Ten thousand dollars will go a long way in Mexico, and I like my motorcycle just fine, so I've changed my mind," he said.

"What about all that money y'all got by robbing an ephedrine truck?" She looked up into the rearview mirror.

"That won't last a long time, and besides, me and the boys like adventure, so we'll get back together after a few months, just like always," he answered.

Billy Tom had probably been a fairly good-looking kid as a teenager, Nikki thought. He had a square jaw and nice green eyes, but the life he'd chosen had made him hard and downright mean. Now he made her skin crawl. One thing for absolute sure, she would not be spending an hour with him, much less a month. Someone would come get her before that happened. Emily checked on her every day, and Tag would know something was wrong when he found her purse lying on the ground outside the cabin.

"You going to call your thug friends and tell them we're close?" she asked as she turned off the engine, undid her seat belt, and opened the car door. "Do I go to the bathroom first or pump gas?"

"No, I'm not calling my buddies. They know I'm on the way," he told her. "Pump the gas and then we'll go inside."

That meant she had no way to leave a message on the gas pump for the folks in the car who waited behind her. After she'd filled the tank, Billy Tom got out of the back-seat, threw half a dozen empty beer bottles into a nearby trash can, and followed her into the small convenience store.

"Bathrooms?" Nikki asked.

The young lady behind the counter pointed toward the far corner of the store. Nikki felt as if she'd never had a shower or washed her hair as she entered the two-stall ladies' room. When she left the restroom, an older woman with gray hair passed her in the doorway, but Billy Tom was standing not three feet away with his hand inside his nasty vest.

"Thought I might have to wait in line, judgin' by all the cars out there, but looks like it's empty," the lady said.

"It's all yours." Nikki smiled.

"You done good," Billy Tom growled as he grabbed her arm. "I was ready to pull the trigger and drop that old bag where she stood."

When they got close to the beer cooler, Billy Tom grabbed a case. "We'll take the boys a little something. They're probably spittin' dust since they can't go to a store."

Paying for the beer aggravated Nikki so badly that she almost refused, but then the lady from the bathroom set a candy bar and a root beer on the counter and leaned over the counter to hug the cashier, who didn't look a day older than eighteen. "How's things goin' today, darlin'?"

She stretched over the top of the counter and hugged her back. "Slow, Granny, but it's a job. The money will help with my college fees this fall. Then it's on to grad school."

Nikki paid for the beer with her debit card, hoping all the time that the police were already tracing the places she'd used it. Without incident, they got back on the highway and she made the next turn Billy Tom demanded. He yawned several times, but he kept his eyes wide open for the next hour and a half.

*   *   *

Tag cursed every single one of the 250 miles to Tulia.

"She's never goin' to speak to me again," he muttered to himself. Tag couldn't blame her if she didn't. He'd brought all this crap down on her head—Billy Tom might have been the actual culprit, but if Tag hadn't ever been associated with him, then it wouldn't have happened.

Guilt lay on his shoulders like a heavy wool blanket every time he even thought her name, and yet he couldn't stop thinking about her. Had Billy Tom hurt her? Why had he even taken her? He could have demanded her car keys and left her alone. He should have thought of all this at the pizza place. He knew Billy Tom and the guys he rode with—that they were ruthless and wild. He should have protected Nikki better.

When he went through Vernon, Texas, it hit him that he'd never told Billy Tom where his ranch was or that he was staying in a nearby cabin, so how did he know where to go?

"Small town living," he muttered. All he'd had to do was ask someone in Sunset about the Baker boys who'd recently settled there. Everyone probably even knew that he was now staying at the cabin.

He wanted to stop the motorcycle and kick something— a tree, a cactus, even one of those "Don't Mess with Texas" trash cans along the side of the road would do just fine. But he didn't have the time to give in to his anger. He had to keep riding until he got to the hideout—and he just hoped he could beat Billy Tom there.

But what if he doesn't go there? It's been years since you rode with him. He could've changed places.

If that was the case, then Tag couldn't rescue Nikki. He couldn't apologize to her, beg her forgiveness, and own up to the fact that this horrible kidnapping was all his fault. One for being such a stupid teenager, the other for getting her into the mess with Billy Tom to begin with.

He was a ball of nerves, anger, and guilt when he finally reached the turnoff to the cabin. He parked his motorcycle under a big scrub oak tree and dismounted, looked around and caught a movement to his right. Matthew came out from behind a big scrub oak tree and gave him a quick hug. "He's not showed up yet, so you've beat him."

"Thank God," Tag said. "Are you the only one here?"

"No, there are others, but they're well hidden. We didn't want to spook him since he's got the hostage," Matthew said quietly. "I've got to get in position up on that rise over there. You wait until they're parked."

"Y'all goin' to let me go in first?" Tag asked.

"You armed?" Matthew asked.

"No. I didn't even think to bring a gun," Tag answered.

"Good." Matthew laid a hand on his shoulder and squeezed gently. "You don't need one. We've got your back, but if you want to try to talk him into surrendering, you can have the job. But don't worry, we will get her back. Just talk calmly so he don't hurt Nikki." Matthew touched the phone on his shoulder.

"Baker here," he said.

"He's been spotted turning off to the main road," a voice said.

"Thank you, Darrin," Matthew said and then looked at Tag. "That's my cue to get up on that little rise behind an old log. See you when it's over."

"Thanks for letting me be a part of this," Tag said.

Matthew nodded and disappeared across the clearing and into the trees that led up to a high spot.

Tag took a deep breath and leaned on the old log blocking the path to the cabin, his heart pounding, guilt still filling his heart and soul, and hoping with everything in him that Billy Tom hadn't hurt Nikki. If he had, Tag wouldn't need a gun to take care of him.

*   *   *

Billy Tom sat straight up in the backseat and growled, "Make a right at the next gravel road. We'll go about a mile and then turn into a lane. I'll tell you where, and, honey, no cuttin' and runnin'. I'm a damn good shot, and you can't run as fast as a bullet."

Nikki drove slowly, hoping that at any minute she'd see police cars behind her, but there were none. A mile of dust boiled up behind them, and then he motioned with the gun for her to make another right turn. There was nothing more than a rutted path from that point on. She'd only driven a couple of minutes when she saw the old tree lying across the road and remembered the story of how Duke died. She braked and brought the car to a stop.

"We'll walk from here. It ain't far." Billy Tom picked up a case of beer in one hand and held the gun in the other.

Nikki got out of her car and caught a movement in her peripheral vision. Then Tag walked out from behind a fallen down log right in front of her. At first she thought she was seeing things, or dreaming, or maybe Billy Tom put a silencer on the gun and she was dead.

No, she couldn't be dead because Tag had come all that way to rescue her. She had to be alive so she could thank him. Things began to blur around the edges, but she refused to give in to it and faint. She stiffened her back and took several deep breaths so that Billy Tom wouldn't have the satisfaction of winning.

"I think you have something that's mine." Tag didn't

even look her way but locked gazes with Billy Tom. "I want it back."

What was Tag talking about? A few kisses didn't make her his.

"You can have her for ten thousand dollars." Billy Tom leveled the gun at Tag's chest.

"I don't think so." Tag folded his arms over his chest and finally looked Nikki in the eye.

Fear and anger all rolled into one was the message she got, not that she wasn't important enough for the ransom.

"So she's not worth that to you? She's just another one of your bar bimbos after all," Billy Tom taunted. "If she's worthless to both of us, I can just kill her right here."

"I'd give everything I've got for her, but that's not the issue here." Tag's gaze went back to Billy Tom. "You are surrounded by men from the Swisher County Sheriff's Department and the Tulia police. Did I ever tell you that my brother Matthew is a volunteer deputy? He can take the eyes out of a rattlesnake at a hundred yards. If you'll look to your left, you'll see the glint from his gun."

Billy Tom cut his eyes around toward the shiny dot among the trees on the slight hill. His face went gray as the blood drained out of it. "Nobody can make a shot that good."

"Maybe. Maybe not. You willing to take that chance?" Tag asked.

"You think his bullet can get here faster than mine can get to her?" Billy Tom moved the gun to point at Nikki's forehead.

"I wouldn't want to see if Matthew's can, but maybe one of these other fellers' will." Tag held up a hand and motioned.

Uniformed policemen began to circle around him. The one with the sheriff's badge said, "We have already got your buddies from the old shack back there in custody. We've confiscated the money, and you've got nowhere to run, Billy Tom. It's taken us twenty years but this time, boy, you're on your way to prison for a long time. The Montague County police called me a few hours ago and said you were on the way. We've been waiting for you."

Billy Tom glared at Tag and then at Nikki, his eyes shifting from one pistol to another—all aimed right at him. He must've realized he was out of options because he dropped the pistol on the ground, fell to his knees, and put his hands behind his head.

Nikki picked up the gun and, using the butt, hit him square between the eyes. He tumbled backward, squalling like a little girl as he tried to catch the blood flowing from his nose. She dropped the gun in the dirt and turned to see Tag coming toward her, his arms outstretched. She couldn't let him touch her, not when she still had the stench of Billy Tom in her nose. She shook her head. "Don't touch me, not until I get this filth off me. Where's the nearest motel?"

"You can stay at my folks' ranch," he offered.

"No, thank you. I'd rather stay in a motel." Her hands shook so badly that she had to clasp them together.

"I need to talk to you, and we've got showers at the jail," the sheriff said. "I can even get you a set of scrubs if you don't mind orange."

"Then I'll follow you." She started for her car.

"You shouldn't be driving alone," Tag said.

"You're going with this deputy right here," the sheriff said. "I'll take Billy Tom with me."

"I'll drive her car," Matthew offered. "Keys still in it?"

It wasn't easy to let them make decisions for her, but the adrenaline rush was crashing. She nodded toward Matthew. "It stinks of him and beer."

"I'll take care of it, Nikki. You just go with the deputy," Tag assured her. "I'll be right behind you, and thanks, Sheriff, for letting me be part of this."

"Matthew had a lot to do with that. I called him the minute the sheriff from over in Montague County got in touch with me."

"I need a doctor," Billy Tom whined.

"Shut up or I'll tell everyone in the jail that a woman half your size took you down," a deputy told him as he put him into the back of a police car.

Chapter Fifteen

Tag followed Nikki and the deputy to the squad car and opened the passenger door for her. "I can go with you and send someone for my motorcycle."

"I'm fine," she said, but her voice shook.

"Just follow us," the officer said.

"I'll be right behind you, Nikki. Did he hurt you?"

She shook her head. *Define hurt,* she thought as he closed the door. It didn't always mean bruises or cuts. Sometimes it went way deeper than that and couldn't be put into words.

"I didn't hear you answer Tag," said the gray-haired deputy as he took the same route back to town that Nikki had driven. It seemed like hours instead of only minutes.

"He didn't physically hurt me, but he kept a gun pointed at me for the last five hours," she said in a thin voice that she hardly recognized as her own.

"I'm sure that was scary," he said.

Nikki was glad that he didn't have any more questions

because she didn't want to answer them. Tears welled up, but she refused to let the dam loose. She'd been strong right up to the end, and now she might get fired for having a record. That stunt with the gun might get her charged with assault with intent to do bodily harm—which was the God's honest truth.

The deputy pulled into a parking spot and got out of the car. Nikki reached for the door handle, but before her hand even touched it, Tag opened it and said, "I'm going with you."

With Tag on one side of her and the deputy leading the way, they went inside the police station. Nikki took a deep breath, sucking in the smell of cleansers. After inhaling beer and nasty burps all day, she wanted to sit down on the tile and enjoy the scent for hours.

The deputy led the way into an office with his name on the door. "The sheriff is on the way. Can I get you something to drink, Miz Grady?"

She shook her head. "I just want a shower."

"All in due time. Tag, you can wait outside now. This won't take long."

"I'd rather stay," he said.

"There's a chair out there." The deputy pointed.

"I'll be waiting, Nikki," he said.

The sheriff entered the room and motioned for Nikki to take a seat across the desk from him. "Can you answer some questions for me?"

She nodded.

"I will record your interview." He set a recording device on the edge of the desk. "You still look pale. Do you need a few minutes to collect yourself?"

"I'm fine. Let's just get this over with," she answered.

"You are a strong woman, Miz Grady. I admire your strength," the sheriff told her, and then pushed a button on the tiny recorder. "This is Sheriff Lester Roberts taking Nikki Grady's statement. Now tell me what happened today. Don't leave out any details."

His comment about her strength gave her the courage to start talking. "I was kidnapped at gunpoint."

*   *   *

Matthew carried a second folding chair down the hallway and set it up beside his brother. "You okay?"

"Another thirty minutes and I wouldn't have been there," Tag said. "I caused this mess. I needed to be there for her when she got out of that car."

That the two cowboys were related was evident by their clear blue eyes and dark hair, but that's where the resemblance ended. Matthew wasn't as tall as Tag, and he'd always been the serious one of the three Baker boys. Tag was the rebel. Hud was the quiet twin. Matthew was the responsible son. Right then Tag wished he had a helluva lot more Matthew in him.

"Is she going to be all right?" Matthew asked.

"She's tough. Had to be coming from the family she did. It wasn't like ours." Tag removed his hat and laid it on the floor beside him. "Crazy mother. Father who left her after her brother died. She was fourteen when all that happened, and she's made her own way since she was eighteen."

"Then I expect she'll be fine. Did he..." Matthew paused.

"I hope to hell not." Tag took a bandana from his pocket and wiped sweat and dirt from his face. "I really like her, Matthew, but now I've got to back away from her for her own safety. Dammit!" He slapped his knee.

"What?" Matthew asked.

"I need to call Emily. She's been worried sick." Tag jerked his phone from his pocket.

"I talked to her on the way here. Also talked to Mama and Dad. Now all you've got on your plate is her," Matthew told him. "Never saw you like this over a woman."

Tag shrugged. "And now I've ruined it with my past mistakes."

"You need to leave the past in the past and move on to the future," Matthew said.

Tag shook his head. "I'm trying but it keeps coming back to bite me on the ass."

"Give it a chance. Things will take on a new light when you get back to your ranch." Matthew patted him on the shoulder.

Tag drew in a long breath and let it out in a whoosh. "I've got to talk to her."

"I've got a solution. Ride home with her and leave that damned motorcycle here," Matthew said.

"If she'll let me, you can do whatever you want with the cycle. If I ever got on it again, all I'd be able to think about is the fear and anger that had a hold on me the whole way from the ranch," Tag said.

"Aww." Mathew grinned. "My baby brother is growing up."

"Go ahead and say it. I deserve it," Tag said.

"About damn time." Matthew chuckled.

"I'd say it's past time."

"Looks like Lester is finished talkin' to her," Matthew said, and pushed up out of his chair.

Tag settled his hat on his head and got to his feet.

Sheriff Roberts came through the door and extended his hand to Matthew. "Thanks for your help today. We didn't know what we might get into out there. Didn't expect to find them all asleep or for it to be so easy. I sure felt better knowin' you was up there on that little hill with your rifle. Thought for a minute there we might have a killin' on our hands." He turned to face Tag and shook hands with him as well. "I hope you're makin' better friends over in Montague County."

"I assure you I am," Tag said. "Can I talk to Nikki now?"

"Yes, but right now she's in my bathroom getting cleaned up. Here are her car keys and wallet. I gave her a set of orange scrubs to change into."

"Was she"—Tag swallowed hard—"hurt?"

"She said Billy Tom threatened her in all kinds of ways but that's all," the sheriff said. "You wait right here. She'll be out in a few minutes."

"Thank you." Tag sat back down.

"Matt, I think I owe you a cup of coffee," Sheriff Roberts said. "And maybe a piece of apple pie."

"With ice cream?" Matt asked.

"Only way to eat it is with two scoops of ice cream. See you later, Tag, and I sure hope it's never like this again," he said as he and Matt started down the hallway.

Then Matt turned and came back. "Here, brother, trade keys with me. I'll take that cycle out to the ranch. You drive my truck to the motel. I'll make arrangements with the detailer to have Nikki's car fumigated and cleaned up for her by tomorrow morning. Just call me and tell me what motel she's in so we can deliver it to her."

"Thank you," Tag whispered.

"Hey, family takes care of family."

*   *   *

Nikki threw her clothing into the trash can as she undressed, including her flip-flops. She adjusted the water to the right temperature and then stepped into the sheriff's shower. First she let the hot water run through her hair and down her back. Then she picked up the soap and a white washcloth. She soaped her whole body down three times and still didn't feel clean, so she gave it one more lathering. After that she picked up a small bottle of shampoo and squeezed the whole thing into her hair. It didn't matter if it wasn't her usual special volume-building product. It could have been pure lye soap and she wouldn't have complained.

When she finished, she dried herself off with one of the two towels that the sheriff had given her. Her skin was red when she got through, but the well-worn scrubs were soft. She didn't have a bra or underpants, but there was no way she would ever touch those things in the trash can again. She wasn't sure she could even get into her car until all that stuff from the backseat was gone and it had been scrubbed.

With her hair still damp, she went back out into the sheriff's office to find it empty, but the door leading out into the hallway was open and there was Tag. His hat was in his hands and her wallet was on the chair beside him. He stood up when he saw her, but he didn't open his arms like before.

She walked, barefoot, right up to him, went on her tip-toes, and put her arms around his neck. Tears began to flow down her cheeks. "I was mad and afraid, but I kept telling myself you'd find me."

His arms encircled her, drawing her so close that their hearts beat as one. "I was terrified I wouldn't get there in time."

"I can't get in my car," she whispered.

"You don't have to. I'm taking us to a motel in my brother's truck." He kissed her on the forehead. "You ready?"

"As I'll ever be." She picked up her wallet, took out all

the cards and cash, and stuffed them into the deep pocket of her scrubs. Then she tossed her wallet in a nearby trash can.

They walked out of the building, hand in hand. Once they were on the hot sidewalk, Tag scooped her up like a bride. She laid her head on his shoulder, and for the first time since Billy Tom showed up at the cabin, she felt safe. He put her into the big black truck and buckled her in. She closed her eyes, and Billy Tom's leering face appeared. She snapped them open and in that second decided she wouldn't be a victim. She was strong like her daddy. She'd survived having a gun in her back for hours, and she hadn't let Billy Tom intimidate her. The sheriff had said the bloody nose she'd given him was self-defense, as far as he was concerned. She wouldn't have a record.

It wouldn't be easy, but she'd get past the trauma—with Tag's help.

"We don't have a lot to offer in the way of hotels here in Tulia. You'd be more comfortable at my parents' ranch," Tag said as he fastened his seat belt.

"I'm not fit to be around people yet, Tag. You can drop me off at a motel and go on home," she said.

"I'm not leaving you. First we'll pick up some clothes for you and then some food. When did you last eat?"

"Not since breakfast." She was grateful that he was taking charge because her brain was still in a fog, even if the sheriff had assured her that she was a strong woman.

He whipped the truck into the parking lot of a Family Dollar, the only place in town to buy clothing, and snagged a place right in front. "Look, that's an omen if there ever was one." He pointed to a cart filled with rubber flip-flops. "What size do you wear?"

"Ladies size five to six will do fine," she answered.

"Color?"

"I'm not picky," she said. "Anything just so that I don't get thrown out." She nodded toward the sign on the door that said NO SHIRT, NO SHOES, NO SERVICE.

He dug around in the cart, took a pair inside the store, and returned to open her door. "Stick your feet out here, darlin'. You can be Cinderella."

"Does that mean you're Prince Charming?"

"I'll be anything or anyone you want me to be," he told her.

That was guilt talking, and she knew it, but it sounded good to her ears right then. She was surprised that no one stared at her when she entered the store. Then she saw another lady in there in orange scrubs.

"The nurses who work in the local nursing home wear orange," Tag said.

She nodded and threw a package of panties into the cart. Then she sorted through a rack of jeans and tossed in two pairs. Tag stayed right beside her, and finding a couple of bras in her size was more than a little embarrassing. After that, they found T-shirts and a nightshirt and headed toward the shampoo and toothpaste aisle. When she'd gotten everything she needed and they were at the counter, Tag whipped out a credit card.

"You're not buying my underwear," she protested.

"Yes, I am. This is my fault and there's no telling how much of your money you spent today. Your backseat looked like a trash bin and that suitcase of beer wasn't cheap," Tag said.

"Tulia's not a big place," she said softly. "Tomorrow, the fact that you were here with me and bought me clothes will be all over town."

"Good." He accepted the total, swiped his card, and put his signature on the screen. Then he carried the bags out to the truck and tossed them in the backseat with his duffel.

"Where'd that come from?" she asked.

"Hud packed it for me. Matthew put it in the truck when he took my motorcycle back out to the ranch. If you'll give me a ride home tomorrow or whenever you're ready to go, I'll leave my bike here."

That was a huge step for him to take, but she didn't want that burden on her conscience. In six weeks or maybe in six days, he'd resent her for his decision.

"You sure about that? Don't do it out of guilt, Tag," she said. "If I'd gone home last night instead of drinkin' moonshine, I wouldn't have been in the cabin this morning. If I'd brought my purse in, I'd have had my gun. This isn't your fault."

"Yes, it is." He drove away from the store and straight to a small motel. "Wait right here." He ran inside and came back with a key. "It's my fault because of decisions I made as a teenager. Duke might have approved of the crazy stunts that we pulled when I was a stupid kid, but my heart tells me it's time to grow up."

"You should always listen to your heart." She didn't even have to wonder if she was talking to him or to herself.

"We can get something pretty quick at Sonic. That okay with you?"

Food suddenly sounded wonderful. "Burgers and a chocolate shake, and the biggest root beer they make. I'm sick of water," she said.

"Fries?" he asked.

"Tater tots, double order, burger with mustard and no onions."

He nosed the truck into a slot, rolled down the window, and pushed the call button. A lady's voice asked if she could

help him. He looked over at Nikki and said, "Are you serious about wanting that much?"

"If I don't eat it now, I will before bedtime," she said.
"Want my credit card?"

He waved her away, ordered four burgers, two chocolate
shakes, two Route 44 root beers, and a double order of tater
tots and a double of fries. "And add two chicken strip dinners to that," he finished.

"How long are we staying in that motel? You've ordered
enough food for a week," she said.

He turned to face her. "I paid for two nights, but we can
leave earlier than that, or we can extend it as long as you
want. This is going to hit you in a little while. I just hope
you don't hate me when it does."

"This is still Tuesday, isn't it?" In some ways, it seemed
like the incident with Billy Tom had happened a year ago
instead of only that morning. In other ways she felt like if
she looked in the rearview mirror, she would see him sitting
in the backseat grinning with food in his mouth.

"It is," he said.

"Less than twenty-four hours ago, I faced off with my
mother, and I thought that was the hardest thing I'd ever
have to do," she said. "I was wrong, Tag, but I refuse to be
a victim in either case. That gives Mama and Billy Tom—
Seems strange to say their names in the same sentence.
Anyway, that gives them power over me, and I won't let
them make me a victim."

"You have the strength of an elephant, Nikki." Tag
reached out and tucked a strand of damp hair behind her ear.

A young girl brought his order and he paid with cash,
adding a couple of dollars for a tip.

"Now let's get you to the hotel so you can eat and call
Emily. She's frantic to hear your voice." He drove them all

the way to the end of the motel and parked at the last room in the row.

"Food, then talk." Nikki felt faint as she got out of the truck, grabbed the paper bags from the backseat, and followed Tag into the room.

Two queen-size beds with standard blue and green bedspreads took up one wall. A microwave sat on top of a small dorm-size refrigerator. The four-drawer dresser held a television, and there was a small green upholstered chair over in one corner. In the other was a tiny round table with two chairs. The bathroom had a shower above a tub. Looking at it, Nikki decided that she'd take a long, soaking bath before she went to sleep that evening. Maybe that would help her truly get the day out of her mind.

Tag set the paper bags of food on the table, left the door open, and went back out to the truck. He returned with his duffel bag. Kicking the door shut with his boot heel, he said, "Soon as we eat, I'd like to have a shower to get the dust off me."

"Tag, you don't have to stay with me," she told him. "I'm a big girl. I might go to pieces, but if I do, I'll get over it, just like I have in the past."

"I'm not going anywhere. I'll take the bed closest to the door," he said.

She crossed the room and wrapped her arms around him. "Thank you."

His phone rang and she stepped back.

"Hello," he said cautiously.

"I'm calling because I just found your number along with the words HELP ME on a card in a convenience store bathroom," a lady said. "Do you know what that means?"

The woman on the other end was practically yelling and Nikki was close enough to hear every word.

"Yes, ma'am, I do and it's all taken care of now. My girlfriend is safe," he said.

"Well, thank God for that. Y'all have a great day."

"Girlfriend?" Nikki smiled.

"If you'll have an old cowboy renegade like me," Tag answered.

"You came to rescue me. I think that forgives the rebel part," she said.

"If you'd disarmed him, we might have been rescuing him." Tag took her by the hand and led her to the table.

"If I could've figured out a way to get that gun away from him, you'd have been burying him, not saving his sorry ass."

Chapter Sixteen

The adrenaline rush for Tag crashed after he'd eaten a couple of burgers and drank half a milk shake. The whole day had been surreal, from the time the policeman knocked on the door until that moment.

"Are you ready to talk about the day?" he asked.

"I can't remember ever being this tired." She yawned. "Can we take a short nap before we talk?"

"Yes, ma'am. Just promise me if you wake before I do that you won't leave?"

"You've got my word," she said.

"I'm calling Emily and then I'm getting between the sheets—that is, if you'll loan me your phone," she said.

He kicked off his boots and headed to the bathroom with his duffel bag in hand. "I'm taking a shower. I'm too dirty to stretch out for a nap." He kissed her on the cheek, on his way across the floor. His reflection in the mirror above the vanity didn't show much of a change in him. A few flecks

of dust hanging to the scruff on his face, but that was all.
He had expected to see that he'd aged ten years in one day,
maybe even see a few gray hairs.

He dropped all of his dirty, sweaty clothing on the floor
and adjusted the water in the shower. He stepped into the
tub and let the warm water beat down on his back for several
minutes before he even lathered up the washcloth with soap.
He and Hud had made the trip to Bowie on motorcycles
last spring. That trip hadn't tired him out like this one had.
Must've been the tension and worry the whole five hours, he
thought. Or maybe he really was getting old, and it was time
to reassess this business of living like he was dying and just
live—period.

He got out of the shower and wrapped a towel around
his waist. He had a change of clothing plus a pair of pajama
pants and a tank top in his duffel bag. Digging deeper, he
discovered underwear and Hud's go kit that held a new
toothbrush and travel-size containers of toothpaste, mouth-
wash, and deodorant, as well as a disposable razor. Tag
smiled. He didn't need the razor that day, but he appreciated
all the other items.

He found a plastic laundry bag in the closet and stuffed
all his dirty things into it. Then he stopped at the side of
Nikki's bed and watched her sleep for a few minutes. She'd
gotten between the sheets and was curled up in a ball, covers
pulled all the way to her chin, hair flowing out on the pillow
like a halo. But she wasn't an angel. She was a fighter. And
he loved that about her.

He'd looked his fill of her, and then made sure the safety
lock was engaged on the door and turned back the bed-
spread and top sheet on the other bed. He bit back a groan
when he stretched out. The warm water had helped, but
every muscle in his body was still tense. He closed his eyes

and thought about the decisions he had made throughout the day. He was sure he'd made the right one in giving up his motorcycle—but there was no way he'd give up the rush of riding a bull or a bronc.

The room was dark when he awoke. The clock on the nightstand told him that it was ten thirty. Nikki was curled up against his back with one arm thrown around him and a leg hooked over his thighs. For a minute he thought he was dreaming; then she moved.

"I had a nightmare," she whispered.

He laced his fingers in hers but didn't move. "Tell me about it."

"You weren't there at that old tree across the road, and Billy Tom dragged me into that cabin. His friends were all leering at me, and Billy Tom was flashing that gun around and telling me that he'd kill me if y'all didn't pay him ten thousand dollars. That's when I woke up. I…needed to…" she stammered.

"I told you I'm here for you." He flipped over and drew her close to his body. "I might have been a scoundrel, but my word is as good as gold. If you need me to hold you every night, I'll do it."

"Out of duty?" she asked.

"Out of whatever this is between us," he answered.

*   *   *

At first light the next morning, Nikki sat up in bed and wrapped her arms around her knees. "What is this with us?"

"I'm not sure," Tag answered. "But I kind of like it." He propped two pillows against the headboard and leaned back. "Now let's talk about what happened yesterday. Tell me the whole thing, Nikki. I need to know."

"I woke up and found your note," she said. "Had a bowl of cereal. Heard a knock on the door. I thought maybe it was you, that you'd locked it behind you and couldn't get in. I opened it to find Billy Tom right there in front of me. My purse with my gun was out in my car."

"Were you scared?" Tag asked.

"More pissed than afraid—did you even hear anything on the phone when I called you?"

"Loud and clear, and then Red dragged your purse into the front yard. I think that's what really convinced the Montague County sheriff to believe me," he said.

"I drank eight bottles of water on the trip so I'd have to keep stopping to go to the bathroom, and I stayed as long as I could," she said.

"You were very brave and resourceful. Don't blame yourself for any of this, Nikki. I'm the one you should hate," he said.

"It's not your fault that Billy Tom found out where the cabin was and kidnapped me," she said. "I'd have crawled out a bathroom window or screamed for help, but he said he'd shoot everyone in the store if I did. You think he would have? After the way he curled up and bawled like a baby when I hit him with that gun, I'm not sure he'd have the balls to actually kill someone." She stretched her legs out and scooted back to share the pillows with him.

"Billy Tom has always been a loose cannon, so I don't know about killing, but I wouldn't put anything past him." Tag's tone was dead serious. "I stopped right after my twenty-first birthday. I hadn't seen or heard from him in eight years; then a couple of weeks ago, he called me out of the blue, wanting me to go in with them on this big deal."

"Were you even tempted?" she asked.

"No, not a bit. I might still be a rebel, but I'm not stupid."

He held her close and stroked her hair until she fell asleep again.

Sun rays flowed through the split in the window curtains later the next morning when Nikki awoke for the second time. The last thing she remembered was telling Tag about all the emotions that had run through her body on that horrible trip. Her back was against his chest and her stomach was telling her that it was time to eat.

"Hungry?" he whispered.

"Little bit," she answered. "Let's heat up some leftovers. Have you heard from your brother? When are they bringing my car?"

"Turned off the phone after you talked to Emily. I didn't want it to ring and wake you." He threw back the covers. "But we don't have to eat leftovers. They serve breakfast here."

"Give me a few minutes to shower and get into some clothes." She hopped out of bed and went straight to the bathroom, then remembered that she hadn't taken her things with her. He was talking on the phone when she returned, and from the look on his face, it was pretty serious.

She retrieved her new clothes and hung them on the hooks on the back side of the bathroom door. Then she stripped out of the orange scrubs, tossed them on the floor with no intentions of ever wearing them again, and ran a bath. She sank down into the warm water and wondered if she went under, would it be kind of like a baptism? Would she wash away all the fear and anger from the day before, like getting rid of sins and being reborn a new woman?

Sliding even farther down until only her nose was above water, she took a deep breath and lay on the bottom of the tub for a few seconds before she came back up. Water sluiced down her face and neck, but she still felt like Nikki

Grady. There was no washing away the sin of wanting to shoot Billy Tom—because she would still do it in a heartbeat if she had a gun and he threatened her again.

She finally pulled the plug on the tub, got out and dried her hair, and dressed in new clothing right off the rack that she'd have washed before putting on if she'd been home. She wiped the fog from the mirror and brushed her teeth. Tag was still on the phone, but the smile on his face said this call wasn't as serious.

"Talk to you later, Granny, and I'll ask Nikki about supper," he said.

"Supper?" she asked.

"I want to see my folks while I'm here, and Hud sent hugs for Mama. I understand if you don't want to go out to the ranch, though," he said.

"Supper at the ranch sounds fine. I owe Matthew a thank-you for helping rescue me," she said. "But I'm more comfortable staying here. That doesn't mean you have to spend another night protecting me."

"Billy Tom escaped," he said bluntly. "They think he's headed back to Mesquite for his cycle and they've got authorities on the lookout between here and there."

"Then would you please stay with me?" she asked. "And if you've got access to a pistol out at the ranch, would you please bring it with you after supper? But tomorrow morning, Tag, whether Billy Tom is back in custody or not, I'm going home. I have to work Friday night, and I refuse to let that son of a bitch make me afraid or upset my life."

"Deal, but just in case they don't catch him, will you let me sleep on your sofa or stay with me at the cabin or even at Emily's?"

"I'll think about it. Now let's go get some breakfast. What are we doing until supper?"

He wiggled his eyebrows. "Well, we've got this room, and the sheriff did say that you were my girlfriend."

They were back on solid ground one more time. She air slapped his arm and said, "But I don't go to bed with my boyfriend after only one date."

"You did last night—twice," he teased.

"With clothes on," she reminded him. "Know what I'd like to do today?"

"Name it and I'll do my best to make it happen," he said.

"We're close to the Palo Duro Canyon, aren't we? Emily's talked about it and I'd love to see it. The only state I've ever been to, outside of Texas, of course, is Oklahoma. I crossed the Red River a few times when I went to the Watermelon Festival in Terral," she said.

"You want to sightsee?" Tag looked genuinely shocked.

"Unless you need to be at the ranch all day," she said.

"No, ma'am." He grinned. "We'll leave right after we eat. Long as we're at the ranch for cocktails at five o'clock, we'll be fine."

"Cocktails?" She frowned.

"Very informal," he said. "We just like to gather up for a beer or a shot of whiskey before supper. It's not dress-up. You've been there before?"

"Not for cocktails. I went with Emily once, but we weren't there at supper time. Then at the wedding everyone was going every which way to get things done," she said. "Truth is, it scares me just a little to be there in the middle of your family."

He looped her arm into his. "Honey, you faced down Billy Tom. I'm surprised that anything scares you."

She slipped her feet into pink flip-flops at the door. "He's a wicked piece of trash. Your folks know we spent the night together. I can only imagine what they probably think of me."

"I talked to them this morning. They know this room has two beds, and they're happy that you let me stay with you." He locked the door behind them. "You really want to eat buffet, or would you rather go to a little café for breakfast?"

"I'm with you. You make the decision," she said.

"Then good hot food brought to the table, it is." He led her to the pickup.

It was only a short drive to the café. When they were inside, it kind of reminded her of the one in Bowie where she liked to treat herself some Monday mornings after forty-eight hours of ER duty.

They chose a booth in the back corner beside a window, and the waitress brought two coffee mugs and then filled them. "Hey, did you hear Sheriff Roberts has locked up that crazy crew you used to run with? I heard they robbed some big-shot drug dealer's shipment of ephedrine and sold it to someone else. Then the fools came back here to Tulia to that old shack they used to hang out in."

"That's what I heard," Tag said.

"Did you hear that Billy Tom escaped? That piece of slime could worm his way out of hell. Now what can I get y'all this mornin', and are you goin' to introduce me to your lady friend, or not?"

"I'm sorry, Charlene." Tag smiled. "This is Nikki Grady, my girlfriend. Nikki, this is Charlene. She cooked at the ranch for a while when I was a little boy, then opened this café."

"Pleased to meet you. I was at Emily's weddin'. You was the maid of honor, right?" Charlene said. "Y'all don't bother with orderin'. I'll bring you my big country breakfast, and it's on the house."

"Thank you, and it's a pleasure to meet you, Miz Charlene." Nikki smiled.

"You're welcome." Charlene headed back to the kitchen.

"Does she always give you free meals?" Nikki whispered across the table.

"No, ma'am. This is the first time. She must like you." He took her hands in his and brought her knuckles to his lips. "I liked waking up with you all curled up around me."

"The nightmare was so real that I woke up crying," Nikki admitted. "If you hadn't been there, I wouldn't have been able to close my eyes again all night."

"It's kind of nice to be needed and not just wanted." Tag gently squeezed her hands and took a sip of his coffee. "I liked it when you let me comfort you last night, even though I don't deserve it."

"I keep telling you that it's not your fault," she said.

"I'm glad that you believe that, but I'm not sure I'll ever forgive myself."

Chapter Seventeen

The landscape in the western part of the state was very different from back where Nikki had grown up. Here the land was flat, almost treeless and reached all the way out to the sky. By stretching the imagination a little, she could almost see the place where the earth actually rounded off a little. Back around Bowie, rolling hills were covered with scrub oak and mesquite trees and lots of cow tongue cactus.

But then a few miles out of Silverton, a town not much bigger than Montague, Tag suddenly cut the speed and they were going straight down into a big canyon. It was eerily beautiful that morning. Burnt umber and ochre, the two colors that she'd used in art class back in high school, came to her mind as she tried to take the whole scene all in with one glance.

The narrow road took them around curves, up hills, and down the other side. On every side of her were amazing rock formations, some reaching so high that she had to strain her neck to see the tops, and others looking like sand castles a child would build on the beach.

"This is awesome," she said. "No cafés, nothing commercial, just a big hole in the ground with all kinds of gorgeous sights. This must be the best kept secret in the whole state," she whispered.

*   *   *

Tag had grown up around Palo Duro, but seeing the canyon through Nikki's eyes opened it up in a whole new light for him. He hadn't thought of her travel being limited because of the disruptions in her family and then her decision to move out and live on her own at such a young age. Suddenly, he wanted to take her every place he'd ever been. Granted, most of them had been family vacations to wherever a rodeo was held, and the majority of them had been in the United States. But they had gone on a couple of cruises. He'd been bored out of his mind most of the time and had even considered jumping overboard and seeing if he could swim back to Texas. Now he wondered what it would be like to see the Mayan ruins and go snorkeling in the Gulf with Nikki.

"Look at that." She pointed.

"That's called the chimney," he said. "I've seen bald eagles sitting up there a few times. This was one of my favorite places to ride my motorcycle."

"Tag, you don't have to give it up. If you love riding, then you should keep it."

He shook his head slowly. "I don't think I can ever ride one again without flashbacks of worrying about you. When I talked to Mama this morning, I told her to donate it to the police department. Seemed fitting since they're the ones who really saved you."

"They couldn't have done it if you hadn't known where to send them."

Tag didn't know how to answer that comment, so they rode in silence for more than half an hour. He drove slowly all the way through the canyon. When they came up on the other side and reached the small town of Claude, he finally asked, "Do you want to go back the same way we came or go through Amarillo?"

"Let's hit that little convenience store right there for a bathroom break and maybe something cold to drink, and then go right back the way we came. The light will be coming from a different angle that way. And could we stop at that place at the top and take a couple of pictures?" she asked. "We'd have to use your phone. Mine is still in my purse at your ranch."

"Sure thing," he said. "Want to pick up some snacks and have a picnic? There's a table for that at the lookout over the canyon."

"Sounds great. Let's have junk food and root beer," she suggested.

He held her hand on the way into the store. She headed off to the bathroom and he gathered up candy bars, chips, and a six-pack of root beer, set it on the counter, and handed the young man a twenty-dollar bill. The guy dropped his change and had to bend down to pick it up, then fumbled when he was putting the food into a bag.

"Sweet Jesus! You're like a bad case of the itch that just keeps showing up." Tag heard Nikki raise her voice at the back of the store.

"He's got a gun," the clerk whispered.

Tag dropped his wallet on the counter and headed toward Nikki but didn't get there before she had kicked off her flip-flops and landed a square kick in Billy Tom's crotch. He rolled forward, and she picked up a gallon of motor oil from a display and swung it like a Louisville Slugger. When it made contact with the side of his head, he fell backward, taking out a stand of Twinkies on the way down.

"Tell that kid I need some duct tape and call Sheriff Roberts," she hollered at Tag. "I believe we've got something that belongs to him. And he doesn't have a gun. If he did, he'd be brandishing it like he was a badass. He was bluffing."

"Did you kill him?" Tag caught the roll of duct tape the kid threw toward him.

"I wouldn't be so lucky." She took the tape from Tag's hand and peeled off a length wide enough to tape Billy Tom's mouth shut. "He'll wake up in a minute. It'd take more than that tap on the head to keep him down. He's high as a kite on something. I can tell by his eyes." She stuck the tape firmly across his mouth, then made two wraps around his legs. "You can work on his wrists. Do a good job or he'll break free. I'll be waiting in the truck. I've seen more of this sumbitch than I want to for the rest of my life."

"She's one badass woman," the kid said. "I was terrified of him, but she scares me more. He got out of a semi that was filling up on gas. Guess he was hitchhiking. He told me that I would give him the keys to my motorcycle when he came out of the restroom and if I called anyone, he'd go to the school and shoot all the kids on the playground. I got a niece in kindergarten."

"He was bluffing. Get on your phone and call the Claude police. Tell them to come get Billy Tom, the guy who escaped from the Swisher County jail last night." Tag wrapped the tape from Billy Tom's wrists to his elbows and did the same from ankles to knees, then trussed the man's hands and feet together like a calf at a roping.

Billy Tom groaned and his eyes fluttered open. He tried to sit up, but Tag had roped him down really well. If it had been possible, he would have shot fire from his eyes at both Tag and the kid.

Tag leaned down and whispered right in Billy Tom's ear. "If you ever, ever come after Nikki or any member of my family again, I will go on the stand and testify to all your past sins. Some of those will put you so far back in jail you'll never see daylight."

Billy Tom's eyes popped out and all the color drained from his face. He struggled against the tape, but it wouldn't budge.

Tag kept talking. "You know that I don't make idle threats. But if that don't work, they will never find your body. Nod if you understand what I'm saying."

Billy Tom shot him a dirty look, but his chin bobbed up and down.

"That's good, and you might pass it on to your buddies. The same goes for them."

Another nod.

The kid made the call and turned to Tag. "He'll be here in five minutes. Could you stick around?"

"Sure thing, but I already hear the sirens. They'll be here right soon," Tag said.

"Thanks," the kid said. "I'd just feel better if..."

Tag nodded and pointed out the window. "They're here now and will be coming in soon. My lady is waiting. I think you can handle this until they get in here. Just go on back to the cash register. He can't get loose." Tag picked up his purchases and wallet as he passed the counter and walked out.

On his way out, he passed two police cars, and four officers were running toward the store with guns drawn. Tag recognized one of them from the bar down in Palo Duro that he used to frequent on Saturday nights. "Hey, Kyle. That's Billy Tom in there and you might want to keep part of that tape on him. He's high on something and slippery as a slug."

"Thanks for the heads-up." Deputy Kyle Robertson kept running. "We might be callin' you about this later."

"You got my number," Tag hollered back.

He was more than a little surprised to see his own hands shaking when he put the bag of snacks in the backseat of the truck. When he got behind the wheel, he leaned over the console, took Nikki's face in his hands, and kissed her—long and lingering and then passionate. When the kiss ended, his nerves were as steady as a rock.

"What was that for?" she asked.

"For just bein' you," he answered.

"Well, I got to admit I was trembling from head to toe when I got out here, but your kiss settled me right down. If that sorry sucker escapes again, I vote that we put out an order to shoot first and ask questions later," she said.

A surge of pure happiness swept through Tag. She had acknowledged that his kiss had affected her the same way it had him. He turned the key to start the engine and Elizabeth Cook was singing "Sometimes It Takes Balls to Be a Woman."

Nikki shot a sideways glance toward him and giggled. He chuckled and before he could put the truck in gear, they were both laughing so hard they could hardly breathe.

Tag finally wiped his eyes. "Talk about perfect timing and something taking all the tension out. You sure you're all right?"

The laughter stopped as suddenly as it had begun, and Nikki looked like she might start crying any minute. Tag had never been good with weeping women, not even his sister or mother, who seldom shed tears. He followed her gaze, and there was Billy Tom, his hands now cuffed behind his back and all the duct tape gone, and he was looking straight at Nikki. The noise from the radio blocked the evil words spewing from his mouth, but Tag could read his lips. Nikki was right. If he escaped again, they should put out a shoot-on-sight order.

Tag laid a hand on her arm. "Are you okay?"

"I am strong. I can do this. I will not be intimidated." She recited the words like a mantra.

"Okaay." Tag dragged the word out.

"I'm not losing my mind." She covered his hand with hers. "'I am strong and I can do this' is what I would say to myself after my brother died and my dad left, and I had to deal with my mother's problems. That last part I've added since I moved out on my own," she said. "Sometimes I have to say it a dozen times before I begin to believe it. I refuse to let the likes of Billy Tom or his evil looks put fear in my heart, even if I have to stand in front of a mirror and repeat it for a whole hour." She inhaled deeply and removed her hand.

"You are strong, and you can do this. I believe in you," Tag said as he drove west out of Claude toward the highway that would take them south and back through the canyon.

*   *   *

Nikki was glad for Tag's faith in her, but her stomach was still twisted up like a pretzel. Kicking Billy Tom like that had been pure impulse. Thank God for that display of motor oil at her fingertips, because even on his knees and groaning, he looked like he could break her in half like a twig.

They started descending into the canyon, and Tag handed

her his phone. "Snap away. Just tell me if you want me to pull off to the side of the road so you can get a better view of something."

"That sounds great. I'm already thinking about a collage to go above my sofa." She started taking pictures, one after the other.

"We'll stop and get copies made of whatever you want on the way home tomorrow," he offered.

"Or we can wait and let me study them before we do that." She took several more out the car window.

When they reached the turnout to the picnic area, two hours had passed and she'd snapped more than a hundred pictures. The tiny place had a couple of big empty trash cans, one picnic table, and an awesome view of several formations. Tag got the snack bag from the backseat and set it on the table. Nikki headed straight for a fenced walkway that overlooked miles and miles of the canyon. She'd snapped a dozen more pictures when she turned around to see Tag sitting on the concrete table with his feet on the bench. She motioned for him to join her.

Without asking why, he meandered that way. "I've seen this place dozens of times. Even donated a few empty beer cans to those trash bins over there."

"But I haven't. And I want a picture of you right there." She pointed to the end of the fenced area. Tag propped one arm on the fence and looked right at her with those clear eyes that matched the cloudless sky behind him and the blue of his Western shirt. He'd rolled the sleeves up to his elbows, showing off arms that had seen lots of hard work. His black cowboy hat against the sky set off the whole picture. In the distance to the right was a huge ochre-colored formation.

"Should I smile?" he asked.

"Not in this one," she said. "Just look at me and follow me with your eyes."

"No problem there. You look pretty damn cute today."

She took a couple dozen pictures. "That should do it."

"No sexy come-hither grin?" he asked.

"Give me the best you've got." She focused on him one more time.

"This works better than a grin anytime." He slid an eyelid shut in a sexy wink. She caught the picture perfectly and decided that would probably be the one in the center of her collage.

"Now it's time to reverse the situation. Give me the phone and you come out here right where I'm standing and let me take a few pictures of you."

"Are you sure? The wind is blowing my hair every which way. I don't have makeup on."

He took the phone from her hand and nodded. "Very sure. Face me and the wind will blow your hair out of your face."

When he'd taken half a dozen shots, he shoved the phone in his pocket and held out his hand. The sparks that danced around like dandelion blossoms in the wind didn't surprise her at all. The place where they were standing wasn't roses and champagne, but it was magical to her. It erased all the fears of that morning and left behind only peace. Tag had rescued her and then hadn't said a word when she'd taken care of matters. This man was worth a chance, no matter what his past had been.

Chapter Eighteen

Tag's mother, Anne, poured three glasses of white wine and handed one to Nikki. "Glad to have you with us this evening. You've surely been through a lot the past couple of days. I understand that Billy Tom is back in the Swisher County jail now, thanks to you." She lowered her voice to a whisper. "He's been bad news his whole life."

Anne stood a full head taller than Nikki and had flaming red hair that she wore in a ponytail at the nape of her neck. That she was Emily's mother wasn't a surprise, but Anne was slim built and Emily was a curvy woman.

"I can believe that," Nikki said.

Tag's grandmother Opal, a gray-haired lady not nearly as tall as Anne, touched her wineglass to Nikki's and smiled. "Would you like a sawed-off shotgun, just in case that sorry sucker shows up in your neck of the woods again? I've got a couple of extras."

"Thank you, but I have a gun."

"Pistol?" Opal asked.

"Yes, ma'am. And I practice often," Nikki answered.

"They're fine, but up close, nothing brings about fear like the sound of racking a shell in a sawed off," Opal said.

"A little red dot does pretty good." Nikki smiled and then took a sip of the wine. "Especially if you move it slowly from their heart to the zipper in their jeans."

"Girl after my own heart," Opal chuckled.

Why in the name of all that was good and right in the world couldn't God have given her to Anne instead of Wilma Grady so that Opal could be her grandmother?

Because that would make you Tag's sister, a pesky voice in the back of her head said loudly.

She glanced across the room to find Tag staring right at her. She held up her glass, and he gave her a long, slow wink as he raised his beer bottle.

Supper was served family style—fried chicken, mashed potatoes, gravy, and all the trimmings. Proper manners, according to Wilma, said a lady ate like a bird when in polite company. Nikki figured she was adhering to her upbringing when she had a second helping just like Opal and Anne did. Wilma hadn't said a sparrow. She'd said a bird and ostriches were classified as birds.

"I like a woman who enjoys good food," Tag whispered.

"I don't get a supper like this very often," she said.

"I hear there's a ranch rodeo this weekend over in your neck of the woods," Matthew said. "And you're not going to believe this, but there's a bull named Fumanchu they say is meaner than Devil Dog."

Tag's eyes glittered. "Oh, yeah, when exactly?"

"Friday night. I heard that no one will sign up to ride him. After that song you play all the time, I figured you'd want to give it a try," Matthew said.

"Dammit!" Opal hit the table hard enough to rattle the dishes. "Why'd you have to tell him that?"

"There's a few things he's got to get out of his system." Matthew grinned. "But now that he's had two run-ins with Billy Tom, maybe he's given up on that song."

"Not hardly," Tag said. "I been waitin' more than ten years for this. I'll check into it soon as supper is over."

Nikki's breath caught in her chest. That pink line of scar under the scruff on his face would be nothing compared to what it would look like if a mean bull trampled him. Maybe all this with Billy Tom had only slowed him down, not ended his rebel days. But then would she care as much for him if he didn't have just a little bit of wild in him?

That's a question that needs an answer. This time it was Emily's voice in her head.

A visual of Tag being carried into the emergency room on a stretcher with a broken leg—or worse, with a broken neck—flashed into her mind. Tears welled up in her eyes, but she refused to let even one fall down her cheek. Could she ever commit one hundred percent to a man who was constantly living on the edge?

Opal nudged her with an elbow. "You ever listen to Miranda Lambert?"

Nikki nodded.

"I like her stuff and the Pistol Annies too. Ever heard her do 'Storms Never Last'?"

Another nod.

"Don't give up on him, Nikki. Storms don't last forever. He's fightin' his way out of a web of guilt, and we see a lot of progress," Opal whispered.

*   *   *

Tag was so excited about the bull that he called the ranch rodeo number on the website as soon as supper was over. With adrenaline climbing almost as high as it had the day before when he faced off with Billy Tom, he gave the lady his information and told her he'd bring the entry fee with him on Friday.

"Want to enter in the bronc as well?" she asked. "We're having it before the bull ride, and we're saving Fumanchu for the last ride of the night, because he's one mean son of a gun."

"Can I bring my own saddle?" he asked. "I'm kind of partial to it."

"We encourage that," she answered.

"Then yes, ma'am. I'll come prepared to ride a bronc and the bull," he told her.

"You should be here by seven thirty, then," she said.

"You can count on it." He ended the call, picked up Nikki, and swung her around until they were both dizzy.

"You're crazy." She wobbled when he finally set her firmly on the floor.

"I might be. I wish you could be there to see me," he said.

"She'll be waiting at the hospital to fix you up afterwards," Matthew teased.

"I'll make sure there's a cubicle ready. He's in luck. Dr. Richards is on duty again, and he's the best at stitchin' and mendin' broken bones," Nikki said.

"Y'all goin' to come watch me?" Tag asked.

Opal shook her head. "I'm not drivin' five hours to watch an eight-second ride."

"Eight seconds?" Nikki chuckled. "The song says that he just has to stay on the bull for two point seven seconds, don't it? And then he has to go skydiving to finish up the list, right?"

"I thought there was something about fishin' in there," Anne said.

"He's done that." Nikki nodded. "I'll sign the affidavit for that part."

"And on that note, I think Nikki and I'd better be going. I've got a couple of places I want to show her before the sun goes completely down. Mama, Hud sent a hug from him, so you better hug me twice," Tag said.

"Long as you promise you won't swing me around like you did Nikki, I'll take both those hugs." Anne walked into his open arms. "You take one back to Hud and the other boys for me. I bet Maverick and Paxton are missing their folks."

"Truth is, we've been so busy tryin' to get fences up that we drag in at dark, ready for sleep," he answered. "We're hopin' to get things in shape before winter sets in. They tell me there's not as much snow out in that part of Texas, but it can still get bitter cold and there's the occasional ice storm."

Matthew clamped a hand on his younger brother's shoulder. "After this little vacation, you should really work by the light of the moon until about midnight to make up for your lost time."

"Coming from the Baker boy who stays in an office ninety percent of the time?" Tag teased.

"Hey, now, I've offered to show you the ropes when it comes to the paper end of a ranch. Which brings me to the question—who's doin' that at your place? Have you roped Nikki into it? Which also reminds me." Matthew dug into his pocket and brought out a set of keys. "Nikki's car's been delivered to the motel. I told the guys to leave it in the parking lot. I'll send one of the hired hands to get my truck tomorrow. Just give the keys to Clarissa at the front desk."

Nikki shook her head. "Thank you, Matthew. You can't

begin to know how much I appreciate this. And about the book work at the ranch, Tag has not talked me into doing it. I can get around my tablet at work, but all that ranchin' lingo isn't up my alley. I barely know a cow from a goat. I'm a nurse, not a ranchin' woman."

Frank Baker had been quiet most of the evening, but his eyes, so much like Tag's, held a double dose of humor. "What this boy of mine needs worse than someone who can pull a calf or put a roof on a barn is a nurse to take care of all his injuries."

"I'll do my best," Nikki said as serious as she could. "But I don't do miracles."

By the time they said their goodbyes and left the Rocking B Ranch that evening, the sun was just a sliver out on the far horizon, past miles and miles of flat land. "One Wing in the Fire" by Trent Tomlinson was playing on the radio when Tag parked the truck in front of the motel door.

"I'm not sure I want my kids to ever think that I had one wing in the fire," he said seriously. "I want to be there to fix their cars and their hearts like the song says, but I want my kids to think that I have a halo like I thought my grandpa had."

"You think that about your dad too?" she asked.

"Pretty much," he said.

"Must be nice. My dad probably had one wing in the fire and no halo at all," she said.

"But he could have turned into a preacher in a little church over around Dallas," Tag suggested. "Don't judge until you know."

Her temper flared for a split second until she realized that he was right. The letters, the cards, the money, they all said that he hadn't stopped caring for her. And before Quint died, they'd gone to church every Sunday. Now, wouldn't it be a twist if she was dating a rebel and her father was a preacher?

"I thought we were going to see some stuff in town before the sun went down," she said as she reached for the door handle. "Look, there's my car. I'm going to go drive it up close to the motel door."

"You want to go sightseeing or grab a shower and throw back on the bed and watch reruns of whatever's on television? I made up that story because I hate goodbyes, and I wanted to get away from the ranch rather than put it off," he said.

"I've really seen enough for one day. I don't even want to talk to Emily tonight. I can call her on the way home tomorrow." She yawned.

"I'm sure she'll be tied up with Mama and Granny all evening anyway. They were probably lightin' up the cell phone towers between here and there before we even got into the truck. I'll open the door while you get your car. You aren't goin' to take off and leave me stranded, are you?" he asked.

She reached across the console and pinched his cheek. "I wouldn't leave my knight in shining armor behind. I might need rescuing again."

He grabbed her hand and brushed sweet kisses across the palm. "I hope not, darlin'."

Her hand was still tingling when she reached her car, and she fumbled the keys. They landed on the ground by her toes, and when she reached down to get them, a cold chill found its way down her spine. What if Billy Tom had a friend on the outside who'd done something to her car?

She was crawling around on the pavement looking for flashing red lights when she noticed a man's boots on the other side. Her heart leapt right up into her throat. She plastered herself against the driver's door and wished that she'd taken Opal up on that sawed-off shotgun. She could hear whoever it was walking around the car and then a hand shot out and touched her shoulder.

"What are you doing? Did your keys scoot under the car?" Tag asked.

"I guess I don't have balls after all. I'm as paranoid as my mother." She was honest when she told him about being afraid there was a bomb under her car.

"You never know with Billy Tom." He extended a hand and pulled her up to a standing position. "Billy Tom isn't smart enough to make a bomb, and besides, he's never going to bother you again. He and I had a little visit after I got the duct tape on him. I'll drive the car up to the motel. Door is open."

She tossed him the keys and stood perfectly still until her vehicle was parked in front of their room. When she started walking, he met her halfway and they walked to the door together.

"What did you tell him to make you so sure that he'll never bother me again?" she asked.

"Just that I knew a lot of stuff about him and his past that could get him a long time in the county jail or maybe even some prison time. I did say that if he threatened you again, they wouldn't find his body."

"That's pretty strong," she said.

"It wasn't a threat. It was a promise."

"Thank you for being honest with me," she said. "It means a lot, but I do wish I'd taken your grandmother up on her offer to let me have one of her sawed-off shotguns."

Tag closed the door behind them and locked it. "I've got one at the ranch back home that I'll let you have if you really want it." He sat down on the end of the bed and removed his boots, then threw himself backward. "I'd feel better if you'd let me sleep on your sofa, or if you'd stay at

the cabin for a while. From now on there'll be protection at
your fingertips, I promise."

She giggled nervously.

"Why's that funny?"

"I'm on the pill." She kicked off her flip-flops and headed
to the bathroom. "I don't need your protection."

He popped up to a sitting position. "You are a lesson in
confusion, woman. One minute you're thinking bombs and
the next condoms."

"One can blow you to an up-close-and-personal visit
with St. Peter. The other can change everything on this earth
for the rest of your natural life. And the confusing thing—
well, darlin', that keeps you on your toes." She shut the
bathroom door, but it didn't keep out his laughter.

She took a short shower and washed her hair and then
stepped out and wrapped a towel around her body and one
around her hair. After she was dry and dressed she towel
dried her hair and thought about what her mother would say
if she were to move in with Tag. Wilma Grady might even
curl up and die at the very idea of her daughter living in sin.

That brought up a picture of a long black hearse, which
looped around and made her think of the black Lincoln
she'd seen several times in and around Bowie. Could that be
her father? Holy hell! Had he been keeping tabs on her all
this time?

She slung open the door and announced, "Tag, I want to
find my father. I think maybe he's been looking for me." She
told him about the black Lincoln and the glimpses of the
guy in sunglasses and a cap.

"Only way to find out for sure is to ask him." Tag unbuttoned his shirt and took it off on his way to the bathroom.
"You sure you're ready for that? Want to let this all settle
before you take that on?"

"Nope, I want to know. I'm going to that address on the envelopes and cards this week." She couldn't take her eyes off his ripped abdomen or the little patch that was just the right amount of hair on his chest. Her fingers itched to see if it was as soft as it looked, so she sat on the bed and tucked her hands under her thighs. He undid his belt, laid it on the dresser, and emptied his pockets. Thinking about him taking off his jeans put a crimson blush on her cheeks.

He stopped at the bathroom door. "So what evening do you want to do this?"

"Monday I have to talk to Mama or the world will come to an end. Tuesday or Wednesday probably," she said. "Why?"

"I'll go with you. Pick you up at seven on Wednesday?"

"You don't have to do that, Tag."

In a couple of long strides he crossed the room, bent so their eyes were on the same level, and gave her a quick kiss on the lips. "I want to go. I can stay in the truck or go up to the door with you. Your choice, but I'll be there for support."

"Thank you," she said softly. "And you don't have to sit in the truck."

Chapter Nineteen

Tag went to sleep alone on Wednesday night, but when he awoke on Thursday, Nikki was curled up against his back again. Before he could turn over, she slipped out of bed and went to the bathroom. When she returned, she was fully dressed.

"Nightmares again?" he asked.

"Oh, yeah," she said. "But they say the third time is the charm, so after tonight they won't be there anymore."

"I'd still feel better if you'd either let me stay at your place or you'd sleep at the cabin or with Emily." He sat up in the bed and stretched.

"I wouldn't put Emily at risk. He knows where the cabin is, and he doesn't know where I live," she said. "But he does know my car, and I just remembered, I have to get my real license plate back."

"Why?" He stood up and headed for the bathroom.

"Billy Tom switched plates at one of the service stations.

Or at least he said he did. God, I hope the nightmares end soon."

"If we get to Bowie before they close, we can stop on the way. Nikki, I apologize again for everything, but most of all for the horrible dreams that bring it all back to you."

"I'm just glad that you've been there the past two nights to comfort me." She sat down on the edge of the bed.

She'd never know how much it meant to him that she accepted his apologies and let him stay with her. The whole way to Tulia, he'd figured that she would never speak to him again, and then when she wouldn't even let him touch her after Billy Tom was handcuffed, it seemed like he'd been right.

He heard her humming when he'd finished brushing his teeth and was getting dressed, but he couldn't figure out what the song was. At least she was happy. He scanned the bathroom one more time to make sure he'd remembered everything and then went on out to talk to Nikki.

Her things were all in plastic bags and waiting with the snack sack from yesterday on the end of her bed. She was organized and neat, which was another plus in his book.

"Want to eat breakfast in the hotel dining room before we leave or get something on the way?" he asked.

"Food here is free, so we might as well eat." She picked up the bags on her bed. "We should be home by early afternoon, right?"

"You anxious to get there, are you?"

"I imagine Goldie is getting pretty hungry. She may decide to run away from home if I treat her like this very often," Nikki answered.

"I'm picturing a goldfish holding a stick tucked up under her arm. There's a little sack of food at the end, and she's bouncing down the stairs on her fat little belly," he chuckled.

"Well, what can you expect? You gave her to me, so she's probably a renegade just like you." Nikki threw her bags into the backseat of her car. "Man, this looks and smells new, like it did the first day I bought it."

"We've got a real good detail guy. He even takes care of Granny's vintage '59 Chevy pickup."

"You're kiddin'. She's got a sixty-year-old truck?" Nikki asked as they started toward the motel.

"Yep, Grandpa was driving it when they went on their first date. She wouldn't let him trade it in or sell it. She gets it out at least once a week to 'blow the cobwebs out of the engine.'" He put air quotes around the last phrase.

"What color is it?"

He held the door open for her to enter the lobby first. "Two tone. Gold on top. White on bottom. It has a special stall in the barn and stays covered except for her weekly trip to town or once a year when she has it detailed. But when Grandpa was alive, they used it every year on their anniversary. They'd usually leave the ranch for a week."

"Where'd they go?" Nikki asked as she scanned the small dining area with its buffet laid out on one side.

"Road trips. No reservations. No plans. Grandpa said they went where the wind took them. They ate when they got hungry and stayed in hotels whenever they were tired. Granny looked forward to the trips all year. I'll get two cups of coffee and set them on that table." He nodded toward one at the back of the room where he could watch the door. He'd feel a lot better when Billy Tom was in a more secure place than the county jail.

"That kind of travel sounds amazing." She picked up a paper plate and started down the line.

Tag was thinking about a week on the road with Nikki and overflowed the first coffee cup. He dumped enough to get the lid on the cup and then wiped down the outside. His thoughts went back to where he'd like to take Nikki, and he did the same thing with the second cup.

"A little distracted?" She was already seated when he set the coffee on the table.

"Little bit." He spun around and headed toward the buffet. The beach at Florida would be a nice stop for a couple of days, he thought. When he realized what he was doing, his plate had a mound of scrambled eggs on it big enough for three lumberjacks. He couldn't scrape them back, so he covered them with sausage gravy and added a couple of biscuits to the side.

Nikki's eyes popped out at the sight when he set it on the table. "You need sideboards for that."

"Distracted again," he muttered.

"Billy Tom?"

He took a sip of the coffee. "No, I was thinking about a road trip with you."

"Oh, really, and where are we going?"

"East to Shreveport, south to New Orleans, then over to a little secluded beach in the panhandle of Florida, maybe back up through Montgomery, Alabama, and Nashville, Tennessee," he said.

"Do we get to take Opal's truck?" She spread cream cheese on a bagel and then added strawberry jam.

"She doesn't even let Emily drive that truck, and Emily is her favorite," Tag chuckled. "If you could do a weeklong road trip, where would you want to go?"

"That one you said would be pretty nice for a starter. I've always wanted to see the ocean," she said.

"The beach I had in mind is in the panhandle, so it would be the Gulf of Mexico, not the ocean," he said between bites.

"Is the water salty?" she asked.

He nodded.

"Then it's the ocean to me, but as much fun as it is to think about that kind of trip, I don't see it happening," she said.

"Me neither. At least not for two or three years until we get the ranch going good. If things were to work out on a long-term basis for us, maybe we'll never sell my truck."

"So you've got hope that this chemistry between us could be more than a flash in the pan?" She finished off her bagel and sipped at the black coffee.

"Oh, my hopes are mighty high." He polished off the last of his breakfast. "How about a coffee refill for the road?"

"No, thanks." She covered a yawn with her hand. "Am I driving or are you?"

"I'll be glad to," he offered. "Looks like you're still sleepy. I'm wide awake."

"Thank you. It was a rough night. I'd love to catch a little more sleep," she said as she got into the passenger seat and leaned it back as far as it would go.

For the first hundred miles, he constantly kept an eye on the rearview mirror. He wouldn't have been surprised at any minute to see a motorcycle coming up fast, but it never did. He settled down to listen to the radio and let his thoughts wander back to the conversation about a road trip. They'd just passed the city limits sign to Childress when Nikki roused.

"Where are we?"

"You've slept a little less than two hours. We're on Highway 287. It will take us all the way to Bowie," he answered.

"Can we stop at that Pilot station up ahead for something cold to drink and a bathroom break?" she asked.

"Of course. No nightmares?" He flipped on the turn signal to get off at the next exit.

"Nope. Slept like a baby," she answered.

The parking lot was crowded, but he snagged a place right in front of the store. Nikki was out of the vehicle and practically jogging to the store before he could be a gentleman and open the door for her. Once he stepped outside the car, he understood her rush. The heat was downright oppressive, and it was only midmorning. He hurried after her, pressing the button on his key fob and listening for the click to tell him the doors were locked. As much as he'd loved his motorcycle, he was glad that he wasn't riding it that day.

He made a sweep through the place before he went to the men's room. There was no one who even resembled one of Billy Tom's gang in the store or in the restroom. When he came back out, Nikki was standing in front of the glass doors where the cold soda pop was displayed.

"Root beer is over there." He pointed.

"I'm trying to decide if I want something in a bottle or a fountain drink with ice," she said.

"I'm getting a big sweet tea with ice. It'll stay cold for at least another hundred miles and then we'll stop for lunch," Tag said.

"That sounds really good." She headed toward the drink machine at the front of the store.

They didn't have to stand in line, so they were back in the car and on the way in a few minutes. Tag groaned when he slid behind the steering wheel. "I miss my truck."

"I guess my car is a little small for you, isn't it?" she said. "What about your motorcycle? Do you miss it?"

"Not in this heat." He took a long drink of the tea and then put it in the cup holder in the console.

"Y'all rode out to Bowie and back when you came to visit Emily last spring," she reminded him.

"And the weather was fairly cool. Come to think of it, where were you while we were there?"

"Working and studying to take my test to be a registered nurse. If anyone had told you what would be happening this past couple of months back then, would you have believed them?"

He pulled out of the parking lot and merged with the traffic on the highway. "I could have believed that we'd own the ranch. Hud and I have been looking for something we could afford for the past couple of years. I wouldn't have believed that we could talk Maverick and Paxton into moving with us so we'd have some help. Or that you'd finally agree to go out with me."

"Maverick and Paxton seem more like brothers to you and Hud than distant cousins. I'd think they'd be happy to join you," she said.

"They've been with the Rocking B since they got out of high school, and we've been through a lot together even before that. It's complicated. Granny's cousin went to Ireland when he was in the military and brought home an Irish wife. She and Granny became fast friends and have remained so all through the years."

Tag watched the landscape change from flat as a pancake to rolling hills. Sometimes he missed what he'd grown up around, too, and a day didn't go by that he didn't miss his family. "How'd you handle it when your dad left?"

"I was mourning for my brother, so I guess I kind of clumped it all together and grieved for him like he was dead too. I don't know where I got it, but since Mama was so…" Nikki frowned like she was searching for the right word, then finally threw up her hands in defeat. "Well, you've met her and I told you what she said when Quint died, so you can guess how she was. I felt like I owed it to both of them to grieve for a whole year. It sounds insane, but a year passed before I had the first little bit of closure."

"When did you have it all, the closure, I mean?" he asked.

"I still don't, not any more than you do for Duke," she answered.

"Giving up the motorcycle has helped," he said.

"Seeing my father in person might do it for me." She reached into the backseat and brought up the snack bag, dug around until she found a package of chocolate doughnuts and a bag of peanuts. "Can I open something for you?"

"Maybe a candy bar if there's one left," he said. "Something about riding makes a person hungry."

"Why did you decide to give up your motorcycle?" she said.

"I haven't ridden it since we bought the ranch. But more importantly, I thought about it all the way to Tulia. Granny told me once that if I was arguing with myself, then I should go somewhere quiet and take five minutes to imagine not doing whatever it was. And then spend another five minutes imagining doing it. Whichever vision delivered peace at the end was the way I should go."

"So you did that?" Nikki bit off half a miniature doughnut.

"I was going down this very stretch of highway. I didn't have a clock, so for twenty miles from this spot I tried to remember all the really good times I'd had on the bike. There was only one that I could really say was fun and not dangerous. That was last spring when Hud and I rode our cycles to Bowie. Then I thought about the fun times I'd had in my truck and on the ranch, especially Canyon Creek with the guys and with you. It wasn't a tough decision after that."

"You think if I think about not seeing my father and then seeing him, it will do the same for me?" she asked.

"I thought you were already resigned to going to see him on Wednesday evening," Tag answered.

"Give me ten minutes. Don't talk to me, but you can turn on the radio. Sometimes songs help me more than words," she said.

He found a country music station and set the volume low. He looked at the digital clock on the dashboard and got ready for ten minutes of nothing but soft music and no talking. Three songs later, Nikki turned to him and said, "I'm going to see him on Wednesday. The last card he sent was dated three months ago, so I hope he still lives there."

"Then I guess we've both made the right decision," Tag added. "Any of those songs help you?"

"Not a single one." She finished off the doughnuts and picked up her tea. "How much farther is it to Bowie?"

"If we only take thirty minutes to eat dinner, we'll be there by one," he answered.

"After that breakfast and our road food, we don't really need to stop, do we?"

"I'm game if you are," he answered.

"And now a classic from 1996," the DJ said. "Let's give it up for Deana Carter."

"1996," Nikki said. "I was just a little girl back then."

"Me too. Born in August 1990."

"July," she said.

"I always did like older women." He grinned.

*   *   *

Nikki stayed just long enough at the ranch to drop off Tag and retrieve her purse and phone. Of course, the phone's battery was dead, so she couldn't call Emily on the way to her apartment. It seemed like a year since she'd seen her friend, but she wanted to get home, collect her thoughts, and feed Goldie.

She parked in her usual spot and climbed the stairs. She was about to unlock the door when she heard the crunch of tires on gravel. She whipped around to see Emily getting out of her van. She unlocked the door and held it open while Emily took the steps two at a time and almost bowled Nikki over when she wrapped her up in a hug. Then she stepped back and eyed Nikki from her toes to the top of her head. "He didn't hurt you, did he?"

"No, just made a lot of threats," Nikki answered.

"I'll get out the ice cream and two spoons and then you're going to tell me every single detail." Emily headed straight to the freezer while Nikki fed Goldie a double amount of food.

Emily carried the container of ice cream and two spoons to the sofa, kicked off her shoes, and sat with her legs drawn up under her. Nikki took the spoon Emily handed her, sat down on the other end, and dipped deep, bringing up lots of chocolate bits.

"Talk," Emily said.

"How much do you already know? What did Tag tell you?" Nikki asked.

"I haven't seen Tag. Mama called and said that she'd talked to him, that y'all were home and he was going out to help the guys for the rest of the afternoon. I knew you would come straight home. This is your nest, like my apartment used to be mine. So start from the beginning and tell me the whole story. I hear you and my brother shared a hotel room. Did you?" She raised an eyebrow.

"We did *not*." Nikki put emphasis on the last word.

"I'm sure you know the basics. Kidnapped. Threatened. Rescued."

"Just start talking or I'm not sharing this ice cream," Emily said.

"It's my ice cream," Nikki reminded her.

"But I'm bigger than you are, so I can keep it away from you," Emily laughed. "I want to hear, so please start talking before my head explodes. I've been so worried. Here's your phone and your purse."

Nikki had told the story twice already—once to the sheriff and then to Tag—but there were certain details she'd left out. The sheriff didn't need to know how bad Billy Tom smelled or the way he made her skin crawl when he leered at her, and neither did Tag.

"Okay, it all actually started Monday night when I went to see Mama." Tears streamed down her face as she told Emily what her mother had said about never wanting her and wishing her father had taken her with him rather than leaving her behind.

"Oh. My. God!" Emily gasped. "I knew Wilma had mental issues but that's downright cruel."

Nikki pulled a tissue from a box on the end table and blew her nose. "Then I read everything in that box of letters and cards from my father." She pointed. "There's probably three or four thousand dollars in those cards. Every birthday, Valentine's Day, Christmas, graduation for the past fifteen years, he sent me a hundred-dollar bill. I'm going to see him on Wednesday, and Tag is going with me."

"Good." Emily took the ice cream back to the freezer and put on a pot of coffee. "Go on."

"I couldn't sleep, and I wouldn't call you because it was way late at night, so I went to the cabin and wound up sleeping on the sofa." Nikki went on with the story from there.

Little by little, word by word, from friend to friend, it all came out, and when she had finished the telling, Nikki felt something like closure. Not the kind that she needed where her dad was concerned, but hopefully that would come later.

"After all that, you've got to come home with me, or at least stay at the cabin with Tag," Emily said. "If I beg, will you let Tag sleep on the sofa here in your apartment for a while?"

"I'll be fine right here," Nikki insisted. "And no, you can't stay either. You belong in bed with your husband."

"Okay, okay!" Emily put up both hands. "You're mean and tough and you don't take no shit off nobody."

"Just like John Wayne," Nikki giggled.

"I should be getting home. Oh, I almost forgot," Emily said. "We're having brunch tomorrow morning at ten for you and the Fab Five. They've been every bit as worried as I have. And you'll have to tell the whole story one more time. Claire is going to close up shop for a couple hours so she can be there too, and Retta is coming."

"Want me to come early and help get things ready?" Nikki asked.

"That would be great." Emily gave her a kiss on the cheek and disappeared outside.

"It's just you and me now, Goldie. Did you miss me?" Nikki asked as she plugged her phone into the charger. "Of course you did. I'm the one with the fish food."

She sat down on the sofa and called her mother.

"Why are you calling me? This isn't Monday," Wilma said.

"Did you hear that I was kidnapped?" Nikki asked.

"They had a prayer circle at church. Guess God heard them because you're home, right?" Wilma asked.

"Yes, I am."

"Then we'll talk Monday like we always do." Wilma ended the call.

Nikki sighed and bit back tears, reminding herself that her mother was ill, and nothing Nikki did or said would change that.

Her phone rang, and thinking it might be her mother with an explanation for hanging up on her, she didn't even look at the caller ID.

"Nikki, we're calling it a day," Tag said. "We ran out of fence posts and the place we get them is closed until tomorrow. Are you sure I can't stay with you?"

"I'm fine. Really, I am. If I don't see you again, good luck on that bull tomorrow night," she said.

"Thanks, but you'll see me before that. Good night," Tag said.

"Night, Tag," she said.

She was truly now in her nest as Emily called it. Her phone was working. Her pistol was on the counter just in case. And she felt almost as safe as she did when she snuggled up to Tag in the bed at the hotel.

Chapter Twenty

The Fab Five—Otis, Larry, Sarah, Bess, and Patsy—came into Emily's new house that morning like a whirlwind.

"Are you okay? I don't mind spending the rest of my years in jail if you want me to kill that sumbitch." Otis was the first one to reach Nikki and hug her.

Otis and Larry had always reminded her of the two old cartoon characters Mutt and Jeff. Otis was short with a round face and a mischievous look in his eyes, and Larry was the opposite—tall and lanky.

"Me neither," Larry declared. "And I'm meaner'n Otis. I'll make him suffer." He bent to hug Nikki.

"Thank you, both, but he's locked up and far away." She peeked around Larry. "Where're the ladies?"

"Right here, darlin'." Sarah patted her gray hair as she entered the dining room. "Damn wind. I just got my hair done yesterday. I didn't know them two could move so fast. At home they can barely get up and down off the kitchen chairs." Like Larry, she was tall and thin and had to bend to give Nikki a hug.

"We had to hurry," Otis said. "Once y'all get in here, we wouldn't have a chance."

"Or to get a word in." Larry nodded.

"You've had your time. It's mine now." Patsy wiggled her round body between Sarah and Nikki. Not any taller than Nikki, she was the firecracker of the Five. Her short, kinky hair was dyed red, and trouble followed her around like a puppy.

Patsy and Bess were twins, but they were as different as night and day. Bess wore her gray hair in two long braids twisted around her head, but she and Patsy were built alike and had the same eyes. Attitude was what made them different.

A lot like Hud and Tag, Nikki thought as Bess finally got her turn to give her a hug. *Tag is the rebellious one like Patsy. Hud is the grounded one like Bess.*

"Honey, they're all a bunch of hot wind. You want something done, you leave it to me. I won't go to jail because I won't get caught," Bess told her.

"I appreciate y'all so much." If only her mother could be as supportive as these folks.

None of them have the mental issues your mother has. Was that her father's voice she was hearing? *It would have been better if you'd had a different childhood, but her example was a lesson in how to not live your life.*

She stood very still, but evidently that was all that her father had to say for now.

"Brunch is on the bar. It's buffet style," Emily said. "We have champagne and orange juice for mimosas, but no more than one for each of you."

"This is a celebration," Otis said. "Nikki lived through a life-threatening ordeal. We should get at least two."

"One." Emily held up a forefinger. "Besides, by the time we each have one, the champagne will be all gone."

"Then I'll take Bess's," Patsy said. "When I hear this story, I'm sure I'll need it."

"Over my dead body," Bess declared.

"Someone can have mine," Retta said as she and Claire arrived through the back door. "I'll be glad when this little girl gets here so I can have a beer again."

"It'll be a year past her birth before you can do that if you breastfeed," Sarah said. "I've been readin' up on birthin' and breastfeedin' and all that, just in case we have to help you. Never know when a tornado will come blastin' through the state, blow a tree down over the road to the hospital, and we'll need to deliver the baby."

"I did that once," Bess said. "Our neighbor's wife went into labor during a blizzard and they couldn't get to the doctor. Wound up at our place and I helped Mama deliver the baby. Patsy fainted."

"It wasn't because of that. The room was too hot, and I hadn't eaten supper. That's what made me get weak in the knees," Patsy protested as she loaded her plate and headed for the table. "We're not here to talk about the one weak moment in my life. We need to hear the whole story about what Nikki had to live through."

Nikki carried the chilled champagne and the carafe of orange juice to the table and filled the fluted glasses. "It was hair-raising at the time, but looking back, I think Billy Tom wanted me to believe he was a tornado, but the truth is that he's just a big bag of wind."

Patsy giggled and gave her another hug. "That's the spirit, darlin'."

They all took their places and she went on to tell the story for what seemed like the hundredth time. When she finished with the part about hitting him with a gallon jug of motor oil, Otis clapped his hands and said, "That's my girl. I wish it would've broken open and gotten all over him."

"Would've been poetic justice to have a slime ball like that all slick with oil," Larry agreed.

"I wish you'd have had on your cowboy boots. That would have put his balls all the way to his throat," Patsy said.

"Are you sure you're all right?" Claire asked. "I remember when Levi came through the cabin door and scared the bejesus out of me and my niece last winter. I can't imagine how I'd have reacted if he'd been like Billy Tom."

"You'd have shot him," Nikki said. "You had a gun trained right on his chest if I heard the story right. If I'd had my gun, Billy Tom would be dead instead of sobering up in a jail cell."

"Have you had any nightmares?" Retta asked as she poured herself a second glass of orange juice and passed it off to Nikki.

"First two nights I did." Nikki set the carafe on the table, and opted for a second cup of coffee. "But last night I was in my own nest, as Emily calls my apartment, and I slept fine."

"I bet your mama was worried out of her mind," Bess said.

"My mama"—Nikki took a deep breath—"has severe mental problems. She's OCD and she's a hypochondriac. Lately, she's even gotten paranoid and she's pretty negative. I never said anything about it before, because I don't want anyone to think I might be like that too."

"Wouldn't that make her even more worried?" Sarah asked.

Nikki's smile was forced. "Mama is too self-centered to worry about anyone other than herself and her schedule."

"Well, honey, you got three mamas right here," Patsy said. "And we were all worried plumb crazy."

"And us two old grandpas here, we wanted to load our shotguns and come after you, but Emily wouldn't let us. She said Tag and her cop brother would take care of it, and she was right," Otis said. "And you old hens need to look at the clock. If you're going to get to the beauty shop on time, we should be going."

Patsy poked Otis on the arm. "Don't you call me an old hen."

"That's better than callin' you a sow or a heifer, ain't it," Larry chuckled.

"You try that and I'll poison you," Bess told him. "But Otis is right. We need to get going. I feel bad that we don't have time to help with cleanup."

Retta patted her on the shoulder. "Honey, we'll have this put to order in no time with four of us working at it. Y'all go get beautified. You might be called upon if a tornado knocks down a tree, and I need some help delivering this baby."

"You just call and we'll be here if we have to ride the tornado's tail wind to get here," Sarah said. "Y'all are the kids we never got to have, and we love you all."

Nikki passed Retta a napkin when she got all misty eyed. She dabbed at her eyes and said, "I appreciate that so much. My baby girl is going to have lots of sweet grandparents."

Emily followed the Five out to the porch. When she returned, the other three women had the table cleared and were busy loading the dishwasher. "We've got to put them on the list to call as soon as you go into labor, Retta. They want to be there when the baby is born."

"Good Lord!" Retta gasped. "The waiting room will be overflowing."

"What waiting room?" Tag poked his head in the door

and then led the other three guys into the house. "I'm not planning on getting hurt tonight, so y'all don't have to reserve a waiting room."

"I hate to burst your bubble, Taggart Baker, but the world does not revolve around you," Emily said.

"Ouch! That had to sting." Maverick grinned.

"Don't tell him there's no Santa Claus too," Hud teased. "He couldn't take that much heavy news all in one day."

"And be very, very quiet about the Easter Bunny," Paxton whispered.

Tag removed his hat and held it over his chest. "Y'all are breakin' my poor little heart, talkin' like that. But if you'll feed us the leftovers from your party this mornin', I'll forgive you, sis."

Emily pointed to the bar. "You're welcome to what's left. The mimosas are all gone, but there's a gallon of sweet tea in the fridge. Help yourselves."

"Okay if we wash up here in the kitchen?" Maverick asked.

"Sure." Emily nodded.

Hud rolled up his sleeves. "I'll go first."

"I'm not above stealing food off your plate if you don't leave anything for us," Maverick said, getting in line behind Hud. "I haven't had a good quiche since we left the panhandle."

Paxton elbowed his brother in the ribs. "Real men don't eat quiche."

"That's an old wives' tale," Maverick told him. "Real men eat whatever they want, and if anyone says anything about it, they beat the shhh...crap out of them."

Tag got in line at the very end, which put him right next to where Nikki was standing. "Did you sleep all right last night?"

"Yes, I did," she said. "You?"

"Not worth a damn. Kept waking up and worrying about you. You could let me stay at your place or you could stay in the cabin, just to help me out," he said.

"We heard there was a party here." Justin came through the door and joined the crowd.

"So did we," Levi said right behind him.

Cade brought up the rear. "And we thought we'd help get rid of leftovers."

Nikki looked at what food was left: part of a pan of quiche, half a pan of cinnamon rolls, and very little fruit in a bowl. The bacon platter was empty and the biscuits were all gone. There wasn't nearly enough to feed that many hungry cowboys.

"Good thing I'm prepared for emergencies," Emily said. "Justin, be a darlin', and help me bring out the second round for these late comers."

"Yes, ma'am." He stopped to give her a kiss on the forehead. "And since we crashed the party, we'll do cleanup afterwards."

"What can I do to help?" Hud asked.

"Follow me," Justin said.

"Please let me stay with you, for my own peace of mind," Tag whispered in Nikki's ear.

"I go to work at midnight tonight and don't get off until my last shift ends at midnight on Sunday. I'll be fine," Nikki said. "But you are still plannin' to go with me on Wednesday, right?"

"Yes, ma'am, and is it all right if I come over at eight on Monday? That's after you talk to your mama, right?"

"Of course. I'll make supper for us," she said.

"I'll be there on the dot." He grinned. "Looks like it's my turn to wash up. I wanted to hug you or kiss you or both when I came into the kitchen, but I've been working outside all morning, and I'm not fit."

Nikki started to hug him, but he turned away too quickly and headed for the sink. Emily and Justin brought out four more quiches from the pantry, and Hud carried in a large pan of biscuits.

"How'd you keep that warm?" Nikki asked.

"There's a warming oven in there. I had all this finished and warming when you got here this morning. I knew the guys were all coming around to eat," Emily answered. "Justin, honey, if you'll bring out the crockpot of sausage gravy, I'll get the platter of bacon, and we'll see just how hungry seven old cowboys really are."

"You are amazing," Nikki said.

"She grew up on a ranch," Hud said.

"But I'm still amazing," Emily teased.

"Yes, you are." Tag slung an arm around her shoulders. "And we love you best when you make us food."

Nikki slipped back into the corner so she could enjoy the huge family and all the banter between them. This was exactly what she'd want if she could be absolutely certain that once she had children, she wouldn't feel about them what her mother felt about her.

*   *   *

Tag came in fourth place with the bronc riding that evening. That didn't get him a prize, but it wasn't too shabby. When he finished his ride, he spent the better part of the rest of the evening sitting on a sawhorse right outside Fumanchu's pen, trying to getting to know the big bull. The beast glared at Tag as if he were trying to get a feel for his next challenge, but Tag stared right back at him without blinking.

"I don't care if you throw me halfway to the stars and I land on my head coming back down," Tag told him. "I don't even care if I can't hang on for eight seconds. If I can make it for two point seven seconds like the song says, I'll have accomplished something."

The bull pawed the ground and snorted, and they continued to stare at each other for the next hour.

It was near eleven o'clock when the announcer finally said, "And the last event of the evening is coming up. Y'all remember this?" He played "Live Like You Were Dying," and the crowd went wild, stomping and singing along, screaming even louder when Fumanchu was mentioned in the song.

"I'm sure that's where this bull got his name, but few cowboys have had the nerve to crawl on his back, and he's never been ridden for the full eight seconds," the guy said. "So let's give it up for Taggart Baker, who's agreed to give it a shot."

"You don't have to do this." Hud stepped onto the first board of the corral. "That's one mean sumbitch."

"I can't let the crowd down." Tag shoved his hands down into his gloves, settled his hat on his head, and eased down from the top board onto the bull's back. Fumanchu snorted and pawed at the ground, but his big body practically filled the chute, and there was nowhere for him to wiggle and very little room for Tag's legs.

"It's gonna hurt." Hud tried to dissuade him.

"Well, yeah, but it's Fumanchu," Tag said. "This ain't a kitty cat, brother. He weighs more'n a ton."

"And he ain't that buckin' barrel Daddy built us when we were kids, or like any other bull you've ever ridden," Hud said.

"Don't expect him to be." Tag tucked his hand under the

rope around the bull's massive body, raised the other one, and nodded toward the guys to open the gate. "Be nice to me, boy. Give the folks a little something to brag about."

The gate opened and Fumanchu came out with his head practically on the ground and his hind feet doing their damnedest to reach the stars. Tag moved with the bull, keeping his balance and waving his fist in the air. His butt hurt like hell when the bull came down with a thud and then twisted his hindquarters to one side as they shot for the moon again.

"Three seconds," the guy in the press box yelled.

Tag had made it past his goal, but now he wanted more. He concentrated on the ride and managed to stay on through the bull's next twist. The crowd was on their feet chanting his name.

"Five seconds!"

He thought he'd figured out the old boy's next move, but he had misjudged it, and suddenly he was flying through the air. The breath was knocked out of him when he landed square on his back. Fumanchu must not have appreciated someone sticking to him that long because he decided to do a victory kick. Hind legs up, front legs firmly on the ground, and then one of the animal's hooves came down—right on the end of Tag's cowboy boots. The clowns rushed out to draw the bull away, and Tag managed to stand up and wave at the crowd.

"Six point seven seconds!" the announcer yelled into the microphone. "It's the longest anyone has ever stayed on this bull. Congratulations to Taggart Baker."

Tag took a bow and threw his hat into the noisy crowd, and then did his best not to limp on his way back to the chute where Hud, Maverick, and Paxton waited.

"How bad is it?" Hud asked.

Maverick patted a wooden box. "Hand or foot?"

Tag sat down and held up a foot. "Hand will be bruised and sore, but a ton of bull on toes doesn't work."

Paxton pulled off his boot and jerked off his sock. "Big one looks good, but we'd better take you to the hospital and get the others X-rayed."

"Hell of a thing to go through to see your woman," Maverick said.

"But I stayed on more'n two point seven seconds." Tag tried to smile but it came out a grimace.

"You're not going to lay up on the sofa because of this," Hud told him. "You already took three days off to go rescue your woman, so you can work with a busted foot."

"Just get me to the hospital," Tag said.

Maverick pulled on his arm. "Stand up. Me and Paxton will be your crutches. Don't put any weight on it until we see what's goin' on. Looks like we might get there at the same time as Nikki checks in for her shift. Don't she go on at midnight?"

"Yep." Hud threw his brother's saddle up onto his shoulder. "The things my brother does for a date."

"Rejection is tough." Paxton grinned.

"He's proven her right, hasn't he?" Maverick said. "She told him she'd be waiting for him in the ER."

"Didn't want to disappoint her. I'm sure she had her heart set on seeing me tonight." Tag's toes throbbed with every beat of his heart. Who'd have thought that toes could hurt even worse than his jaw did when it was laid open with a broken beer bottle? And as much as he wanted to see Nikki, he wished he could stroll into the hospital with the news that he'd stayed on the bull's back for the full eight seconds, then pick her up and twirl her around like he had in Tulia.

It was only ten minutes to the hospital, but it seemed to

Tag like it took an hour. Maverick and Paxton helped him inside while Hud parked the truck, and the first face he saw was Nikki's. She looked so damn cute in her scrubs and her dark hair pulled up in a ponytail that he almost forgot the pain in his foot.

"Where's the blood?" She grabbed the nearest wheelchair and rolled it toward the three guys.

"Bull trampled his foot," Paxton said.

"But I stayed on for more'n six seconds," Tag told her. "Almost went to the full eight."

"Almost only counts in hand grenades and horseshoes," she said as she pushed him toward the doors. "Y'all can come on back if you want. It's startin' off to be a slow night, so there's no one else here."

*　　*　　*

"Nikki, I'm dyin'." Sue Ann's voice cut through the air.

"I'll get the pretty cowboy." Rosemary took the wheelchair from her. "Don't worry. I'll be gentle with him. You're the only one who can talk Sue Ann down. Thank God you're here."

Nikki turned around and barely caught Sue Ann as she ran past the check-in desk and fell into her arms. The woman reeked of booze, and her eyes were completely glazed over.

"I tried to be good for Mama, but I got bored," she whined.

"Okay, let's get you back to a bed and talk about this." Nikki kept one arm around her so she wouldn't collapse and took her to the second cubicle, right next to where Rosemary was examining Tag's foot.

Sue Ann stretched out on the bed and crossed her arms

over her chest. "Tell them to bury me in a dress and granny panties. Mama will be really mad if she sees these." She pulled down the waist of the fake black leather leggings to show a bright red lace thong. "But if they can, they could put a pint of tequila in the edge of the coffin just in case Mama don't let me into heaven. I might as well have a drink or two if I got to go to the other place."

"I thought you were in rehab getting some help," Nikki said.

"I was, darlin'." Sue Ann pushed her hair back out of her eyes. "But that place wasn't no fun. So me and Gilbert, we escaped."

"Who's Gilbert?" Nikki asked. "And can you tell me what you've drank tonight and did you take pills with it?"

"Gilbert is my buddy. He's been my friend since I was a little girl. Mama says he's not real, but he is. And I had a lot to drink, but I didn't take any pills. No, ma'am, I did not." She giggled. "But me and Gilbert smoked some stuff. He wouldn't eat the worm but I did. You got to get it out of me."

"We can fix you right up." Nikki patted her bony arm. If she had to compare Wilma to someone, it should be Sue Ann, not the Fab Five, she thought. Then her mother didn't look bad at all. "I'll get in touch with the on-call doctor, and we'll get you a bed."

"I knew you'd know what to do. When I die, promise you'll tell them about the panties?" Sue Ann whispered. "And don't call Darla June. Mama said she's dead."

"You got my word," Nikki said as she picked up her tablet and stepped out into the hall. When she found Dr. Richards, he told her to do exactly what she thought he would. Send Sue Ann back to the psych ward and tell them to watch her closer this time.

She poked her head back into the room to find Sue Ann

curled up in the fetal position and snoring like a hibernating bear. She made the phone call to the right people and sat
with Sue Ann until two orderlies arrived. They released the
brakes on the bed, and she awoke with a start.

"Nikki, where are they taking me? Am I dead like Darla
June?" Sue Ann asked.

Nikki held up a hand for the orderlies to stop. "No,
you're not dead, and who is Darla June?"

"Shhh…" Sue Ann put a finger over her mouth. "Don't
tell Mama I said her name. Darla June is dead to us. Mama
said so when she got pregnant and she wasn't married. We
can't say her name."

"Do you have a sister, Sue Ann?" Nikki asked.

"I did have, but Mama says she's dead now." Sue Ann
pulled the sheet up over her and closed her eyes. She was
snoring before they were out of the exam room.

Nikki stepped out of the cubicle to find Dr. Richards
coming straight at her. "Guess our cowboy has had a run-
in with a bull this time rather than a beer bottle. I heard he
rescued you from a kidnapper this past week. Reckon you
might talk some sense into him."

"Don't think I'm that much of an influence on him,"
Nikki answered.

"Honey, if he rode a motorcycle all the way to the panhandle in this unbearable heat to get you, surely you have
some kind of influence on him. Let's go see what he's done
now."

"Rosemary is taking care of him this time," she said.

"She was. You are now. She can have the next one," Dr.
Richards said.

"Why?"

"Because I said so." Dr. Richards pulled back the curtain.
"Rosemary, there's a little guy coming in with a bean up his

nose. You take that one since it's your son. The rest of you cowboys can go to the waiting room."

"Good God." Rosemary rushed out with Maverick, Paxton, and Hud behind her.

"I always thought God was pretty good myself." Dr. Richards examined Tag's foot. "The two smallest toes are broken. We'll get an X-ray to see how badly and to prove I'm right. Also to be sure none of the other small bones in your foot are fractured."

"What happens then?" Tag asked. "A cast?"

"I'll tape them to the toe next to them, and you'll have to wear something other than boots for about a month until they heal. Takes four to six weeks. Ice packs help and elevation does wonders," Dr. Richards said. "What's it going to take for you to stop punishing your body like this?"

Tag shot a look toward Nikki.

"Maybe he will stop once he's gone skydiving." Nikki frowned.

Chapter Twenty-One

W hat's the verdict?" Hud asked when Nikki pushed Tag out in a wheelchair.

"Ice, elevate, and stay off it as much as possible for four weeks," she answered. "He's got a follow-up appointment with the doctor in a month, and he can't wear a cowboy boot on that foot until it's healed."

"Well, that'll keep your ornery ass in the house." Hud grinned. "You can use the time to get acquainted with the bookkeeping program Matthew set up for us. This settles the argument about who's going to do the paperwork for the ranch."

"It's my left foot, so I can still drive," Tag protested.

"Good." Maverick nodded. "When we need posts or wire or stuff to work with, you can go get it, and we'll keep working."

"I'll bring that shoebox full of receipts and the laptop over to your cabin in the morning," Hud told him.

Tag groaned. "I hate computers. You know anything about them, Nikki?"

"Not me." She shook her head. "I'm lucky just to run the little patient tablet that I use."

The doors swung open, and a nurse pushed a wheelchair with Retta in it down the hall. Nikki stopped in her tracks and asked, "Is it time?"

Retta grimaced and laid a hand on her bulging stomach. "I thought it was false labor all day, but I was wrong."

"Has everyone been called? Does Emily know? Have you talked to the doctor?" Nikki was so excited that she forgot all about Tag for a minute.

"No one has been called yet. Would you please…" Retta moaned. "The pains are less than a minute apart now."

"I'll get a hold of Emily and the rest of the family," Nikki said.

"Might as well turn around and take me back to the baby waiting room," Tag said. "Where's Cade?"

"Parking the truck. He'll be here real soon," Retta panted.

The hall was wide enough that Nikki and a nurse's aide pushed the wheelchairs side by side toward the maternity area.

"You ready to have this baby?" Hud asked. "I bet Cade is a nervous wreck."

"I'm so ready," Retta said. "And you're right about Cade. Knowing y'all are here for him means the world to me."

"I can't believe that we're going to have a new baby in the family. This is beyond exciting, Retta. She's going to be here before long," Nikki said.

Retta brushed away a tear. "But she's a little early."

"Not enough to hurt her," Nikki assured her. "She'll be fine."

"This is where we part company." The nurse pushed the button to open the doors into the maternity part of the hospital. "Nikki will show the rest of you to the waiting room."

Nikki rolled Tag into a large room with sofas and chairs grouped into several seating areas. "I have to get back to the emergency room, but I'll run by and check on things every chance I get." She pulled a chair over and propped his leg on it. "I'll send an ice pack up with Cade."

"Thanks for everything," Tag said.

"Hey, I'm not anywhere near even with you for rescuing me," she told him.

"Then you'll come over through the week and do all that book work for me?" He looked up at her with those mesmerizing blue eyes.

"I don't owe you that much." She blew a kiss as she left the room.

On her way back to the ER, she met Claire and Emily almost jogging down the hall. "Are we too late?" Emily asked.

"I was just fixin' to call you," Nikki said. "How did—"

"Cade called Justin about a minute ago. We were all on our way home after the ranch rodeo, so we just whupped a U-turn in the middle of the road and came right back. Can you believe it? We're getting the first Maguire grandbaby tonight," Emily said.

"It could be tomorrow if she decides to make an entrance and hold out until after midnight," Nikki told them, and then gave them directions to the waiting room. They rushed off in that direction, and Nikki turned to find Cade, Justin, and Levi coming around the corner.

"How is she?" Cade looked like he might faint any minute.

Nikki laid a hand on his arm. "She's fine, but I bet she'll be glad to have you in the room to hold her hand." She pointed to the signs on the wall leading to the maternity section and returned to her post in the ER.

Rosemary jerked the curtains back on a cubicle and startled Nikki so badly that she jumped. "Didn't mean to scare you. We just now got that bean out of my kid's nose. Damned thing had swollen up and filled his whole nostril. It's a wonder he didn't have to have surgery. How's your cowboy?"

"He's got two broken toes that's going to keep him off bulls and out of boots for a month or more. Retta Maguire just checked in to have her baby, so the maternity waiting room is going to be full all night." Nikki helped Rosemary straighten up the room.

Through the week, nurses' aides did that kind of work, but weekends were a whole different matter. Not that Nikki minded. She liked staying busy.

"And Sue Ann?"

"Was high and drunk, and Doc sent her right back to the psych ward. Trouble is that she signs herself in, so she has the authority to sign herself out. She said that she had a sister. I wonder where she is. I feel so sorry for her, but I realized something tonight. Mama has plenty of problems, but at least she's not as bad as Sue Ann," Nikki said.

"I've known Wilma my whole life, and you're right. But, honey, that don't make it any easier on you to deal with, just easier to accept. You know it seems like I remember Sue Ann's older sister. She was maybe sixteen when Sue Ann was born, so she was quite a bit older than me. I wonder if she's on any of the social media sites." Rosemary piled the dirty linens into a bin and pushed it out into the hallway. "Now tell me more about this cowboy and the kidnapping.

We haven't had a free minute since we got here. Let's get a cup of coffee and wait until the next round hits. Bars close at two, so you know we'll have some business then."

"It'll be a miracle if we don't." Nikki followed Rosemary to the break room. They'd each poured a cup of coffee when Rosemary's phone rang.

"I told Steven to call me when they got home. Be right back." She stepped out into the hallway to take the call from her husband.

Nikki's thoughts went to the real miracle that was going on in the maternity section of the hospital that night, not in the ER. A baby was coming into the world. One who would be so loved that the waiting room was packed with people who could hardly wait to see her for the first time. Nikki wondered if there'd be that many people supporting her if and when she had a child.

"Hey, that lady out there said I'd find you here." Tag rolled his wheelchair through the door. "Cade just came to tell us that Retta is ready to push. I don't know how he's keeping his cool. If my wife was having a baby, I'd be spinnin' around on my head."

"Holy smoke! She must've been in labor all afternoon and didn't tell anyone until the last minute." Nikki set her cup down. "I figured y'all would be here until morning."

"Emily swears that Retta knew exactly what she was doin'. If they'd called her mother-in-law this afternoon, she'd be here already and she would be tryin' to take over the whole show. I saw how bossy that woman can be when we were moving Emily into her new house, so I don't blame her a bit." Tag maneuvered the chair around and started back out the door. "I'll come back and let you know when the baby arrives."

"I'm not busy right now. I'll push you." Nikki grabbed

the wheelchair handles. "So you'd be spinnin' on your head, huh? That brings up a pretty funny picture in my mind."

"How about you? What if you were the one in Retta's shoes?"

She slowly shook her head. "I don't let myself go there."

"You ever go down to the nursery and look at the newborns?" Tag asked.

"Yep. Especially if it's been a hectic night and I can't settle the adrenaline rush of running from one patient to another. Sometimes I even volunteer to rock a baby if there's more of them than the pediatric nurse can take care of," she said.

"How does that make you feel?" he asked.

"All warm and cuddly," she answered.

He reached over his shoulder and covered her hand with his. "You've got so much kindness in your heart, Nikki, that you'll make a great mother."

"How can you know that—not just say it, but know it?"

He removed his hand and tapped his chest. "This right here tells me so."

Could he possibly be right? She thought again about the way she felt with a baby in her arms. She often sang a simple lullaby that her father had sung to her when she was a little girl and couldn't sleep. For her thirteenth birthday he'd given her a music box that played the song. It sat on her dresser and had become part of her birthday ritual. She was about to turn the wheelchair into the room when she caught sight of Cade coming down the hall.

"She's here and she's perfect, and I'm a father," he said loudly.

Nikki pushed Tag's chair, and they followed Cade to the waiting room.

"And we're the first to know," Tag said. "Is that the same as catchin' the bouquet at a wedding? Are we next?"

"Not unless we have another case of immaculate conception," Nikki said.

Tag chuckled. "I reckon we could have a normal wild child."

"Tag Baker, are you askin' me to be your baby mama?" she teased.

"No, ma'am, I want more than a baby mama when I have children," he answered.

"Our baby girl is here," Cade announced to everyone in the waiting room.

"What's her name?" Emily asked.

"How much does she weigh?" Otis wanted to know.

"Is Retta okay?" Justin asked.

"When can we see her?" Patsy clapped her hands.

Poor old Cade had trouble answering them.

"Right now I'd give up all my rebel ways to be in his shoes," Tag whispered.

"Now that's a line you should put in your little black book," Nikki, leaning down, whispered in his ear.

"Didn't think I'd ever say that or feel this way," Tag said.

Nikki's phone pinged. She pulled it out of her pocket to find a text from Rosemary. Two ambulances had been dispatched to a wreck north of town. They'd be bringing in six injured patients in a few minutes.

"Got to go," Nikki said. "Keep that foot up and don't be too macho to take the pain pills Dr. Richards prescribed."

Tag stood up, balanced on one foot, and pulled her close to his chest. "It's going to be a long weekend, but the light at the end of the tunnel is that I'll get to see you Monday evening." Then he tipped up her chin and kissed her, right there in front of everyone.

Chapter Twenty-Two

Any other morning, Tag would have simply crawled through the barbed-wire fence or hopped over it and walked from the cabin to the ranch house, but on Saturday he drove. He hopped on one foot from the truck to the porch and used the railing to help him maneuver the steps. Hud threw open the door and handed him a set of crutches before he reached the top step.

"Guess Granny was right to insist that we bring these with us," he said.

"I never knew how much two toes could hurt," Tag admitted. "When I busted my arm in two places, it didn't hurt like this."

"That's because you were young. Kids heal faster than adults. It was Maverick's turn to make breakfast. He's still flippin' pancakes if you're interested." Hud led the way to the kitchen.

"I thought maybe I could at least string barbed wire on

one foot." Tag sat down at the table and propped his foot on an empty chair. Maverick stacked four huge pancakes onto a plate and set them in front of him.

"You'd do it in a wheelchair to get out of all the paperwork, wouldn't you?"

"Thank you. And you're right. I hate to paint, too, but I'd do the whole barn to get out of what y'all are making me take on." Tag slipped pats of butter between the layers and then covered the top with warm maple syrup.

"Too bad." Paxton set a cup of coffee by Tag's place.

"Thanks for waiting on me," Tag said.

"We'll drop in when we break for noon each day, and maybe if you go to church tomorrow, we'll let you take time off if you talk Emily into inviting all of us to Sunday dinner," Hud said. "Other than that, you're going to spend an eight-hour day in front of the computer learning what Matthew does. Everything has to be input from cows to bulls to fence posts, and how much winter wheat seed we bought. After the initial input, the job shouldn't take but a day a week, according to what Matthew told me this morning."

"And I'll be the only one, other than Matthew, who knows how to do it, right?" Tag groaned.

"You can always take care of that part of the business on Saturday when Nikki's at work." Hud refilled his coffee cup and sat down at the table.

"What's she got to do with this?" Tag asked between bites.

"You're in love with her. You might not know it yet, but you are, and in another year, two at the most, you'll be the one coming to tell us about your new baby." Maverick set a plate full of pancakes in the middle of the table. "You can fight it, but when a good woman grabs you by the heart, you're a goner."

"I'm not in love," Tag protested. "I like Nikki a lot, and for the first time in my life, I'm calling someone my girl-friend, but we've only made out a few times, and gone out together twice. How does that mean the L-word, much less talk about babies?"

"It was obvious to some of us at Emily's wedding. You looked across the room at her in that pretty blue dress and it was all over," Paxton told him. "Just mark our words. And that idea of doing all the drudge work when she's at the hospital is a good thing. Besides, it'll keep you out of the bars, off bulls, and hopefully away from the hospital."

Tag shot a dirty look his way but had to acknowledge, albeit silently, that Paxton was right. And it would give him something to do over the weekends when he couldn't see Nikki. But that stuff about being in love—that might happen on down the road, like in a couple of years—but not now.

*   *   *

When things slowed down in the ER that morning, Nikki slipped into Retta's room to find her sleeping. Annie was in a little portable crib beside her. Her eyes were wide open, but she wasn't fussing. Nikki gently picked her up and held her close to her chest as she sat down in a rocking chair and began to sing to her.

They'd named her Annabelle and planned to call her Annie. Nice and simple. Nikki loved it and thought the name fit the little angel who had a full head of dark hair. She breathed in the clean baby-fresh scent and wished that she was holding her own child.

Cade slipped into the room and smiled down at Retta with so much love in his face that Nikki felt guilty for even sharing space in such an intimate moment. "Want to hold Annie?"

He sat down on a sofa and held out his arms. "I'm a little afraid of her, Nikki. She's so little, and I'm such a big man. I'm terrified that I'll hurt her. I've never been around a baby this small."

Nikki settled Annie into the crook of his arm. "Just support her head and hold her close. She's listened to her mama's heartbeat the whole time, and hearing yours will bring her comfort. The fear is natural. All new daddies feel that way with their first child."

"So you've been around lots of babies?" he asked as he gently touched Annie's tiny hand with a forefinger. "She's so beautiful that it almost makes this rough old cowboy cry."

"I was never around babies until I had pediatric clinical training for my nursing degree. Sometimes I go down to the nursery here and help out. It calms me," she admitted.

Annie wrapped her hand around his finger.

"Look!" Cade whispered. "How can someone so small make me feel like a king?"

"It's called the miracle of life," Nikki whispered.

"You are going to be a great mother," Cade said, but he didn't take his eyes off his little girl.

She was thinking about what Cade said as she climbed the stairs to her apartment that night. She didn't notice the black Lincoln parked across the street until she heard a noise and turned to see it pulling away from the curb. If that was her father, she sure wished he'd just get out and talk to her. But then why would he if he thought that she'd ignored him all these years? And if it wasn't her father? A shiver went up her spine at the thought.

She stopped long enough to feed Goldie and then stripped out of her scrubs, put them into the washer with other laundry, and started the cycle. The load would wash while she slept most of the day. She took a shower and slid beneath the sheets. Her eyes were closed when her head hit the pillow. The last thing she remembered thinking was that she should have set the alarm.

When she awoke and glanced at the clock, it said three thirty-five. She'd been asleep more than twelve hours, but that wasn't unusual for Monday. She threw back the covers, slipped on a robe, and was on the way to the kitchen when her phone pinged.

She dug through her purse and found three messages from Emily and one from Tag. The ones from Emily included pictures of Annie and Retta from Sunday morning when they had brought the baby home. Looking at them set Nikki's biological clock to ticking loudly. Tag sent a selfie of him holding a whole sheaf of papers and a message that said: Save me!

She sent one back that said: Hang on until 8. I'll bring supper.

He sent back an emoji blowing kisses to her.

She sang as she cleaned Goldie's bowl and then fed her, hummed as she stripped the bed, tossed her scrubs into the dryer, and threw the sheets into the washer. Then she cleaned her little place. Never would she let herself get into a habit of doing anything by the clock or the day of the week like her mother did.

She was starving by the time she finished her chores, so she made herself a peanut butter and jelly sandwich. That would have to do until she picked up some tacos to take out to the cabin for supper. She watched a rerun of *Law & Order* while she waited on her mother's call. The show ended and she did a countdown from ten. When she got to number one, the phone rang.

"Hello, Mother," she said.

"Why are you callin' me that? You've always called me Mama before. You wanted me to be honest with you and I was, so why are you acting like this? You know it raises my blood pressure when you are ugly," Wilma said.

"Let's start all over," Nikki said. "Hello, Mama. How's your week been?"

"Well, for starters, Mrs. Thomas got a cat and it's been walkin' on my porch and leaving footprints. I have to go out there every day and shoo it away, and then take a dust mop to the porch. If she has to have a pet, she should keep it in her own house," Wilma said. "And I'm down to seventeen nerve pills, so you need to call the pharmacy because they said they can't refill it until they're all gone. What if I'm short one on a day when things are going bad for me like that rotten cat traipsing across my porch?"

"How many do you take each day?" Nikki rolled her eyes and thought about the difference in cat prints and getting kidnapped.

"I take three a day. I can't be without them. You should call the pharmacy tomorrow and demand that they bring me a new bottle."

"I'm sure they'll bring your medicine as soon as they can," she said. "What else has been going on?"

"That man you hired to mow my yard left a whole lot of grass on the sidewalk again. You just can't get good help anymore," Wilma said.

"Were you worried when I was kidnapped?" Nikki asked.

"Did you flirt with that man? Is that why he stole your car and made you drive him way out there to West Texas? You must've done something to encourage him," Wilma said. "You're like your daddy that way. He flirted with every woman he saw."

"Oh, yeah? What did he do that made you think that?"

"He used to smile at every single woman who checked us out in the stores and chat with them. And he always smiled at all the women in church like he wanted to get to know them better. He said he was just being cordial. I told him I hated it when he did that, but did he listen to me? Oh, no! Not your daddy! I bet you smiled at that man, didn't you?" Ice dripped from Wilma's words.

Nikki closed her eyes tightly and reminded herself: *Think about Sue Ann. Don't let her negativity get to you.*

"Are you still there?" Wilma yelled.

"I'm here, Mama. Did you go out today? It's been up in the nineties." Nikki changed the subject. Surely the weather wouldn't be something that would get her in trouble.

"Lord, no! I don't go out on Monday." Wilma went into her normal tirade about everything, and all Nikki had to do was murmur now and then.

Her mother finally brought their conversation to an abrupt end. "It's eight o'clock and I have things to do. Good night, Nikki. We'll talk again next week."

"Love you, Mama," Nikki said.

"Okay, goodbye." Her phone screen went dark.

You tried, her brother Quint's voice whispered in her head. *That's all anyone can do.* He'd told her the same thing so many times when they were kids that his words were burned into her brain.

Tears welled up in her eyes. She tossed the phone into her purse and headed for the door. "Hold the fort down, Goldie. Don't wait up for me. I might be late." She swiped at her tears with the heel of her hand. A swing by the drive-through netted a bag full of tacos and burritos. She made another stop at a convenience store for a six-pack of beer and one of root beer. Then she drove out of town straight for the cabin.

When she arrived, she carried the bag and beer up to the door and started to knock with the edge of the six-pack. Tag startled her when he swung the door open before her knuckles even hit it.

"I heard you drive up. That stuff smells wonderful." He stood back and let her enter the cabin; then using one crutch, he followed her to the table. "But seeing you beats all the food in the world. You are gorgeous."

She turned around to find that he'd laid the crutch down and opened his arms.

"I missed you," he said.

She took two steps and his arms wrapped around her. Rolling up on her toes, she cupped his face in her hands and brought his lips to hers. One kiss and it didn't matter what Wilma had said or what she was afflicted with. Nikki was at peace for the first time in her life right there in Tag's arms.

He hopped over to the sofa and pulled her down onto his lap. One kiss led to another, going from a sweet brush of the lips to something deeper and deeper, until they were both panting. His hand slipped under her shirt up to her bra, and in one swift motion, it was undone, and he began to massage her back. She unbuttoned his shirt and slid it from his shoulders.

"Honey," he nibbled on her ear, "we either need to stop this or take it to the bed."

"Bed." In one swift motion, she pulled her shirt and bra off and tossed them toward the end of the sofa. His soft hair against her breasts felt just like she thought it would, and the touch of it sent tingles from her scalp to her toes.

"I'd carry you, but I'm afraid I can't hop that far," he said.

Nikki pulled him up and draped his arm around her shoulders. "I'll be your crutch. You sure you…"

Together they made it to the bed, where he pulled her down and the make-out session started all over again. "I don't need my toes to make love to you."

She wasn't sure when her jeans and underpants came off or even her shoes. But they were both naked and his blue eyes were staring into hers as he stretched out on top of her. Wrapping her legs around his waist, she reached between them and gasped when she realized how ready he was. She drew him into her and began to rock with him. On that miraculous night, he brought her to heights she'd never known, taking her right to the edge of a climax and then backing off until finally he said her name in a growl and together they reached the mind-blowing end.

"There are no words," he panted as he collapsed on top of her.

"Yeah, right. As many notches as you've got on your bedpost, you can't say…" Her breath came out in short bursts.

"Honey, what we just had deletes all those notches."

"Are you serious?" she asked.

"More than I've ever been in my whole life," he said.

"Ready for round two." She rolled over on top of him.

"Kiss me, darlin'. One kiss and I will be," he said.

The next morning, Nikki awoke to the smell of coffee and bacon. Sun rays flowed through the window and onto the quilt that covered her. That meant it had to be at least seven o'clock. "Good mornin'," she said.

"Awww, I meant to wake you with a kiss and breakfast in bed. I was trying to figure out how to hop over there with a tray." He smiled.

She sat up, wrapped the quilt around her body, and eased her feet to the floor. "If you'll share it with me, I'll do the carrying."

"And then we might see if morning sex is as good as it was at midnight, right?" he asked.

"I've got a feeling that whenever we have it, it'll be fabulous." She tiptoed for a kiss.

"Me too, darlin', me too," he said.

Chapter Twenty-Three

I spent the last two nights with Tag." Nikki held Annie close to her chest and rocked the baby in an antique chair.

"You've done that before," Retta said as she sipped from a cup of hot chocolate. "The way you are with babies, you should have a dozen."

"I would love that." Nikki's thoughts went back to the short conversation that she and Cade had in the hospital. She'd been on her own for so long that somehow she'd thought she'd have to raise a child without help if she ever had one. But seeing Cade and Retta together, both so eager to help with little Annie, had changed her mind. Even with her tough schedule, with help, she could have a career and a family both—just like her friend Rosemary.

"Time isn't our friend to have that many." Emily brought a plate of cookies to the living room and set them on the table. "And you've got to have sex to have a baby—at least in the normal way."

"Tag and I had sex the past two nights. I think it was a little better than plain old normal." Nikki bent to kiss Annie on the top of her head.

Retta spewed hot chocolate on her shirt. "You mean you didn't before?"

"Holy smoke!" Emily gasped. "Tag's reputation is ruined for sure. He spent at least three nights with you and didn't sweet-talk you into bed?"

"Didn't even try." Nikki's frown told them she was being honest.

Retta wiped the brown spots from her paisley shirt. "Get out the brides' magazines, Emily. We've got a friend on the way to the altar."

"Not just yet. Annie is chewing her fists. I think she may be hungry." Nikki kissed the baby again and handed her to Retta. "Neither of us are ready for that step. He's still getting over the death of his friend Duke, and I've got this thing with my father tonight. We both have to close the door to the past before we can open the one to the future."

Retta lifted her shirt and held the baby to her breast. "It's hard to believe that less than a week ago, this little darlin' wasn't even born. She's stolen my heart and got her big old cowboy daddy wrapped around her finger. Cade and I are living proof that sometimes the future slips up on you real fast, Nikki."

"I can believe it." Emily nodded. "Your little angel has inspired Justin and me to have a baby of our own. I stopped taking the pill this morning."

"Hello, everyone. Is it my turn to hold the baby?" Claire made her way into the living room. "Did I hear right about you and Justin?"

"It's your turn when she finishes eating," Retta said.

"And yep, you heard right. When are you and Levi going to do the same?" Emily answered.

"Already did. We're announcing it at Sunday dinner this next week. I went to the doctor this morning and the due date is Christmas."

"Oh!!" Retta squealed. "Annie will have a playmate. How has Levi ever kept this a secret? You must be two months along."

"It hasn't been easy," Claire laughed. "I've had to figure out ways to dump mimosas and wine so y'all wouldn't suspect. But we wanted to see the doctor and be certain before we told anyone. My jeans are already tight around the middle, so you would've figured it out soon anyway."

"The ranch is growing." Emily shot a look at Nikki. "The Canyon Creek needs a baby too. You and Tag need to get that crap about his past settled and move on to the future."

"One step at a time," Nikki said. "And baby steps for us. But I will admit that I'm bullfrog green with jealousy right now."

"Good!" Emily said. "You know I'd love to have you for a sister and an aunt to our kids."

"Oh, honey, I'll be their aunt no matter what. It don't take blood to make folks kin to each other, and sometimes blood don't mean jack squat," Nikki said. "I should be going. Tag is picking me up in an hour. I'm still torn about what to even wear, and after the last two nights, I can't imagine what I'll say to my father."

"Keep it simple," Emily suggested.

"That's what Tag advised."

"That's exactly what I'd tell you too," Claire offered. "We'll all be thinkin' about you this evening."

"Thanks. That means more than you'll ever know."

Nikki felt that the three women might never know the extent of her sincerity, but what she said came from her heart. It had taken her a while to understand that family didn't always share DNA.

*   *   *

When Nikki got back to her apartment, she changed clothes three times before she decided on a simple black and white sundress and a pair of sandals. She whipped her long, dark hair up into a ponytail, applied a little makeup, and was about to change her mind about her choice of clothes when she heard a vehicle. She picked up her purse, rushed outside, and hurried down the stairs.

"I was hoping you'd have pity on a poor cripple and not make him climb those steps," Tag joked as he held the truck door open for her.

"Cripple, my butt," she sassed as she got inside.

"Your butt is much too pretty for anybody to cripple it, and if I may say so, darlin', you look amazing tonight."

"Yes, you may say so and thank you. You clean up really nice yourself, for an old cowboy with only one boot," she said.

"Had to give the other guys a fightin' chance. It wouldn't be fair to them for me to have two boots," he teased as he shut the door and crutched his way around the front of the truck.

"Nervous?" he asked when he'd settled into the driver's seat.

"Yep."

"How much?"

"More than I was when Billy Tom was in the backseat.

Almost as much as I was when he had a gun pointed at you. And a little more than I was when I knocked on your cabin door that first night," she answered.

"Don't be. If it goes well, you will have a father in your life. If it doesn't, then you've still got your friends, the Fab Five, and me," he reassured her.

"That's what I've been tellin' myself all afternoon," she sighed. "And I appreciate every one of you." She stopped short of saying that she loved all of them, but she did. Maybe in different ways, but the love was there.

He reached across the console and took her hand in his. "I miss the trucks that had a bench seat. Our old ranch work truck doesn't have a console. Someday I'm going to get one like that so you can sit all snuggled up beside me."

She let go of his hand, flipped the console up and slid over to the narrow seat. "Like this?" she asked.

"Exactly." He slipped an arm around her shoulders and drove with one hand. "You've got such a big personality that sometimes I forget how small you are."

"I'll take that as a compliment." She laid a hand on his thigh. "I used to envy the big, tall girls. Don't tell Emily, but I've been jealous of her too. She's curvy and looks so cute in her clothes, and now she's so damned sugary happy that it makes my teeth ache."

Tag chuckled. "I have to admit that her honeymoon glow makes me jealous too."

"Is that what's going on with us?" Nikki asked. "Are we caught up in their happiness, and we want what they've got?"

"Maybe, but then it could be that what we see in them is waking us up to what we might have if we want to work at it. They didn't just sit down on a quilt under a shade tree and fall in love. They had to jump through fire hoops and go through obstacle courses too," he answered. "When she came home last spring after one of their arguments, we figured it was all over between them, but they got through it."

"What if six months down the road one of us decides we're tired of all the work it takes? I've got a lot of baggage for you to contend with," she said.

He drew her even closer. "What you've got is nothing compared to the burdens I'm bringing into this relationship."

She looked up at him and raised a dark brow. "This is a relationship?"

"I think it just might be." He kissed her on the forehead. "I've never slept with the same woman two nights in a row, so it must be special."

A little streak of jealousy shot through Nikki when she thought of all those other one-night stands, but then she reminded herself that she had by no means been a virgin. And she realized that what each of them had done in the past shouldn't affect the future they might have. What happened going forward was the important issue.

Looking back from Emily's wedding to now, she tried to figure out the exact time when their easy banter turned into something more than mild flirtation. It had happened gradually, she realized, and she couldn't narrow it down to a date or an incident.

They rode in comfortable silence for the first thirty minutes of their two-hour trip toward Dallas. But when Tag made a turn onto Highway 380 and headed east, butterflies started flitting around in her stomach. She wanted to tell him to turn around at the next exit and take her home, but after that comment about her being such a strong person, she couldn't do it.

"You're fretting," he said. "You've gone all tense."

"Walk a mile in my shoes right now," she said.

"Okay, but since my toes are hurt, it'll take me a little longer than normal. Let me just imagine I'm doing it. Give me ten minutes. I can usually do a mile quicker than that, though, just for the record," he said.

"Sounds fair to me," she said.

They passed an exit for Denton before he spoke again. "My feet hurt from walking in your shoes. Even at my worst, my mama would fight a forest fire for me. And even when my dad was dealin' out the discipline, and that was often in my case, I knew it was because he loved me. So you have every right to fret. What can I do to help?"

"I'm not sure anyone can actually help, but I appreciate the concern and the understanding. How much farther is it?" she asked.

"Less than half an hour. Would you turn on the radio? I've only got two hands, and they're both doing something pretty important."

She turned the dial and found a country music station in that area. Catching the middle of Blake Shelton's song "I Lived It," she hummed along with it. When that one ended, Miranda started singing "The House That Built Me." The irony that those two songs played back-to-back didn't escape either of them.

After some thought, Tag spoke. "Kind of poetic, ain't it?"

"How's that?" she asked.

"You've lived it. Maybe not like what Blake talks about. And your mama's house built you. It taught you what you don't want to be, and sometimes that's as important as learning what you should be. I know because you're teaching me that same thing. I don't want to live like I'm dying anymore."

Alison Krauss started "When You Say Nothing at All."

"This is my song to you," she said.

"She's right. I would catch you if you fall," he said. "And thank you for the song, and for everything that it means."

She looked up to see a sign welcoming them to the city of McKinney. "I can do this," she whispered.

"Yes, you can," he reassured her. "Plug the address into your phone and navigate for me."

They found the house on the south side of McKinney. She stared at the small brick home that was set back on a large lot. Two huge pecan trees shaded the wide lawn, and the front porch had a swing on one end and a rocking chair on the other. A sliver of light flowed out from between the drapes covering the living room window.

The driveway was empty, but there were two black Lincolns parked across the street. Was one of them her father's? She slid across the seat, took a deep breath, and wrapped her hand around the door handle, but she couldn't force herself to open it.

"You sure about this? We've made progress. We know where he lives," Tag said. "If you're not comfortable, we can go back home and meet him another day."

She shook her head. "We've made the trip. It won't be a bit easier in a week or a month than it is right now."

"Okay, then." He opened his door, got his crutches out of the backseat, and rounded the rear of the truck. When he opened the door for her, she leaned out and kissed him.

"Thank you," she whispered.

"You are very welcome."

They walked up the sidewalk side by side. She rang the doorbell and waited. The guy who opened the door was as tall as Tag, but he was slim built, rather than muscular. His dark hair needed to be cut even worse than Tag's did, and his brown eyes reminded her of someone, but she couldn't figure out who.

"We're looking for Don Grady," she said. "Is this his address?"

"It was, but he moved last week over to Alvord. I'm just here to give the new owners the keys," he answered. "Can I ask you why you're looking for him?"

"I'm his daughter, Nikki Grady," she answered.

"I can believe that. You have his eyes. He's out of town on business right now, but he'll be home tomorrow evening if you'd like to stop by his place then."

"Yes, I would," Nikki said. "Alvord is just south from where I live in Bowie."

"How about that? And you drove all the way here to find him. Should I tell him that you'll be coming to see him tomorrow evening?"

"Sure," Tag answered for her. "How do you know him?"

"It's a long story and he'll want to tell you himself. I'm Lucas, by the way, and I'm sure Don will be glad to see you." He smiled.

The hair on Nikki's neck prickled. "Does my dad drive a Lincoln?"

"No, ma'am. He's got a Dodge Ram truck, kind of a chocolate brown color," Lucas said. "I'm sorry. Where are my manners? Would you like to come inside? There's nothing in here, and all I've got is a couple of bottles of water in the refrigerator, but you're welcome."

"No, that's all right," Nikki said. "If you give me his address, we'll be going."

"Sure thing." Lucas rattled it off.

She typed it into her phone. "Thank you."

"Well, those are the new owners coming up the sidewalk. I guess it's time for me to give them the keys and be on my way," Lucas said.

"Thank you again," Tag said.

He nodded at the property's new owners as they passed and said, "Good evening."

"Is this a sign for me to forget this?" Nikki asked when they were back in the truck.

"Or is the fact that he lives close to you a sign that you need to at least ask him a few questions?" Tag asked. "You reckon Lucas is an employee of his? He sure didn't want to answer questions, did he?"

"Or maybe he's a driving buddy of my dad's. He was a trucker for years and might still be doing that," Nikki said.

"Guess we'll find out tomorrow evening. What time do you want me to pick you up?"

"Seven, but don't climb the stairs."

"You are goin' home with me tonight, aren't you?" he asked.

"I should stop by the apartment to feed Goldie first, and maybe pack a bag."

"Pack for two days," Tag urged. "After tomorrow night, you should stay with me, no matter which way the chips fall." He glanced over at her. "Are you terribly disappointed?"

"That I'm staying the night with you again or that I didn't get to meet my dad?"

"Both." He started the engine.

"Never on spending time in your arms. Yes on seeing my dad. Now my stomach will have to get tied in knots again, but I'm determined to do this. He needs to know that I never got his letters."

Tag traced her jawline with his forefinger. "It would be so easy to fall in love with you, Nikki."

"But you never take the easy way out of anything, do you?" She pulled his face to hers for a long, lingering hot kiss.

Chapter Twenty-Four

Nikki arrived at the café a few minutes before noon the next day and was waiting to be seated when Emily joined her. They were escorted to a booth and a waitress appeared immediately with menus.

"What can I get y'all to drink?" she asked.

"Sweet tea," Emily said.

"Same." Nikki nodded.

"Be right back with some chips and salsa and your drinks." She started to walk away and then turned. "Lemon?"

"Lime," Emily and Nikki answered at the same time.

"I'm sorry you didn't get to meet your dad last night. Are you more nervous or less now that you know he's not that far away?" Emily turned her focus back to Nikki.

"Even worse than yesterday," Nikki answered. "I've thought of a thousand questions I should have asked Lucas since last night."

The waitress returned with a tray bearing chips and

drinks. Emily squeezed the slice of lime into her tea and took a drink. "Like what?"

Nikki did the same thing with the lime. "Like how did he know my dad? Does he work for him? Is he kin to him? Daddy never mentioned that we might have cousins somewhere. Relatives never came to visit us, but lookin' back I can understand why. If anyone came before I was born or when I was a toddler, Mama's attitude would have sent them runnin' for the hills. And maybe Daddy didn't tell us because he knew we'd want to get to know them."

"Well, you'll find out tonight," Emily said. "You ever worry that this can of worms you're opening might be as bad as what your mama said last week?"

"Yep, I have." Nikki loaded a chip with salsa and popped it in her mouth.

"I'm glad Tag is going with you. I can't believe how much he's settled down since he moved here and you two started seeing each other. I've thought that he and Hud would figure out real quick that being boss of their own place was tougher than they'd imagined. But they've surprised me." Emily used a chip to dip deep into the salsa.

"Me too. He's so"—Nikki searched for the right word— "different from how he was at your wedding."

"It's amazing. Mama and Daddy are over the moon with the way he's taking on responsibilities now. Matthew says it won't last if the guys make him keep doing the book work, but I think it just might," Emily said. "But enough about Tag. We're here to talk about your visit this evening. I have faith in you. If you don't like where this journey takes you, you can slam the door on it. But good Lord, girl. Think about all those letters and cards and all that money. He didn't forsake you even when he thought you'd turned your back on him."

"It would have been easier if he'd been in McKinney last night. Now that he's less than thirty miles away, it'll be harder on us both if things don't go right," Nikki said.

The door opened and Nikki looked up to see Tag maneuvering his way inside on his crutches. She waved and he smiled as he made his way around tables and chairs. "Mind if I join y'all?"

Nikki scooted over. "Not at all. We haven't ordered yet."

"What are you doing in town?" Emily asked.

"Had to make a run in to get some lumber and corrugated sheet metal for the guys. The barn roof is leaking and we're planning to start cuttin' hay next week. We'll need a dry place to put it, so they're working on that today." Tag laid a hand on Nikki's thigh. "Thought I'd get some lunch and some takeout for the guys before I go back home. What's on your agenda for the rest of the afternoon?"

"I'm driving a hay wagon for Justin," Emily said.

"I'm going to buy groceries for the next couple of weeks. Want me to pick up anything for you?" It seemed only natural that Nikki would ask, but then she wondered if that was too much and got a little flustered.

His hand moved a little bit higher. "We're out of everything at the cabin. Just buy whatever you think we need, and keep the receipt so I can reimburse you."

"Are y'all living together?" Emily asked.

"No!" Nikki put a hand on his to stop it.

"Well, that was pretty definite," Tag chuckled.

"My mama would put out a hit on me if... Wait a minute." Nikki frowned. "I'm almost thirty. If I want to live with someone, that's my business."

Tag gently squeezed her leg. "That's my girl."

"Does that mean you might live together sometime in the future?" Emily asked.

"Mind your own business, sis." Tag removed his hand, picked up a chip, and dipped it into the salsa.

"Nikki?" Emily asked.

"Let's just get through tonight, but the question is kind of moot since I haven't been asked. I don't think, at this point in our relationship, it's time for that anyway."

Before they could continue with the conversation, the waitress came with another menu and asked Tag what he'd like to drink.

"Coke with a wedge of lime, please," he said. "And some more chips and salsa. If the ladies are ready to order, I know what I want."

The waitress whipped a pad from her pocket. "Yes, sir?"

"The taco plate with refried beans and rice and an order of guacamole on the side. And while we're eating, would you fix up three more of those for me to take with me?"

"You got it." She turned to Emily.

"That sounds good. I'll have the same."

"And you, ma'am?" she asked Nikki.

"Two chicken taco plates, no beans on the side, double the rice." Nikki glanced out the window in time to see a black Lincoln pull up to the curb. "Tag, let me out, please."

He slid out of the booth and stood to one side. "The bathrooms are at the back."

"Not going that way." She made her way through the tables and stepped out on the sidewalk in time to see the vehicle back out onto the road. Lucky devil didn't even catch a red traffic light at the next corner but sped right through a green light and made a left-hand turn before she could read the license plate.

It wouldn't be her father because Lucas said he drove a pickup truck, so who in the hell was stalking her?

"Did you get a look at him?" Tag asked so close behind her that she jumped.

"Nope, but I could swear it's the same car that was parked across the street from my dad's old place last night," she said. "Next time I'm going to get his license number and call the police."

"Billy Tom?" Emily gasped right behind Tag.

"Nope, can't be. This has been going on since before Billy Tom even showed up at the pizza place. We might as well go on back inside. Let me get the door for you."

"A gentleman opens the door for his lady," Tag muttered. "I hate these crutches."

"So I'm your lady? Is that the same as your girlfriend?" Nikki raised an eyebrow.

"I hope so." Tag finally smiled.

*   *   *

Nikki had a full cart of food by the time she'd finished shopping. She divided it as she set it on the conveyor belt. What she planned to take to her apartment would be in separate sacks from what she'd bought to go to the cabin. She paid the bill, shoved it into her purse, and piled all of it into the trunk of her car. It took two trips up the steps to get all of her things into her place. Once it was put away, she fed Goldie and told her not to wait up for her because she might not be home until morning again.

Face it. You are practically living with Tag, and you've only known him a month. Quint's voice in her head put a smile on her face.

"But I feel like I've known him forever," she muttered as she locked the door and went down to her car.

When she got to the cabin, Tag was sitting on the porch,

his crutches lying next to him on one side and Red sprawled out on the other. He waved and started to get up when she parked. She shook her head at him.

"Just sit still. I can get this. Thought I'd make some supper before we leave. It'll give me something to do until it's time to go," she said.

He got up, hopped over to the door without his crutches, and held it open for her. "I can think of something better to do than cooking."

"Oh, yeah, well, let me get this stuff put away, and you can show me what you've got in mind." She lined grocery bags on her arm and carried them into the house.

"It's got something to do with giving you a massage for doing all this for me, and then we'll see where that takes us," he said. "But first you have to get naked."

"I've never had a massage from a sexy cowboy. This could be interesting." She set the bags on the kitchen table and put away the food as she unloaded it.

"Well, today is your lucky day," he told her as he went back for his crutches.

Red dashed into the cabin ahead of him and went straight to Nikki.

"Look at those big old sad eyes," she crooned as she ripped open a package of doggy treats. "He knows who loves him the most."

"If I get a sad look in my eyes, will you treat me?" Tag asked.

"You can have as many bacon-flavored little bites as you want," she told him. "But first you'll have to sit up and beg for them."

"Red don't have to beg," Tag protested.

"Red is a puppy. You're a big sexy cowboy." Nikki put the last of the groceries away and kicked off her shoes and socks.

"I'll get the oil. You just get naked and stretch out on the bed," Tag said.

"Oil? How many women have you…" She stopped. The past was the past and was none of her business.

"None, but while I was in Walmart this morning, I saw this stuff and thought it would be fun," he said. "I also bought the shower gel to go with it. It smells like coconut, and it reminded me of the beach. You said you'd love to see the ocean, so you can pretend that you've got your toes in the water."

"I shouldn't have asked." She pulled her T-shirt over her head, and then her bra came off. She laid both over the back of a kitchen chair.

Red curled up on the end of the sofa and put his paw over his eyes.

"He's pouting because it's my turn to spend time with you." Tag's eyes went all dreamy as he watched her undress. "You are stunning, in and out of clothes."

"I've always felt like I'm too small." She took off her underpants and threw them on the pile.

"You are perfect," he told her. "Now stretch out on your stomach and let me take your mind off all your worries." He leaned the crutches against the wall and picked up the oil from the nightstand.

She tossed the pillow that she used at night to the side and stretched out. "Did you plan this?"

"I cannot lie to you, darlin'. Yes, ma'am, I did, and I've been pretty aroused just thinking about it since you agreed to get groceries for me," he said.

He applied oil to her back and began to gently rub it in. Then he got serious. He started at her neck and slowly worked his way to the bigger shoulder muscles.

"Where did you learn to do this?" she asked.

"YouTube," he chuckled. "I watched several videos while I waited on you."

"You were supposed to be doing ranch paperwork," she reminded him.

He stopped long enough to nibble on her ear. "It's all done and caught up. Besides, the videos were way more interesting."

"I bet they were." Nikki sighed in contentment as he worked out a particularly large knot in her shoulder. "What are you going to do all weekend if you've caught up on work?"

"I'm going to another ranch rodeo to watch the guys ride bulls. But don't worry, I'm going to be a spectator, not a rider. And I've been thinking that when I get around to the skydiving thing, we just might do it together," he said.

"Honey, I go skydiving every time you make love to me." She relaxed and he worked his way down her entire body.

Every part of her was tingling when he reached her toes and then worked his way back up. It wasn't until he reached her shoulders and flipped her over that she realized he was as naked as she was.

"Oh, when did that happen?" she asked.

"What? The fact that just touching you aroused me or that I took off my clothes?"

"All of the above," she gasped.

He stretched out beside her and ran a hand down her ribs, causing even more fire to build up in her insides. "You had your eyes closed, enjoying the massage. I took off a piece at a time. Your skin is so soft. It's like wrapping these old rough hands in silk."

"We've had enough foreplay, cowboy." She moaned as she rolled over on top of him. "Do we need a YouTube video for what comes next?"

He flipped her over onto her back and his lips found hers in a string of kisses that left them both panting. "Honey, I think we can manage this part just fine."

Afterwards, they curled up together in a quilt cocoon and fell asleep. Nikki's breasts were pressed against his chest, and his arms were around her. Then like a bolt of lightning hit him, he jumped out of bed and spit out a long string of swear words. It startled her so bad that she bounced to her feet in the middle of the bed and looked around for a mouse or a spider or even a snake.

"What's wrong?" she asked.

"God, my toes hurt." He fell backward on the bed.

His weight caused her to bounce and fall flat on her butt. "You aren't supposed to put weight on them. What happened?"

"Damn Red cold nosed my bare leg. I thought it was something crawling on me," he answered breathlessly.

She giggled. "Looks like you scared the poor pup half to death. He's cowering under the table."

"Well, he did the same to me." Tag laughed with her. "Next time, he's going outside."

"Oh, there's going to be a next time?" she asked.

"You bet there is, and according to the clock, it can be right now," he said as he pushed her back on the bed and strung kisses from her neck to her lips. "We've got lots of time before we go to Alvord to see your father."

Chapter Twenty-Five

For the second night in a row, Nikki sat in Tag's truck in front of a house. This one was a two-story frame house set back at the end of a lane lined with pecan trees. Half a dozen rocking chairs were lined up behind the railing of the wide front porch.

"I remember this house," she said.

"You've been here before?" Tag asked.

"No, but I saw something like this in a magazine when I was a little girl. I told Daddy when I got big, I wanted a two-story house," she said.

Lights poured out of several windows, both upstairs and down. A brown pickup truck was parked at the curve of a circular driveway. Tonight there was definitely someone at home, but there wasn't a black car anywhere in sight. That meant Nikki's stalker wasn't her father.

"Whoa!" Nikki said. "I just assumed that whoever is driving that black Lincoln is tracking me. But what if they were following me because of you? What if you have some baby-mama out there somewhere and they want to know exactly what's going on between us," she said.

"Whoa there, darlin'," Tag said with a laugh. "I think your nerves have made your imagination run wild. Relax and take a deep breath. Let's just get through tonight, okay?"

"You didn't answer my question." She folded her arms over her chest.

"I would always do right by a child if it's mine, but I wouldn't marry for that reason," he said. "Now let's go talk to your dad. This isn't something that we need to discuss tonight."

She didn't wait for him like she usually did, but got out of the truck and headed up the sidewalk. He'd answered honestly, but it made her think what percentage of the time the pill failed. There was a slim chance that she was pregnant.

Tag caught up to her just as she rang the doorbell. "Why are you mad at me?"

"I'm not," she said.

"And pigs can sprout wings and fly," he said.

The door opened and her dad said, "Hello, Nikki."

"Daddy, I'd like you to meet my boyfriend, Tag Baker."

"Please come in." Don stood to the side and motioned them inside. "It's a pleasure to meet you, Tag. I'd shake your hand, but it looks like you've got both of them pretty tied up. This is Lucas, but then y'all met him last night. I'm so glad you're here, Nikki."

"He always talks too fast when he's excited." Lucas came out of a doorway. "But I really can't say much, because I do too. Y'all come on in the living room. We aren't totally unpacked yet, but this room is done, and we've laid out a little snack on the coffee table. Can I get you a glass of wine? A drink? Maybe some coffee?"

The look on her father's face was like those times when she was a little girl and he didn't quite know what to do—whether to say he was sorry for the words that had just spewed from her mother's mouth or to give Nikki a hug. She wanted to comfort him, but the moment was awkward.

She took a deep breath and stepped forward. "It's been a long time, Daddy." She rose up on tiptoes and wrapped her arms around his neck. "I've missed you so much."

With tears rolling down his cheeks, Don hugged her tightly. "Oh, Nikki, I've waited for this moment for years. We've got so much catching up to do."

"Yes, we do." She took a step back and looped her arm in his.

Lucas led the way into the living room. Nikki looked around, and her head began to swirl. She thought for a minute that she would faint right there. A collection of framed photographs of her and Quint were lined up on the fireplace mantel. A collage of photographs above the sofa included one of her in her cap and gown at her high school graduation, one at her capping ceremony when she became an LPN, and another had been taken when she received her RN degree. Scattered among them were pictures of Lucas at various functions.

She turned toward her dad. "You were there?"

"At every single thing you ever did." He sat down on the end of the sofa and patted the cushion next to him. "Sit beside me and tell me all about yourself."

She eased down onto the buttery soft leather sofa. "I didn't get any of your letters until last week. Mama kept them in a shoebox. I had no idea that you'd offered to let me live with you."

"I'm so sorry. I came to the house several times, but I couldn't make myself go inside." He pulled a tissue from a nearby box and wiped away his tears. "So I wrote the letters and sent them to you. I had no idea that Wilma would keep my mail from you. Let's have a drink to settle our nerves. Lucas, will you pour for us? And forgive me, Tag. I'm so excited to see y'all that I'm being a bad host. Please sit in the recliner and prop up your foot. What happened to your leg? You want a beer?"

"A mean bull stepped on my foot at a rodeo. Guess he wanted to show me he was still the boss. And a beer sounds great." Tag eased down in the chair and nodded toward the pictures on the wall. "Quite a collection you've got there."

"Thank you," Don said.

Nikki slid long, sideways glances at her father. His hair was gray and wrinkles around his eyes and mouth testified that he was an older man now, but he could easily pass for much younger than the fifty-five or -six that he had to be.

"You've grown up." Don handed her a glass of white wine.

"Not much taller but a lot older." She smiled.

Lucas removed the cap from a bottle of beer and waited until Tag was comfortable in one of two recliners before he put it in his hand.

"I understand y'all met Lucas last night," Don said. "I should tell you about him before we get into catching up. Lucas is my son and your half brother. He's about seven years older than you, Nikki."

She almost shot wine out her nose. "You were married before?"

"No, ma'am. Your mama was my one and only wife. I swore I'd never make that mistake again, and I haven't. His mother was my high school sweetheart. We started college together, and we both dropped out after a year. She moved to California with her parents, and I got a job driving trucks.

She died about a year after Quint's death, but she told Lucas all about me before she passed away."

Lucas sat down in a rocking chair. "Mother married my stepfather before I was born, so I just figured he was my father. He died when I was sixteen and Mama died after a short fight with cancer when I was twenty-one. It was my last year of university up in Weatherford, Oklahoma. Academic scholarship," he answered her unasked question. "I finished up the year and got a job in Dallas. Figured I might as well see if I could locate Don Grady, who Mama said was my biological father. I found him in McKinney and we hit it off. I lived with him a couple of years before I 'fell in love.'" He put air quotes around the last three words. "I got married. It lasted about four years. And I moved back in with Dad. Last year I sold my company and retired. Now I'm writing books on running a business and retiring early in life. I'm probably making more with them than I did with a computer software company. So that's my story. I'm your half brother. I've always wanted to know you beyond those pictures up there."

"Why didn't your mama tell my dad she was pregnant?" Nikki asked.

"Mother told me that she wasn't sure she ever loved him, that what they had was a high school fling," Lucas answered.

Nikki glanced over at Tag. Would they grow apart like that?

He raised his beer bottle to her. "Can you believe you've got a brother?"

Have a brother? she wanted to scream. *I had a brother. His name was Quint. His pictures are on the mantel. I don't know this man.*

"I'm in shock." Nikki drank the rest of her wine and refilled the glass. "Are you retired, Dad?"

"Yes, as of six months ago. After your mother and I divorced, I worked hard, bought the trucking company I was driving for, built it up to be a fairly prosperous business, and then sold it last year. I stayed on for six months to help the new owners with the transition. I bought this place because it's secluded and quiet. I don't want to hear the noise of the city. You'll have to come sometime in the morning and see the deer. There's a big deck we can sit on and watch all kinds of wildlife. Remember when you used to sit still by Canyon Creek and watch for rabbits?"

"I remember." She smiled. "Over on Longhorn Canyon Ranch, there's a bunny that comes up all the time. His name is Hopalong, and he lets us pet him." This was all surreal. A father and a brother, all at once, and they both acted like they wanted her in their lives.

"Are you going to get bored here?" Tag looked over at Don.

"Haven't so far, but then we've had the move to think about," Don said. "I understand you own a ranch near Sunset."

"How…" Nikki started and remembered the black car. "You're the one who's been spying on me."

"Yes, I am." Lucas nodded. "I couldn't figure out why you didn't send him at least one letter all these years, so I'm the one in the black Lincoln that's been watching you. Besides, I've always wondered what it would be like to have a sister, so…" He shrugged.

Tag raised both eyebrows at her. "Never thought it would be a brother, did you?"

"Not in my wildest dreams," Nikki answered.

"I kept thinking that you might show up at my door after I sent that first letter to you, but months went by and then years. I thought maybe you blamed me for Quint's death and never wanted to see me again. I had no idea that Lucas was spying on you until about a month ago. That's when he found out the Baker boys had bought old man Johnson's ranch. And that they were your best friend, Emily's brothers. I was at the retirement home where you worked last year the night of your Valentine's party."

"No!" Nikki gasped. "I would have known you."

"I stayed in the shadows and I wore a baseball cap and glasses. Have to have them now when I read," he said. "You wore a pretty red dress and the residents there loved you. Especially five who sat together at a table with Emily's boyfriend."

"The Fab Five," she whispered. "Did you know that I moved out into my own place when I graduated from high school?"

"I did," Don said. "I wanted to help you, but I was afraid you'd spit in my face since you didn't acknowledge my letters and cards. But I couldn't stop sending them."

"We've sure wasted a lot of time, haven't we?" she said.

"Yes, we have," Lucas answered for him. "And to make up for it, we'd like for you and Tag to come down tomorrow night for a real meal with us. Dad is a fantastic cook."

"He wasn't when we were kids," Nikki said.

"I learned." Don grinned. "Try one of my homemade taquitos."

She picked one up from the plate on the coffee table and bit off half the tiny tortilla wrapped chicken and cheese mixture. "This is great. You've got to share your recipe."

"Gladly."

"And one of those little sugar cookies," Lucas said. "If he made those all the time, I'd weigh five hundred pounds."

Nikki ate one of the cookies and then put three of the spicy tidbits and an equal number of cookies on a napkin and passed them across the coffee table to Tag. "You've got to have these. They're fantastic."

Tag ate one and told her, "If you ever make this at the ranch, the guys will take you away from me. And Maverick has a terrible sweet tooth, so he'd love these cookies, but not as much as I do."

"You'll come tomorrow night?" Don asked. "I've got more pictures you might want to see. I couldn't put them all on the walls or the mantel."

"I have to work tomorrow night," Nikki told him. "Monday night I talk to Mama. So how about Tuesday night? You got anything planned, Tag?"

He shook his head. "Not until these toes heal and then I'm making a date with a skydiving company."

She shivered. "That comes from 'Live Like You Were Dying,' a song he's lived by since he was a teenager."

"Did you stay two point seven seconds on a bull named Fumanchu?" Lucas asked.

"Six point seven seconds," Tag answered.

"Been fishin'?"

"Yep, couple of times a year at least." Tag nodded.

"Then all that's left is skydiving. Sounds like fun. Want some company?" Lucas asked. "I've loved that song ever since it came out."

"Nikki is going with me, but you can tag along if you want," Tag said.

"The hell I am!" she said. "I'm not on a guilt ship with that song as my sails."

Don guffawed so hard that they all laughed with him. "I worried about you living with your mother for nothing, girl," he said between hiccups. Finally, he opened a bottle of beer and took several swallows. "You speak your mind like my mother did."

"Do I have any other family? Cousins? Grandparents still living?"

Don shook his head. "No, darlin', what you've got is right here in this room. You said you talk to your mother on Mondays. So she's still alive?"

"You should know. You send her money every month," Nikki said.

"I put that in my lawyer's hands when I bought the company. I told them when she died, not to even tell me. Other than having you and Quint, like I said, that marriage was a mistake. I mistook her neediness for love. But why do you talk to her on Monday? Don't you keep up with her all week?"

"Nope," Nikki said. "Mama only wants to talk on the phone on Mondays. When I was kidnapped, if she worried about anything, it was that I wouldn't be there on Monday so her schedule wouldn't be interrupted."

"Kidnapped?" Lucas asked.

Tag spoke up and told the shortest form of the story that he could, taking all the credit for the trouble.

"So that's why you were gone those days. I thought maybe you and Tag slipped off for a little midweek getaway," Lucas said. "I was afraid to ask too many questions in town for fear I'd get caught."

Don's face registered pure shock. "I'm so sorry. I had no idea. If I had known, I'd have helped in some way. I know people all over the country from my truck driving days."

"It's okay. It's all over now. Billy Tom is locked up," Nikki said. "And we should be going."

"So soon?" Don asked.

"Dad, it's after ten." She pointed at the clock on the far wall.

"We'll be back Tuesday." Tag put the footrest down,

popped another cookie into his mouth, and picked up his crutches. "What can we bring?"

"Not a thing but a healthy appetite." Don and Lucas both stood up and walked them to the door. "Nikki, this has been great. I just knew when I found this house that someday you'd visit me in it."

"That's not what he told me," Lucas laughed. "He said that someday he'd sit on the front porch in one of those rocking chairs and watch his grandchildren play on the lawn. I told him he'd better get in touch with you because I have the Grady curse. That means I don't do well with women."

"You sound like my friend Maverick, who works with me and my twin brother on the ranch. He says he has the Callahan curse," Tag said.

After hugs and handshakes, Nikki's father and brother waved at them from the porch until they were out of sight. She wrapped her arms around herself and wondered if it had all been a dream.

"Well, that went well," Tag said.

"Yes, but I'm mentally exhausted," she sighed.

"Then let's go home and fall into the bed."

"Tag, I need some time alone to process this. I think it's best if I go to my apartment tonight," she told him.

Tag was more than a little disappointed. "Whatever you want, darlin', but I'm here for you whenever you need me for anything."

Chapter Twenty-Six

Nikki was doing laundry the next morning trying to decide how she really felt about having a brother and whether she'd be dishonoring Quint if she decided that she liked Lucas. Lucas had stepped in to fill a void in her dad's heart not long after Quint had died, and Don had thought Nikki had forsaken him forever. She was jealous of that, even if it wasn't right. Lucas had had a mama and a stepdad who evidently loved him enough to see to it that he had an education and followed his dreams. She and Quint had had to pretty much fend for themselves.

It's not his fault, Quint said softly in her mind. *Don't ever blame Lucas for what we didn't have. And don't be afraid to let Tag into your life. Not just for a night or a week, or even for a year. Open up your heart and let love into it.*

"I made a mistake the last time I did that. The guy was married," she said as she made a round through the bedroom and back to the kitchen.

Don't judge Tag by his past or by some other bastard.

Nikki giggled. "You said a dirty word. Mama would have a fit. God, my head hurts." She cupped her cheeks with her hands and rubbed her temples with her fingertips. If she couldn't get these roller-coaster emotions settled before she went to work the next night, maybe Rosemary could give her some advice. Emily had met Wilma only once. Rosemary had known her all her life, so she'd understand what Nikki was facing. If she could just put one thing to bed forever that night, it would be the absolute fear that she'd become like Wilma and be a burden to Tag. Maybe she should make a trip to Sunset tomorrow before she went to work and talk to the ladies of the Fab Five. None of them had been married, but they were pretty sage in their advice.

While the wash cycle ran, she stretched out on the sofa and fell asleep. She dreamed that she and Tag were naked in the bed at the cabin when a tornado ripped through the county. They barely made it into the tiny bathroom and were huddled together in the shower that was so small it made one person feel crowded. Tag's arms were around her when the cabin's roof was suddenly ripped off, and she could feel the vacuum inside the vortex of the tornado sucking her away from him. She held on as tight as she could, but the force of nature finally pulled her away from him. She awoke flailing her arms and hanging on to a throw pillow.

Her hands hit Goldie's fishbowl and sent it flying across the room and upended against the wall. When she realized what she'd done, she ran across the room and chased the poor flopping fish all over the floor before she finally got her in her hands. She ran to the kitchen, put her in a bowl, and ran water straight from the tap, hoping that it was the right temperature and wouldn't kill the thing.

"There, there, now, you're going to be all right. It was

time to clean your bowl anyway. Just swim around in there until I can get my heart to settle down, gather the pieces, and clean up your bowl. Thank God it didn't break." Nikki talked to the fish in the same tone she used for Sue Ann and her other patients.

She could hear Wilma's voice in her head as she scraped up the rocks from the carpet and put them back into the bowl. *That's why you can't have a pet. You're not responsible enough to take care of one properly. Now look at this mess you've made. I'll probably step on those sharp rocks and get sepsis in my foot. When I'm dead and in my casket, you'll wish you'd have taken better care of me.*

Nikki had heard those words so many times that it wasn't even surprising that they came back to haunt her that morning. Would she ever say something like that, even in anger, at her child?

"Hell no!" she said aloud, answering her own question, just as the doorbell rang.

She peeked out the peephole to see her father standing there on the tiny landing. She opened the door and said, "Daddy?"

"Is it a bad time? After I rang the bell, I figured I should have called first. I shouldn't just drop in like this."

"Come on in. Watch your step. I just knocked over the fishbowl and haven't cleaned up the mess yet," she said.

"I'll help," Don said. "Where do you keep the vacuum?"

"In that closet." She pointed. "But you don't have to..."

"I want to," he said as he headed into the kitchen. "I see your faucet is dripping. I could fix that, too, while I'm here. I carry wrenches in the car."

"Did you come here to fix all my problems?" she asked.

"I wish I could do that, honey," he sighed. "I came so we could visit without Lucas and Tag. I wanted to talk to you, just the two of us. But I don't mind helping with whatever you need while I'm here." He pulled the vacuum out into the living room floor and quickly cleaned up all the rocks.

When the machine was back in the closet, he asked, "Mind if we both sit down for a visit?"

"I'm sorry, Daddy. Yes, please sit. Can I make you a cup of coffee? Get you a glass of sweet tea?"

"I'm good for now." He sat down on the sofa.

She took a place beside him. "Okay, I'll go first. It's going to be tough to accept Lucas. Quint wouldn't want me to be that way, but…"

He covered her hand with his. "It'll take time. It did for me. I'm having trouble accepting Tag. Sounds like he's kind of a daredevil, riding bulls and wanting to go skydiving. And to tell the truth, I'm having a terrible time thinking of you in a relationship. To me, you're still fourteen."

"And to me, it's just days after Quint died, and you're coming home for the weekend," she said.

Don patted her hand. "I guess time stood still at the same time it moved ahead with warp speed, didn't it? If you'll give Lucas a chance, I'll be more open-minded about Tag. Deal?"

"Deal," she said. "Now how about a beer? I could sure use one."

Don shook his head slowly. "I'd love one. It's still hard to see my little girl with a wineglass in her hands or think about her drinking a beer."

"Your little girl isn't so little anymore, Daddy." She leaned over and kissed him on the cheek. "I'll get those beers."

*   *   *

Tag reached for Nikki when he awoke on Friday morning, but all he got was a pillow. He threw it across the room, hit the end of the sofa, and woke Red. The dog jumped up and started barking.

"It's okay, boy," he said as he flipped the covers back and, holding on to furniture for balance, hopped to the door and let the dog outside. "You probably need to get out for a minute anyway, but I'll prop the door with my boot so you can come back to eat when you're done."

Red scampered out and back in before Tag could get dressed in pajama pants and pick up his crutches. "I hate this toe stuff worse than the stitches in my jaw," he muttered as he headed toward the kitchen area to make coffee.

The puppy came back into the house and jumped around in excitement wanting to be fed, and Tag almost tripped over him. "Okay, okay, give me a minute. This feller needs his coffee since his lady isn't here to brighten his morning."

Maverick came into the cabin without knocking. "Where's Nikki? Her car isn't out there. Did you ruin things with her?"

"Good morning," Tag said. "Nikki needed some time to sort out her feelings after seeing her father. I hope to hell I didn't ruin anything."

"I brought over a whole envelope full of papers that Hud found on the top of the refrigerator that needs to be put into the computer. Don't shoot the messenger, but you could give him a cup of coffee." Maverick put the envelope on the top of the microwave.

Tag motioned toward the kitchen table. "Have a seat. It'll be done in a few minutes, and I won't shoot you this morning. I'll get to those papers eventually, but today I'm going to straighten up the tack room in the barn. I can do that with one crutch, and I feel the need to do something physical."

"To keep your mind off Nikki, right?" Maverick pulled out two chairs and sat down in one. "What happened last night?"

Tag told him about what had happened when they went to see her father. "It had to be overwhelming for her because it was for me. It was the first time I'd met any girl's father. I've seen Nikki's mother at church, and we ran into her that time in Walmart, but that's not like actually meeting her."

"And what'd you think of her father and her brother?" Maverick pushed the chair back and poured two large mugs of coffee.

"Thank you." Tag blew on the top and took a sip. "I liked them both. They seemed honest and genuine."

"So you're wonderin' about your past? If you're really settling into this lifestyle? Or if you'll go back to being a rebel?"

"Yep, that's exactly it," Tag admitted.

"Are you missin' your old way of life?" Maverick asked.

Tag thought about it for a minute and then shook his head. "No, I like where I am now with Nikki, and I like sharing the ranch with y'all. I don't think I ever want to go back, but how can I convince Nikki of that?"

"You can't. You have to continue to keep living every day without doin' crazy stuff that will get you killed and show her, not tell her. All the talk in the world is worthless if you don't have the deeds to back it up," Maverick said.

"You speakin' from experience?" Tag asked.

"My heart was broken last year when Paxton and I went to Ireland with our Mam. It was love at first sight for me. Her name was Bridget. We had a month together, roaming the green hills of Ireland. I didn't ask her to come with me to America because I didn't feel like I was good enough for her. That was a big mistake not to let her choose. Now she's over there with my heart, so how could I ever give it to another woman?"

"You never told me that before," Tag said. "And you could call her or talk to her, even if she is over there and you're here."

"I tried that. It didn't work. Her phone number had been changed," he said. "We sound like a couple of old women talkin' like this." Maverick went back to the cabinet and brought the coffeepot to the table. "We'll have another cup and then you can give me a ride to the barn."

"I'm very serious. I'm getting cabin fever. I can clean it without a boot on my foot," he said.

"We've got a rodeo tonight and we're going to the Rusty Spur tomorrow night. You ain't much of a dancer right now, but you can sit at the bar and draw in the women like flies to a honey pot and then turn them over to us," Maverick teased.

"Y'all don't need my help, but I'll think about it," Tag said.

"Mam would say that you've done got moonstruck, my friend," Maverick said. "Never knew you to turn down a night in a bar, and this is not your first rodeo on crutches."

"Your grandma might be right." Tag hopped over and took his jeans and a work shirt from a dresser drawer.

"Mam also told me that if you can't tell a girl that you love her in six months, you should move on and not waste any time for either of you," Maverick said.

"Did you tell Bridget that you loved her?" Tag tugged a knit shirt over his head.

"No, I didn't and that was a mistake for sure. I thought it should be six months so I didn't say the words. But when we got home and I was moping around like a lovesick puppy, Mam told me that I hadn't showed my Irish blood one bit, and she was disappointed in me. She said when everything clicks with a woman, then there will be no doubt in your mind. It will overtake you like a web around a cocoon. It will calm you. And it will inspire you. I lost my Bridget. Don't you make the same mistake."

"It's only been a month for me and Nikki." Tag removed his pajama pants, tossed them on the bed, and pulled on his jeans.

"Ask yourself if it's clicking and if you are calm, and if she's inspired you to be a better man. I'm going to finish my coffee while you finish getting dressed, and then we'll go to work. Sometimes hard work is better than a therapy session. When you're working with your hands, your mind can figure things out," Maverick said.

"Amen." Tag shoved one foot into a cowboy boot and the other into a sneaker. "Let's go to work."

Chapter Twenty-Seven

The ER was full when Nikki checked in to work that Friday night. They spent a few minutes getting caught up, and then she and Rosemary hit the floor in a run. Another type of influenza had hit the area and every cubicle was full and folks were practically standing in line in the waiting room.

There was no letup until dawn, when everyone had been treated and either admitted or sent home. Nikki and Rosemary collapsed into chairs behind the nurses' desk, leaned back, and closed their eyes.

"I'm putting in for a day shift soon as summer is over," Rosemary said.

"Why'd you ever start working weekends?" Nikki asked.

"We don't have to hire a babysitter or pay for day care. I take care of them through the week while my husband works. He spends time with them on Saturday and Sunday while I work. But the youngest will be in preschool this fall, so I can go to days," she said. "I'll miss working with you."

"Me too," Nikki said.

"So how'd things go with the cowboy this week? I didn't hear of him having to get on his white horse and go rescue you," Rosemary said.

Nikki gave her a rundown of the week, ending with "How do you know when you can fully trust someone? I've tried it a couple of times and got burned."

"First of all, you ask yourself if that person has ever given you a reason not to trust him. Has he lied to you? Cheated on you? That kind of thing. Then you ask yourself what it is that makes you distrust him. If it's that fool that you let into your life and then found out he was married, it's not fair to the cowboy. My granny used to call that judgin' one person by another's half bushel. Never did figure out what all that meant," Rosemary said.

"Makes sense to me." Nikki stood up.

"How do you know that?" Rosemary asked.

"I hear sirens."

The ambulance backed up to the ER doors, and EMTs brought in an older man who thought he was having a heart attack. His wife came with him, sat down behind the curtain with her purse in her lap, and watched every move Nikki made.

"I been with that man sixty years. We got married when we was sixteen and eighteen, and I ain't about to leave him, so don't tell me to," she said.

"Congratulations," Nikki said. "You don't hear of folks stayin' together like that so much anymore." She thought of her own parents and the horrible marriage they'd had.

The gray-haired lady smiled. "Thank you. He was a rounder, that one was. Took me a while to tame him."

"Really?" Nikki put in an IV, checked all his vital signs, and then hooked him up to an EKG machine. At that young age, surely he couldn't have gotten around that much. If they wanted to see a real rebel, she could introduce them to Taggart Baker.

"Honey, he was outrunnin' girls when he was thirteen, and kissin' them behind the barn at fourteen. Don't let them wrinkles and that bald head fool you. He was quite a handsome feller in his youth," she said.

"I'm layin' right here, Inez," her husband said. "And all that talk ain't goin' to keep me from dyin' if it's my time."

"Hush," Inez said. "I'll tell you when it's your time, and it ain't today."

"I'll take over here." Rosemary popped into the room. "You're needed down in cubicle one."

"Did Sue Ann escape again?"

"One of your cowboys is hurt. He's askin' for you," Rosemary said.

"I didn't have time to input information into the tablet. EKG is running. Blood pressure is good. IV is in place." Nikki pulled back the curtain and hurried down the hall. Trust, hell! Tag had promised he wouldn't ride tonight.

She slipped inside the room to find a worried Tag beside the bed where Hud was lying. Both of them looked pale and frightened.

"Bronc?" she asked.

"No, he fell off the barn roof," Tag said. "He said he was fine but his eyes looked dilated to me and he could have a concussion."

Nikki took her penlight from her pocket and checked. Tag was right. Pupils were bigger than Sue Ann's after she'd mixed booze and pills. "Are you hurting anywhere other than your head, Hud? Can you raise your arms and wiggle your toes?"

"Yes," he answered, and showed her. "I'm not broke, but my head hurts. Where's Grandpa? He was there when I fell."

From what Tag had told her, their grandfather had been dead for a long time. She picked up the phone and called Dr. Richards. "I think we've got a concussion in exam room two." When she hung up, she said, "We'll be taking him for a scan, but you're probably right, Tag. You had these before, I suppose."

"He's had everything before," Hud chuckled. "Broken bones and stitches. He's the bad twin. I'm the good one."

"Maybe you're switchin' places." Nikki took all his vital signs.

"What did he hit when he fell?" she asked.

"The last of a few broken bales of hay," Tag answered. "I was in the tack room. Maverick and Paxton were on the roof with him. His foot slipped and he fell through the rafters. If they'd had the last piece of sheet metal up there..."

Nikki touched his arm. "We'll take good care of him."

"I know you will. That's why I wouldn't let anyone else near him." Tag patted her hand.

"Hud, we're going to roll this bed out of here and take you down to radiology for a scan. Can you tell me your name?"

He gave her a dirty look. "I'm Hudson Baker and that is my twin brother, Taggart Baker. I'm fourteen years old. I live on the Rockin' B Ranch and Grandpa told us to stay off the old barn roof, so don't tell him."

"I won't tattle on you," she said. "Tag, you can go as far as the door and wait outside."

She pushed the bed out of the waiting room and met the

technician coming down the hall. "I hate to be on weekend call. Is this our heart attack patient?"

"No, he'll be in next. This is our concussion patient, Hud Baker," Nikki said.

"Well, wheel him in here," the technician said.

Tag sat down in one of the two folding chairs against the wall and laid his crutches on the floor. Nikki was a few minutes getting Hud situated in the right place. When she returned, Tag had his elbows on his knees and his head in his hands.

"They'd just gotten up on the roof when it happened. I'm the one who gets hurt, not Hud." His voice sounded hollow. "Now I know how he feels every time I've been carted off to the hospital."

"Still want to go skydiving?" she asked.

Tag raised his head. "No, I don't. I don't ever want to put anyone through this kind of pain again. Not my brother. Not my sister. Not my parents. And especially not you, Nikki. Are you disappointed?"

"About skydiving? Not in the least. I'm afraid of heights. It took me a while to get used to the landing outside my second-floor apartment. I still don't look down from there." She slipped her hand into his.

He brought her hand to his cheek. "I'm scared, Nikki. Really, really scared. What if he's like this the rest of his life?"

"Then we'll deal with it, but mostly people with concussions usually come out of it in a few hours. He might remember the fall, and maybe not the day before if it's a minor one. We'll hope for that." She scooted closer to him and laid her head on his shoulder.

"Thanks for being here for me," he said.

"It's my job."

"This part isn't. Just having you here beside me right now helps," he said.

"Tag, I'm always here for you. You're my knight in a shiny pickup truck." She kissed him on the cheek.

*   *   *

Lying on the bed with his eyes closed, Hud almost looked fourteen again. Tag removed his boot and sneaker and propped his feet on the extra chair in the room. Maverick peeked in and whispered, "Okay if we come in for a minute?"

"Sure it is," Tag said. "They're going to keep him for at least twenty-four hours for observation. If he comes out of it by tomorrow, he can go home. If not, they said they'd reevaluate the whole thing."

"We'll go on home, then," Paxton said. "No need in all of us missing a day's work and we need to get that hay cut soon as we nail down that last piece of sheet metal."

Tag nodded. "I should be there, but I can't leave him. He thinks he's fourteen. He's remembering the time Grandpa told us not to go up on the roof, but we did anyway and I fell. He thinks it was him."

"It's that twin thing," Paxton said. "You stay with him. We'll hold down the ranch until y'all get home. If you need anything, just give us a call and we'll have it here soon as we can."

"Thank you both. I'm learning it's different when you're at the side of the bed instead of in it," Tag said.

Maverick clamped a hand on his shoulder. "Kind of gives you something more to think about, don't it?"

Tag swallowed the lump in his throat and nodded. The Callahan brothers slipped out as quietly as possible and closed the door behind them.

Tag's job was to wake Hud every hour all night, ask him if he recognized him and if he knew his name. The sun was up when Hud roused on his own, looked at Tag with a frown, and said, "I'm Hudson Baker. You're my twin brother."

Tag had spent time in rooms almost just like this one with an IV in his arm like what Hud had. He'd had a couple or three concussions, and like Hud had said, broken bones and stitches. Who knew what kind of damage all that knocking his brain took might lead to in the future? When he got to be old and gray, arthritis would set in where the bones had snapped. And the scars wouldn't be nearly so sexy in sagging skin. Nikki deserved better than that.

As if she knew he was thinking about her, she pushed into the room with a tray in her hands. "I brought food. You need to eat. And there are two bottles of water for you to sip on this afternoon. How is he?"

"In and out. Sleeping, groaning a little. I've been where he is, so I know he's got a killer headache," Tag said. "I really hate this, Nikki."

She bent down and brushed a sweet kiss across his lips. "I remember when Quint was in the hospital and how much I hated feeling helpless, so I understand. I've got to get back to the on-call room and catch a few winks so I'll be ready for the next eight hours. Call me if he wakes up and is lucid or if you need me for anything."

He pulled her lips to his for a more passionate, lingering kiss. "I love you, Nikki."

She blinked several times but didn't say a word. Maybe he'd only thought the words and hadn't actually said them out loud. He'd never told a woman that before, so perhaps it was normal for them not to answer and leave the room immediately.

"I love you, too," Hud muttered. "I've always loved you, Cactus."

Tag jerked his head around to stare at his brother. "Oh, really? Cactus who?"

"Cactus Rose O'Malley. I've always been in love with her. Shh...Grandpa. Don't tell Tag. If she sees him, she'll like him better," Hud muttered.

"I don't remember anyone by that name. Have you been keeping secrets from me?"

Hud's eyes popped wide open. "Where are we? Where's Grandpa?"

"You're in the hospital. You've got a concussion," Tag said. "Do you know who I am?"

"Of course, Tag." Hud's brow drew down so tightly that his eyebrows almost touched. "What happened?"

"You tell me," Tag said. "Where's Grandpa?"

Hud continued to look totally confused then his expression changed as if a light bulb went off.

"He died years ago, didn't he? Am I dying, too?" Hud asked.

"No, you're not dying," Tag answered. "What's the last thing you remember?"

"Stayin' on the bronc for eight seconds. Did he throw me?" Hud tried to sit up.

"Be still and let me call a nurse." Tag pushed the button on the side of the rail to raise the bed. "You fell off the barn roof, not a bronc. They think the concussion is minor, but you've got to stay here for twenty-four hours."

"Bullshit! You fell off the barn, not me. You've made me trade places with you, haven't you?" Hud said.

"Not this time," Tag told him. "Hungry?"

"No. The thought of food makes my stomach turn over. Are you serious? This isn't a joke?"

Tag smiled. "No, it's not a joke and it's very serious. It's a good sign that you woke up so quickly and that you remember riding the bronc Friday night."

Hud stared at his brother. "I don't remember falling off the barn or coming here."

"Nikki says that's normal," Tag told him. "But you need to rest. I'll be right here with you until we can take you home."

"You don't need to stay here. I'm a big boy. I can sleep without you by my side."

"How many times have I said that to you, and you never left me for a minute?" Tag asked.

"I don't have enough fingers and toes to count that far," Hud answered as his eyes slowly closed and he began to snore.

Tag dug his phone out of his pocket and called Nikki.

"Hello," she said.

"He woke up and he remembers some things, but not the fall. He's asleep now," Tag said. "I hope I didn't wake you."

"You didn't, and, Tag, I love you too," she said.

"Say that again?" he whispered.

"I love you," she said. "I was about to call and tell you. I couldn't go to sleep without saying the words."

He was completely speechless for several seconds. "Will you tell me in person next time we're together?"

"Yes, I will. See you later, Tag."

"Sleep tight, my darlin'."

Chapter Twenty-Eight

In some ways, the weekend lasted forever; in others, it went by at warp speed. And then it was midnight on Sunday, and Nikki was free to go home. She and Rosemary walked out together into the sweltering night air, the concrete still hot from the boiling sun pounding on it all day.

"It was strange not seeing Sue Ann this weekend," Nikki said. "But I'm glad her sister from Oklahoma stepped in and offered to take her for some real help. With Sue Ann signing herself into the psych ward at the hospital and then either walking out or signing herself out, she wasn't getting the long-term help she needs."

"Me too. I'm glad you tracked her sister down and told her about Sue Ann," Rosemary said.

"Families can sure screw things up, can't they?" Nikki sighed.

"If you let them, they can. Maybe now Sue Ann can get clean and have a decent life. Darla June seemed to really want to help. The expression on Sue Ann's face when she saw her sister for the first time in years almost brought tears to my eyes," Rosemary answered.

"Mine too," Nikki agreed.

"I'm getting all misty eyed again just thinking about it, so let's talk about something else," Rosemary said. "How are things with the cowboy and his brother?"

"Hud went home today, and I told Tag that I love him," Nikki said.

"How'd it make you feel?" Rosemary stopped by Nikki's car.

"At peace," Nikki answered.

"Then it was the right thing to do. Girl, I sure hope this week is better for you than the past two have been. I'll be waiting to hear all about it next Friday." Rosemary gave her a hug and headed on down the row of vehicles to her own car.

Nikki drove to her apartment, fed Goldie, and shoved a couple of outfits into a bag. As she made her way down the stairs, she caught sight of a flash in the sky and saw her very first shooting star. A warm glow filled her from the inside out as she remembered her father telling her that when she saw a star falling from heaven that she got to make one wish.

"I wish for a lifetime with Tag," she said as she got into her car, tossed her bag into the backseat, and headed toward the cabin.

When she arrived, the lights were still on, so she rapped on the door lightly before she entered. Tag was sitting on the sofa, the laptop on the coffee table, and Red was curled up in front of the fireplace.

"I was hoping you'd come," he said.

"I'm glad you're still up." She sat down beside him and laid her head on his shoulder. "How's Hud?"

"No physical work for a week until the doctor sees him again, and then maybe not for a while after that. But Justin is sending us two of their hired hands to get the hay cut tomorrow and he's loaning us their big round baler so we can stack it outside instead of in the barn. And Emily is coming to help out too." Tag draped an arm around her shoulders.

"I'll help any way I can," she said.

He pushed a strand of hair behind her ear. "Darlin', you are helpin' just by bein' here beside me. But if you want to go with me to the tack room and help get it organized tomorrow, I'd love to spend the time with you."

"Done." She yawned.

"I'd carry you to bed, but…" He glanced down at his foot.

"I'd carry you, but…" She grinned.

"Let's just lean on each other and go get some sleep," he said.

"That sounds great." She stood up and got her bag from the end of the sofa where she'd dropped it. "And, Tag, I love you."

"Never thought I'd say those words or hear them either. They're pretty powerful, aren't they?" Tag stood and draped an arm around her shoulders.

"Me neither. And yes, they are. They can still a restless heart." She served as his crutch to the edge of the bed. He sat down, and she dug around in the bag for a nightshirt.

"I like it better when you come to bed naked," he said.

"Tonight we'd better sleep in clothing."

"Why?"

"Because we don't have the energy to make love all night and then work all day tomorrow." She yawned again. "I just want to fall asleep in your arms."

"I can be satisfied with that tonight." He slid between the sheets and waited, then gathered her close to his body when she joined him.

*   *   *

Tag awoke to the aroma of coffee and bacon. When he sat up in bed and opened his eyes, he saw Nikki in the kitchen area making breakfast. "Good morning. You sure look sexy in that outfit."

"What, this old thing?" She tugged at the bottom of her faded nightshirt. "I wore it to a White House dinner, and then to tea with the queen."

He laughed out loud. "And I bet you wore diamonds with it to one and pearls to the other."

"One can't meet the queen without her pearls. Pancakes are ready. Need your crutches or can you hop," she said.

"I can actually walk a little on the foot now, if I'm careful. Trouble is I look like an old man." He got out of bed and eased his way across the floor to the table.

"Honey, we all get old eventually." She waited until he was seated and gave him a kiss and then handed him a cup of coffee. "Eat up. We've got a tack room to clean this morning, and we need to check on Hud."

Tag would have liked to spend an hour in bed before they left, but Nikki rushed through breakfast, did the cleanup, and got dressed so fast that he didn't have time to seduce her. Oh, well, he'd make up for that later that evening, after she'd talked to her mother.

They passed Maverick and Paxton, each operating a John Deere tractor that morning. The smell of fresh-cut hay filled the cab of the truck. It reminded Nikki of Saturdays when her father mowed the grass. She always thought it was a big privilege when he let her push the lawn mower for a few rounds.

Tag's phone rang and he didn't even check the caller ID before answering it.

"Hello."

"Hud is in the tack room," Maverick said. "Paxton and I took four-hour shifts like you suggested all night, but we figured it'd be easier on you to take care of him in the barn. Just giving you a heads-up. He's an old bear."

"Thanks for everything. I'll take it from here, and I owe you," Tag said.

"It's just through today and then he should be fine," Maverick said. "And we volunteered. Did you tell her yet?"

"I did," Tag answered.

"Good for you," Maverick said. "Holler if you need us."

"Will do." He ended the call and turned to tell Nikki what was going on.

When he finished, she simply nodded. "I'll watch the time for you."

They found Hud stretched out on the worn-out sofa in the tack room. He was snoring loud enough to wake hibernating grizzly bears all the way up toward the northern part of the States.

Nikki checked her watch. "He can sleep until nine o'clock. Now, where do we start?" Her eyes scanned the messy room.

"We don't have to do it all today. I don't think Eli Johnson threw away anything." Tag picked up a jar filled with bent nails.

"I remember his wife. She and Mama could've been sisters. Not so much in looks but in their attitudes. The two of them were always comparing medicines and illnesses. I bet Eli spent hours out here." Nikki picked up a box of empty milk jugs. "We probably need a whole box of big trash bags to start with." She turned around slowly, taking in the whole room. "There's a bathroom right there. Has it got a shower?" She crossed the room and stepped inside. "Yep, it does, and you're not going to believe this, but it's above an old claw-foot tub. I bet this was his doghouse. When she was on a rampage, he probably lived out here. My dad's escape was the cab of a truck. Eli's was this tack room."

Tag slipped his arms around her waist and buried his face in her hair. "Am I going to need a doghouse?"

"No, but you do need a bunkhouse, and I'm seeing a possibility here. If you knock out that wall and claim the two stalls on the other side, throw up some drywall and insulation, you could have a really nice bunkhouse right here. Or you could just cut a door through right about here and make two bedrooms."

"You are a genius." He leaned his crutches against the work table and envisioned the area as a small apartment. "Or this could be a living area and the room beyond it could be a bedroom. With water already out here, we could even put in a small kitchen. I bet Justin could draw some plans pretty quick."

"We?" she asked.

"Darlin', I can't offer you dinner at the White House or tea with the queen, but this is doable real soon. Will you live with me in this five-star bunkhouse when it's finished?"

"Let's get it done and then we'll talk about it." She hopped up on the work table. "My rent is paid for June. Offer me a closet, and I might consider it."

"I think we can manage that." Tag turned to face her and his lips found hers in a long, hot kiss.

"Are we jumping into this too fast?" Her breath came out in short gasps.

"Hey, it's a whole month away. That's not fast enough in my book," Tag said.

"Well, before we can do anything, we need to get our future living room cleaned up," she said.

"Hey, what are y'all doin' in my bedroom?" Hud sat up and scratched his head. "Oh, I forgot. Maverick and Paxton made me come out here. Give me something to do. I'm going crazy with boredom, and they kept waking me up all night. Really, what are y'all doing?"

"We're going to make an apartment out of this room and a couple of stalls next door. We need plans drawn up, but first we have to get things in order," she answered.

"Do I get the apartment?" Hud asked. "I refuse to live with those Callahan cowboys if they're going to wake me up all the time. It's just a concussion."

"No, it's for me and Nikki," Tag said.

"Will you make one of them Callahan cousins move to the cabin so we have more room in the house?"

"You got it," Tag agreed.

Hud eyed the room. "A doorway over there and you could take it all the way to the end of the barn for a bedroom. This could be the living room. If you knock out the wall on the other side of the bathroom and close it on this side, it could be a private bathroom."

"I'd say he's doing much better," Nikki said.

Tag kissed her on the forehead. "He had an amazing nurse."

*   *   *

Nikki couldn't think of a single reason to put off telling her mother that she planned to move in with Tag as soon as their tiny barn apartment was finished. But she wasn't nearly as prepared for the Monday night conversation as she thought she would be. When the phone rang at exactly seven o'clock, she'd already had her shower and Tag was taking one.

"Hello, Mama, how are you tonight?" Nikki answered.

"My gout is acting up. I was drinking cherry juice twice a day, but it caused me to have colon problems."

In the Grady house, no one said diarrhea or constipation. "Colon problems" covered both maladies. Women didn't get pregnant. They were in the family way. The word *sex* was spoken in whispers when used at all.

"I'm sorry. Have you talked to your doctor?"

"He's a quack. I keep tellin' you that I want to change doctors, but you won't do a thing about it. He's going to let me die and it'll all be your fault."

Nikki inhaled deeply and let it out slowly. "I'm going to move in with Tag Baker at the end of June or before if we get our apartment finished. We're building a two-room apartment in the barn on his place."

"You've lost your mind! You never were real smart, but this takes the cake." Ice coated every word Wilma said. "Do you know what people will say about me?"

"Mama, this isn't about you. I love Tag. We want to spend time together, so we're going to do this. I've been spending most of my nights with him anyway, ever since I was kidnapped," she said.

"I'll never be able to hold my head up in town again," Wilma sighed. "You've ruined my reputation. I've just built it back from when your worthless father divorced me."

"If you don't want to talk to me, we can hang up now," Nikki suggested.

"It's not eight o'clock, yet," Wilma told her.

"Okay, then, I'll also tell you that I'm having dinner with

Daddy and he came to see me in my apartment." Might as well get it all out in the open.

Dead silence for several moments, and then Wilma said, "You've always been more like him than me. Quint took after me. He never was healthy, poor little darlin' boy. I still miss him."

Nikki rolled her brown eyes toward the ceiling. Add narcissism to the long list of her mother's mental problems. When it suited her purpose to be the victim, she rewrote reality. "So you aren't going to give me grief over visiting with Daddy and having dinner with him?"

"It's not time to hang up, but I need to go to the bathroom. I guess the cherry juice is affectin' me. Goodbye, Nikki. We'll talk again next week," Wilma said.

A click ended the call before Nikki could say another word.

Tag came out of the bathroom wearing nothing but a towel and a smile, and suddenly it didn't matter one bit what her mother, her father, or anyone else on the face of the earth thought. She wanted to be with Tag for the rest of her life.

"Let's go for a walk down to the creek," she said. "I need a breath of fresh air."

"Your mama upset you?" Tag dropped the towel and got a pair of jeans from the dresser.

"Nope, she reacted to the idea of me living with you just like I figured she would," Nikki said. "Everything always has been and always will be about her. Nothing is going to change. The thing I have to learn is to accept it and move on. It'll be interesting to see what Daddy says about us living together. Somehow I think he might be happy for us."

"Me too," Tag said. "Darlin', you're forgetting that I'm still on crutches, so how about we drive over to Canyon

Creek and sit on the banks of the creek for a while? Will that do?"

"Oh yeah," Nikki said.

The radio was playing Rascal Flatts's "Back to Life" when they got into the truck. "This is my song to you tonight," Tag said. "Listen to every word. Just like the song says, you really do bring me back to life."

"This is one of my favorite songs. It should be our song, because you pull me up every time I feel like I'm going under," she said. That's when the idea hit her and she smiled. She took her phone from her pocket and found the right karaoke music.

He parked as close to the creek as possible and got out of the truck. "I'll have to use the crutches on this uneven ground. I like it back here. Someday we'll build a house in this copse of pecan trees," he said.

"I'd like that, Tag, but I'll be content in our little corner of the barn until we can afford to build," she said as she let herself out of the truck. She walked down to the edge of the water and removed her boots and socks.

"Going to do some wading," he asked. "Reckon it would hurt my foot if I joined you, Nurse Nikki?"

"If it doesn't hurt them to take a shower, then this creek water shouldn't either," she said. "But I had something other than wading in mind," she answered. "I betcha I can get undressed faster than you can." She tugged her shirt over her head.

"You're on." He tossed the crutches to the side, sat down, and jerked the boot off his good foot, his sneaker off the other one, and then his socks. She tossed her clothing on the ground and would have beat him if he'd worn underwear. But while she was pulling off those cute little black lace panties, he was already on his feet.

"It's not deep enough to swim," he said.

"Who said anything about swimming?" Nikki pushed a button on her phone and tossed it on the ground with her clothing. The music to "Live Like You Were Dying" started playing. When it got to the chorus, she sang about going fishing and riding a bull named Fumanchu, but when it came to the part about skydiving, she substituted "skinny-dippin'."

Tag laughed out loud as he waded into the cool bubbling water. "I'd rather go skinny-dipping with you than skydiving any day. Have I told you today what a lucky cowboy I am?"

"No, but don't ever forget it," she said.

He bent at the waist and splashed water on her. "My rebel days are over."

She grabbed his hand and pulled him down into the water with her, then shifted her position so that she was sitting in his lap. The fast-moving current flowed around them at waist level. "I love my rebel cowboy in the bedroom, but outside of it, I'd sure breathe easier if he took those stickers off his truck."

"Anything for you, darlin'." He scooped water up into his hands and poured it down her back.

"Will you tell me if you begin to regret any of this or change your mind?"

"Yes, I will, but it ain't happening. I've finally got closure. How about you?"

"I do." Nikki nodded.

"Maybe someday in the not too distant future, you'll say those two words in a church."

Nikki cocked her head to one side. "Tag, are you propos-ing to me?"

He ran a hand down her naked sides. "If and when I do, do you reckon you'll say yes?"

"Probably."

"What do you mean, probably?"

"You'll have to ask me to find out. I'll tell you right now I want the whole nine yards—you down on one knee with a ring in a velvet box. I'm not real crazy about a wedding like Emily's. Can't you just see my mama and daddy in the same room? It would be a total nightmare. A trip to the courthouse will be fine with me, but I want the big engagement so I'll have the memory to hold on to."

"Darlin', you will have everything you want, however you want it. And I'll always be your bedroom rebel." Tag pulled her face to his and sealed the promise with a kiss.

Looking for more hot cowboys?
Forever has you covered!

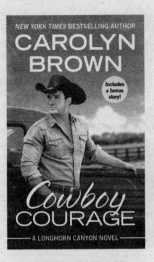

NEW YORK TIMES BESTSELLING AUTHOR
CAROLYN BROWN

Includes a bonus story!

Cowboy COURAGE

A LONGHORN CANYON NOVEL

COWBOY COURAGE
by Carolyn Brown

Heading back to Texas to hold down the fort at her aunt's bed-and-breakfast will give Rose O'Malley just the break she needs from the military. But while she may speak seven languages, she can't repair a leaky sink to save her life. When Hudson Baker strides in like a hero and effortlessly figures out the fix, Rose can't help wondering if the boy she once crushed on as a kid could now be her saving grace. Includes a bonus novella!

Discover bonus content and more on read-forever.com.

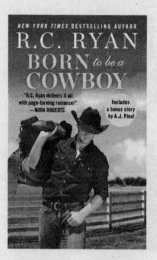

BORN TO BE A COWBOY
by R.C. Ryan

After running wild in his youth, Finn Monroe is now on the other side of the law as the local attorney. Between his practice and the family ranch, his days aren't as exciting as they used to be—until Jessica Blair steps into his office. Gorgeous and determined, Jessie has a hunch her aunt is in trouble, and Finn is her last hope. When she and Finn start poking around, it becomes clear someone wants to keep them from the truth. But as danger grows, so does their attraction. Includes a bonus novella by A.J. Pine!

ROCKY MOUNTAIN HEAT
by Lori Wilde

Attorney Jillian Samuels doesn't believe in true love. But when a betrayal leaves her heartbroken and jobless, an inherited cottage in Salvation, Colorado, offers a fresh start—until she finds a gorgeous and infuriating man living there! Tuck Manning has been hiding in Salvation since his wife died and isn't leaving the cottage without a fight. They resolve to live as roommates until they untangle who owns the cottage. As their days—and nights—heat up, they realize more than property is at stake ...

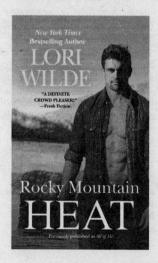

Connect with us at Facebook.com/ ReadForeverPub

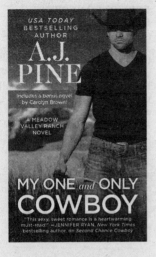

MY ONE AND ONLY COWBOY by A.J. Pine

Sam Callahan is too busy trying to keep his new guest ranch afloat to spend any time on serious relationships—at least that's what he tells himself. But when a gorgeous blonde shows up insisting she owns half his property, Sam quickly realizes he's got bigger problems than Delaney's claim on the land: She could also claim his heart. Includes a bonus novel by Carolyn Brown!

UNFORGIVEN by Jay Crownover

Hill Gamble is a model lawman: cool and collected, with a confident swagger to boot. Too bad all that Texas charm hasn't gotten him anywhere in his personal life, especially since the only girl he ever loved has always been off-limits. But then Hill is assigned to investigate her father's mysterious death, and he's forced back to the town—and the woman—he left behind. Includes a bonus novella by A.J. Pine!

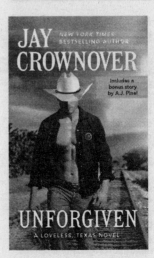

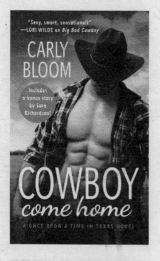
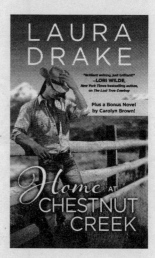